W9-CSY-340

THE BOOK

A complete and totally enthralling novel in itself, *THE TEMPLE OF DAWN* is the third book in *THE SEA OF FERTILITY* tetralogy, a work of cosmic scope and poignant human drama that charts, with satirical verve and resonant feeling, the progress of a soul through several incarnations.

THE AUTHOR

Yukio Mishima is one of Japan's most celebrated novelists. He has been compared to Proust, Gide, Sartre, and Hemingway. A highly disciplined and extremely prolific writer, he was, as well, an actor, expert in the martial arts, and commander of his own private army.

THE ACCLAIM

"Once more," declared *The National Review*, "we are in that world of decadence and perversion Mishima pictured so brilliantly in *FORBIDDEN COLORS*."

Books by Yukio Mishima

THE SEA OF FERTILITY,
  A Cycle of Novels:

  Spring Snow
  Runaway Horses
  The Temple of Dawn
  The Decay of the Angel

Published by POCKET BOOKS

Yukio Mishima

The Temple of Dawn

Translated from the Japanese by
E. DALE SAUNDERS and
CECILIA SEGAWA SEIGLE

WASHINGTON SQUARE PRESS
PUBLISHED BY POCKET BOOKS NEW YORK

WSP A Washington Square Press Publication of
POCKET BOOKS, a Simon & Schuster division of
GULF & WESTERN CORPORATION
1230 Avenue of the Americas, New York, N.Y. 10020

Japanese edition, *Akatsuki no Tera*, copyright
© 1970 by Yukio Mishima. English translation,
The Temple of Dawn, copyright © 1973 by
Alfred A. Knopf, Inc.

Published by arrangement with Alfred A. Knopf, Inc.
Library of Congress Catalog Card Number: 73-7277

ISBN: 0-671-44534-0

First Pocket Books printing September, 1975

10 9 8 7 6 5 4 3

WASHINGTON SQUARE PRESS, WSP and colophon are
trademarks of Simon & Schuster.

Printed in the U.S.A.

The Temple
of Dawn

Part One

1

IT WAS the rainy season in Bangkok. The air was saturated with a continuous fine drizzle, and often drops of rain would dance in a brilliant ray of sunlight. Rifts of blue were always visible here and there; and even when the clouds clustered most thickly round the sun, the sky at their circumference was dazzlingly blue. Before an approaching squall, it would turn ominously dark and threatening. A foreboding shade would shroud the predominantly green, low-roofed city dotted with palms.

The name of the city dates from the Ayutthaya dynasty, when it was first called *bang*, "town," *kok*, "olives," because of its many olive trees. Another ancient name is Krung Thep, or "City of Angles." The metropolis, situated less than six feet above sea level, is completely dependent on canals for transportation. When roads are constructed by piling up dirt, canals are inevitably created. And when ground is excavated in building a house, ponds immediately form. Such pools connect up naturally with streams; and thus these "canals" run in every direction, all flowing into the mother waters of the Menam, gleaming the same brown as that of the inhabitants' skin.

In the center of the city there are European-style three-storied buildings with balconies and numerous two- and three-storied brick constructions in the foreign concession. The roadside trees, once the city's most beautiful feature, have been felled here and there in the path of highway construction, and some streets have been partially paved. Mimosa trees, intercepting the

1

strong rays of the sun, form pools of deep shade on the roadways, covering them with black veils of mourning. After a thunder squall the leaves, shriveled in the heat, suddenly revive, and refreshed, raise their heads.

In its prosperity the town reminds one of some southern Chinese city. Numberless two-seated pedicabs ply their way with shades drawn on the sides and in back. Sometimes buffalos from the rice paddies near Bangkap are led through the streets, crows still perching on their backs. Here and there the luminous skin of a leprous beggar glows in the shade like a dark smudge. The boys run about quite naked, while the girls wear a metal pleating over their sex. Exotic fruits and flowers are on sale in the morning market. In front of the Chinese banks glitter chains of pure gold suspended like bamboo jalousies.

But when evening falls, Bangkok is left to the moon and the star-filled sky. Apart from hotels with independent electric systems, only the homes of the wealthy, which are provided with generators, sparkle festively here and there. For the most part, people resort to lamps and candles. A single taper burns throughout the night at the Buddhist altars in all the low-lying houses along the river, and only the gilt of the Buddhist images gleams dimly in the depths of the bamboo-floored structures. Thick, brown incense sticks burn before the statues. Candlelight from the houses on the opposite bank glimmers in the river and is interrupted now and then by the silhouette of a passing boat.

In 1939—last year—Siam officially changed its name to Thailand.

The reason why Bangkok is called the Venice of the East does not stem from any external resemblance between the two cities, which cannot be compared either in design or in scale. First of all, both employ a plethora of canals for maritime transportation, and then both contain many holy edifices. There are seven hundred temples in Bangkok.

Buddhist pagodas soar up through the greenery and

are the first to receive the light of dawn and the last to retain the rays of the evening sun, changing with the light into a multitude of colors.

Wat Benchamabopit, the Marble Temple, constructed by Rama V Chulalongkorn in the nineteenth century, though a modest edifice, is the newest and certainly the most sumptuous temple.

The present monarch, Rama VIII, or King Ananda Mahidol, succeeded to the throne in 1935 at the age of eleven, but he soon went to study in Lausanne; and now at the age of seventeen, he is still there devoted to his research. During his absence, the Prime Minister, Luang Phiboon, assumed totalitarian powers, and now the nominal parliament serves merely in an advisory capacity. Two regents were set up: the first, Prince Achitto Apar, was pretty much of a decoration, while the second, Prince Prude Panoma, held the real power.

Prince Achitto Apar, a devout Buddhist, often visited one or another of the sanctuaries in his spare time. One evening it was announced that he intended to go to the Marble Temple.

The edifice stood on the bank of a stream bordered by the mimosa trees of Nakhon Pathom Road.

The reddish brown portals of the Marble Temple, protected by a pair of stone horses with mandorlas like white crystal flames in the ancient Khmer style, stood open. On either side of the straight flagstone walk leading from the entrance to the main building set in glistening emerald-green grass, stood a pair of pavilions in classic Javanese style with upturned roofs. The mimosa trees on the greensward were cut in round shapes and blossoming; frolicking white lions on the eaves of the pavilions trampled flames underfoot.

The white columns of Indian marble directly in front of the main building, the pair of guardian marble lions, the low European-type balustrade, and the facade, also of marble, reflected the dazzling rays of the westering sun and formed a pure white canvas that served to bring out the rich decorative patterns of gold and vermilion. The inner frames of the pointed-arch windows were limned in scarlet and encircled by ornate golden flames that rose, engulfing them. Even the white columns of the facade were decorated in brilliant gold with coiled *naga*-serpents that sprang abruptly from the capitals. Rows of golden snakes with raised heads edged the upsweeping roofs, composed of tier upon tier of red Chinese tiles, and the tips of each subordinate roof were formed of thin, golden serpent tails, like the spike heels of a woman's shoe, thrusting upward, as if in competition, to the blue sky, to the very heavens. All this gold shone rather darkly in the sun, enhancing the white of the pigeons that idled along the gables.

But when the white birds, startled, suddenly flew up into the gradually darkening sky, they were as black as particles of soot. The soot from the golden flames, repeated in the ornaments of the temple, became birds.

In the garden the towering palms seemed petrified in amazement, arboreal fountains like bows, shooting their greenery farther and farther skyward.

Plants, animals, metal, stone, and Indian red, mingling in harmony, frolicked in the light. Even the marble heads of the white lions guarding the entrance appeared to be for all the world like sunflowers. Serrated seedlike teeth lined their gaping mouths; their lion faces were angry white sunflowers.

Prince Achitto Apar's Rolls Royce drew up in front of the gate. The Young Men's Military Band, dressed in red uniforms, had lined up on the lawn by the pavilions and were playing their instruments, brown cheeks puffing. The polished mouths of the horns reflected minutely the figures of the youths in their bright uniforms. Under the tropical sun no instrument was more appropriate.

A servant clad in a white coat and red sash followed the Prince, holding a grass-colored parasol over the royal head. The Prince, wearing decorations on his white military jacket, entered the temple escorted by a chamberlain in a blue sash, holding offerings, and ten royal guardsmen.

His visits usually lasted some twenty minutes. During

this period spectators waited on the grass, roasting in
the sun. At length came the sound of a Chinese viol
in the inner precincts, mingled with delicate chimes,
and the footman bearing the parasol moved to the entrance. He raised the umbrella, to the tip of which was
attached a delicate golden pagoda, to his shoulder, and
four guardsmen wearing monklike hats with flaps hanging down over the napes of their necks lined up on the
stone steps. The interior, hidden from view, was so dark
that one could barely glimpse the flickering of the candles
inside. Voices chanting a sutra rose rapidly to a crescendo,
then stopped at the sound of a single bell.

The servant opened the green umbrella, respectfully
holding it over the departing Prince, and the guardsmen
saluted by hoisting their swords. The Prince passed
quickly through the gate and entered his Rolls Royce.

After a while the spectators who had watched the
departure scattered, the military band left, and the quiet
of evening gently settled over the temple. Some of the
saffron-garbed priests strolled out to the riverbank; some
read books, other conversed. Withered red flowers and
dead fruit floated in the water that reflected the mimosa
on the opposite bank and the beautiful clouds in the
evening sky. The sun sank behind the temple, and the
grass darkened. At length only the marble pillars, the
lions, and the facade of the temple retained a fading
evening whiteness.

* * *

Wat Po.

There one must push one's way through the crowds
streaming among the late-eighteenth-century pagodas
and the central hall constructed under Rama I.

Blazing sun. Azure sky. Still the great white columns
of the gallery in the main temple are stained like the
legs of a white elephant.

The pagoda is decorated with small fragments of porcelain, whose smooth glaze reflects the sun. In the purple Great Pagoda are chiseled tiers of blue mosaic,

and innumerable pieces of ceramic, on which are painted countless flowers with petals of yellow, red, and white on a bluish purple ground: a ceramic Persian carpet towering high in the sky.

To one side stands a green pagoda. A pregnant bitch, black-spotted pink teats hanging pendulously, staggers down the flagstone walk as if crushed by the hammer of the sun.

In the Nirvana Hall a great gilded statue of Shakyamuni reclining rests its mass of golden curls on a box-pillow of blue, white, green, and yellow mosaic. His golden arm is stretched far out to support his head, and at the other end of the somber hall gleam his golden heels.

The soles of his feet are inlaid with fine mother-of-pearl; and in each segment, against a finely wrought black background in gleaming iridescent shellwork, are depictions of the Buddha's life, all decorated with peonies, shells, altar accessories, rocky crags, lotus flowers rising from swamps, dancers, strange birds, lions, white elephants, dragons, horses, cranes, peacocks, ships with three sails, tigers, and phoenixes.

The open windows shine like polished brass panels. Under the lime trees a group of priests passes by in shimmering orange robes, their brown right shoulders bare.

Outside, the air itself seems stricken with some tropical fever. Over the stagnant pond between the pagodas, glistening green mangrove trees let fall their mass of aerial roots. Pigeons while away the time on a center island with rocks painted blue. An immense butterfly is depicted on the rocky facade, and at the crest stands a small, inauspicious black pagoda.

And Wat Phra Keo, guardian temple of the royal palace, famed for its principal statue—an emerald Buddha.

It has never been damaged since its construction in 1785.

A golden *garuda,* half woman, half bird, flanked on either side by gilded spires, glistens in the rain at the top of the marble stairs. The green-bordered tiles of

Chinese red sparkle more brilliantly than ever in the luminous rain.

The gallery walls of the Mahamandapa are covered with a series of murals illustrating episodes in the *Ramayana*.

Rather than the virtuous Rama himself, the monkey god, Hanuman, the flamboyant son of the wind god, appears throughout the painted story. The golden beauty, Sita, with teeth of jasmine flowers, is being kidnapped by the fearful *rakshasa* king. Rama fights his many battles with fixed, bright eyes.

Colorful palaces, monkey gods, and battles of monsters appear against mountains painted in the manner of the southern Chinese school or in that of the somber early Venetian landscapes. Above the tenebrous *paysage* soars a god in the seven colors of the rainbow, mounted on a phoenix. A man in golden robes whips a clothed horse that sits motionless. A monstrous fish, rearing its head far above the sea, is about to attack some soldiers standing on a bridge. There is a faint blue lake in the distance; and Hanuman, sword unsheathed, lurks in a bush as he stalks a white horse with a golden saddle that paces silently through the dark forest.

"Do you know the real name for Bangkok?"

"No, I don't."

"It's *Krung thep phra mahanakorn amon latanakosin mahintara shiayutthaya mafma pop noppala rachatthani prilom.*"

"What does all that mean?"

"It's almost impossible to translate. Thai names are like the temple decorations, unnecessarily pompous and flowery, ornate purely for the sake of ornateness.

"Well, *Krung thep* means roughly 'capital,' and *pop noppala* is 'a nine-colored diamond'; *rachatthani* is 'a large city'; and *prilom* means something like 'pleasant.' They choose exaggerated and ostentatious nouns and adjectives and string them together like beads on a necklace.

"In answering a simple 'yes' to the king, protocol

of the country demands that you say: *phrapout chao ka kollap promkan saikrao sai klamon,* which roughly translates as: 'Your humble and obedient servant makes reverent obeisance to Your Majesty.'"

Honda, ensconced in a rattan chair, listened to Hishikawa's words with detached amusement.

Itsui Products Limited had sent this encyclopedic but somewhat strange and seedy character—doubtless a one-time artist—to serve as interpreter and guide for Honda. Already at forty-six, the latter considered it a kind of courtesy to himself to leave things to others, especially in such a sweltering country as this.

He had come to Bangkok at the request of Itsui Products. If a business transaction based on Japanese law has been closed in Japan and a dispute with a buyer arises abroad, even though the suit is brought before a foreign court, it is settled according to international civil law. Furthermore, foreign lawyers are invariably ignorant of Japanese law. In such cases, some eminent Japanese counselor is invited to explain Japanese legal intricacies to the native lawyers and thus to help settle the suit.

Itsui Products had exported one hundred thousand cases of Calos antifever pills to Thailand in January. Of them thirty thousand had been damaged by damp and had been discolored, thereby losing their affectiveness. The cases were dated, indicating a reduction in potency after a given time limit, but that served no purpose now that they were spoiled. Such civil problems should have been solved by reference to the law concerning default of obligation, but the buyers had brought charges of criminal fraud. According to article 715 of the Civil Code, Itsui Products should, of course, have assumed responsibility for indemnifying a non-negligence default for any flaw in merchandise issued by a subcontracting drug company. But they could do nothing without the assistance of a capable Japanese lawyer like Honda in matters of this nature which involved international civil law.

Honda had been assigned a room in the Oriental

Hotel—the natives pronounced it Orienten Hoten—with a lovely view of the Menam River. The room was ventilated by a large white ceiling fan, but at nightfall it was better to go out to the garden along the river and enjoy the slightly cooler breezes there. As he sipped his aperitif with Hishikawa, who had come to guide him for the evening, he let his companion take over the conversation. Honda was overcome with weariness; even the spoon felt too heavy for his fingers to raise, and conversing was even more burdensome than a silver-plated spoon.

On the opposite bank, the sun was sinking behind Wat Arun, the Temple of Dawn. An all-pervading evening glow filled the vast sky over the flat vista of the Thon Buri jungle, broken only by two or three spires silhouetted against the horizon. Like cotton the green of the forest absorbed the glow, changing it to a truly emerald hue. Sampans passed by, crows gathered in great numbers, and a soiled rose color lingered in the river water.

"All art is like the evening glow," said Hishikawa, watching as he always did when he was preparing to express an opinion, for the effect his words would have on his listener. Honda felt annoyed by these points of silence even more than by Hishikawa's continuous chatter.

Hishikawa's profile with its cheeks of Siamese swarthiness and the non-Siamese pasty, taut skin gleamed in the last rays of the sun that came from the opposite bank.

"Art is a colossal evening glow," he repeated. "It's the burnt offering of all the best things of an era. Even the clearest logic that has long thrived in daylight is completely destroyed by the meaningless lavish explosion of color in the evening sky; even history, apparently destined to endure forever, is abruptly made aware of its own end. Beauty stands before everyone; it renders human endeavor completely futile. Before the brilliance of evening, before the surging evening clouds, all rot about some 'better future' immediately fades away. The present moment is all; the air is filled with a poison of color. What's beginning? Nothing. Everything is ending.

"There's nothing of substance in it. Of course, night has its own intrinsic nature: the cosmic essence of death and inorganic existence. Day too has its own entity; everything human belongs to the day.

"But there's no substance in the evening glow. It's nothing but a joke, a meaningless, but impressive joke of form and light and color. Look . . . look at the purple clouds. Nature seldom offers a banquet of such a lavish color as purple. Evening clouds are an insult to anything symmetric, but such destruction of order is closely connected with the breakup of something much more fundamental. If the serene white daytime cloud may be compared to moral exaltation, then these riotous colors have nothing to do with morality.

"The arts predict the greatest vision of the end; before anything else they prepare for and embody the end. Gourmets and good wines, beautiful forms and sumptuous clothes—every extravagance human beings can dream up in one era is crammed into the arts. All such things have been awaiting form. Some form with which to pillage and destroy in the shortest time all of human living. And that is the evening glow. And to what purpose? Indeed, for nothing.

"The most delicate thing, the most fastidious aesthetic judgment of the minutest detail—I refer to the indescribably subtle contours of one of those orange-colored clouds—is related to the universality of the vast firmament; its innermost aspects are expressed in color, and uniting with external aspects, they become the evening glow.

"In other words, evening glow is expression. And expression alone is the function of the evening glow.

"In it, the slightest human shyness, joy, anger, displeasure is expressed on a heavenly scale. In this great operation the colors of human intestines, ordinarily invisible, are externalized and spread over the entire sky. The most subtle tenderness and gallantry are joined with Weltschmerz, and ultimately affliction is transformed into a short-lived orgy. The numerous bits of logic which people have so stubbornly cherished during the day are all drawn into the vast emotional explosion of the heavens and the spectacular release of passions, and people realize the futility of all systems. In other words, everything is expressed for at most ten or fifteen minutes and then it's all over.

"The evening glow is swift and possesses the characteristics of flight. It constitutes perhaps the wings of the world. Like the wings of a hummingbird which change into rainbow colors as it flutters about sucking the honey from flowers, the world shows us a brief glimpse of its potentiality for soaring; all things in the evening glow fly rapturous and ecstatic . . . and then in the end fall to the ground and die."

As Honda listened desultorily to Hishikawa's words, the sky above the opposite bank was already slowly sinking into dusk, leaving a faint gleam on the horizon.

Had he claimed that all art was evening glow? Yet there stood the Temple of Dawn!

* * *

Honda had crossed over to the other bank on a hired boat early the previous morning and visited the Temple of Dawn.

He had done this precisely at sunrise, a most fitting time. It was still darkish, and only the very tip of the pagoda caught the first rays of the rising sun. The Thon Buri jungle beyond was filled with the piercing cries of birds.

As he approached, he realized that the pagoda was all inlaid with countless fragments of Chinese porcelain of either red or blue glaze. Each tier was marked by a balustrade; the one on the first story was brown, on the second green, and on the third a purplish blue. Countless porcelain dishes that had been placed there formed flowers: yellow ones represented the cores from which extended petals of plates. Some had a core of inverted lavender wine cups and here colorful golden dishes formed the petals. Chains of such flowers ascended to the summit. The leaves were all tile; and from the top, four white elephant trunks hung down at the four cardinal points.

The repetitiveness and the sumptuousness of the pagoda were almost suffocating. The tower with its color and brilliance, adorned in many layers and graduated toward the peak, gave one the impression of so many strata of dream sequences hovering overhead. The plinths of the extremely steep stairs were also heavily festooned and each tier was supported by a bas-relief of birds with human faces. They formed a multicolored pagoda whose every level was crushed with layers of dreams, expectations, prayers, each being further weighted down with still other stories, pyramid-like, progressing skyward.

With the first rays of dawn over the Menam River, the tens of thousands of porcelain fragments turned into so many tiny mirrors that captured the light. A great structure of mother-of-pearl sparkling riotously.

The pagoda had long served as a morning bell tolled by its rich hues, resonant colors responding to the dawn. They were created so as to evoke a beauty, a power, an explosiveness like the dawn itself.

In the eerie, yellowish brown morning light reflecting ruddily in the Menam River, the pagoda cast its shining reflection, presaging the coming of still another sweltering day.

"I'm sure you've had enough of temples. Tonight I'll take you someplace amusing," said Hishikawa. Honda was gazing absently at the Temple of Dawn, now completely enveloped in darkness.

"You've seen Wat Po and Wat Phra Keo. And when you went to the Marble Temple, you were lucky enough to see the Regent's visit. And yesterday morning you saw the Temple of Dawn. There's no end to temple-visiting if you've got a mind for it, but I think you've had enough."

"Hm. I suppose I have," Honda replied vaguely, reluctant to let the thoughts in which he was so deeply absorbed be interrupted.

He had been musing about Kiyoaki's old Dream Diary, which he had not glanced at for so long, but which he had brought along in the bottom of his suitcase, thinking he might read it again to help pass time during his journey. Because of the intolerable heat and his weariness, he had not had the opportunity to do so until now. But the brilliant tropical colors in the description of a dream about which he had read long ago were still vivid in his mind.

Indeed, being so busy, Honda had not accepted the trip to Thailand for purely business reasons. In his school days, at a most sensitive age, he had, through Kiyoaki, become acquainted with two Siamese princes and had witnessed the pathetic end of Chantrapa's love story and the loss of Prince Pattanadid's emerald ring. Because of the overwhelming realization that he was destined to be an observer, the hazy picture in his memory had been ultimately preserved in a strong and solid frame. Long ago he had firmly resolved that he must visit Siam one day.

Yet on the other hand, Honda at forty-six had become most wary of his slightest emotions; unconsciously he had fallen into the habit of detecting deceit and exaggeration in them. He mused that his last passion had been for saving Isao, the boy whom he had discovered to be the reincarnation of Kiyoaki. He had even given up his judgeship. It had led to naught, and he had experienced only a shattering failure that had borne home to him the total futility of altruism.

Having abandoned altruistic ideals, he had become a much better lawyer. No longer having any passions, he was successful in saving others in one case after the other. He accepted no assignment unless the client was wealthy, no matter whether the case was civil or criminal. The Honda family prospered far more than in his father's time.

Poor lawyers who acted as though they were the natural

representatives of social justice and advertised themselves as such were ludicrous. Honda was well aware of the limitations of law as far as saving people was concerned. To put it candidly, those who could afford to engage lawyers were not qualified to break the law, but most people made mistakes and violated the law out of sheer necessity or stupidity.

There were times when it seemed to Honda that giving legal standards to the vast majority of people was probably the most arrogant game mankind had thought up. If crimes were often committed out of necessity or stupidity, could one not perhaps claim that the mores and customs upon which such laws were based were also idiotic?

After the incident with the League of the Divine Wind in the Showa period that ended in Isao's death, many similar events had taken place, but internal turmoil in Japan had stopped with the events of February 26, 1936. The China Incident, which had begun shortly thereafter, remained inconclusive even after five years of fighting. And now the pact binding Japan, Germany, and Italy had provided a strong stimulus; and the danger of war between Japan and the United States had become a frequent topic of discussion.

But as Honda was no longer interested in the passage of time, political battles, or the imminence of war, he no longer felt any emotion about them. Something had collapsed in the innermost recess of his heart. He knew that he was powerless to arrest events which went storming on like rain squalls, drenching every insignificant person, beating indiscriminately upon the individual pebbles of fortune. But it was not clear to him whether all fortunes were ultimately pathetic. It was history's wont to progress by granting the wishes of some and by denying those of others. No matter how distressing the future might prove to be, it did not necessarily disappoint everyone.

However, one must not suppose that Honda had become a complete nihilist and cynic. Compared to the past he was quite cheerful and gay. His manner of speech, which he had been so careful of throughout the period of his judgeship, had changed considerably; and his taste in clothes was more liberal. He even wore a checkered hound's-tooth sports jacket and had begun telling jokes and acting more magnanimously. But since he had come to this sweltering country pleasantries no longer came readily to his lips.

His face now displayed a grave dignity suited to his years. He had long since lost the clean-cut profile of his youth, and his skin, once as plain as washed-out cotton, having known the taste of luxury, had taken on the texture of satin damask. As he was well aware that he had never been handsome, he was not altogether displeased with the opaque veil age had imposed.

Furthermore, he now possessed his future much more surely than any youth could. The reason why young men patter on about the future so was simply that they didn't yet have it. Possessing by letting go of things was a secret of ownership unknown to youth.

Just as Kiyoaki had not influenced the times in which he had lived, Honda too did not affect his. In place of the era when Kiyoaki had perished on the battlefield of romantic emotions, a new period was coming when young men would die on real battlefields. Its forerunner was the death of Isao. In other words, Kiyoaki and his reincarnation, Isao, had died contrasting deaths on contrasting battlefields.

And Honda? There was no sign of death in him! He had never desired death passionately, nor had he ever tried to evade its onslaught. However, now that he had suddenly become the target of the fiery shafts of the tropical sun that poured down on him the livelong day, the beautiful, dense, luxuriant greenery all about seemed possibly the stunning luxuriance of death itself. "A long time ago, perhaps twenty-seven or twenty-eight years, when two Siamese princes came to Japan to study, I was privileged to know them for some time. One was the younger brother of Rama VI, Prince Pattanadid; and the other was Prince Kridsada, his cousin, a grandson of Rama IV. I wonder what they're doing now. I had hoped to see them when I got to Bangkok, but it seems presumptuous to impose myself on people who have surely forgotten me."

"Why didn't you tell me before?" said the omniscient Hishikawa, hastening to reproach Honda's reserve. "Whatever you ask, I can find a solution."

"Well, then, do you think I might be able to see the two princes?"

"I shouldn't go so far as to say that. Rama VIII, their uncle, depends very much on them, and they are both in Lausanne with him now. Most of the important members of the royal family have gone to Switzerland and the palace is empty."

"I'm sorry to hear it."

"But there's a possibility of seeing a member of Prince Pattanadid's family. It's a strange story. His Royal Highness's youngest daughter, a little girl about seven, is staying in Bangkok alone with her ladies-in-waiting. The poor thing is practically a prisoner in a small mansion they call the Rosette Palace."

"Why is that?"

"It would be an embarrassment to the family if they took her abroad; she's thought to be retarded. Ever since the Princess was able to talk, she's been saying: 'I'm not really a Siamese princess. I'm the reincarnation of a Japanese, and my real home is in Japan.' She won't change her story no matter what people say. If anyone objects, she throws a tantrum. So the rumor is that all her attendants have gone along with her delusion and brought her up to believe whatever she wishes. An audience is rather difficult, but since you have relations with the royal princes, I think I can do something— depending on how I approach those responsible for her."

2

HAVING HEARD the story of the poor little mad Princess, Honda was not at once moved to seek an audience.

He knew that she would be within his reach like some brilliant, little golden temple. And just as temples never fly away, he felt that the Princess too would always be there. Madness in this country would surely be like its architecture or its monotonous, elegant dances that went on and on in their eternal splendor. Another day, he thought, when his mood had changed, he would request an audience.

Perhaps this procrastination came in part from the listlessness one experienced in the tropics and in part from his advancing years. His hair was turning gray, and his sight would have been growing less acute too were it not, fortunately, that he had been slightly nearsighted since childhood. He still managed well without the assistance of an old man's spectacles.

His age enabled him to use the laws taught him by experience as measurements, and he could foretell the outcome of most situations. Actually, except for natural calamities, historical events occurred, no matter how unexpected they might seem, only after long maturation. History is as hesitant as a young maiden before a romantic proposal. For Honda there was always a hint of the artificial in any event that corresponded precisely to his own wishes and that approached at a pleasing speed. Therefore, if he wanted to entrust his actions to the laws of history it was always best for him to adopt a reserved attitude toward everything. He had seen too many instances where one could get nothing one wanted and where determination had ultimately been quite futile. Even things which one should have been able to obtain if one had not craved them managed to slip away simply because they had been coveted too much. Suicide seemed so completely dependent on one's own desire and resolve, yet Isao had had to spend a whole year in prison in order to carry it out successfully.

However, on reflection, Isao's act of assassination and his suicide seemed like brilliant evening stars, harbingers, in a night filled with glittering constellations, that led the way to the February Twenty-Sixth Incident. To be sure, the assassins had hoped for dawn, but what materialized was night. And now, be the times what they may, that night was almost spent, and an uneasy, stifling morning had settled in, one that none of those activists would have imagined.

The treaty drawn up by Japan, Germany, and Italy had angered a segment of the nationalists and those who were pro-French and pro-English; but the great majority of those who liked Europe and the West and even the old-fashioned proponents of a pan-Asia were pleased about it. Japan was to be married, not to Hitler, but to the German forests; not to Mussolini, but to the Roman pantheon. It was a pact joining German, Roman, and Japanese mythology: a friendship among the beautiful, masculine, pagan gods of East and West.

Honda, of course, had never submitted to such romantic prejudice, but he sensed that the times were somehow tremulously ripening and it was clear that some dream was forming. And now that he was here, away from Tokyo, the sudden rest and leisure resulted curiously in fatigue, and he could do nothing to prevent this plunge into reminiscing about things past.

He had not abandoned his idea, the one he had stressed long, long ago when talking with the nineteen-year-old Kiyoaki: the will to engage oneself in history is the essence of human purpose. Yet the instinctive fear that a nineteen-year-old boy has about his own character turns out, at times, to be extremely prophetic. While proclaiming such a concept, Honda at the time was in reality expressing despair in his own makeup. This despondency increased as he grew older and finally became a chronic ailment. But his personality had never changed in the slightest. He recalled a most terrifying

passage from the chapter on the Three Recompenses *
in the *Treatise on the Establishment of Reality*, which
was among the two or three Buddhist texts recommended
by the Abbess of the Gesshu Temple:

> That one takes pleasure in doing evil
> Is because that evil is not ripe.

Thus, Honda took a listless, tropical pleasure in the
gracious reception he had met in Bangkok, in what he
heard and saw, and even in what he ate and drank,
But that was not really proof that he had been guiltless
of evil acts in the nearly fifty years of his life. His evil
was surely not yet so ripe as the fragrant fruit ready
to fall of itself from the branch.

In Thai Theravada Buddhism with the artless concept of causality found in the Southern Buddhist Canon,
Honda recognized the causality of the Laws of Manu
that had impressed him so deeply in his youth.
Throughout, Hindu deities show their grotesque faces.
The sacred *naga*-serpent, the mythical *garuda,* half giant,
half eagle with golden body, white face, and red wings,
which adorn the eaves of the temples, still recount the
stories of the *Nagananda,* the seventh-century Indian
epic, and the filial piety of *garuda* is acclaimed by the
Hindu Vishnu.

Since coming to this land, Honda's former intellectual
curiosity had been piqued, and he was eager to discover
how Theravada Buddhism explained the mystery of
transmigration. It was this concept that provided him
the opportunity of casting aside half a lifetime of rationality.

According to scholars, Indian religious philosophy
is divided into six periods:

1. The period of the *Rig Veda.*
2. The period of the *Brahmanas.*

---

* That is, recompensation in the present life for deeds already done, in
the next rebirth for deeds now done, and in subsequent lives. (Translators'
note.)

3. The period of the *Upanishads,* which extends from the eighth to the fifth centuries B.C., an era of self-conscious philosophy, establishing as its ideal the unity of Brahma, the ultimate ground of all being, and atman, "self." The idea of a cycle of births and deaths—samsara—appeared clearly for the first time in this period, and when linked to the concept that acts (karma) bring inevitable consequences the law of causality came into being. By coupling that with the idea of atman, a philosophical system emerged.

4. A period of schism among various schools of thought.

5. The period of perfection of Theravada Buddhism, occurring between the third and first centuries B.C.

6. The ensuing five hundred years which saw the rise of Mahayana Buddhism.

The problem is the fifth period, in which the Laws of Manu were compiled. Honda had been surprised when in his youth he had discovered that the concept of samsara was applied even to law codes. The idea of karma as it appears later in Buddhism was distinctly different from that in the *Upanishads:* the difference lay in Buddhism's denial of atman, for such denial is the essence of this religion.

One of the three characteristics which differentiate Buddhism from other religions is that of the selflessness of all the dharmas. Buddhism advocated selflessness and denied atman, which had been considered to be the main constituent of life. It followed that Buddhism rejected the idea of "soul," which is the extension of atman into the hereafter. Buddhism does not recognize the soul as such. If there is no core substance called soul in beings, there is, of course, none in inorganic matter. Indeed, quite like a jellyfish devoid of bone, there is no innate essence in all of creation.

But then the troublesome question arises: if good acts produce a good subsequent existence and evil acts a bad one, and if, indeed, everything returns to nothingness following death, what then is the transmigrating substance? If we assume there is no self, what is the basis of the birth-and-death cycle to start with?

The three hundred years of Theravada Buddhism constitute a period of dispute and conflict among many schools which resulted in no satisfactory logical conclusion for any given one. All were embarrassed by the contradictions and inconsistencies that existed between the atman, that Buddhism denied, and karma, which it inherited.

For a credible philosophical answer to this question, mankind had to await the Mahayana school called Yuishiki, or "consciousness only." But when the Theravada Sautrantika school evolved, the concept of "seed perfuming" was established, according to which the effect of a good or bad deed remains in one's consciousness, permeating it as the fragrance of perfume permeates clothes, and thus forms character. This power of forming was the origin of the causal theory. The doctrine was the precursor of later Yuishiki ideas.

And now Honda realized what was behind the constant smile and the melancholy eyes of the two Siamese princes. It was a feeling of heavy, golden listlessness, of lulling breezes beneath the trees—the constant evasion of any organized logical system; oppressed and languid in the sun, the people of this land of sumptuous temples and flowers and fruits faithfully worshipped the Buddha and believed implicitly in reincarnation.

Prince Kridsada aside, the intelligent Prince Pattanadid had had, surprisingly, the sharp mind of a philosopher. Yet the violence of his emotions swept away any dispassionate intellectualism. Honda still remembered most vividly, more than any words the Prince had spoken, the sight of him fainting that end of summer on the lawn chair at Kiyoaki's southern villa on hearing the news of Chantrapa's death. His tanned arm dangled limply from the white armrest. Honda could not see if the Prince's face, resting against his shoulder, had turned pale, but his brilliant white teeth were visible between slightly parted lips.

His long, elegant brown fingers, meant for the subtle

caresses of love, hung loosely, almost touching the green summer grass, as though all five had momentarily followed in death the deceased object of his desire.

However, Honda feared that the princes' recollection of Japan might not be very pleasant, though the passage of time could well have made them miss it even more. Their isolation, their language difficulties, the different customs, Prince Pattanadid's loss of his emerald ring, and the death of Princess Chantrapa had made their stay in Japan something less than enjoyable. But what had ultimately turned away their understanding was the intimidating Swordsmen's Team spirit at the Peers School. This had alienated not only the princes but also ordinary students like Honda and Kiyoaki and the liberal and humanistic young men of the White Birch literary society. Unfortunately, the real Japan was not easily found among the friends of the princes, but was much more present among their enemies; the princes themselves were probably vaguely aware of this. An uncompromising Japan, as proud as a young warrior in scarlet silk, and yet as sensitive as a young boy challenging to battle before he is taunted and charging to his death before accepting insult. Isao was different from Kiyoaki, for he lived in the center of this radical world and believed in the existence of the soul.

Approaching fifty, Honda now possessed one advantage: he was probably free of prejudice. Of authority too, for he himself had once been authority; and even of reason, since he had once been the personification of cerebration.

Even the spirit of the Swordsmen's Team in the second decade of the century was one of youth in uniform; it pervaded the entire era. And Honda too, who had never been a part of it, now that he was older did not hesitate to identify in his memory those youthful days with an aggressive spirit.

This temper, further distilled and purified, formed Isao's world, one Honda had not shared with him in his younger days, one he had observed only as an outsider.

THE TEMPLE OF DAWN • 23

Noting how Isao's youthful Japanese mind, struggling in absolute isolation, had destroyed itself, Honda could not but realize that what had permitted him to live the way he had was the strength of Western thought, imported from the outside. Unfertilized thinking brings death.

If one wished to live, one must not cling to purity, as Isao had done. One must not cut oneself off from all channels of retreat; one must not reject everything.

Nothing had ever forced Honda to probe the question of an unadulterated Japan more deeply than had Isao's death. Was there any way to live honestly with Japan other than by rejecting everything, than by rejecting present-day Japan and the Japanese people? Was there no other way of living than this most difficult one, in which ultimately one murdered and then committed suicide? Everyone was afraid to say, but had not Isao given proof by his acts?

On reflection, in the purest of tribes there was the smell of blood and the taint of savagery. Unlike the Spaniards, who preserved their national sport of bullfighting despite the accusations of animal lovers throughout the world, the Japanese, when the nation had embraced a new culture and ethic at the end of the last century, turned their efforts to eliminating the barbaric customs of preceding generations. As a result, the genuine, unadulterated national spirit was subordinated, its energy erupting from time to time in explosions of violence which repelled and alienated the people even more.

However, whatever frightening mask it might assume, the national spirit in its original state was of pristine whiteness. Traveling through a country like Thailand, Honda realized more clearly than ever the simplicity and purity of things Japanese, like transparent stream water through which one could glimpse pebbles below, or the probity of Shinto rites. Honda's life was not imbued with such spirit. Like the majority of Japanese he ignored it, behaving as though it did not exist and surviving by escaping from it. All his life he had dodged things fundamental and artless: white silk, clear cold water, the zigzag white paper of the exorciser's staff fluttering in the breeze, the sacred precinct marked by a torii, the gods' dwelling in the sea, the mountains, the vast ocean, the Japanese sword with its glistening blade so pure and sharp. Not only Honda, but the vast majority of Westernized Japanese, could no longer stand such intensely native elements.

But if Isao, who believed in the soul, had indeed gone to heaven—and this was an example of a good cause producing a good effect—if he had entered the cycle of births and deaths and been reborn as a human, what could the process be?

Now that he thought about it, Honda wondered if Isao, when he had determined to die, had not indeed secretly held some premonition of another life. There seemed to have been some indication of this. When a man strove to live his life in so pure and extreme a fashion, was he not naturally led to the supposition of another existence?

Honda recalled the Japanese shrine, and in the heat the very thought made him feel drops of clear cool water on his forehead. To the visitor climbing the stone steps, the torii, that seems merely a well-defined frame for the main shrine building, on his exit seems to change into a frame of clear blue sky. Strange that one frame should contain a lofty shrine from one side and empty blue sky from the other. The form of the torii seemed like that of Isao's soul.

For Isao had lived a well-defined life that resembled a torii, lofty, beautiful, simple. And inevitably it was ultimately filled with clear blue sky.

No matter how far the dying Isao's mind had drifted from Buddhism, this very paradox seemed to point up to Honda the relationship between the Japanese and Buddhism. It was as though the muddy waters of the Menam were to be filtered through a sieve of white silk.

Late the same night that he had heard the story of the Princess from Hishikawa, Honda rummaged

through his suitcase in the hotel room and brought out
Kiyoaki's Dream Diary wrapped in purple silk.

The diary had been read and reread and the binding
had begun to fall apart; Honda had clumsily but carefully
mended it himself. Kiyoaki's hasty, youthful writing
was still vibrant, but the color of the ink had faded
during the thirty years since it had been written.

Yes, just as Honda remembered, Kiyoaki had had
a vivid dream of Siam which he had entered in the diary
shortly after the Siamese princes had visited his home.

Kiyoaki was seated in a fine chair in a palace with
a ruined garden. He wore "a high, pointed, gold crown
inlaid with jewel clusters." In the dream he was a member
of Siamese royalty.

Many peacocks were perched on the beams, letting
fall their white droppings, and Kiyoaki wore Prince Pattanadid's emerald ring on his finger. "The lovely face
of a small girl" was mirrored in the stone. This must
have been the face of the little mad Princess he had
not yet seen, and the reflection in the emerald with its
downcast eyes was presumably Kiyoaki's own. It seemed
beyond question now to Honda that the Princess was
indeed the reincarnation of Kiyoaki by way of Isao.

It was not unexpected that he should have had such
a dream after receiving the Siamese princes in his house
and listening to the fascinating tales of their country.
But after several experiences, Honda was forced to accept
the fact that Kiyoaki's dream was another manifestation
of his transmigration.

It was now self-explanatory. Once he had surmounted
the problem of faulty logic, everything fitted together.
Isao had never told Honda, nor had Honda ever discovered, whether Isao had had any other omens; Isao
too might well have dreamed during his prison nights
about the girl in the tropics.

Hishikawa diligently looked after Honda's needs
during the latter's stay in Bangkok. And the lawsuit
was going well, thanks to Honda's efforts. He had un-
covered an oversight on the part of the buyers.

According to article 473 of the Thai Civil Code, which was founded on Anglo-American law, sellers need not assume responsibility for flaws in their merchandise in one or more of the following instances:

1. If the buyer was aware of the flaw at the time of purchase, or could have been had he been ordinarily observant.

2. If the flaw was evident at the time of the delivery of the merchandise, or if the buyer accepted the merchandise without reservation.

3. If the merchandise was sold at public auction.

As Honda investigated further, it became clear to him that the buyers could have been guilty according to either the first or second instance. If he could follow this up and get sufficient proof, they might well drop the charges.

Needless to say, Itsui Products were grateful, and Honda himself was quite relived. He felt inclined to ask Hishikawa to get on with arranging an audience with the Princess. But he was such a bore.

Honda had never had any desire to make friends with artists, and indeed, he had never had a friend who could be called one. Nor had he ever expected to be introduced to an arty dropout in such a remote place as this.

It was all the more exasperating then that Hishikawa should be so helpful as a guide for the unaccustomed traveler, never the slightest reluctant to do whatever Honda asked. Furthermore, he possessed all sorts of back-door entrées in this country where any entrance through the front was strictly impossible. He was indeed a priceless guide, and he himself knew it.

But Hishikawa had retained the disagreeable affectations of an artist, whatever the work was he had produced in the past. He depended on guiding travelers to earn his living, and yet in his heart he was contemptuous of the Philistines whom he squired about. As this was transparently clear to Honda, he amused himself by being the very image of the Philistine Hishikawa thought him to be. He talked intentionally about his wife and mother in Japan, about his unhappiness in having no children. He enjoyed observing as Hishikawa unsuspectingly acted out the role of being sympathetic.

In fact, artists who were not only immature, but who made it a practice to flaunt immaturity as a dishonest alibi to fend off criticism of their works were hideous beyond measure when compared to the guileless immaturity which Kiyoaki or Isao had displayed. Artists dragged this immaturity throughout their lives . . . into their eighties. It was as if they made the swaddling clothes they hauled along into merchandise.

If there was anything worse it was the pseudo-artists; their indescribable arrogance together with their particular brand of obsequiousness gave off an odor peculiar to lazy men. Hishikawa was simply a sloth living by hanging onto others, but he pretended to be the elegant, listless aristocrat living in the tropics. Honda was irritated by his habit of saying at restaurants, wine list in hand: "Since Itsui Products are footing the bill anyway . . . ," and of then proceeding to order the more expensive wines. Honda was not all that fond of wine.

While he hoped he would never be put in the position of defending such a man, it would be a breach of etiquette on his part, as an invited guest, to ask to have his guide replaced.

Every time the obese branch manager asked Honda in the waiting room at court or at a dinner party: "Is Hishikawa doing all right by you?" Honda would answer: "He's very capable, yes," concealing in his words a certain bitterness. The manager seemed satisfied to take his reply at face value, and Honda was irked that he made no attempt to read behind the words.

Familiarity with the covert human relationships in this country, which were like the dank jungle undergrowth rapidly rotting away beneath the surface green that shone in the blistering sun, had enabled Hishikawa to develop his talent for smelling out rottenness in human matters faster than anyone else. And that was the source of

his income. He would have rested his powerful, housefly
wings of gold on the leftovers in the manager's plate.

"Good morning!"

Honda was awakened from deep sleep by a familiar
voice on the interphone at his bedside, a voice he heard
every morning—Hishikawa.

"Did I wake you? Forgive me. The court people think
nothing of making you wait for hours, but they're terribly
fussy about visitors being punctual. I called early to
be on the safe side. Take your time shaving. What?
Breakfast? No, no, don't worry about that. Well, to tell
the truth, I haven't yet, but I can do without. Oh? In
your room with you? Well, thank you very much indeed.
I'll accept the invitation and come on up. Shall I let you
have five minutes? Or ten? Well, since you're not a lady,
perhaps I don't have to be so punctilious."

This was not the first time that Hishikawa had partaken
of the Oriental Hotel's sumptuous, multicourse English
breakfast in Honda's room.

Shortly, dressed in a well-cut white linen suit,
Hishikawa walked in, busily fanning his chest with a
panama hat. He stopped squarely under the large, white,
sluggishly rotating blades of the fan.

"Before I forget," said the pajama-clad Honda, "what
shall I call the Princess? Is it proper to say 'Your
Highness'?"

"No, no!" replied Hishikawa with assurance. "She's
the daughter of Pattanadid and he's half brother to the
king. His title is Pra Ong Chao; you address him as
'Your Royal Highness' in English. But the daughter
is Mon Chao, and you should call her 'Your Serene
Highness.' Anyway don't worry. I'll take care of everything."

The unrelenting heat had already invaded the room.
Having left his sweat-dampened bed and standing under
the cold shower, Honda felt for the first time the morning
on his skin. The experience was a strangely sensuous
one. He who never contacted the external world without
first filtering it through rational thought, here felt through

his skin; only through his skin sensing the brilliant green of the tropical plants, the vermilion of the mimosa flowers, the golden decor adorning the temples, or the sudden blue lightning could he come into contact with the world about him. This was a totally exotic experience for him. The warm rains, the tepid showers. The external world was a richly colored liquid, and it was as if he were constantly bathing in it. How could he have anticipated all this in Japan?

While waiting for breakfast, Hishikawa paced back and forth around the room like a European, scoffing at the mediocre landscape that hung on the wall. The heels of his freshly polished black shoes reflected the patterns of the carpet as he outrageously postured. Honda was suddenly tired of the game where Hishikawa played the artist and he the Philistine.

Abruptly turning, Hishikawa removed a small purple velvet case from his pocket. Handing it to Honda, he said: "You mustn't forget this. Hand it directly to the Princess."

"What is it?"

"A present. Royalty has made it custom here never to receive a visitor who arrives empty-handed."

Honda opened the case and discovered a fine pearl ring.

"Oh, I see. I never thought of that. Thank you for reminding me. How much do I owe you?"

"Oh, nothing. Really it's not necessary. I told Itsui Products you needed it for a royal audience. Anyway the manager probably picked it up cheap from some Japanese. You don't need to worry."

Honda immediately understood he should not ask further about the price for the time being. But Itsui Products should not be expected to pay for his private expenditures. He would repay the manager. Hishikawa had probably charged them a fat commission. He would have to overlook that and reimburse the local representative, whatever the cost.

"Well then, I accept your kindness with gratitude." Honda arose, and slipping the small case into the pocket of the jacket he was going to wear, casually asked: "By the way, what is the Princess's name?"

"Princess Chantrapa. I hear Prince Pattanadid named his last daughter after a fiancée who died long ago. Chantrapa means 'moonlight.' What a coincidence she's a lunatic," Hishikawa commented smugly.

3

ON THE WAY to the Rosette Palace, Honda saw from his car window some boys in the Yuwachon Movement marching in khaki uniforms reputedly modeled on those of the Hitler Jugend. Hishikawa, seated next to him, complained that American jazz was rarely heard in town those days, and that Prime Minister Phiboon's nationalism seemed to be taking effect.

It was the kind of transformation Honda had already witnessed in Japan. Just as wine slowly turned to vinegar or milk to curd, matters long neglected slowly change in response to the various forces of nature. People have long lived in fear of too much freedom, too much carnal desire. The freshness of the morning after an evening when one has abstained from drinking wine. The pride one feels on realizing that water alone is essential. Such refreshing, new pleasures were beginning to seduce people. Honda had a vague idea where such fanatical ideas would lead. It was a realization that had been born of Isao's death. Single-mindedness often gives rise to viciousness.

Honda suddenly recalled Isao's drunken, incoherent words two days before his death. "Far to the south . . . Very hot . . . in the rose sunshine of a southern land . . ." Now, eight years later, he was hastening to the Rosette Palace to meet him.

His was the joy of a parched and feverish land awaiting the drenching rains.

It seemed to Honda that in experiencing such emotions as these he was brought face to face with his innermost self. As a youth he had judged his fears, his sorrows, and his rationality to be his true inner core, but none was real. When he heard about Isao's suicide, he had felt a kind of sudden frustration instead of the sharp pain of sorrow; but with the passage of time, this had changed into the expectant pleasure of meeting him again. Honda realized in his heart that in moments like this, his emotions contained not one human element. His inner self was ruled perhaps by some extraordinary pleasure not of this world. It must be so, for he alone, in Isao's case, had escaped the sorrow and pain of parting.

Far to the south . . . Very hot . . . in the rose sunshine of a southern land . . .

The car drew up before an elegant gate beyond which lay a stretch of greensward. Hishikawa got out first and spoke to the guard in Siamese as he handed him a calling card.

From the car window Honda could see an iron gate of repeating octagon and arrow motifs, while beyond, the smooth green lawn quietly soaked up the intense sun. Two or three bushes with white and yellow flowers, trimmed into round shapes, cast their shadows on the grass.

Hishikawa escorted Honda through the gate.

The building was too insignificant to qualify as a palace; it was merely a small two-story structure with a slate roof, painted a faded yellowish rose. Except for a large mimosa tree to one side, soiling the wall with its severe black shadow, only the expanse of yellow soothed the harsh brilliance of the sun.

They met no one as they walked along the winding path over the lawn. As Honda approached his goal, and despite the joy that he knew was metaphysical, he felt as though the sound of his footsteps were that of the sharp claws of some jungle beast stalking its prey with drooling fangs. Yes, he had been born for just this pleasure.

The Rosette Palace seemed confined in its own stubborn little dream. The impression was enhanced by the shape of the building itself. It was a little box with neither wings nor extensions. The ground floor displayed so many casement windows that it was difficult to discern which was the entrance. Every one was paneled in wood carved into roses, above which octagons of yellow, blue, and indigo glass encircled small, five-petaled, purple rose-shaped windows in the Near Eastern style. The French windows facing the garden were half open.

The second floor bore a panel of fleur-de-lis, and three windows opening on the garden formed a triptych. The central one was higher than its neighbors, but all were bordered with carved rosettes.

The entrance itself at the top of three steps consisted of a French window of the same design. As soon as Hishikawa rang the bell, Honda indiscreetly peeped through the small rose pane of purple glass. Inside all was dark violet, like the ocean floor.

The French door opened and an old woman appeared. Honda and Hishikawa removed their hats. The white-haired brown face with its flat nose wore a smile of friendly greeting in the characteristic Thai manner. But the smile was a formality, nothing more.

The woman spoke with Hishikawa for a few moments. Apparently there had been no change in the appointment he had arranged.

Four of five chairs were lined up in the foyer that was too small for a reception hall. Hishikawa handed a package to the woman and she accepted it after joining her hands respectfully. Opening the central door, she at once led them into a spacious audience hall.

After the morning heat outside, the musty, stagnant coolness of the room was pleasant. The two men were invited to sit in red and gold Chinese chairs supported by legs in the form of lion paws.

While waiting for the Princess, Honda took the opportunity to scrutinize the room. There was no sound save the faint buzzing of a fly.

The reception hall did not give directly onto the windows. A pillared gallery supported a mezzanine; only the throne was heavily draped. And directly above it a portrait of King Chulalongkorn was displayed in the upper gallery. The Corinthian pillars of the gallery were painted blue with vertical incisions inlaid with gold, while the capitals were adorned with golden roses in the Near Eastern style instead of the usual acanthus leaves.

The rosette pattern was tenaciously repeated throughout the palace. The gallery, painted gold and bordered in white, had openwork balustrades of golden roses. An immense chandelier suspended from the center of the lofty ceiling was also decorated with gold and white roses. When Honda looked down at his feet, he saw that the red carpet had a rosette pattern.

A pair of gigantic ivory tusks placed behind the throne—an embracing pair of white crescent moons—was the sole traditionally Thai decoration. The impressive polished ivory gleamed yellowish white in the gloom.

Upon entering, Honda discovered that the French windows occupied only the forepart of the house facing the front garden. The open ones looking out on the rear garden, barred by a corridor, were only chest high. It was through the northern windows that a light breeze entered.

As his eyes wandered toward the windows, he suddenly glimpsed a black shadow flitting by the window frame. He shuddered. It was a green peacock. The bird perched on the sill, stretching its long elegant neck that glittered a greenish gold. The plumed crest on its proud head was like the delicate silhouette of a miniature fan.

"I wonder how long they're going to make us wait," Honda whispered into Hishikawa's ear, thoroughly bored.

"It's always like this. It doesn't mean anything. They're not trying to impress you particularly by making you wait. You know by now that you mustn't rush things in this country. In the days of Chulalongkorn's son, King Urachid, His Majesty used to go to bed at dawn and arise in the afternoon. Everything was slow and easygoing; day and night were reversed. The Minister of Palace Affairs put in his appearance about four in the afternoon and returned home only in the morning. But in the tropics perhaps that's the best way. The beauty of these people is the beauty of fruit; fruit should ripen lazily and gracefully. There's no such thing as diligent fruit."

Honda was annoyed with Hishikawa's typically long, whispered disquisition, but before he could turn away to avoid his bad breath, the old woman reappeared. Joining her hands respectfully, she indicated the approach of the Princess.

There was a hissing from the window where the peacock perched. It was not the warning sound used in the ancient Japanese court to signal the arrival of royalty. They were simply chasing the peacock away. There was a flutter of wings at the window, and the bird disappeared. Honda saw three old ladies coming down the northern corridor. They walked in a straight line, keeping an equal distance between them. The Princess was led by the first lady-in-waiting, her one hand held by the woman, the other toying with a garland of white jasmine. As the little seven-year-old Princess Moonlight was led toward the great Chinese chair before the ivory tusks, the old woman who had first met the guests at the door immediately knelt down on the floor and kowtowed in the manner called *krab* in Thai. She was presumably of low rank.

The first lady-in-waiting put her arm around the Princess and sat down with her in the center Chinese chair. The other two seated themselves in small chairs to the right of and facing the throne. The third lady was now next to Hishikawa. The woman who had knelt down had already vanished when Honda looked around.

He imitated Hishikawa, who stood up and bowed deeply, then sat down on the red and gold Chinese chair. The women seemed to be close to seventy, and the little Princess appeared more their charge than their mistress.

The little girl was not wearing the old-fashioned *panun*, but a Western-style blouse of some white material embroidered in gold, and a printed Thai cotton skirt called *passin* that resembled a Malayan sarong. On her feet she wore a pair of red shoes decorated in gold. Her hair was cut short in the characteristic Thai style. This traditional coiffure honored the brave maidens of Khorat who long ago, dressed as men, had fought against an invading Cambodian army.

Her lovely, intelligent face showed no sign of insanity. Her delicate, well-shaped brows and lips were commanding, and her short hair made her look more like a prince than a princess. Her skin was a golden tan.

Audience to her was receiving the two men's obeisance; this over, she toyed with her jasmine wreath and swung her legs over the edge of the high chair. She looked intently at Honda and whispered to the first lady-in-waiting; the latter rebuked her with a single word.

At Hishikawa's signal Honda brought out the purple velvet case with the pearl ring. It was passed to the third lady, then by way of the second and the first, respectively, it finally reached the Princess's hand. The time spent as it made its way to her seemed to deepen the torpor of the summer heat. As the case had been examined by the first lady, the Princess was deprived of the childish delight in opening it herself.

Her lovely brown fingers carelessly discarded the jasmine garland and took up the pearl ring. She inspected it intently for some time. Her unusual quietness that signified neither emotion nor lack of emotion lasted so long that Honda began to think this might be one of the symptoms of her madness. Suddenly a smile, like a bubble in water, broke out on her face, showing her white, childishly irregular teeth. Honda was relieved.

The ring was returned to the case and given back to the first lady-in-waiting. The Princess spoke for the first time in a clear, intelligent voice. Her words were then transmitted through the three ladies like a green snake slithering from branch to branch in the sun-touched shade of the palms and finally, translated by Hishikawa, reached Honda. The Princess had said: "Thank you."

Honda asked Hishikawa to translate for him. "I have for long been an admirer of the Thai royal family, and I understand Her Serene Highness likes Japan too. If I may, I should like to send her a Japanese doll after I return. Would she accept it?" The Thai sentences spoken by Hishikawa were rather simple, but as they were passed on by the third and the second ladies-in-waiting, they grew longer and more numerous, and by the time the first lady-in-waiting conveyed the import to the Princess, they seemed endless.

And the Princess's words when they returned to Honda were devoid of any sparkle of emotion or charm after they had traveled through the ladies' dark and wrinkled lips. It was as though the meat of the young Princess's vivacious expressions had been sucked out in the process, chewed up by their ancient dentures, leaving only unsightly refuse for Honda.

"They say that Her Serene Highness is pleased to accept Mr. Honda's kind offer."

Then a strange thing happened.

Catching the first lady off-guard, the Princess jumped off the chair, covered the three feet that separated her from Honda, and clung to his trouser legs. Honda rose in alarm. Quivering and still clinging to him, the Princess cried out, weeping loudly. He bent over and put his arms around the fragile shoulders of the sobbing girl.

The ladies-in-waiting, nonplussed, were unable to pull her away. They clustered together, whispering uneasily among themselves as they stared at her.

"What does she say? Translate!" Honda called to Hishikawa who was standing in amazement.

Hishikawa translated in a shrill voice: "Mr. Honda! Mr. Honda! How I've missed you! You were so kind, and yet I killed myself without telling you anything. I have been waiting for this meeting to apologize to you for more than seven years. I have taken the form of a princess, but I am really Japanese. I spent my former life in Japan, and that is really my home. Please, Mr. Honda, take me back to Japan."

Finally the Princess was brought back to the chair and somehow the propriety of an audience was restored. Honda looked from where he stood at the black hair of the girl who was still weeping, now leaning against the first lady-in-waiting. He cherished the child's warmth and fragrance which still lingered on his knee.

The ladies requested that the audience be terminated since the Princess was not feeling well; but Honda begged, through Hishikawa, to be permitted two brief questions.

"What year and what month was it that Kiyoaki Matsugae and I learned about the visit of the Abbess of the Gesshu Temple on the central island of the lake in the Matsugae estate?" was the first.

When the question was conveyed to her, the Princess partly raised her wet cheeks from her attendant's lap as though still cross and pushed back a strand of hair that adhered to her cheek.

"October of 1912," she answered readily.

Honda was secretly surprised, but he was not sure whether, like an illuminated picture scroll, she kept in her mind a clear and detailed record of the events of two former lives. He was not certain either, despite Isao's words of apology spoken so fluently, whether she knew the background details and circumstances. As a matter of fact, the accurate words had dropped from the Princess's emotionless lips as though numerals picked and arranged at random.

Honda asked the second question: "What was the date of Isao Iinuma's arrest?"

The Princess seemed to be growing sleepy, but she answered unhesitatingly: "December first, 1932."

"That should be enough," said the first lady, rising and thus pressing her charge to leave immediately.

The Princess suddenly sprang to her feet, climbed up on the chair in her shoes, and shouted to Honda in her shrill voice. The first attendant scolded her in

whispers. The Princess, still shouting, clutched at the
old woman's hair. She was evidently repeating the same
words, judging from the similarity of the syllables. As
the second and third ladies ran over to hold her arms,
the Princess started to cry madly, her piercing voice
echoing from the high ceiling. From among the old
women who were trying to pull her down, her smooth,
pliant arms shot out, catching hold here and there. The
old women withdrew, crying out in pain, and the Princess's voice rose even higher.

"What was that?"

"She insists on inviting you to the Detached Palace
of Bang Pa In when she goes there for a visit day after
tomorrow, and the ladies are trying to prevent it. This
is going to be some show," said Hishikawa.

A discussion began between the Princess and her
attendants. Finally she nodded and stopped crying.

"The day after tomorrow," said the first lady, still
out of breath, straightening her disheveled clothes and
speaking directly to Honda, "Her Serene Highness will
drive to the Bang Pa In Palace for amusement. Mr.
Honda and Mr. Hishikawa are invited. We should very
much like them to accept. As we shall lunch there, it
would be well if they were here by nine o'clock in the
morning."

The formal invitation was immediately translated
by Hishikawa.

In the car returning to the hotel, Hishikawa kept
up his interminable chatter, ignoring the fact that Honda
was lost in thought. The lack of consideration for others
displayed by this self-styled artist bespoke his threadbare
sensitivity. Had he deemed sensitivity to be an unnecessary, Philistine characteristic and had he adhered to
this view, at least he would have had the virtue of consis-
tency; but in truth Hishikawa took pride in his delicacy
and sensitivity in human relationships, which he thought
far exceeded those of other guides.

"It was very astute of you to ask those two questions.
I didn't understand what it was all about. But you were

putting her to a test because she showed you a special closeness in pretending to be the reincarnation of your friend. Isn't that right?"

"Quite," Honda replied perfunctorily.

"And were both the answers right?"

"No."

"Was one, at least?"

"No. I'm sorry to say both were wrong."

Honda lied to be let alone, and his despairing tone conveniently concealed the deception, whereupon Hishikawa broke into loud laughter, believing Honda was telling him the truth.

"Is that right! All of them wrong? She said the dates so seriously. Well, too bad. The transmigration business wasn't very convincing then. You're not very kind, though, testing such a lovely little princess as if you were examining a quack fortune-teller on some street corner. By and large, there's no mystery in human life. Mystery remains only in the arts, and the reason is that mystery makes sense only in art."

Honda was again surprised by Hishikawa's one-track rationalism. He glimpsed something red outside the car window, and looking out, saw a river and among the coconuts with trunks of flaming red bordering the road baboonlike, the smoky scarlet of poinciana along the bank. Heat waves were already quivering around the trees.

Honda turned to the problem of how he could get to the Bang Pa In Palace without Hishikawa, even though that meant he would be unable to communicate with the Princess.

4

HONDA'S WISH materialized unexpectedly. "I'm not in the mood for another session with the mad princess," Hishikawa said patronizingly, "but if I don't go, you'll have trouble. The attendants speak only a few words

of English." Contrary to his wont, Honda replied: "I
shall enjoy the Thai language as if it were music, even
though I don't understand it. I'd rather do that than
be bothered with the nuisance of a translation each time."
He hoped that this would more or less bring to a close
his dealings with Hishikawa.

Subsequently Honda would recall again and again
the delightful outing that day.

The car could approach only partway to the Bang
Pa In Palace. The remaining distance was covered on
a court-style pleasure boat, which moved along a water-
way consisting of both the river and flooded rice fields.
From time to time a water buffalo would awaken from
his nap in a paddy and suddenly rear up, his muddy
back glinting in the sun. When the boat skirted a forest
of tall trees, the Princess was delighted at the sight of
numerous squirrels scurrying up and down the branches
along the riverbank. On one occasion a small green
snake, his head erect, could be seen leaping from one
low branch to another.

Golden spires rose above the jungle, each one freshly
gilded, thanks to the donations of believers. Honda knew
that the gold leaf was made in Japan and exported to
Thailand in considerable quantity.

He vividly recalled the few moments during which
Princess Moonlight ceased her constant childish chatter
and motionlessly leaned against the side of the boat,
staring blankly into the distance. The female attendants,
engrossed in their own merriment, were quite accustomed
to such whimsical action on the part of the little girl
and paid her no attention. Honda noticed immediately
what it was she was watching and was quite shaken.

A great cloud that had appeared from beyond the
horizon now hid the sun. The sun was already high,
and the cloud had to stretch its tentacles far to cover
it. The black cloud reached out to overlay just the sun
and, with some difficulty, succeeded. The highest part
in the blue sky over the disk was a dazzling white, giving
the lie to the ominous black density of the thicker area.
Nor was that all; the extension had made the cloud

too thin and resulted in a large rift in the lower portion, through which a radiant light streamed, as though the shining effulgence were blood endlessly spurting from a great wound.

The distant horizon was covered by low-lying jungle. The foreground sparkled in radiant green, as though it were part of another world, grasping the sunshine that poured from the rift in the cloud. But the jungle farther away under the lower black portion was drenched by rains of such violence that fog seemed to be rising. The rain hung like some elaborate fungoid network, wrapping the dark jungle in its misty vapor. The rain net, which covered only a part of the distant horizon, was distinctily visible, and one could discern the horizontal movement of the drops whipped by the wind. The heavy shower, as if imprisoned, seemed concentrated in that area alone.

Honda knew immediately what the child was looking at: she was seeing simultaneously time and space. That is to say, the area beneath the squall belonged to some future or past undetectable by the human eye. To be beneath a clear blue sky and perceive so clearly a world of rain meant that different time periods and different spaces coexisted. The rain cloud permitted a glimpse of the gap between separate times, and the vast distance involved testified to the hiatus between the two spaces. The Princess was staring into the deep chasm of the universe.

Her tiny, pink, wet tongue was absentmindedly but earnestly licking the pearl ring Honda had given her—the lady-in-waiting would have scolded if she had noticed. It was as if the tiny Princess, by licking the pearl, were testifying to the revelation of such a miracle.

Bang Pa In.
The name had become unforgettable.
The Princess insisted on holding Honda's hand as she walked along; and ignoring the ladies' frowns, he let himself be guided by the tiny, damp fist. Thoroughly familiar with the land, the Princess led him to a Chinese

villa, then to a French arbor, a Renaissance garden, an Arabian tower, to one spot after another, all of which pleased his eye.

The floating pavilion in the center of a spacious artificial pond was particularly beautiful, like a fine objet d'art set upon the water.

The stone stairs at the water's edge had been invaded as the water rose and the bottom step was hidden in the depths of the pool. The white marble in the water was green with algae. Waterweed had wrapped itself around, covering it with tiny silver bubbles. Princess Moonlight wanted to dip her hands and feet into the water, but her attendants repeatedly forbade her to do so. Honda could not understand her words, but she seemed to think that the bubbles, like her ring, were pearls she wished to gather.

When Honda stopped her, she calmed down immediately and seated herself on the stone steps beside him and looked out at the chapel that seemed to float in the center of the pond.

It was not really a chapel, but a small pavilion used merely as a resting place while boating. Inside, it was quite empty, as one could see when the breeze parted the faded buff-yellow curtains.

The simple building was enclosed by walls of thin black rods decorated in gold. Through the interstices the greenery of the opposite shore, the curling clouds, and the sky heavy with light were all visible. As Honda stared at the panorama, the magnificent clouds and the forest visible through the screen of rods took on the appearance of a picture composed of strangely long, vertical strips of colors. And, of course, the roof of the small pavilion was highly decorative, being constructed of four tiers of thick layers of brick-red, yellow, and green Chinese tiles and a brilliant thin spire of gold which pierced the blue sky.

Whether he had thought of it then or whether the vision of the pavilion overlapped with that of the Princess later, Honda could not remember. But in his mind the slim black rods of the pavilion somehow turned into the ebony bodies of dancing girls momentarily poised for dance, adorned with many gold filigree ornaments and wearing their pointed headgear.

5

ALL RECOLLECTED EVENTS that happen without any verbal communication—especially those during which there is no special attempt made to establish such communication—become effortlessly so many beautiful miniature paintings, all equally edged in ornate golden frames. The time Honda had spent at the Rosette Palace was indelibly etched in his memory because of those moments of aesthetic pleasure. Segments of such sunny instants would suddenly well up, at times forming a momentary portrait of the little Princess: the childish roundness of her hand stretched out to the pearl bubbles on the steps submerged in the water; the delicate, clean lines on her fingers and her palms; the deep black of her short hair hanging against her cheek; the long, almost melancholy eyelashes; and on her dark forehead the reflection of water, flickering like mother-of-pearl against black ebony. The time was aglow, the air in the garden was filled with the humming of bees, and the mood of the strolling ladies was cheerful too. The essence of the moment was like coral, beautiful and exposed. Yet, in those moments, the Princess's innocent, unclouded happiness and the series of agonizing and bloody events of her former two lives were combined like the clear and rainy skies of the distant jungle they had seen on their way to the palace.

Honda felt as if he were standing in the center of time, as if in some enormous hall in which all partitions had been removed. It was spacious and free, not like the mundane dwellings to which he was accustomed. There, black pillars stood in serried ranks and he felt almost as if his eyes and voice could reach areas normally unattainable. In this great expanse created by the Princess's happiness, behind the multitude of black pillars stood Kiyoaki and Isao and a myriad of other transmigrated shades lurking breathlessly as though in a game of hide-and-seek.

The Princess laughed again. Rather, in her merrymaking she smiled constantly, but frequently her moist pink gums would suddenly flash in real laughter. With each outburst she would look up into Honda's face.

Once at the Bang Pa In the old ladies quickly put aside their formality. Forgetting their stiff decorum, they giggled and ran about in high spirits. The formality gone, their age was all that remained of their ceremoniousness. They occupied themselves in picking at betel nuts together, quite like greedy, wrinkled parrots clustering around a bagful of seeds. They also scratched wherever they itched, thrusting their hands under the hems of their skirts. They would cackle noisily as they strutted sideways in imitation of young dancing girls. One mummied dancer with wiglike white hair shining over her brown face stretched her betel-stained mouth in gaping laughter and raised her sharp elbows, thrust sideways as she danced; the exposed, dry bones of her angular arms cut sharp shadow-pictures against the background of blue sky with its layers of dazzling clouds.

The Princess spoke, and at once the ladies stirred about. They surrounded the child and bustled off with her like a rolling whirlwind, leaving a surprised Honda alone. He grasped the meaning of their actions when he saw the small building that was their destination. She wanted to go to the bathroom.

A princess going to the toilet! Honda was aware of a sharp pang of affection. He had previously imagined having a small daughter and feeling a fatherly love for her, but having never had any child, his imagination had always been limited. His response to the charming idea of the little Princess going to the bathroom was an intimation of flesh and blood and a totally new emotional experience. He wished it was possible for him

to hold the Princess's smooth brown thighs in his hands
as she urinated.

She was shy for a while upon returning, saying nothing
and avoiding looking at him.

After lunch they played games in the shade.

Now Honda could not recall how the games went.
They had sung simple, monotonous songs over and over,
but he was ignorant of their meaning.

He could recall only the scene where the Princess
stood in the center of a sun-dappled lawn under the
trees, and around her the three old ladies were sitting
at ease, one with one knee raised, the others with their
legs crossed. One of them seemed to have entered the
play just to be sociable; she kept smoking tobacco
wrapped in lotus petals. Another had a lacquered water bottle inlaid with pearl shells by her knee in readiness
for the Princess who complained so often of thirst.

Probably the game had something to do with the
Ramayana. The Princess resembled Hanuman when
she wielded a tree branch like a sword, assuming a hunch-
backed stance and holding her breath in a comical way.
Each time the ladies clapped their hands and chanted
something, she changed her stance. By tilting her head
slightly she was a delicate flower nodding to a fleeting
breeze or a squirrel stopping to cock its head in the
midst of its travels through the tree branches. Again,
transformed into Prince Rama, she pointed gallantly
heavenward with the sword held by a dark, slender arm
extending from her gold-embroidered white blouse. At
that instant a mountain pigeon swept down in front
of her, obscuring her face with its wings. But she did
not move. Honda discovered that the towering tree behind
her was a lime. The broad leaves hanging at the tips
of the long stems on the gloomy growth rustled at every
soft touch of the breeze. Each green leaf was stamped
with distinct yellow veins, as though tropical sunbeams
had been woven into it.

The Princess grew warm. Rather peevishly she asked
something of the old ladies. They consulted together,
and standing up, signaled to Honda. The party quit

the shade of the woods and moved on to the boat landing. Honda gathered they must be going home, but he was wrong. They gave the boatman an order, whereupon he brought out a large piece of printed cotton.

Holding the fabric, they moved along the shore with its coiling mangrove roots until they found a more secluded spot. Two of the ladies lifted their skirts and walked into the water, holding either end of the cloth, which they completely opened when the water was hip high, so as to provide a screen that shut out the view from the opposite shore. The remaining lady accompanied the now naked Princess. The light reflected from the water on the emaciated thighs of the old women.

The Princess cried out in delight when she caught sight of some small fish that had gathered round the mangrove roots. Honda was surprised that the ladies-in-waiting should act as though he were simply not there, but he assumed that that too must be some aspect of Thai etiquette. Seating himself at the base of a tree on the bank, he watched the Princess bathe.

She was never quiet. Lit by the sunbeams dancing through the stripes in the cotton print, she smiled constantly at Honda. She made no effort to conceal her quite plump, childish belly as she splashed water on the ladies. When she was scolded she dashed away. The stagnant river water was not clear, but rather a yellowish brown, similar to the Princess's skin. But even that turned into limpid, sparkling droplets when splashed in the light that filtered through the cotton print.

Once the little girl raised her arm. Involuntarily Honda looked intently at her left side, at her small flat chest usually hidden by her arms. But he did not see the three black moles that should have been there. Whenever he could, he stared at the area until his eyes watered, thinking that perhaps the light moles were indistinct against the tan skin.

6

THE LAWSUIT Honda was handling came to an unexpected conclusion when the plaintiff, realizing he was at a disadvantage, suddenly dropped charges. Honda could have gone home at once, but as a token of their gratitude Itsui Products wanted to present him with a bonus in the form of a pleasure trip. He wished to go to India and expressed this desire. The administration replied that it would probably be the last opportunity for anyone to go to India since there were signs of approaching war; they promised that all Itsui offices would do their best to assure his every comfort. Honda prayed that that would not entail the kind of consideration they had imposed upon him by assigning Hishikawa as his guide.

Honda sent word to his family in Japan. At once he took pleasure in scheduling his itinerary with the aid of an Indian timetable featuring steam engines that traveled only fourteen or fifteen miles an hour. Upon consulting a map, he saw that the places he wished to visit—the Ajanta caves and Benares on the Ganges—were so far apart that he almost felt faint. Yet each attracted equally the magnetic needle of his desire for the unknown.

His intention of taking leave of Princess Moonlight was dampened as he was faced with the nuisance of asking Hishikawa to interpret for him. Using the urgent preparations for his trip as an excuse, he simply wrote a thank-you note on hotel stationery for the outing to Bang Pa In. He sent it off to the Rosette Palace by messenger moments before his departure.

Honda's trip to India was marked with colorful experiences. But it is enough to describe one profoundly moving afternoon spent in the Ajanta caves and the soul-shaking sight of Benares. In these two places, Honda witnessed things extremely important, things essential to his life.

7

His itinerary included a voyage by boat to Calcutta; then one whole day by train to Benares, which was 350 miles from there; a trip by car from Benares to Mogulsarai; then two days by train to Manmad; and finally another car trip to Ajanta.

Calcutta in early October was bustling with the annual Durga festival.

The goddess Kali, the most popular of the Hindu pantheon and especially venerated in Bengal and Assam, had innumerable names and avatars, as did her husband Shiva, the god of destruction. Durga is one of Kali's metamorphoses, but her bloodthirstiness is less pronounced. Gigantic effigies of the goddess had been erected everywhere in the city. They showed her in the act of punishing the deity of water buffalos, and beautiful, angry eyebrows were depicted on the valiant face. At night the statues, standing out sharply against the bright lights, received the adulation of the crowds.

Calcutta is the center of Kali worship, with its temple, the Kalighat; and the activity there during these festivals defies the imagination. As soon as he arrived in the city, Honda hired an Indian guide and paid a visit to the temple.

The core of Kali is *shakti,* the original sense of which is "energy." This great mother goddess of the earth imparts to all female deities throughout the world her sublimity as mother, her feminine voluptuousness, and her abominable cruelty, thereby enriching their divine nature. Kali is depicted in an image of death and destruction, doubtless the two essential elements of *shakti,* and she represents pestilence, natural calamities, and various other powers of nature which bring death and destruction to living things. Her body is black, and her mouth is red with blood. Fangs protrude from her lips and her neck is adorned with a necklace of human skulls

48

and freshly severed heads. She dances madly on her husband's body which lies prostrate in fatigue. This bloodthirsty goddess brings epidemics and calamities as soon as she feels thirst, and constant sacrificial offerings are necessary to keep her appeased. It is reputed that the sacrifice of a tiger quenches her thirst for one hundred years, that of a human for a thousand.

Honda visited the Kalighat one sultry, rainy afternoon. Before the entrance, hordes of people were noisily jostling about in the rain while beggars everywhere pleaded for alms. The temple precinct was extremely small, and the temple itself was packed with people. A throng had congregated around the high shrine with its marble base, jostling, eddying back and forth, packed so closely together that there was no place to stand. The marble base, wet with rain, gleamed especially white, but it was daubed with brown mud by the feet of the worshippers who were trying to climb up and with spatterings of the cinnabar that was to be applied to their foreheads along with a blessing. It seemed like a sacrilegious turbulence, but the intoxicating din went on and on.

A priest, his black arm extended outside the temple, was painting small, round holy dots of red cinnabar on the foreheads of the devout who had thrown a coin in the box. In the pressing crowd of those wishing to be so decorated were a woman with a blue, rain-drenched sari that slung to her body, molding the contours of her round back and buttocks, and a man in a white linen shirt, whose neck was a pile of shiny black wrinkles. They were all jostling toward the red-stained black fingertip of the priest. Their movements, their paroxysms, and their devotion reminded Honda of the crowd depicted in the "Almsgiving of Saint Rocco" by Annibale Carracci, a painter of the eclectic Bolognese school. However, in the inner part of the temple, somber even in the day, a statue of the goddess Kali, with her protruding red tongue and her necklace of fresh heads, quivered in the candlelight.

Honda followed his guide to the back garden, with

its irregular, rain-drenched flagstones, that occupied an area of less than four hundred square yards. He found only a few people there. A pair of pillars stood like low, narrow gateposts, with a trough of carved stone at their base. There was also a small, partitioned enclosure like a sort of washing place. Then immediately beside them stood smaller but exact replicas. The shorter pair of posts was wet with rain; and in the trough at their base lay a pool of blood, and dots of blood smudged the rainwater on the stone floor. The guide explained to Honda that the larger one was the altar where water buffalo were sacrificed and that it was no longer in use. The smaller replica was one used to sacrifice goats; and particularly during important festivals like that of Durga, four hundred goats would be slaughtered there.

When Honda looked at the back of the Kalighat which had previously not been clearly visible because of the crowds around it, he found that only its base was constructed of pure white marble, the central stupa and surrounding chapels being decorated with a mosaic of brilliantly colored tiles reminiscent of the Temple of Dawn in Bangkok. The rains had washed the dust from the exquisite floral patterns and arabesques of affronted peacocks, and the brilliantly colored edifices towered arrogantly over the gory mess below.

Large raindrops fell in sporadic flurries; and the water-laden air, carried inside, created a misty warmth.

Honda saw a woman unprotected by her umbrella kneel reverently in front of the smaller altar. She had the round, sincere, intelligent face found so frequently in middle-aged Indian women. Her light green sari was drenched. She carried a small brass kettle containing holy water from the Ganges.

The woman poured the water over the pillars, lit the oil burner which functioned even in the rain, and scattered miniature vermilion java flowers around it. Then she knelt on the bloodstained stone floor, and pressing her forehead against the post, began fervently to pray. The holy red spot on her forehead was visible through her rain-plastered hair all during the ecstatic prayer, as

THE TEMPLE OF DAWN • 51

though it were a spot of her own blood offered in sacrifice.

Honda was deeply moved, and at the same time his emotions were mixed with an indescribable abhorrence close to rapture. As he examined his own feelings, the scene about him receded and only the figure of the praying woman was sharply, almost uncannily focused. Just as the clarity of detail and his horror became so overwhelming that he felt unable to cope with either, the woman suddenly vanished. For a moment he thought it must have been an illusion, but no. He saw her walking away past the unclosed back gate of openwork wrought-iron arabesques. However, there was no connection between the woman who had been praying and the one walking away.

A child led in a young black kid. A vermilion holy spot shone on its shaggy, wet forehead. As holy water was poured on the daub, the kid shook its head and kicked its hind legs, struggling to escape.

A young man with a moustache, wearing a soiled shirt, appeared and took the animal from the boy. As he placed his hand on its neck, the goat began to bleat pathetically, almost irritatingly, writhing and backing away. The black hair on his rump was disheveled in the rain. The youth forced the goat's neck between the two posts of the altar, face down, and inserting a black bolt between them, he pushed it home over the imprisoned animal. The victim reared its hips and struggled desperately, bleating piteously. The youth poised his crescent-shaped sword, its edge glittering silver in the rain. It descended accurately, and the severed head rolled forward, eyes wide open, its whitish tongue protruding grotesquely. The body remained on the other side of the posts, its front quivering delicately while the hind legs kicked wildly around its chest. The violent movements gradually weakened, like those of a pendulum abating with every swing. The blood flowing from its neck was relatively scant.

The young executioner grasped the headless kid's hind legs and ran out through the gate. Outside the sacrificed goats were hung on pickets where they were then dismembered and swiftly disemboweled. Another headless kid lay in the rain at the youth's feet. Its hind quarters were still trembling as though in the throes of some dreadful nightmare. The borderline between life and death, which had just been drawn so skillfully, so painlessly, had been passed almost unconsciously; only the nightmare remained to torment the animal.

The young man's skill with the sword was remarkable; he was following faithfully and unemotionally the practice of this holy, yet abominable profession. Holiness dripped in the most ordinary way, like perspiration, from the blood spotting his soiled shirt, from the depths of his deep, clear eyes, and from his large, peasantlike hands. The festival-goers, accustomed to the sight, did not even turn around, and holiness with its dirty hands and feet sat confidently in their midst.

And the head? The head was offered on an altar protected by a crude rain cover inside the gates. Red flowers had been scattered in the fireplace burning in the rain, and some of their petals were scorching; it was the fire of the shrine dedicated to the worship of Brahma. Seven or eight black goat heads were arranged by the fireside, each red, open end blooming like a java flower. One of these was the one that had been bleating just a few minutes ago. Behind them an old woman, crouching low, appeared to be intently sewing, but her black fingers were earnestly stripping away the smooth, gleaming entrails from the inner lining of the skin of a carcass.

8

DURING HIS TRIP to Benares, the sight of the sacrifice came again and again to Honda's mind.

It was a bustling scene as if in preparation for something else. He felt that the sacrificial rite did not end there at all; it was as though something had begun, and

a bridge had been built to something invisible, more
sacred, more abominable, more sublime. In other words,
the series of rituals was like a strip of red carpet un-
rolled in welcome for some indescribable being who
was approaching.

Benares is the holy of holies, the Jerusalem of the
Hindus. At the point where the Ganges curves in an
exquisite crescent, accepting the melted Himalayan
snows where the god Shiva resides, is situated on its
western bank the city of Benares, the Varanasi of old.

It is a city dedicated to Shiva, husband of Kali, and
has come to be considered the main portal to paradise.
It is also the destination of pilgrims from throughout
the country. The bliss of paradise is achieved on earth
by bathing in the waters at this juncture of the five holy
rivers: Ganges, Dutapapa, Krishna, Jamna, and Saras-
vati.

The *Vedas* contain the following passage concerning
the efficacy of the water:

> The waters are medicine.
> The waters cleanse sicknesses of the body
> And fill the body with vitality.
> Indeed the waters are healing
> And will cure all sickness and evil.

And again:

> The waters are filled with eternal life.
> The waters are the protection of the body.
> The waters have miraculous efficacy for healing.
> Forget not ever the awful powers of the waters,
> For they are medicine for body and soul.

As eulogized in these passages, the ultimate of Hindu
rituals, which start with the cleansing of the heart by
prayer and the ablution of the body by water, is enacted
on Benares's innumberable ghats.

Honda reached Benares in the afternoon and immediately unpacked and bathed in his hotel room. Then

he arranged for a guide. He felt no fatigue after the long train ride, and he found his strangely youthful inquisitiveness had put him in a gay and restless frame of mind. The stifling light of the setting sun pervaded everywhere outside the hotel windows. He felt as if he could instantly grasp its mystery by dashing out into it.

Yet, Benares was a city of extreme filth as well as of extreme holiness. On both sides of the narrow, sunless alleys stalls for fried food and cakes, astrologers, grain and flour vendors were all crowded together; and the area was filled with stench, dampness, and disease. As one passed through and emerged on the flagstone square by the river, clusters of crouching leprous mendicants had gathered; they had come from all parts of the country as pilgrims, and now they begged for alms while awaiting death. Flocks of pigeons. Sultry late-afternoon sky. A leper was sitting in front of a tin can containing a few coppers; his one eye was red and festered and his fingerless hands like the stumps of felled mulberry trees were raised to the evening sky.

There was deformity of every kind. Dwarfs were running about, and bodies were arranged like some undeciphered ancient writing, lacking any common symbol. They appeared deformed not because of corruption or dissipation, but because the wretched, twisted shapes themselves, with freshness and feverishness, spewed out a repulsive holiness. Blood and pus were carried like pollen by thousands of fat, shiny, green-gold flies.

On the right-hand side of the slope that led down to the river, a colorful tent with holy insignia on it had been pitched, and cloth-wrapped corpses had been deposited beside the crowd listening to a sermon by some priest.

Everything was afloat. Under the sun lay exposed multitudes of the most ugly realities of human flesh with their excrement, stench, germs, and poisons. Everything hovered in the air like steam evaporating from ordinary reality. Benares. A piece of carpet, hideous to the point of brilliance. A riotous carpet joyously hoisted day and night by temples and people and children—fifteen hundred temples, temples of love with red pillars and black ebony reliefs illustrating all of the possible positions of sexual intercourse, the House of Widows whose inmates earnestly await death, loudly chanting sutras night and day . . . inhabitants, visitors, the quick, the dead, children covered with pox, dying children clinging to their mother's breast . . .

The square sloped down to the river, leading visitors naturally to the most important ghat: the Dasasvamedha, the "Sacrifice of Ten Horses." Tradition has it that the creator Brahma once made a sacrifice of ten horses at this spot.

The river with its opulent ochre waters was the Ganges! The precious holy water which filled the small brass kettles to be poured on the foreheads of devotees and sacrificial victims in Calcutta was now flowing down the vast river before Honda's eyes. An unbelievably generous feast of holiness.

It was only reasonable that here the sick, the healthy, the deformed, the dying should all be equally filled with golden joy. It was only reasonable that the flies and vermin should be plump and besmeared with bliss; that the characteristically dignified and suggestive facial expression of the Indians here should be so filled with reverence as to verge on blankness. Honda wondered how he could fuse his reason with the blazing evening sun, the unbearable odor, with the river breezes like faint swamp vapors. It was doubtful he could immerse himself in the evening air which was everywhere like some thick woolen fabric woven with chanting voices, tolling bells, the sound of beggars, and the moaning of the sick. He was afraid his reason might, like the sharp edge of some knife he alone concealed in his jacket, slash this perfect fabric.

The important thing was to discard it. The edge of the knife of reason, which he had regarded as his weapon since youth, had barely been preserved, considering the nicks already inflicted on it by each substantiation of transmigration. Now he had no choice but to abandon it unperceived in the perspiring crowds covered with germs and dust.

Numerous mushroomlike umbrellas for bathers stood on the ghat, but for the most part they were unoccupied now that evening sunbeams darted deep beneath them. It was long after bathing time, which had reached its peak at sunrise. The guide went down to the shore and started to negotiate with a boatman. Honda could do nothing but wait to one side throughout the interminably long dickering, feeling the hot iron of the evening sun scorching his back.

Finally the boat carrying Honda and his guide put out from the shore. The Dasasvamedha was located approximately in the center of the many ghats along the western bank of the Ganges. Sightseeing boats for the most part went downstream to the south to see the other ghats, then turned upstream to reach those north of the Dasasvamedha.

Whereas the western shore was considered to be holy, the eastern bank was sorely neglected. It was said that people who lived there would transmigrate into the body of an ass, and therefore all avoided that side. There was not so much as the shadow of a house, just the low jungle green in the distance.

Once the boat started downstream, the bright evening sun was at once cut off by buildings and provided only a brilliant halo for the magnificent view formed by the many imposing ghats with their columns at the back and the mansions supported by pillars. Only the Dasasvamedha ghat, backed by the square, allowed the setting sun its way. The evening sky was already casting its gentle rose color over the river; passing sails dropped dusky shadows on the water.

It was a time of opulent, mysterious luminescence before the dusk of evening. A time controlled by light, when the contours of all things were perfect, every dove painted in detail, when everything was dyed a faded yellow-rose, when a languid harmony reigned with the exquisiteness of an etching between the reflection on the river and the glow in the sky.

The ghats are great architectural structures suitable precisely to this sort of light. They consist of colossal staircases, like those of palaces, or great cathedrals, that lead down to the water, and behind each one stands a great monolithic wall. The columns and arches forming the background from the ghats are only pilasters, and the arcades have blind windows. The staircase alone has the dignity of a sacred place. Some capitals are Corinthian in style, others are quite syncretic in the Near Eastern fashion. On the pillars white lines are drawn as high as forty feet, the heights reached in the yearly flood disasters, especially the notorious ones of 1928 or 1936. Above the staggeringly lofty pilasters, cantilevered arcades jut out for the people who live at the top of the walls, and rows of pigeons perch on the stone balustrades. Over the rooftops a halo of evening sun paused, gradually fading in brilliance.

Honda's boat was nearing one of the ghats called Kedar. There a man was fishing with a net near his boat. Kedar ghat was quiet, and the thin, ebony bathers as well as the spectators on the steps were all lost in prayer and meditation.

Honda's attention was caught by a man who had come down the center of the great staircase and was about to bathe. Behind him stood a line of magnificent ochre columns, and in the fading glow everything was clear and distinct, even to the ornamented crannies in the capitals. He was standing in the midst of holiness, yet it was questionable whether he could be called a man at all, so great was the contrast of his skin with that of the black bodies of the tonsured priests about him. A tall, stately old man, he alone was a radiant pink.

He wore a small topknot of white hair on his head, and with his left hand he held a heavy scarlet loincloth around his hips. The rest was an ample expanse of slightly slackened pink nudity. His eyes were rapturously transfixed, as though no one existed about him, and he gazed vacuously at the sky above the opposite bank. His right hand slowly stretched heavenward in adoration. The skin of the face, chest, and abdomen was a

fresh pinkish white in the evening light, and his nobility
completely removed him from his surroundings. But
remnants of the black skin of this world remained here
and there on the upper half of his arms, on the backs of
his hands, or on his thighs, almost peeling off, but still
forming blotches, marks, and stripes. These remnants
made his glowing pink body appear even more sublime.
He was a white leper.

A multitude of pigeons took flight.

As the boat started upstream, the movement of one
startled bird was instantly transmitted to the others,
and the sudden flutter of many wings took Honda by
surprise. His attention was drawn from the foliage of
the lime trees stretching out over the river surface between
the many ghats. Each leaf was said to house for ten
days the soul of one just deceased while it waited to
be reborn.

The boat had already passed the Dasasvamedha ghat
and was alongside the House of Widows, a building
of red sandstone by the river. The window frames were
decorated with green and white mosaic and the interior
was painted green. Incense wafted from the windows,
and bells and the chanting of *kirtana* could be heard
echoing from the ceiling and spilling over the river surface.
Here widows gathered from all corners of India to
await their death. Emaciated by sickness and anticipating
the salvation of extinction, for these people their last
days in Mumukshu Bhavan, or the "House of Happiness,"
in Benares were their happiest. Everything was conveniently close. The crematory ghat was situated to the
immediate north, while just above rose the golden spire
of the Nepalese Temple of Love, on which the sculptures
honored the thousand postures of sexual intercourse.

Honda's eyes picked out a package wrapped in cloth
floating beside the boat. He remarked that the shape,
bulk, and length suggested the corpse of a two- or three-
year-old child and was told that that was precisely what
it was.

Honda glanced at his watch. It was forty minutes

past five. The evening dusk was gathering. At that instant, he distinctly saw a fire in front of him. It was the funeral pyre of the Mani Karnika ghat.

Facing the Ganges, it consisted of five-tiered platforms of varying widths on a Hindu-style base. The temple was formed of a group of stupas of different heights that surrounded a large central one, and every structure had a Mohammedan-style arched balcony in the shape of a lotus petal. As this gigantic brown cathedral was smoke-stained and stood on high colonnades, the closer Honda's boat approached the more its gloomy, imposing silhouette, uninhabited and smoke-swathed, loomed like an ominous hallucination in the sky. But a vast muddy stretch of water still lay between the boat and the ghat. On the darkening surface of the water, a profusion of flower offerings—including the red java flowers he had seen in Calcutta—and incense came floating down like trash; and the inverted reflection of the towering flames of the funeral pyre played clearly on the water.

The pigeons inhabiting the stupas fluttered about in confusion, mingling with the sparks that rose high in the sky. The heavens had turned a dark indigo touched with gray.

A sooty stone grotto stood near the water, and flowers had been placed before the statues of Shiva and one of his wives, Sati, who had flung herself into a fire in order to uphold her husband's honor.

Many boats piled high with wood for the funeral pyres were moored in the area, and Honda's craft hung back from the center of the ghat. Behind the brightly burning fire a small flame was visible deep under the temple arcade. It was the sacred, eternal flame, and every funeral pyre received its fire from it.

The river breeze had died and a suffocating heat hung over the area. Like everywhere else in Benares, noise rather than silence prevailed here too; it mingled with the constant movement of people, cries, children's laughter, and the chanting of sutras. People were not the only bathers; emaciated dogs followed the children into the water; and from the dark depths away from the fires, there where the extremity of the ghat steps lay submerged, the sinewy, shiny backs of water buffalo suddenly emerged one by one, herded on by the cackling shouts of their keepers. As they teetered up the steps, the funeral fires were mirrored on their wet black backs.

Sometimes the flames were enveloped in white smoke and flickering red tongues would appear through rifts. The smoke wafted up to the temple balconies and eddied like some living thing in the dark recesses of the building.

The Mani Karnika ghat offered the ultimate in purification: it was the outdoor, public crematorium in which all was out in the open in Indian fashion. Yet it was full of nauseous abomination, the inevitable ingredient of all things deemed sacred and pure in Benares. Beyond question this location marked the end of the world.

A corpse wrapped in red cloth was propped against an easy slope of steps adjoining the grotto of Shiva and Sati. It had been soaked in the waters of the Ganges and now awaited its turn for cremation. The red wrapping around the human form showed that the body was that of a woman. White cloth was reserved for men. Relatives waited with tonsured priests under the tent in order to fulfill their duty by throwing butter and incense upon the corpse after the pyre was lit. Just then another white-swathed corpse arrived, borne on a bamboo litter and surrounded by chanting priests and all the relatives. Several children and a black dog chased each other around their feet. As observable in any Indian town, the living were all very much alive and making considerable noise.

It was six o'clock. Flames suddenly rose in four or five places. As the smoke was blown away in the direction of the temple, the offensive odor did not reach Honda in the boat, but he could see everything clearly.

To the extreme right all the ashes were gathered together and left to soak in the river water. Individual characteristics that had so obstinately clung to each body were no longer, and the ashes of all, conjoined and finally dissolved in the holy water of the Ganges, thus returned to their four elemental constituents and the vast Universe. The under part of the ash mound was inextricably mixed with the damp earth of the area before being soaked in the Ganges. The Hindus do not build tombs. Honda suddenly recalled the shudder that had gone through him at the Aoyama Cemetary when he had visited Kiyoaki's grave, the horror he had felt that Kiyoaki was quite definitely not under the gravestone.

The corpses were laid on the fire one after the other. As the binding cords burned away and the red and white shrouds were consumed in the fire, a black arm would suddenly rise or a body would curl up in the fire as though turning over in sleep. The corpses that had been placed on the pyre first turned a dark gray. Sizzling sounds, like those of a pot boiling over, could be heard across the water. The skulls did not burn easily, and a cremator constantly walked about, poking a bamboo pole through the ones that were still smoldering well after the bodies had been reduced to ash. The sinews in his strong black arms that powerfully drove the pole through the skulls reflected the flames, while the crunching sounds he made reverberated against the temple walls.

The slow progress of purification of the human body, returning its parts to its four elemental constituents . . . the resistant human flesh and its useless odor lingering after death . . . something red opening in the flames, something shiny writhing, black powdery particles dancing up with the fiery sparks. There was a flashing animation in the flames, as though something were being created. From time to time, when suddenly the firewood noisily collapsed and part of the fire disappeared, the cremator would pile on more wood; and from time to time unexpectedly lofty flames would leap upward, almost licking at the temple balcony.

There was no sadness. What seemed heartlessness was actually pure joy. Not only were samsara and reincarnation basic belief, but they were actually accepted as a part of nature, constantly renewing itself before one's eyes, the rice paddy and its growing plants, the trees bringing forth their fruit. Some assistance from human hands was necessary, just as harvest and cultivation required human intervention; people were born to take their turns in this natural progression.

In India the source of everything that seemed heartless was connected with a hidden, gigantic, awesome joy! Honda was afraid of grasping such delight. But having witnessed the extremes he had, he knew that he should never recover from the shock. It was as though all of Benares were afflicted with a holy leprosy and that his very vision had been contaminated by this incurable disease.

But his impression of having seen the ultimate was incomplete until the following moment arrived, one that struck Honda's heart with a crystalline thrill of fright.

It was the moment when the sacred cow turned toward him.

In this crematorium there was a white cow, one of those sacred animals permitted anything anywhere in India. The sacred cow, accustomed to the fires, had been chased off by the cremator and stood just out of reach of the flames in front of the dark temple arcade. Inside was total blackness; and the white of the animal seemed awe-inspiring and full of sublime wisdom. The white belly reflecting the flickering flames appeared like cold Himalayan snow bathed in moonlight. It was a pure synthesis of impassible snow and sublime flesh in the body of an animal. The flames were smoke-logged; sometimes flashes of red dominated, again to be hidden by the swirling smoke.

Just then the sacred cow turned its majestic white face to Honda through the vague smoke rising from the burning bodies and looked directly at him.

That night, as soon as he finished dinner, Honda left word that he would be leaving before dawn the next morning, asd fell asleep with the help of a nightcap.

Legions of phantasmagoria cluttered his dreams. His

dream fingers brushed a keyboard they had never touched before, producing strange sounds. They examined like an engineer all corners of the structured universe so far known to him. The limpid Mount Miwa suddenly appeared, then the Offing Rock, reclining rock of horror on the peak of which dwelt the gods; blood spouted from a crevice and the goddess Kali emerged, her red tongue protruding. A burned corpse rose in the form of a beautiful youth, his hair and loins covered with the brilliantly pure leaves of the sacred sakaki tree. Then the obscene scene at the temple instantly turned into the cool precincts of a Japanese shrine covered with clean pebbles. All ideas, all gods were jointly turning the handle of the gigantic wheel of samsara. The great disk like a spiral nebula was slowly turning, carrying masses of people who, unaware of the effects of samsara, were simply happy, angry, sad, or joyful, quite like those who lived their daily lives totally unaware of the rotation of the earth. It was like a ferris wheel at night all decorated with lights in the amusement park of the gods.

Perhaps Indians knew all this. This fear had followed Honda into his very dreams. Just as the fact of the earth's rotation is never detected through any of the human senses and is barely recognizable by scientific reasoning, samsara, karma, and reincarnation too were perhaps not discernible through ordinary perception and reason, but only through some supernatural power, some extremely accurate, systematic, intuitive super-logic. And perhaps this perception made the Indians appear so listless, so resistant to progress, and so devoid of all those human emotions—joy, anger, sorrow, and pleasure—that are common standards for measuring ordinary human beings.

Of course, these were the rough impressions of a traveler who had barely scratched the surface of the land. Dreams often combine the highest level of symbols and the most vulgar of thoughts. Perhaps Honda was following in his dreams the old habit of his judgeship days: a cold, prosaic, speculative process had inad-

vertently put in its appearance. His professional habits
and his character seemed like a cat's tongue, too sensitive
to hot food, forcing him to cool at once any warm,
unidentified elements and to transform them into con-
ceptually frozen food. He was probably using this same
old automatic defense mechanism, exactly like so many
others who are particularly cautious in their dreams.

Far more than the ambiguity and strangeness of the
dream, what he saw in reality was a much greater mystery
to him, one that stubbornly rejected understanding or
interpretation. When he awoke he perceived that the
heat of this fact lingered clearly in his body and mind.
He felt as though he had contracted a tropical fever.

Near the dim light of the front desk at the end of
the hotel corridor, his bearded guide stood joking and
chuckling with the bellboy on night duty. He recognized
Honda approaching in his white linen suit and bowed
respectfully from a distance.

Honda's reason for leaving the hotel before the dawn
was to see the crowds waiting to worship the sunrise
at the ghats.

Benares was dedicated to the concept of the one from
the many, the unity of Brahma, who was a transcendent
godhead, being the One that contained the many. The
solar disk was the embodiment of his divinity, and his
godliness was greatest at the moment the sun rose above
the horizon. The holy city of Benares and the heavens
had been treated as equals in Indian religion. The pundit
Shankara once said: "When God put the heavens and
Benares on the scale, heavy Benares sank to the land
and the lighter heavens rose."

Hindus perceive the highest consciousness of the
godhead in the sun and consider it the symbol of ultimate
truth. Thus Benares is filled with devotion to and prayer
for the solar disk. People's consciousness frees itself
from the rules governing the earth, and thus Benares
itself, like a floating carpet, is elevated by the efficacy
of prayer.

Unlike the day before, Dasasvamedha ghat was now

swarming with masses of people, and the candles under countless umbrellas were flickering in the dusk before sunrise. In the sky above the jungle on the opposite side of the river, there was a hint of the approaching dawn below the tiers of clouds.

People had placed benches under each large bamboo umbrella and decorated the lingam stone, symbol of Shiva, with red flowers. Some were mixing red cinnabar powder in small mortars, preparing to paint their foreheads after the bath. Beside them attendant monks were mixing the paste with Ganges water in brass jugs which had been dedicated and blessed at the temple. Some people had already descended the stairs in order to be in the water to meet the sunrise. After worshipping the water, which they scooped up in their hands, they slowly immersed their entire body. Some awaited the sunrise kneeling under the umbrellas.

As the first light of dawn broke over the horizon, the scene on the ghat instantly assumed outline and color; women's saris, their skin, flowers, white hair, scabies, brass vessels—all began to cry out with color. The tortured morning clouds, slowly changing shape, gave way to the expanding light. Finally, just as the tip of the vermilion morning sun appeared above the low jungle, all at once a reverent sigh escaped from the lips of the people who had filled the square almost rubbing shoulders against Honda. Some of them knelt in devotion.

Those who were in the water pressed their hands together or opened their arms, praying to the red sun which gradually rose to display its full disk. The shadows of their torsos, cast far across the purplish golden river waves, reached to the feet of the people on the steps. Great rejoicing was heard, all directed toward the sun over the opposite shore. And all the while, one after the other, people stepped into the water, as though guided by some invisible hand.

The sun hung now above the green jungle. The scarlet disk, which had permitted itself to be looked upon, now turned in a trice into a cluster of brilliance that rejected even a momentary glance. It had already become a pulsating, threatening ball of flame.

Suddenly Honda knew! The sun which Isao had constantly seen in his suicide dream was this!

9

BUDDHISM suddenly deteriorated in India sometime after the fourth century of the Christian era. It has been rightly said that Hinduism stifled it in its friendly embrace. Like Christianity and Judaism in Judea and Confucianism and Taoism in China, Buddhism had to be exiled from India for it to become a world religion. It was necessary for India to turn to a more primitive folk religion. Hinduism perfunctorily retained the name Buddha in a far corner of its pantheon, where he was preserved as the ninth of the ten avatars of Vishnu.

Vishnu is believed to assume ten transfigurations: Matsya, the fish; Kurma, the land tortoise; Varaha, the boar; Narasimha, the man-lion; Vamana, the dwarf; Parashurama; Rama; Krishna; the Buddha; and Kalki. According to the Brahmans, Vishnu, assuming the form of the Buddha, purposely introduced a heretical religion so that believers would be led astray, thus presenting the opportunity for the Brahmans to lead them back to their true religion—Hinduism.

Thus, along with the decline of Buddhism the cave temples at Ajanta in western India fell into ruin and became known to the world only twelve centuries later, in 1819, when a British Army corps chanced upon them.

The twenty-seven stone caves in the cliffs of the Wagora River were originally excavated in three different periods: in the second century B.C. and in the fifth and seventh centuries A.D. With the exception of caves 8, 9, 10, 12, and 13 constructed during the Hinayana period, all the rest belong to the age of Mahayana Buddhism.

After visiting the living holy land of Hinduism, Honda

wanted to seek out the ruins of Buddhism, now extinct in India.

Ajanta was where he must go. Somehow it was his destiny.

This idea was substantiated by the fact that the caves themselves and the hotel and its surroundings were extremely quiet and simple, devoid of surging crowds.

As there were no facilities for lodgings around Ajanta, Honda registered in a hotel in Aurangabad with the thought of visiting the famous Hindu site of Ellora. Aurangabad was only eighteen miles from there, but sixty-six from Ajanta.

The best room in the hotel had been reserved for him by Itsui Products, and the finest car placed at his disposal. These advantages along with the Sikh chauffeur's deferential attitude turned the English tourists in the hotel hostile. That morning in the dining room before setting out on the all-day tour, Honda had already felt the silent pact of antagonism that united the Britishers against the lone Asian tourist. It was even expressed overtly when the waiter brought a plate of bacon and eggs to Honda's table before serving anyone else. An arrogant old gentleman with a handsome beard, doubtless some retired Army officer, seated with his wife at the next table, called the waiter over and admonished him sharply and curtly. After that, Honda was served last.

An ordinary traveler would have at once taken umbrage at such a situation, but Honda was obstinately impervious to trivia. Since Benares, some incomprehensible, thick membrane overlay his heart and everything slipped off its surface. Since the excessive respect of the waiter was surely the result of a generous tip paid in advance by Itsui Products, such incidents never affected the withdrawn dignity he had acquired during his term as judge.

The beautiful black car, assiduously cleaned and polished by more than five hotel employees with nothing else to do, stood in readiness for Honda's departure, the various flowers of the front garden reflecting in its shining surface. Soon, with Honda as passenger, it was rolling over the lovely plains of western India.

The vast expanse revealed not a single human figure. Sometimes the supple, dark-brown forms of mongooses splashed in the swamp water beside the road or scurried across in front of the car; or a group of long-tailed monkeys would peer out at him from the branches.

Hope for purification arose in Honda's heart. Purification in the Indian manner was too disgusting, and the sacraments he had witnessed in Benares were still in him like a raging fever. He craved a ladle of clear, cool Japanese water.

The expansiveness of the plains comforted him. There was no rice paddy nor other field under cultivation: only endless, beautiful plains stretching away, dotted with the deep indigo shadows of mimosa trees. There were swamps, streams, yellow and red flowers, and over it all, a brilliant sky hung like some colossal canopy.

There was nothing miraculous or extreme in this natural setting. The dazzling greenery radiantly exuded idle sleepiness. The plain itself had a tranquilizing effect on Honda whose heart had been seared by frightening and ominous flames. Instead of the spatter of sacrifical blood, a virginally white heron fluttered up from the jungle. The whiteness sometimes darkened when it passed before the deep green shade, but would emerge pure white again.

The clouds in the sky ahead were delicately convoluted, and their irregular borders gave out a silken sheen. The blue was fathomless.

Needless to say, a large component of the comfort Honda felt came with his awareness that soon he was to enter Buddhist territory, even though Buddhism had long been extinct.

To be sure, after experiencing the weird and variegated mandala of Benares, the Buddhism he dreamed of was as refreshing as ice, and already he felt a presage of the familiar Buddhist quietude in the bright stillness of the plains.

Suddenly Honda felt nostalgic. He was returning from

a noisy kingdom dominated by living Hinduism to a familiar country of temple gongs, a land which had been destroyed but which had taken on a purity by that destruction. As he thought of the Buddha waiting for him to return from the Absolute he had experienced in Benares, he felt he had perhaps never expected an Absolute in Buddhism. In the tranquility of the homecoming he had dreamed of, he felt an unremitting closeness to what was gradually perishing. Beyond the beautiful, radiantly blue sky, the graveyard of Buddhism itself, the site of its oblivion was soon to appear. Even before seeing it, Honda clearly felt the somber coolness soothing his overheated mind, the coolness of the rock caves, and the limpidity of the water there.

It was a kind of weakening of intent. Perhaps the odiousness of color and the deterioration of flesh and blood had driven him to seek another religion which had petrified itself in solitude. Simple, pure extinction was suggested even by the shapes of the clouds beyond. Here was the illusion of shade, perhaps a reward from a former life, in the beautiful, luxuriant foliage. In this world of absolute morning quiet, still except for the lazy vibration of the car engine, the smooth vista of the plains slowly unfolded beyond the window and slowly but surely carried Honda's heart home.

After a time the car reached the edge of a ravine cutting sharply into the flat plain. This was the first indication of Ajanta. They drove along the meandering road descending toward the bed of the Wagora which glistened at the bottom of the gorge like the sharp blade of a knife.

The teahouse where Honda stopped to rest was aswarm with flies. He looked out of the window immediately before him across the square toward the entrance to the caves. Going in now, giving in to his impatience, he felt, might infringe on the tranquility he was seeking. He bought a postcard, and taking his fountain pen in a clammy hand, he scrutinized for some time the picture of the caves crudely printed on the front.

Again there was a suggestion of noise here as in Benares. Black people in white clothes with suspicious eyes were standing around, and skinny children were shouting in the square, selling souvenir necklaces. The space was filled with bright yellow sunlight that reached to every cranny. On a table in the dark room lay three small dried-up oranges with flies crawling over them. The heavy, acrid odor of fried food wafted from the kitchen. He addressed the postcard to his wife Rié, to whom he had not written for some time. Then he wrote:

I'm here to see the cave temples at Ajanta. The tour's about to start. I can't drink the orange drink in front of me, because I see the edge of the glass is all dotted with fly spots. But don't worry, I'm being very careful about my health. India's really astonishing. You're taking care of your kidneys, I hope. Love to Mother.

Could this be thought of as affectionate? He always wrote the same. The nostalgia and affection that had begun to gather like a haze in his heart had suddenly made him resolve to write. But when he tried to put his feelings into words, his sentences invariably turned out ordinary and dry.

Rié would always welcome his return with the same quiet smile she had displayed at his departure, no matter how many years he might leave her alone in Japan. Though her hair might bear a few more strands of white since he had left, the face which had seen him off and the one which would greet his return would coincide as perfectly as the two identical crests on the sleeves of a formal kimono.

A touch of kidney trouble had made her profile somewhat vague, like a moon in daytime; and this countenance, now that he called it to mind, seemed more suitable for being visualized in memory than seen in reality. Of course, no one could dislike such a woman. In his heart Honda felt deep relief as he wrote the postcard, and he offered thanks to an unnamable something. It was a relief altogether different from the assurance of being loved.

Having written the card, Honda placed it in the pocket of the jacket which he had taken off and stood up. He would mail it at the hotel. As he set out across the sunny square, the guide sidled up like an assassin.

The twenty-seven stone caves had been excavated at midpoint in the cliffs overlooking the Wagora, where there were several layers of rocky outcrops. Starting from the river, the slope gradually steepened, going from rocks to grass; then it became a precipitous cliff covered with coppice. A white stone walkway connected the entrances to the caves.

The first cafe was a *chaitya,* or "chapel." There were the ruins of four chapels and twenty-three *vihara,* or "monks' dwellings"; the first cave was one of the four.

Just as he had expected, the air inside had the musty coolness of dawn. A large image of the Buddha in a central recess was clearly visible; the smooth figure was seated in the lotus posture in the reflection from the entrance from which a patch of light the size of a doormat penetrated. There was not enough radiance to make out the frescoes on the ceiling and the surrounding walls. The ray of the guide's flashlight unsteadily flitted here and there like a bat of light hovering about the cave. Again and again, depictions of an unexpected motley of worldly desires flashed into view.

Half-naked women with golden crowns on their heads and colorful sarongs wrapped around their hips appeared in various postures in the spot of the flashlight. Most of them held the stalk of a lotus flower in their hands. Their faces were all alike, like those of sisters. The extremely long, slanting eyes were half open and new-moons of eyebrows curved above them. The coolness of their intelligent, straight noses was softened by slightly flaring nostrils. The lower lip was voluptuous, while the mouth was pinched as though tied at both ends. Everything reminded Honda of what the face of Princess Moonlight in Bangkok would be when she grew up. The difference between these women in the frescoes and the little Princess lay clearly in their mature bodies. Their breasts were cloves of ripe pomegranate ready to burst, with necklaces of fragile gold, silver, and precious stones hanging loosely over them like ivy clinging to fruit. Some were half reclining, with their back turned, showing the voluptuous curve of their hips; some revealed an overflowing sensual abdomen barely covered by scant sarongs. Some women were dancing and others were on the verge of death. And as the flashlight shifted from one spot to another, to the incessant prattle of the guide spouting his usual lines, the women again disappeared one by one into the darkness.

As Honda emerged from the first cave, the tropical sunlight, like a violently struck gong, at once changed the murals into illusions. Musing in the daylight, one felt as if one had visited the caves in some long-forgotten memory. The only thing that offered reality was the Wagora gleaming below and the barren look of the rocks.

As usual, Honda was annoyed with the guide's indifferent prattle. Thus, letting the others pass on, he remained for some time alone in the deserted ruins of a *vihara* which the guide had coldly passed by and which the other sightseers ignored completely.

The absence of any object enabled him to give free rein to his rich imagination. The *vihara* served this purpose well. There was no statue, no fresco, only thick, black columns standing at either side of the cave. A pulpit was situated in the center of a particularly dark recess inside, while a pair of large stone tables facing each other ran from the entrance to the back. Light streamed in and it seemed as if the monks had just risen to take the fresh air outdoors, leaving the stone tables which they used both for studying and eating.

The absence of color relaxed Honda's mind, although by searching carefully he found a faint red spot of faded paint in a small depression on the stone table.

Had there been someone here who had just left?

Who could it have been?

Standing alone in the cool of the cave, Honda felt

as though the darkness around him suddenly began to whisper. The emptiness of the undecorated, colorless cave awakened in him a feeling of some miraculous existence, probably for the first time since he had come to India. Nothing was more vividly real to his skin—clear proof of a fresh existence—than the fact that his existence had declined, perished, and was extinct. No, existence had already begun taking shape among the odor of the mildew that covered every stone in the cave.

He experienced an animal-like emotion. It was the mixture of joy and anxiety which he always felt when something was about to take shape in his mind; it was the excitement of a fox, who, having caught the distant scent of prey, slowly approaches his victim. He was not sure what it was, but the hand of his distant memory had already grasped it firmly in the back of his mind. Honda's heart was turbulent with expectation.

He came out of the *vihara* and began walking in the outside light toward the fifth cave. The path described a wide curve and a new vista lay before him. The walkway before the caves passed inside some columns inserted in the rocks. The columns were wet, as they were located behind two waterfalls. Honda knew that the fifth cave was close by, and he stopped to look across the valley at the cascades.

One of the two waterfalls was interrupted as it ran over the surface of the rock, while the other streamed down in an unbroken silver cord. Both were narrow and precipitous. The sound of the cascades falling down the yellowish green rock cliff of the Wagora resounded clearly on the surrounding cliffs. Except for the dark hollows of the cave entrances, everything behind and to either side of the falls was bright: the light green clumps of mimosa, the red flowers bordering the water, the brilliant light playing on the falls, and the rainbow formed in the mist. Several yellow butterflies fluttered up and down, as though clinging to the straight line of Honda's gaze as he watched the water.

Honda looked to the top of the falls and was surprised

at the amazing height. They were so lofty that he felt
as if he were in a world belonging to another dimension.
The green of the cliff to either side of the falls was dark
with moss and fern, but at the top it was a pure light
green. There were some bare rocks too; the softness
and brightness of the green foliage was not of this world.
A black kid was grazing there; and above, in the absolute
blue of the sky, an abundance of luminous clouds rose
in magnificent disorder.

There was sound, but complete soundlessness dominated. No sooner was Honda overwhelmed by the silence
than the noise of the waterfalls came wildly to his ears.
He was enchanted by the alternate stillness and the sound
of water.

He was impatient to get to the fifth cave where the
water splashed, but a strange feeling of awe held him
back. It was almost certain that nothing was waiting
there. Yet Kiyoaki's feverish and delirious words fell
like drops of water in his mind.

"I'll see you again. I know it . . . beneath the falls."

Since then, he had believed that Kiyoaki had been
referring to the Sanko falls on Mount Miwa. Probably
so. But it occurred to Honda that the ultimate waterfall
he had meant must be these cascades at Ajanta.

10

THE S.S. *Southern Seas*, of Itsui Shipping, Ltd., on
which Honda left India, was a six-cabin freighter. The
rainy season was over, and the ship headed across the
Gulf of Siam, which lay in the cool northeast monsoon
breeze. After passing by Paknam at the mouth of the
Menam, the ship made its way upstream to Bangkok,
watching for propitious tides. The sky without rain this
November twenty-third was a ceramic blue.

Honda was relieved to be returning to the familiar
city from a land of such pestilence. His mind was at

rest, but he carried a heavy load of terrifying impressions from his journey, and he remained leaning against the railing of the upper deck throughout the voyage, the cargo groaning deep in the hold of his heart.

They passed a destroyer of the Thai Navy, but there was no sign of human life along the quiet bank covered with coconut, mangrove, and reeds. Finally, when the ship began its approach, with Bangkok to the right and Thon Buri to the left, tall stilted houses with palm-thatched roofs could be seen on the Thon Buri side, and the dark skins of orchard workers were visible under the sparkling leaves, cultivating bananas, pineapple, mangosteen, and other fruits.

Betel nut trees, which the climbing fish preferred, thrived in one corner of the orchard. On seeing them, Honda remembered the old lady-in-waiting who chewed on betel wrapped in *kimma* leaves that tinted her mouth all red. The modernist Phiboon had already forbidden its use. The old ladies had apparently dispelled the gloom of the regulation by chewing the nuts away from the capital at Bang Pa In.

Sculled boats carrying water became more numerous, and at length the masts of commercial and naval ships formed a forest in the distance. It was Khlong Toei, the port of Bangkok.

The setting sun added a strange brilliance to the muddy waters, making them appear a smoldering rose color; it added further iridescence to the patches of oil, reminding Honda of the smooth texture of the lepers' skin he had so frequently seen in India.

As the ship drew up to the pier, Honda recognized the obese branch manager of Itsui Products, two or three clerks, the director of the Japan Club, and behind them, Hishikawa, who looked as though he were hiding among the people waving their hats in welcome. Immediately he felt depressed.

As soon as Honda came ashore, Hishikawa grabbed the briefcase from his side before the Itsui clerks had the chance. He acted with unprecedented obsequiousness and diligence.

"Welcome back, Mr. Honda. I'm relieved to see you looking so well. The trip to India must have been very hard on you."

This seemed to be a very impolite greeting to the branch manager, so Honda ignored the comment and thanked the manager.

"I was amazed at the thoroughness of your arrangements for me every place during the trip. Thanks to you, I traveled like a king."

"Now you know well enough that Itsui's not going to be stopped by anything like Britain and America freezing our credits."

In the car on the way to the Oriental Hotel, Hishikawa was quiet, holding the briefcase in the seat next to the driver, while the manager talked about the worsening public feeling in Bangkok during Honda's absence. He advised Honda to be careful, for the populace, taken in by English and American propaganda, had grown extremely antagonistic toward the Japanese. Honda saw from the car window crowds of poor he had not habitually seen before swarming in the streets.

"With the rumors of impending invasion by the Japanese Army and the deterioration of local order, a staggering number of refugees have come into Bangkok from the French Indochina border."

But the English-style businesslike curtness of the hotel management had not changed in the slightest. After getting himself settled in his room and taking a cold bath, Honda felt better.

The manager's party was waiting in the lobby facing the garden to join Honda for dinner, sitting under the large, slowly rotating fan against which beetles sometimes collided noisily.

On the way down from his room, Honda reflectively observed the arrogant behavior of some so-called Japanese gentlemen in Southeast Asia, a group to which he too belonged, he reminded himself. They were quite devoid of any redeeming feature.

Why? he wondered. It would be more appropriate

to say that in that instant Honda really recognized for the first time their ugliness . . . and his own. It was hard to believe that they were the same Japanese as those beautiful youths, Kiyoaki and Isao.

With their excellent English linen suits, white shirts, and neckties, their attire was above reproach. And yet each was fanning himself with inelegant haste, the Japanese cord with its single black bead attached to the fan hanging from their hands. Their gold teeth flashed when they smiled and they all wore glasses. The head man was talking with false modesty about some episode connected with his work, and his inferiors were listening to the old story they had heard so many times, nodding and repeating their perpetual comments: "That's what I call real courage . . . real pluck." They gossiped about vagrant women, the possibility of war, and then, in whispers, about the high-handedness of the military. Everything had the tone of the listless, repetitive sutra chanting of the tropics, and yet was curiously imbued with simulated vivacity. Despite the listlessness they constantly experienced within, despite an itching or the trickling of sweat, they held themselves stiffly erect, occasionally recalling in some corner of their consciousness the pleasures of the night before with its concomitant fear of some disease with sores like red swamp lilies. Perhaps it had been because of his fatigue from the trip, but Honda had not recognized himself as being one of them when, minutes before, he had looked into the mirror in his room. He had seen only the reflection of a forty-six-year-old man, who had once been engaged in matters of righteousness, who had then made a living on the back streets of justice, the face of a man who had lived too long.

"My ugliness is special," he thought, clinging to the confidence which he quickly retrieved, as he descended the red-carpeted steps between the elvator and the lobby. "At any rate, I'm a recidivist of justice; I'm not like those tradesmen."

* * *

That night, after a few cups of wine had been downed at a Cantonese restaurant, in front of Hishikawa, the manager said in a loud voice to Honda: "Hishikawa here is terribly worried about having caused you so much trouble and hurt your feelings. He seems overly sensitive about it, and after you left he told me every day how wrong he had been, how he had been at fault. He's almost neurotic about it. I know he has his weaknesses, but I assigned him to you because he's very useful. I feel responsible for causing you any un-pleasantness. You will be leaving in only four or five days—we've booked a seat in an Army plane—and Hishikawa has done a lot of soul-searching. He says he will do his best to please. I'm going to ask you, Mr. Honda, to be generous enough to forgive him and ac-cept his services for the rest of your stay."

Hishikawa immediately spoke up from the other side of the table, as though beseeching Honda: "Sir, please take me to task as much as you will. I was wrong." He bowed his head almost to the table.

The situation was extremely depressing for Honda.

The manager's words could be interpreted that he still believed he had chosen a good guide for Honda; but that, judging from Hishikawa's attitude, Honda must have been extremely hard to please, that if he changed guides, Hishikawa would lose face. Therefore, there was nothing to do but to let Hishikawa swallow the humiliation and continue to work for the rest of the time until his departure. To achieve this, it was best to pretend that everything had been Hishikawa's fault. Thus, Honda would not be disgraced.

Honda felt a momentary surge of anger, but in the next instant he realized that it would not be to his advan-tage to reject the manager's suggestion. Hishikawa could not himself have confessed actual instances of his being at fault. Furthermore, Hishikawa was congenitally in-capable of realizing why he was disliked. However, he must have sensed that he was and, having thought it over in his own limited way, must have decided to do something to ease his lot. He must have got the manager on his side for him to say such insensitive things.

Honda could forgive the obese manager's lack of sensitivity, but he could not pardon Hishikawa's impudent, hypersensitive play-acting which he had quickly thought up on sensing Honda's antipathy.

Suddenly he wanted to go back home the very next day. But a change of schedule at this point would obviously be interpreted as a childish plan for revenge because of his dislike for Hishikawa, and he realized he had no other choice. By showing generosity in the beginning, he was forced to be even more generous now.

Well, the only thing he could do was to treat Hishikawa like a machine. He protested smilingly that the manager's apology was quite unnecessary and that for the next few days he would have to depend totally on Hishikawa to help him purchase gifts, go book-hunting, and make arrangements for visiting the Rosette Palace to say goodbye. At least he felt satisfaction with his excellent deception in skillfully concealing his true emotions from the manager.

Hishikawa's attitude did change.

First he took Honda to a bookstore where, as at a poorly stocked vegetable vendor's, crudely printed paperbacks in English or Thai were sparsely arranged on a display board. Before, Hishikawa would have contemptuously discussed the level of Thai culture, but he let Honda make his choice without a word.

He could not find any books on Thai Theravada Buddhism, much less any in English concerning samsara and reincarnation. But he was attracted by a thin pamphlet of poetry, apparently a private publication printed on poor-quality paper, its white cover browned by the sun and its corners curled by handling. He read the English preface and realized that it was a collection of poems written shortly after the bloodless revolution of June, 1932, by a young man who seemed to have participated in it. The poet expressed the disillusionment that followed the revolution for which he had been so ready to give his life. By coincidence the collection was published the year after Isao's death. As Honda turned the pages, he saw in the faded print that the poet's English was immature.

Who would have known?
From the sacrifice of youth dedicated to the future
Only the vermin of corruption come forth.
Who would have known?
In debris-strewn fields that once promised rebirth
Only plants of venom and thorn are burgeoning.
The vermin will soon stretch their golden wings,
And the wind passing over the grasses will spread
    pestilence.
In my heart the love I bear my land
Is redder than mimosa flowers in the rain;
Suddenly after the storm, on eaves, pillars, balustrades
The white mildew of despotism reaches out.
Yesterday's wisdom is beclouded in luxurious baths
    of profit,
And yesterday's activist is ensconced in a
    palanquin of embroidered brocade.
There would be nothing better
In the regions of Kabin and Patani,
Where the flowering pear and rosewood and the
    manifan's luxuriant foliage,
The creeping ivy and the thorny rose and the pinks
    mark the byways;
Where the sun and the rain fall upon deep jungles;
Where rhinoceros, tapirs, and buffalos dwell;
If, at times, a herd of elephants in quest of water
Would trample my bones underfoot.
There would be nothing better than
To rip with my own hands the red crescent of my throat
Shining in the dewy underbrush.
Who would know?
Who would know?
I sing my song of sorrow.

Honda was deeply moved by this political poem of despair and thought that he could find nothing better with which to comfort Isao's spirit. Was it not true? Isao had died without bringing about the revolution he had dreamed of for so long, but there was no doubt that he would have experienced even greater disillusionment if one had taken place. Death in success, death in failure—death was the basis of Isao's acts. But the unfortunate human lot is that one cannot take oneself out of time and dispassionately compare two deaths at two different points for the purpose of choosing one or the other. One cannot choose by giving equal priority to a death after experiencing disillusionment in the aftermath of revolution and to one before experiencing it. If one died before experiencing disillusionment, dying afterward would be impossible; and conversely, if one died after experiencing disillusionment, dying before would be out of the question. Therefore, all that one could do was to project oneself into the two deaths in the future and select the one one's intuition commanded. Isao had chosen death before disillusionment could set in. His prophetic choice showed the unclouded youthful wisdom of one who had never wielded the slightest political power.

But the feeling of disillusion and despair—as if one had seen the other side of the moon—which overtakes the successful revolutionary makes death merely an escape from a wilderness worse than death itself. Therefore, however sincere the poet's death was, it must surely be regarded as a pathological suicide that took place in the weary afternoon of revolution.

For this reason Honda wanted to dedicate this political poem to Isao. At least Isao had died dreaming of the sun, but the morning in this poem had opened a festering wound under a cracked orb. However, an endless thread stretched between Isao's brave death and the despair of this political poem, both by chance occurring during the same period. The very best, the very worst, the most beautiful and the most ugly illusions about the future for which people sacrificed their lives were probably to be found in the same place and, what was even more frightening, were probably the same thing. What Isao had dreamed of and had been willing to give his life for had to be the despair expressed in this poem, for the shrewder his foresight, the purer his death.

Honda knew full well that he tended to see things in this way because India had cast its spell on him. India imposed on his thinking a many-layered structure, like lotus petals, and no longer let him think in a direct and simple way. The time he willingly put aside his judgeship in order to help Isao—although he was strongly motivated by remorse for not having been able to help Kiyoaki—was probably the first and last occasion in his life that he had been so altruistic and dedicated. Yet despite his efforts, he had not been able to prevent Isao's futile death, and after that nothing remained but for him to reverse his ideas on reincarnation and see his future outside samsara. And it was India, terrifying India, that had dropped the final hint to Honda, who found it increasingly difficult to entertain "human" emotions.

Whether in success or in failure, sooner or later time must lead to disillusionment; and if foresight of this disillusionment remains only that, it is mere pessimism. The important thing is to act on this foresight even by dying. Isao had achieved that magnificently. Only by action can one see through the glass walls erected at various points in time—glass walls insurmountable by human effort, but which can be seen through equally from both sides. In eager desire, in aspiration, in dreams, in ideals, the past and future become equal in value and in quality: they are coordinate.

Whether or not Isao had glimpsed such a world at the moment of his death was a question Honda could not put off now that he was growing older, if he would discover what he should have to face at the moment of his own death. At least it was certain that at that instant the existing Isao and the Isao to be had looked directly into each other's eyes. By his foresight the existing Isao had grasped the splendor of the unseen on the

other side and his eyes there saw through to this side
with craving. It was certain that the existing Isao had
foreseen the glory of the future Isao, and the eyes of
the Isao to come had looked back yearningly at the
innocent being that had not yet experienced this glory.
By passing through two unrelivable existences the two
Isaos were connected through the glass wall. Isao and
the political poet suggested the eternal link between
the poet who, having passed through life, yearned for
death, and the youth who, rejecting the passing, died.
If that were true, what had become of that which they
had so adently desired, each in his own way. Honda's
theory, unchanged since his youth, was that history could
not be advanced by human volition, but that the intrinsic
nature of human will was to become involved in history.

How, he wondered, could he dedicate these poems,
a most suitable gift, to Isao's soul?

Would it be best to take the book back to Japan
and offer it at his grave? No, Honda knew all too well
that Isao's tomb was empty.

Surely the best way would be to dedicate it to the
little Princess who openly claimed herself to be Isao's
reincarnation. She would be the fastest and most de-
pendable messenger. Honda now became the fleet-
footed courier easily passing through the wall of time.

But no matter how intelligent, could a girl of seven
understand the despair of such poems? Besides, as
Isao's reincarnation had taken such an obvious form this
time, Honda had experienced a twinge of suspicion.
And then, he had not been able to see the three little
moles on the Princess's lovely, dusky body even in the
bright sunlight.

Having decided to take as gifts an Indian sari of
excellent quality and the book of poems, Honda asked
Hishikawa to contact the Rosette Palace. He was
informed that the Princess would grant an audience
in the Hall of Queens at the Chakri Palace, which she
would have opened especially for him, as it had been
closed for some time because of the King's absence.

However, one strict condition was imposed by the ladies-in-waiting. During his trip to India, the Princess had been anxiously waiting for Honda's return to Thailand, insisting that she was going to accompany him to Japan when he returned. She had complained that her attendants had done nothing in preparation for the trip, and they had soothed her by pretending to make arrangements. Therefore, they desired that at the time of the audience Honda make no mention of his departure, much less of the date, and that he pretend that he was staying on in Thailand.

11

THE NEXT DAY, the one on which Honda was to leave for Japan, was beautifully clear, but the wind had fallen and it was extremely hot.

Honda and Hishikawa passed by the royal guard house about nine forty for their ten o'clock audience, suffering in necktie and jacket.

The palace, designed by an Italian architect, had been built in 1882 under King Chulalongkorn and was in style a magnificent mixture of neo-Baroque and Siamese.

It featured an amazingly complex, almost hallucinating facade set against the blue tropical sky. No matter how European the style, the brilliant and overly ornate front possessed the dazzling and intoxicating quality characteristic of tropical Asian architecture. The marble staircases which ascended gracefully to the left and right were guarded at their base by bronze elephants. The main entrance was in the style of the Pantheon in Rome, and the imposing pediment above the arches contained a colorful portrait of King Chulalongkorn. Up to this point, it was purely European neo-Baroque with marble and bas-reliefs and gold. But as one's gaze mounted to the story above, one saw a pavilion in the Siamese style standing in the center of a gallery of pink marble

Corinthian pillars. The ceiling was checkered, alternately maroon and gold on a white base, and the whole structure jutted out impressively like a ship's turret. It bore the candelabrumlike coat of arms of the Chakri dynasty. The upper stories to the very peak of the golden spire rose in pyramids of intricate, authentic Siamese intercalary roofs in red and gold, the ornate end-tiles of the ridges pointing to the blue sky like the raised shoulders of dancers. It seemed as if the whole point of the Chakri Palace was to have the solid, rationally cold European base crushed by the royal dreams of the tropics—superfluously complex, unnecessarily colorful . . . maddening. It was as though a beaked nightmare with sharp talons and bristling gold and red wings were bent over the torso of a recumbent king, dignified, cold, white.

"Is this supposed to be beautiful?" said Hishikawa, stopping and wiping the perspiration from his upturned face.

"Whether it's beautiful or not, what's that to us? We've been invited only to see the Princess."

Honda's unexpected curtness instantly intimidated Hishikawa, who looked at him with fear in his eyes; nothing further was said. Honda regretted that he had not used this effective method at the very beginning of his visit to Bangkok.

The officer of the guards who served as guide intimated that it had been considerable trouble for them to open the long-closed palace just to humor the whimsical Princess. Honda, at a wink from Hishikawa, quickly slipped a suitable amount of money into the officer's pocket.

Once the gigantic doors were open, a dark hall was revealed, on the black, white, and gray mottled mosaic floor of which some twenty rococo chairs edged in mahogany had been arranged. A familiar-looking lady-in-waiting took over from the officer and guided the two guests to a large door on the right. Beyond it was a well-lit room with a high ceiling, a purely European palace hall complete with chandeliers, Italian marble tables inlaid with floral patterns, and red and gold Louis Quinze chairs placed around them.

On the walls hung life-sized portraits of the four royal consorts of King Chulalongkorn and the Queen Mother. Hishikawa explained that three of the consorts were sisters. All the portraits had been painted in Victorian style by some Western painter. Their faces revealed the painter's artistic integrity, his fearful courage, his shameless lies, his malice, his sincerity, and his flattery—all coexisted like waves and sand at the water's edge in the margin of realism. The somewhat melancholy grace suitable to royalty matched the heavy sensuality of the subjects' dark skin, and the tropical feeling of the clothes and the background inadvertently blurred the seemingly realistic surface picture with an illusory quality.

The Queen Mother, Thep Sirin, was a wizened aristocrat, and her face showed the most dark and savage dignity of all. Honda walked slowly, carefully examining each painting as he passed by; he learned from Hishikawa that the first consort, Queen Prephaiphim, was the youngest of three sisters. Next came Queen Sawaeng Watana, and then the eldest sister, Queen Sunantha. It was unquestionable to anyone that the eldest was the most beautiful.

Queen Sunantha's portrait hung in one corner of the room, half concealed in the shadows. She was standing by a window, one hand resting on a table. Outside one could see the hazy blue sky filled with evening clouds and orange branches heavy with fruit.

On the table stood a rose-bud vase in cloisonné containing a small lotus flower, a gold ewer, and wine cups. The queen's beautiful bare feet were visible below her gold *panun,* and from one shoulder of her embroidered pink jacket hung a wide cordon. A large medal glistened at her breast, and she held an ivory fan. The tassel of the fan and the carpet both reflected the scarlet of the evening glow.

Honda was struck by her most charming small face. Of the five portraits it somehow bore a marked resemblance to that of Princess Moonlight. There were the same ripe, plump lips, the somewhat stern eyes, and the short-cropped hair. The resemblance faded after he had gazed at the portrait for a while. But after a time the impression like evening dusk crept back from some corner of the room, and again he was convinced of the likeness—the small, dark, quick fingers holding the fan, the curved hand resting on the table, and finally the eyes and lips that were the exact duplicate of those of the Princess. But just as the likeness became most apparent, like the sand of an hourglass, it would once more begin irresistibly to slip away.

At that instant an inside door opened and the three old ladies-in-waiting emerged escorting the Princess. Honda and Hishikawa stood where they were and bowed deeply.

The afternoon at the Bang Pa In Palace seemed to have melted the ladies' hearts, for no one stopped the Princess as she ran toward Honda with a cry of joy. Like a dove picking up scattered peas, Hishikawa busily translated the torrent of words that spurted forth.

"It was a long trip . . . I was lonely. Why didn't you write me more often? Which country has more elephants, Thailand or India? I don't want to go to India, I want to go back to Japan."

Then the Princess took Honda's hand and led him to a spot in front of the portrait of Queen Sunantha.

"This is my grandmother," she said proudly.

"Her Serene Highness has invited Mr. Honda to the Chakri Palace because she specifically wanted to show him this beautiful portrait," offered the first lady-in-waiting.

"I inherited only my body from Queen Sunantha. My heart came from Japan, so really I should leave my body here and only my heart should go back. But to do that I should have to die. So I'll just have to take my body along, like a child with her favorite doll. Do you understand, Mr. Honda? The pretty me you see is really only the doll I carry with me."

Judging from the childish manner of her speech, she must have spoken less sophisticatedly than Hishikawa had translated, but as she spoke, the clarity in her serious eyes moved Honda's heart even before he understood what she was saying.

"There's another doll." The Princess as usual paid no attention to what the adults were thinking; and now she left Honda's side and moved swiftly to the center of the hall, where the sunlight took the shape of the grilled casement windows. She solemnly traced the outline of the creeping vines; then the flowers in the complex floral pattern—there were gaps in the inlay—on the table to which her chest scarcely reached. "There's another doll," she continued as if singing, "which looks just like me in Lausanne. But she's my elder sister and she's not a doll really. Her body's Thai and so's her heart. She's different from me; I'm really Japanese."

She accepted the sari and the poetry collection with delight, but she merely leafed through a few pages of the book and looked no further. One of the attendants explained apologetically that the Princess could not yet read English. Honda's test had not worked.

Entreated by the Princess, Honda talked for a while of his trip to India in the stiff formality of the hall. He noted tears and sadness in the eyes of the Princess as she listened rapturously to him, and he was conscience-stricken at the thought of concealing the news of his departure the next day.

He wondered when he would be able to see the Princess again. Surely she would mature into a very beautiful woman, but he would probably never have the opportunity of seeing her. This might be his last chance. Soon the mystery of reincarnation, like the shadow of a butterfly crossing a tropical garden of an afternoon, might vanish from her memory. Perhaps the soul of Isao, regretful of dying without a word of farewell to Honda, had borrowed the lips of the mad little Princess to deliver an apology. It was easier for Honda to leave Bangkok believing this.

Gradually the Princess's eyes became more moist as she listened to Honda's stories; she must have had some premonition of his departure. He had carefully chosen childish, entertaining episodes to relate, but the sorrow in her eyes kept deepening.

Honda spoke one sentence at a time which Hishikawa would then translate with gesticulations. Suddenly the Princess's eyes opened in astonishment. The ladies glared angrily at Honda who had no idea what had happened.

The Princess suddenly uttered a piercing cry and clung to Honda. The attendant rose and attempted to tear her away, but the child put her cheek to his legs and sobbed loudly.

The drama of the other day was reenacted. At length the ladies succeeded in separating the two and signaled Honda to leave the room. As Hishikawa was translating the sign, Honda was again on the verge of being caught by the sobbing Princess. He ran among the tables and chairs with the little girl in pursuit, and the ladies scrambling after her from three sides. Louis Quinze chairs crashed to the floor, and the palace hall was transformed into a terrain for blindman's buff.

Finally Honda freed himself, passed quickly through the anteroom, and ran down the marble staircase of the central entrance. There he hesitated to make his final departure, as he listened to the sharp cries of the little girl echoing from the high ceiling of the palace. "The ladies are telling us to go quickly," said Hishikawa, urging him on. "They'll take care of her somehow. Let's go!"

Honda dashed through the spacious front garden, soaked in perspiration.

"I'm sorry. You must have been surprised," said Hishikawa to the still panting Honda when the car had started to move.

"No. It happens every time," he replied, trying to freshen up by wiping away the perspiration with a large white handkerchief.

"You told the Princess that you wanted to fly back from India but that you couldn't get a seat on an Army plane."

"I did indeed."

"I made a bad translation there," Hishikawa explained coolly, obviously feeling no guilt. "I didn't think and told her the truth. I said that you were going back to Japan, but as you were taking an Army plane you couldn't get a seat for her and so couldn't take her with you. That's why she made such a fuss. She begged you either not to go or to take her with you. The ladies looked so angry because you broke your promise. It was all my fault. I don't know how to apologize."

12

REGULAR AIR TRANSPORTATION between Japan and Thailand had commenced the year before, in 1940. But after Japan had begun to send observers into French Indochina in order to control the supply routes to Chiang Kai-shek, the Indochinese no longer resisted, and a new southern air route was opened via Saigon, this in addition to the already existing Taipei—Hanoi—Bangkok run.

It was a civilian line administered by Greater Japan Air Lines. But Itsui Products considered military planes more sophisticated in handling important guests. The planes did not provide the most comforable transportation, but they were speedy and powered by an excellent engine. Furthermore, a military plane gave the impression of an important official tour to friends of the traveler who might come to the airport to meet him or to see him off, and it would simultaneously demonstrate the extent of Itsui's influence with the military.

Honda was sorry to leave the tropics. When the golden pagodas had faded away in their distant jungle setting, his chancing on indications of reincarnation there began to seem like a fairy tale or a dream. Because of the Princess's extreme youth, it could all be no more than a children's song, in spite of the many proofs he had had. He did not know the life story or the cause-and-effect element in the Princess's dramatic beginning nor how she would end, as he had in the case of Kiyoaki and Isao. He had merely witnessed episodes in the life of the little girl as though he were watching the outlandish floral float of some festival passing before a traveler's curious eyes.

How strange it was that even a miracle required the commonplace! As the plane approached Japan, Honda realized with relief that he was returning to the familiar daily routine and had escaped the miracle of Benares. Finally, he had lost not only the process of reason, but even measure for his feelings. He felt no particular sorrow in leaving the Princess, and he felt neither annoyance nor any other emotion toward the officers on the plane who were heatedly discussing the approaching war.

He was naturally pleased to see his wife at the airport. Just as he expected, he felt that the Honda who had left Japan and the one who had come back had immediately fused into the same unchanged person. His wife's sleepy face, somewhat swollen and white, had acted as a catalyst to effect this fusing. The time interval between his two phases disappeared, and the deep, raw wound inflicted by the Indian trip seemed to vanish without a trace.

His wife stood at the rear of the crowd of friends who had come to meet him. She removed the dull-hued shawl from her shoulders.

"Welcome home."

She bowed to him, thrusting under his nose her familiar bangs, which she always rearranged herself after each permanent done at a beauty parlor whose styling she did not like. Her hair gave off the faint scorched odor of some chemical that had been used.

"Mother is well, but the nights have turned chilly and I didn't want her to catch cold. She's impatiently waiting at home."

Honda experienced a surge of tenderness when Rié talked about her mother-in-law without being asked, yet there was no touch of obligation in her tone. Life was again exactly as it should be.

"I want yout to go to a department store as soon

as possible, maybe tomorrow, and get a doll," said Honda on the way home in the car.

"All right."

"I promised the little princess I met in Thailand to send her a Japanese doll."

"An ordinary one with a little girl's haircut?"

"That's right. I don't think I'd send a very big one . . . one about so," he said, holding his hands in front of his chest and abdomen to indicate the size. Momentarily he thought of sending a boy doll to stand for the transmigration of a boy's soul, but he thought it might seem strange, and decided against it.

His mother was there to greet him in the vestibule of the house in Hongo, her old hunched shoulders clad in a dark silk striped kimono. She had dyed her bobbed hair a pitch black and the thin gold earpieces of her glasses passed over it. Honda thought he would suggest sometime that she should not wear her glasses in that way, but whenever it occurred to him the time never seemed right.

He walked along the matted corridor to the inner room of his familiar spacious house, now dark and cold, accompanied by his mother and wife. He realized that his manner of walking resembled that of his deceased father when the latter had used to return home.

"I'm so relieved you could get back before the war broke out. I was worried." His mother, once a zealous member of the Women's Patriotic League, panted as she walked through the corridor swept by chilly night drafts. The old woman feared war.

After two or three days of rest, Honda resumed the trip to his office in the Marunouchi Building, and his busy but peaceful days recommenced. The Japanese winter rapidly awakened his reason that resembled a seasonal winter bird—he naturally had not seen that in Southeast Asia—some crane that had again migrated to the frozen bay of his heart as it returned to Japan.

On the morning of December eighth, his wife came

into the bedroom to awaken him. "I'm sorry to wake you earlier than usual," she said quietly.

"What is it?"

Thinking that his mother's health might have taken a turn for the worse, he scambled to his feet.

"We're at war with the United States. Just now, on the radio . . ." Rié seemed still apologetic for having awakened him so early.

That morning, excited over the news of the attack on Pearl Harbor, no one in the office could settle down to work. Honda was amazed at the ceaseless and irrepressible laughter of the young office girls and wondered if women knew no other way of expressing patriotic exultation except through physical joy.

Lunch time came. The staff discussed going to the Imperial Palace Square together. After sending them off, Honda locked the office and set out alone for an afternoon stroll. His steps led him of their own accord toward the square in front of the palace.

Everyone in the Marunouchi area seemed to have had the same idea, and the wide boulevard was jammed with pedestrians.

He was forty-six, Honda mused. Nothing of youth, power, or pure passion remained in either his physical or spiritual being. He would have to prepare for death, perhaps in another ten years. More than likely he would not die in the war. He had had no military training; and even if he had, there was no danger of being called to the battlefield.

All he had to do was to stay behind and applaud the patriotic acts of the young. So they had gone to bomb Hawaii! It was a glamorous action from which his age had absolutely excluded him.

But was it only age? No. He was basically unsuited for any physical action.

Like everyone else, he had lived by approaching death step by step, but he did not know any other way. He had never run. Once he had tried to save a man's life, but he had never been placed in any position where the efforts of another had been required to save him.

He lacked the requisite quality for being saved. He had never given people the feeling of impending crisis where they would feel compelled to extend their hand in help, where they would be forced to try to rescue that certain glorious something that was in danger. The quality was charisma, and regrettably Honda was totally self-reliant and completely devoid of that.

It would be an exaggeration to say that he was jealous of the excitement about the attack on Pearl Harbor. He had simply become the captive of the egoistic and melancholy conviction that henceforth his life would definitely end and he would never achieve greatness. But had he ever really desired that in life?

On the other hand all glamorous and heroic acts faded away against the hullucination of Benares. Was it perhaps because the mystery of transmigration had warped his mind, robbed him of courage, made him recognize the futility of all brave actions, and in the end taught him to utilize all his knowledge of philosophy merely for the sake of self-love? Like a man skirting around the lighting of firecrackers, Honda felt that his mind shrank violently from the sight of such mass paroxysms.

The little flags waving and the shouts of *banzai* sounding in front of the Imperial Palace could be seen and heard from a considerable distance. Honda maintained a good stretch of the pebbled square between himself and the demonstrators; from a distance he noted the color of the dead grass covering the banks of the moat around the palace and the wintry hue of the pines. Two girls in dark blue office smocks passed by laughing, holding hands, running toward the bridge at the entrance to the palace, their white teeth flashing and glistening moistly in the winter sun.

The beautiful, bow-shaped winter lips of the women created a momentary crevice, attractive and warm, in the clear air as they passed by. The heroes in the bombers must dream at times of just such lips. Young men were always like that, seeking the most rigorous and yet attracted to the most tender. Could the tenderest thing they seek be death? Honda himself had once been a young man of promise, but not one attracted to death.

Suddenly the expanse of pebbled space beneath the winter sun became in Honda's eyes a vast and barren field. The image in the photograph labeled "Memorial Service for the War Dead, Vicinity of the Tokuri Temple," shown him by Kiyoaki thirty long years ago, returned vividly to his mind. It was Kiyoaki's favorite picture from the entire collection of photographs of the Russo-Japanese War. It now superimposed itself upon the scenery before him and finally occupied his entire consciousness. That was the end of one war, and here was the beginning of another. At any rate, it was an ominous illusion.

A mountain range in the distant left rose in the haze, trailing its long skirt of spacious plains; the horizon on the opposite side dotted with clumps of trees disappeared in yellow dust, and instead of mountains, a line of trees rose to the right, through which peeked a yellow sky.

Such was the background of the photograph. The center was occupied by a small altar covered with white cloth fluttering in the breeze, on which had been placed a bouquet of flowers and an unpainted wooden grave marker. Thousands of soldiers with bent heads surrounded it.

Honda saw the image most vividly. Again the voices shouting *banzai* and the waving flags returned to his consciousness. The vision left an indescribable sorrow in his heart.

13

DURING THE WAR Honda used his spare time entirely for his own study of samsara and transmigration and found pleasure in hunting for old books on these subjects. As the quality of new publications gradually deteriorated, the dusty luxury of wartime secondhand bookshops increased. Only there were freely available the knowledge and the pursuit of a hobby that transcended the times. And compared to the increase in the cost of everything else, the price of both Japanese and Western books remained low.

Honda gleaned considerable information from these tomes which expounded on Western theories concerning life cycles and reincarnation.

One theory was attributed to Pythagoras, the Ionian philosopher of the fifth century B.C. But his ideas on life cycles had been influenced by the earlier Orphean mysteries that had swept all of Greece in the seventh and sixth centuries. Orphean religion had in turn evolved from the worship of Dionysus that had ignited fires of madness throughout the preceding two hundred years of war and instability. The fact that the god Dionysus had come from Asia and fused with the Earth Mother and agricultural rituals throughout Greece suggested that the two had really originated from one source. The Earth Mother's vibrant figure still lived in the Kalighat in Calcutta that Honda had seen. Dionysus embodied the life cycle of nature that was manifest in the northern country of Thrace. He arrived with the beginning of winter, died at its height, and was resurrected with spring. No matter what lively, wanton figure he might simulate, Dionysus was the personification of young spirits of grain, of whom Adonis was one—beautiful youths who died prematurely. Just as Adonis indubitably had united with Aphrodite, Dionysus too unvaryingly united with the Earth Mother in mystic rituals observed in various lands. At Delphi, Dionysus was enshrined with the Earth Mother, and the chief deity in the mystic worship of Lerna was the holy ancestor of both.

Dionysus had come from Asia. His worship, which brought frenzy, debauchery, cannibalism, and murder, had its roots in Asia and posed the all-important problem of the soul. The paroxysms of this religion permitted no transparency of reason and no firm, beautiful form for either man or god. It was a religion that attacked the fertility of Greek fields in their Apollonian beauty like a swarm of grasshoppers darkening sun and sky, ravaging them, consuming their harvests. Honda could not but compare this to his own experience in India.

Everything abominable—debauchery, death, madness, pestilence, destruction . . . How was it that such things could so entice the heart and allure the soul outward. Why did souls have to "exist," discarding easy, dark, and quiet dwellings? Why was it that the human heart rejected tranquil inertness?

That was what happened in history and with individuals. If men did not do thus, it was because they surely felt that they could not touch the wholeness of the universe. Inebriated, disheveled, tearing their clothes, and exposing their genitals, blood dripping from the raw flesh in their mouths—by such actions, they must have felt they could scratch the surface of that wholeness.

This was indeed the spiritual experience of *enthusiasmus,* being god-possessed, and *extasis,* exiting from self, which had eventually been refined and ritualized by the Orpheans.

What had turned Greek thought to the concept of samsara and reincarnation was this *extasis* experience. The deepest psychologic source of reincarnation was "ecstasy."

According to Orphean mythology, Dionysus was called Dionysus Zagreus, Zagreus being the child born to Zeus and Persephone, daughter of the Earth Mother. He was the favorite of his father and destined to be his successor and the future universal ruler. It is said that when Zeus, Heaven, fell in love with Persephone, Earth, he transformed himself into a great serpent, betokening the essence of earth, in order to make love to her.

His love for the maiden aroused the wrath of his jealous wife, Hera. She summoned the subterranean Titans, and they enticed the baby Zagreus with a toy. Once captured, he was murdered, dismembered, cooked, and eaten. Only his heart was offered to Zeus by Hera.

In turn, Zeus gave it to Semele, and a new Dionysus was reborn.

Meanwhile, Zeus was infuriated by the Titans' act and he attacked them with thunder and lightning. When they were completely destroyed, man was born of their ashes.

Thus, mankind was given the evil character of the Titans and at the same time possessed godlike elements transmitted by Zagreus's flesh that the Titans had consumed. Accordingly, the Orpheans proclaimed that man must worhip Dionysus by *extasis* and reestablish his holy origin by self-deification. The ritual of the sacred feast persists in the Christian sacrament of the holy eucharist.

Orpheus the musician, murdered and dismembered by Thracian women, seems to reenact the death of Dionysus; and his death, rebirth, and the mysteries of Hades became significant Orphean doctrines.

As wandering souls who left their bodies by *extasis* were thought to be able to make contact for a short time with the mysteries of Dionysus, men were clearly aware of the separation of body and soul. Their flesh was formed of the evil ashes of the Titans and their soul embraced the pure fragrance of Dionysus. Furthermore, the doctrine of Orpheus taught that earthly suffering did not end with corporeal death; the soul, having escaped its dead body, was obliged to spend some time in Hades before reappearing on earth and transmigrating into another human or animal body. Thus was it destined to traverse limitless "cycles of life."

The immortal soul, originally holy, must traverse such a dark passage because of the original sin of the flesh: namely, the Titans' murder of Zagreus. Man's earthly life added new sins, and they renewed themselves. Thus, mankind is eternally incapable of escaping from the suffering of this cycle of lives. A man is not necessarily reincarnated in human form, but depending upon the gravity of his sins, may be reborn as a horse, sheep, bird dog, or cold snake fated to crawl in the dust.

The Pythagoreans, who had been called the successors of the Orpheans and credited with developing their theories, held to the unique doctrines of samsaric reincarnation and Universal Breath.

Honda could detect a trace of the latter principle in King Milinda's concept of life and the soul; he had long meditated on Indian philosophy. It also bore a resemblance to the mysticism of ancient Shinto.

Compared to the fairy-tale cheerfulness of the *jataka,* tales drawn from the various lives of the Buddha, in Theravada Buddhism, the Western theory of reincarnation, darkened by gloomy Ionic melancholy, depressed Honda in spite of the fact that both came from the same source. Consequently he tended to heed Heraclitus who had claimed that all things were in flux.

Enthusiasmus and *extasis* merged in this philosophy of transitory unity, according to which one was all, one came from the all, and all from the one. In the area which transcended time and space, ego disappeared, unity with the universe was easily accomplished, and man was able to become through this divine experience every thing. There, man, nature, bird, animal, forests rustling in the breeze, streams sparkling with the scales of fish, cloud-capped mountains, blue seas dotted with islands—all were able to disengage themselves from their earth-bound existence and unite in harmony. It was such a world that Heraclitus talked about.

> The living and the dead,
> The awake and the sleeping,
> The young and the old are all one and the same.
> When the ones change, they become the others.
> When those shift again, they become these.

> God is day and night.
> God is winter and summer.
> God is war and peace.
> God is fertility and famine.
> He transforms into many things.

Day and night are one.
Goodness and badness are one.
The beginning and the end of a circle are one.

These lines represent the sublimity of Heraclitian thought, and when Honda came into contact with it, was blinded by its brilliance, he experienced a certain liberation; but at the same time he was cautious lest he remove too hastily the hands with which he covered his dazzled eyes. For one thing, he was afraid of going blind; for another, he felt that he was still too immature in his sensitivity and ideas to accept such boundless illumination.

14

FOR THIS REASON Honda averted his eyes for a while and concentrated on his studies of the theories of samsara and reincarnation that had been revived in seventeenth- and eighteenth-century Italy.

Tommaso Campanella, a monk living in the sixteenth and seventeenth centuries, believed in the theory of the life cycle and reincarnation. This heretic and rebellious philosopher was welcomed in France after spending twenty-nine years in prison. There he was happy and much honored during the last years of his life. When Louis XIV was born, he dedicated to him an *éloge* in which he claimed that the royal birth was proof of his theory of reincarnation.

Campanella learned the Brahman theory of samsara and transmigration from Botero and there discovered that the souls of the dead transmigrated even into monkeys, elephants, or cows. Borrowing the Pythagorean belief in the immortality of the soul and in reincarnation, he designated the inhabitants of his principal work, *Città del sole,* to be "wise men who had originally come from India to escape the pillage and atrocities of the Mogul." "Pythagorean Brahmans," he called them, yet he left their belief in samsara ambiguous. Campanella himself claimed that after death, the human soul did not go to hell, purgatory, or heaven.

It is said that his Caucasian Sonnets vaguely suggest the theory of samsara. In these poems, he expressed his emotions of sorrow. "I cannot believe that my death will bring improvement to mankind; frequently, even if misfortune be averted, evil prospers more than ever. Human senses survive eternally after death; such senses simply forget the suffering endured during life in this world. If we cannot even know whether our former lives were spent in torture or in peace, how shall we know anything of the afterlife?"

In contrast to the jubilation Honda had witnessed in Benares, the Europeans who discoursed on reincarnation were especially depressed by the adversity and sorrow of this life. Furthermore, they did not seek joy in a hereafter, but hoped merely for oblivion.

On the other hand, the eighteenth-century philosopher Giovanni Batista Vico, a ferocious opponent of Descartes, advocated reincarnation and a return to eternity, and his bravery and militancy in his struggle made him a forerunner of Nietzsche, who held the same views. Honda read with pleasure one passage from Vico, in which he praised the Japanese as being heroic, even though he had but a vague knowledge of Japan. "The Japanese eulogize the heroic man as did the Romans at the time of the Punic Wars. They are fearless in military affairs and speak a language similar to Latin."

Vico interpreted history through his concept of recurrence. In short, he maintained that each civilization came to its final phase with "Premeditated Savagery," which is far worse than the earlier "Natural Savagery." The latter signifies a noble naïveté, but the former indicates cowardly cunning and insidious trickery. Thus the venomous "Premeditated Savagery" or "Civilized Savagery" must necessarily perish, after centuries of progress, by a renewal of "Natural Savagery."

Honda felt that an example was to be found in the brief history of modern Japan.

Vico believed in the order of the universe as propounded by Catholicism; yet he was close to the theory of causation through karma. "God the creator," he said agnostically, "and the created are separate entities. The raison d'etre and essence of things are individual in each entity; therefore, the created is an entirely different entity from the godhead as far as its essence is concerned."

If one holds the created—that which appears to be an entity—to be dharma and atman and if one regards its raison d'etre to be karma, then deliverance is simply attaining the entity of the creator on another dimension.

Vico claimed in his theology that God's creation changed "internally" into the created and "externally" into matter, and thus the world was created in time. He also said that the human spirit, being God's reflection, was able to grasp the concept of infinity and eternity and was immortal. It is not confined by the body and consequently is not limited by time. But he did not provide an answer to the question why the limitless being was shackled by limited things, claiming this to be unknowable. But this is the very point at which the wisdom of the theory of samsara and reincarnation should begin.

On reflection, it is surprising that Indian philosophy, persistently insisting on the power of knowledge, did not reject fantasy or dreams and never developed its own agnosticism.

15

WHEN HONDA DISCOVERED that a Western tradition of reincarnation had been feebly handed down by lone and solitary thinkers, he mused that it was only natural that King Milinda, who had ruled northwestern India in the second century B.C., seemed to have quite forgotten the Pythagorean philosophy of ancient Greece when he met the Elder, Nagasena, and plied him with questions. He was most interested in, and at the same time skeptical of, the more profound Buddhist theories of samsara and transmigration.

The first volume of *The Questions of King Milinda*, as it appears in the Japanese translation of the Buddhist canon, opens with the following description of the ruler's capital:

Thus I have heard: In one of the regions colonized by the Greeks, there is a city called Sagara. It is a great center for commerce and foreign trade and is marked by purple mountains and clear water, parks, woods, and fields, forming a pleasant, natural paradise on earth; and its inhabitants are devoutly religious. Furthermore, their enemies have all been driven away, so that they feel not the slightest insecurity or oppression. The king's castle is surrounded by fortifications, a variety of ramparts, majestic, forbidding side gates, high white walls, deep moats, and the protection provided is complete. The city's squares, crossroads, and marketplaces are most aptly designed: beautifully decorated stores are filled with countless invaluable merchandise. Several hundreds of charitable hospitals add dignity to the city, while several thousand mansions and high pavilions tower like the Himalayas high in the clouds. And in the city streets, throngs of people are visible, men like pines, women like flowers, priests, warriors, farmers and traders, serfs—people of all classes pass by in groups.

All the citizenry welcomes scholars and teachers of various religions and doctrines. Thus, Sagara appears as a nest for elders and academicians of all persuasions. Also in the streets stand eave to eave both large and small dry goods merchants who handle goods woven in Benares called *khotumbari* and all other kinds of goods and fabrics. Lavish fragrance wafts from the flower and incense market, purifying the air of the city. Other shops handle wishing pearls and divers other gems and goods of gold, silver, copper, or stone. It is as though one has stepped into a dazzling mine of jewels. Then, as one turns in another direction, there are great stores for grain and warehouses full of priceless merchandise, shops with all manner of food and drink and cakes; nothing is lacking. In short, Sagara rivals Uttarakuru in wealth, and its prosperity compares well with that of Arakaman-dar, the city of heaven.

Extremely self-confident and excelling in elocution and debate, King Milinda was contemptuous of Indians as being intellectual chaff. And it was in the midst of this ravishing and glorious city that he met the elder, Nagasena, for the first time, a sage superior in intellect to the King.

"O Wise One, when I call you Nagasena, exactly who is this Nagasena?" asked the King.

The Elder answered with a question: "What do you think Nagasena is?"

"O Wise One, I think Nagasena is what exists within a body, a life or soul which enters it as wind or breath."

The King's reply reminded Honda of the Pythagorean theory of the Universal Breath. That is to say, *psyche* in Greek originally meant "breath," and if human psyche was breath, man was sustained by air, and thus the whole universe was maintained by air and breath. Such was the Ionean theory of natural philosophy.

The Elder further asked why it was that the breath of one who blows a conch, flute, or horn never returned once it was released, and yet the blower did not die. The King was unable to reply. Thereupon Nagasena made a statement which pointed up the fundamental difference between Greek and Buddhist philosophy.

"The soul is not breath. Inhaled and exhaled, breath is merely the body's latent energy or power."

Honda immediately felt he could anticipate the dialogue that would follow; it did in fact appear on the next page.

The King asked, saying: "O Wise One, is anyone and everyone reborn after dying?"

"Some people do, some do not."

"What sort of people would they be?"

"Those who have committed sins will be reborn; those who are sinless and pure will not be reborn."

"Are you going to be reborn, O Wise One?"

"When I die, if I am attached to life in my heart, I shall be reborn; but if not, I shall not be reborn."

"I understand."

From this point on, a zealous desire for learning was kindled in King Milinda's heart, and pertinaciously he posed question upon question concerning samsara and transmigration. The King pursued the Elder with the spiral investigation of Greek dialogue, asking for proof of the "selflessness" of Buddhism and the question why men who possess no "self" go through samsara, and concerning the essence that is subject to the law of samsara. Because if samsara occurs through a sequence of causes and effects—a good cause producing by reward a good effect, a bad cause a bad one—there must be an eternal host substance responsible for causal actions. But atman, which was recognized in the days of the *Upanishads,* had been categorically denied in the Abhidharma teachings that characterized the school to which Nagasena belonged. Because of the doctrine and because of his ignorance of the elaborate system of the Consciousness Only school that developed later, Nagasena merely answered: "There is no samsaric subject as essence."

But Honda saw an indescribable beauty in the parable which Nagasena used to explain samsara and transmigration, that of a sacred taper, whose flame is not quite the same in the evening, at midnight, and at dawn, and yet not different either as it continues on the same wick burning throughout the night. The karmic existence of an individual is not substantive existence but merely a succession of phenomena similar to the flame.

And so Nagasena taught that time was the existence of samsara itself, almost in the same manner as the Italian philosophers who espoused it many centuries later.

16

IT WAS ONLY NATURAL that King Milinda should choose a Buddhist as his companion in these dialogues, for the ruler, being a foreigner, was necessarily excluded from Hinduism. One not born within the Indian caste system, sovereign or not, was arbitrarily rejected by this religion.

Honda's first encounter with the words "samsara" and "reincarnation" had occurred thirty years before, at the house of Kiyoaki Matsugae, where, having listened to the sermon of the Abbess of the Gesshu Temple, he had on his own read the *Laws of Manu* in the French translation of Louis Delongchamps. These laws, which were compiled sometime between the second century before and the second century after the birth of Christ, inherited the idea of samsara established at the beginning of the eighth century B.C. in the *Upanishads* with their belief in the unity of Brahma and atman. The *Brihadaranyaka Upanishad* states:

> Indeed the person performing a good deed will become benevolent and one performing a bad deed will become evil; one becomes pure by pure acts and black by evil acts. Therefore it is said: A human being is composed of *kama,* or "desire"; by following *kama,* one creates will; by following will one creates karma; and through karma, samsara comes into existence.

In retrospect, Honda's experience in Benares might have been predestined since that day when, at nineteen, he had become familiar with the *Laws.* The *Laws of Manu* encompasses all of religion, morality, custom, and law, beginning with the creation of heaven and earth and ending with samsara. During their rule of India, the British wisely permitted these laws to continue in effect as practical rules for the Hindus who resided there.

After a second reading of the *Laws,* Honda was for the first time able to touch upon the origin of the jubilation and adoration that he had witnessed in Benares. He read in the impressive first chapter the description of the birth of Brahma, the ancestor of the entire world, where it is told how a divinity coming into being spontaneously expelled the chaos of darkness and began to shine. First he created water and placed a seed in it. The seed grew and became a golden egg as brilliant as the sun. A year later, he broke the egg and from it Brahma was born. And the water that had nurtured the god was that of Benares.

The principle of reincarnation expounded in the *Laws of Manu* classifies human rebirth as being roughly of three kinds. Three natures govern the bodies of all sentient beings: wisdom (*sattva*), which is joyous, serene, and filled with pure, shining emotions, is reborn as a god; ignorance (*rajas*), which likes business enterprises, which is indecisive and tends to follow dishonest works and is addicted to sensuous pleasures, is reborn as man; and anger (*tamas*), which follows a life of indolence and dissipation, slothfulness, cruelty, unbelief, and evil, is reincarnated as an animal.

Transgressions that bring about transmigration into animals are itemized in detail: the murderer of a Brahman will enter the body of a dog, pig, donkey, camel, cow, goat, sheep, deer, or bird; a Brahman who steals money from another Brahman will be reborn a thousand times as a spider, snake, lizard, or aquatic animal; one who invades the bed of a noble person will be born a hundred times as grass, bush, vine, or flesh-eating animal; one who steals grain will become a rat, a honey filcher will become a horsefly; a milk thief will be born as a bird; a herb scrounger will be a dog; a meat stealer will be reborn as a condor; a thief of fat meat will become a cormorant; a salt filcher will transmigrate as a cricket; a robber of silk will be a partridge; a linen stealer will be reborn as a frog; a cotton thief will become a crane;

a cow poacher will be an iguana; a filcher of incense will become a muskrat, a vegetable thief, a peacock; a stealer of fire, a heron; a furniture thief, a wasp; a horse thief, a tiger; a woman abductor, a bear; a stealer of water, a cuckoo; and a fruit poacher, a monkey.

17

NONETHELESS, the Theravada Buddhism of Thailand was sustained by the naïve doctrinces of the *jataka,* or "birth stories," in the Southern Buddhist Canon that retained much of the flavor of the original Pali texts. It was not even considered strange for Shakyamuni, who had made no transgression as a bodhisattva in his former lives, to be reborn as a rat or a golden swan.

The southern teachings current in Thailand were unknown in Japan until the late nineteenth century. Within one to two hundred years after the death of the Buddha, they were divided into many schools, usually called the Eighteen Theravada Sects; and their teachings, brought to Ceylon by Mahinda under the rule of King Ashoka in the third century B.C., are still practiced there and in Burma, Thailand, and Cambodia.

In the Theravada Canon, written in Pali, the minute regulations set forth in the *vinaya,* or "rules" section, still regulate the daily lives of Siamese cenobites. Monks are subject to two hundred and fifty precepts, nuns to three hundred and fifty.

Honda was anxious to learn about the Thai concept of samsara and transmigration, how it differed from the Yuishiki doctrine that attributes the existence of the exterior world to inner ideation, and what sort of characteristics it possessed. Whatever the little Princess's belief, he wanted to know what ideas of samsara were entertained by the ubiquitous saffron-robed monks in Bangkok. He read voraciously.

Thus it was that he discovered that the doctrines of the Eighteen Theravada Sects had originated in the

Abhidharma school to which Nagasena, the Elder who had conversed with King Milinda, belonged. As for the dissemination of the *Questions of King Milinda,* certain scholars claim that the work was probably compiled in northwestern India, where there were then Greek colonies, and later traveled eastward to the region of Magadha where it was transcribed into Pali. Ultimately, with the addition of some material, it reached Ceylon and spread from there to Burma and Thailand, becoming the *Milindapanha* of the Thai canon.

We may thus assume that the particular Thai concept of samsara is approximately the same as that advocated by Nagasena. The basic tenet of this sect is that the karmic essence that causes samsara is thought or will. This is consistent with the *Agamas* and is very close to primary Buddhist thought. The followers of this sect claim that in terms of motivation there is basically neither good nor evil in men or matter in the external world. What makes them good or bad is completely the product of mind, thought, or will.

So far so good. But in explaining "selflessness," or *anatman,* the Abhidharma school proceeds from the fact that the whole material world is *avyakrita,* "unrecordable" as either good or bad—neutral. For instance, imagine a carriage. Despite the fact that all the constituents of this carriage are simple material elements, they can turn into an instrument of crime if the driver runs over a man and escapes. Thus, as mind and will are causes for transgressions and karma, man is fundamentally *anatman,* "without self." However, thought rides in the vehicle of the body and produces samsara and reincarnation through the six karmic causes: passion, anger, wrong views, indifference, non-anger, and correct views. Thought is the cause of samsara, but it is not the migrating body. What this body may be is never explained. The hereafter is merely a continuation of this world, and the taper light burning during one's final evening in this world is the birth light of the next life with which it is linked.

On reflection, Honda seemed to understand better

what must have been going on in the mind of the little Thai Princess.

With every rainy season, the rivers in Bangkok overflowed, the divisions between road and river, river and rice paddies immediately vanished. Roads became streams, and rivers boulevards. It was surely not an unusual event, even in the mind of a child, that a flood of dreams should invade reality, that past and future, breaking their dikes, should overflow into this world. The green spears of rice plants peeked out of the flooded paddies, and the matters of river and paddy were both bathed in the same sun, both reflected the same masses of summer clouds.

Similarly, a flood of past and future might have occurred subconsciously in the mind of Princess Moonlight, and the isolated phenomena of this world, like islands dotting the vast stretch of water clearly reflecting the moon after the rains, might be the more difficult of the two to believe. The embankments had been broken down and all divisions had disappeared. The past had begun to speak freely.

18

HONDA NOW FELT that he could easily return to the Yuishiki theory that had so puzzled him in his youth. He could grasp the system of Mahayana Buddhism that was like some magnificent cathedral now that he had the help of the lovely enigma he had left behind in Bangkok.

Nevertheless, the Yuishiki doctrine was a dazzlingly lofty religio-philosophic structure by which Buddhism, once it had denied atman and soul, provided a most precise and meticulous explanation of the theoretical difficulties concerning the migrating body in rebirth and reincarnation. Like the Temple of Dawn in Bangkok, this consummately complex philosophical achievement pierced the vast expanse of the blue morning sky, which, in that mysterious time before sunrise, was filled with cooling winds and glimmering light.

The contradiction between samsara and *anatman,* a dilemma unresolved for many centuries, was finally explained by Yuishiki doctrine. What body recurs from life to life? What body is liberated in the Pure Land paradise? What can it be?

To begin with, the Sanskirt word for Yuishiki, *vijnapti-matrata,* "consciousness only," was used in India for the first time by Asanga. Asanga's life was already half shrouded in legend by the time his name became known in China at the beginning of the sixth century through the *Chin kang hsien lun,* or "Treatise of Vajrarishi." The Yuishiki theory originated in the Mahayana Abhi-dharma sutras, and as we shall see, one *gatha,* or "verse," in these writings constitutes the core of Yuishiki ideas. Asanga systematized Yuishiki principles in his main work the *Mahayanasamparigraha shastra,* "A Collection of Mahayana Treatises." It is pertinent to note that Abhidharma is a Sanskirt word indicating the last of the tripartite Buddhist canon comprising sutras, rules, and scholastic treatises and is practically synonymous with scholastic treatises.

Ordinarily we function in life through the mental opera-tion of the so-called six senses: sight, hearing, smell, taste, touch, and mind. But the Yuishiki school estab-lished a seventh sense, *manas,* which in its widest import applies to all mental powers that perceive self and indi-vidual identity. But it does not stop there. It further advocates the concept of *alayavijnana,* "the ultimate consciousness." Translated by "storehouse conscious-ness" in Chinese, *alaya* stores away all "seeds" of the phenomenal world.

Life is active. *Alaya* consciousness functions. This consciousness is the fruit of all rewards, and it stores all seeds that are the results of all activity. Thus that one is living indicates that *alaya* is active.

This consciousness is in constant flux like a foaming white waterfall. While the cascade is always visible to our eyes, the water is not the same from minute to min-

ute. New water incessantly pours by, streaming and
surging, sending up its misty vapors.

Vasubandhu expatiated on Asanga's theory, and in
his *Trimshikavi jnaptikarika,* or the "Thirty Eulogies
to Yuishiki," stated: "Everything is in constant flux
like a torrent." This was one sentence that the twenty-
year-old Honda had heard from the lips of the old Abbess
of the Gesshu Temple and had kept locked in his heart,
though he had not been quite himself at the time because
of Kiyoaki.

Furthermore, this thought was connected with his
trip to India, with the memory of the two waterfalls
plunging precipitously into the Wagora at Ajanta, of
the streams which had struck his eyes the moment he
stepped out of the *vihara* that he felt someone had just
left.

And in those probably final and ultimate falls at Ajanta
reflected a mirror image of the Sanko waterfall at Mount
Miwa where Honda had met Isao for the first time and
of the cascade in the Matsugae garden where he had
encountered the old Abbess.

Now *alaya* consciousness is implanted by all seeds
of all results. Not only the results of the seven senses
we have already spoken of and their activity during
life, not only the results of mental activities, but also
the seeds of physical phenomena that are the objects
of such mental activities are implanted in it. Implanting
the seeds into the consciousness is called "perfuming,"
in a manner similar to the way incense permeates clothing,
the process being referred to as *shuji kunju,* or "seed
perfuming."

The process of reasoning will differ depending on
whether one regards this *alaya* consciousness as pure
and neutral or otherwise. If it is assumed to be neutral,
then the power which generates samsara and reincarnation must be an external, karmic force. All temptations,
all things that exist in the external world, or all illusions
of the senses from the first through the seventh constantly
exert influence on the *alaya* through the power of
karma.

According to the doctrine of Yuishiki the seeds of karmic power—karmic seeds—are indirect causes, or "auxiliary karma," and the *alaya* consciousness itself is both the migrating body and generative power of samsara and reincarnation. Asanga claimed that this idea would eventually lead to the logical conclusion that *alaya* consciousness itself was not completely pure, that, being a mixture of water and milk, as it were, its adulterated ingredients generated the world of illusion while the pure part brought enlightenment. The karmic seeds of good and evil it contains will materialize in the future according as they are the reward for good or bad acts in the past. This is the difference between the doctrines of the Yuishiki and the Kusha schools, for the latter stresses the external power of karma. Yuishiki developed its unique concept of the world structure based on the idea that the seeds of the *alaya* consciousness generate this consciousness and form natural law (like causes produce like effects) and that these seeds by means of karmic seeds produce moral law (different causes produce different effects).

Alaya consciousness is thus the fruit of sentient beings' retribution and the fundamental cause of all existence. For example, the materializing of a man's *alaya* consciousness means simply the existence of that man.

Thus, *alaya* consciousness makes the delusions of the world in which we live. The roots of all knowledge, embracing all objects of perception, make these objects materialize. The world is composed of the physical body and its Five Roots,* the natural or material world, and "seeds," that is, the energy that makes all mind and matter materialize. The self, which we tenaciously think of as being our actuality, and the soul, which we presume to continue to exist after death—both are born from the *alaya* consciousness, which is the creator of all phenomena, and therefore both return to this consciousness; all is reduced to ideation.

Yet according to the term *yuishiki*, "consciousness

---

* The five organs of the senses: eyes, ears, nose, tongue, and body as roots of knowing. (Translators' note.)

only," if we think of an object as actually existing in the world and assume all to be merely the product of ideation then we are confusing atman with *alaya* consciousness. For atman under given conditions is a constant entity, but *alaya* consciousness is a ceaseless "flow of selflessness."

In his *Mahayanasamparigraha shastra,* Asanga defines three kinds of "perfuming" pertaining to those seeds which cause the world of illusion to materialize after being perfumed by the *alaya* consciousness.

The first is the seed of name.

For instance, when we say that a rose is a beautiful flower, the designation "rose" distinguishes it from other flowers. In order to ascertain how beautiful it is, we go up to a rose and take cognizance of how different it is from other blooms. The rose first appears as "name"; the concept gives rise to imagination, and when imagination comes into contact with the real object, its fragrance, color, and shape are stored away in memory. Or it is possible that the beauty of a flower we have seen without knowing its name has moved us to desire further information about it; on hearing the name "rose" we conceptualize it. Thus we learn meanings, names, words, and their objects, as well as the relationships among them. All things we learn are not necessarily beautiful names nor always accurate meanings, but everything we acquire by perception and thought has been since time immemorial stored away in memory and brings forth worldly phenomena.

The second seed is that of attachment to self.

When the seventh of the eight consciousnesses, *manas,* gives rise in the *alaya* consciousness to egotism with its differentiation between self and others, that egotism insists on an absolute individual self; by eventually moving the other six consciousnesses it produces a series of "perfumings of self." Honda could not but think that both the formation of so-called consciousness of self in modern times as well as the fallacy of egotistic philosophy found their origins in the second seed.

The third is the seed of the *trailokya.*

Trailokya means the "three worlds" and signifies the entire world of illusion consisting of sensuous desire, form, and the formlessness of pure spirit. *Lokya* represents cause. This seed, which is the cause of the three worlds of suffering and delusion, is the seed of karma itself. The difference of fates, the partiality of fortune and misfortune depend on the merit and demerit found in this seed.

Thus it was clear that what migrated in samsara and reincarnation, what passed from one life to the next was the vast flow of selflessness of the *alaya* consciousness.

19

BUT THE MORE Honda learned about Yuishiki theory, the more he had to know how *alaya* consciousness caused the phenomenal world to appear. For according to Yuishiki concepts, cause and effect dependent on *alaya* occurred simultaneously at a given instant, and yet alternately. For Honda, who could think of cause and effect only in terms of time sequence, this idea of simultaneous, yet alternating causes and effects of the *alaya* consciousness and the phenomenal world was exceedingly difficult to grasp. Yet it was clear that in this concept lay the basic difference between the interpretation of the universe by all of Mahayana (including the Yuishiki school) and that of Hinayana Buddhism.

The world of Theravada Buddhism was like the rainy season in Bangkok when the river, rice paddies, and fields presented an unbroken, limitless expanse. The monsoon floods now must have occurred in the past too and would occur in the future as well. The phoenix tree with its vermilion flowers blooming in the garden was there yesterday and therefore would doubtless be there tomorrow. If it was certain that existence went on, say, even after Honda's death, similarly his past would certainly continue smoothly into the future in repeated reincarnations. Unquestioning acceptance of the world as it was, the natural tropical docility so like the land which accepted the floods, was characteristic of Theravadins. They teach that our existence continues from the past, through the present, to the future; past, present, and future resemble the vast brown waters of a river bordered by mangroves with their aerial roots, its flow heavy and lanquid. The doctrine is called the theory of constant existence in past, present, and future.

Contrary to this, Mahayana Buddhism, especially the Yuishiki school, interpreted the world as a torrential and swift rapids or a great white cascade which never pauses. Since the world presented the form of a waterfall, both the basic cause of that world and the basis of man's perception of it were waterfalls. It is a world that lives and dies at every moment. There is no definite proof of existence in either past or future, and only the present instant which one can touch with one's hand and see with one's eyes is real. Such a world concept is unique to Mahayana Buddhism; reality exists in the present only, there being no past or future.

But why should this be called "reality"?

If we can recognize a narcissus by seeing it with our eyes and touching it with our hands, at least the narcissus and its immediate environment exist at the moment of touching and seeing.

That much is confirmable.

But then, if we are asleep and if a narcissus is placed in a vase by our pillow during the night, can we prove the existence of the flower at every moment during our sleep?

Thus, if our eyes are gouged out, our ears, nose, and tongue cut off, if we depart our body and our consciousness is extinguished, does the world of the narcissus and its environment continue to exist?

But the world *must* exist!

The seventh consciousness, *manas,* may affirm or deny the world, depending on its attachment to self. Honda could say that since there was a self, that as long as that self continued to perceive, even after the loss of all five senses, there existed about him his fountain pen, vase, ink bottle, red glass pitcher and on it the white cross of the window frame forming a smooth curve reflecting the morning light, his copy of the *Compendium of Laws,* paperweight, desk, wall panel, framed pictures—his world which was a carefully arranged extension of these small objects. Or he might say that as long as self-consciousness (the self) existed and perceived, the world was nothing more than a phenomenal shadow, a reflection of the ego's perceptions; the world was nothing and therefore nonexistent. Thus the ego would with arrogance and pride try to treat the world as its own, like a beautiful ball to kick about.

But the world *must* exist!

Yet if order for it to do so, there must be a consciousness that will produce it, make it exist, make the narcissus be, that will guarantee the existence of these things at every moment. This is the *alaya* consciousness, as constant as the North Star, which is awake at every moment during the long dark nights, making such nights exist in fact, incessantly guaranteeing reality and existence.

But the world *must* exist!

Even if all consciousnesses to the seventh should claim that the world were nonexistent, or even though the five senses were completely destroyed and death occurred, the world would exist as long as there was *alaya.* Everything exists through *alaya,* and since it does, all things are. But what if *alaya* were extinguished?

But the world *must* exist!

Therefore, *alaya* consciousness is never extinguished. As in a cascade, the water of every moment is different, yet the stream flows in torrential and constant movement.

Thus, *alaya* consciousness flows eternally in order to make the world exist.

For the world *must* at all costs exist!

But why?

Because only by the existence of the world—world of illusion—is man given the chance of enlightenment.

That the world must exist is thus the ultimate moral

requisite. This is the supreme answer of the *alaya* consciousness as to why the world must be.

If the existence of the world—the world of illusion—is the ultimate moral requisite, *alaya* consciousness itself, which produces all phenomena, is the origin of that moral requisite. But the world and *alaya* consciousness, or *alaya* and the world of illusion that gives birth to phenomena must be said to be interdependent. For if *alaya* does not exist, the world does not come into being; but if the world is not, *alaya* is deprived of samsara and reincarnation in which *alaya* itself is the migrating essence, and the way to enlightenment will be forever closed.

Thus it is through this highest moral requisite that *alaya* and the world are mutually dependent; the existence of the *alaya* consciousness depends on the very necessity that the world exist.

Yet only the immediate present is reality, and if the ultimate authority that guarantees momentary existence is *alaya,* that *alaya* that brings about all worldly phenomena exists at the point where time and space intersect.

Honda was able to grasp, albeit with difficulty, that here was born the unique Yuishiki theory of cause and effect being at once simultaneous and alternate.

Now for Buddhist theory to be authentic, there must be textual proof that it is part of the teaching of Gautama Buddha, and the Yuishiki school found just that in the following *gatha,* the most difficult in Mahayana Abhidharma sutras.

> All dharma are stored in consciousness,
> And consciousness is stored in all dharma.
> The two become mutual causes
> And always mutual results.

Honda interpreted this passage as meaning that according to the law of continuous cause and effect characteristic of the *alaya* consciousness, the world observed at the momentary section of the present might be described as being sliced like a cucumber into momentary slices of present that are observable one after the other.

The world is born and dies at every instant, and on each momentary cross section appear three forms of endless births and deaths. One is "seeds producing the present world," then "the present world 'perfuming' the seeds," and last, "seeds producing seeds." The first is the form in which the seed causes the present world to materialize, and naturally it includes momentum from the past. There is a trail from the past. The second shows the present world being "perfumed" by *alaya* seeds and becoming future phenomena. Naturally uneasiness over the future casts its shadow. But this does not mean that all seeds are "perfumed" by the present and produce present phenomena. Some seeds, even though being tainted, are merely succeeded by other seeds. These are the third kind of seed. And their causes and effects alone do not occur simultaneously, but follow a time sequence.

The world manifests itself through these three forms, and everything occurs in an instantaneous present.

But the first and second seeds are born anew simultaneously, influence each other, and perish in the same instant. The momentary cross sections, inherited only by these seeds, are discarded as the seeds move from section to section. The structure of the human world is formed of thin slices of instants, infinite in number, pierced through by the skewer of the seeds of the *alaya* consciousness. And the thin slices representing so many instants are both pierced and discarded in each minute segment of time.

Samsara and reincarnation are not prepared during a lifetime, beginning only at death, but rather they renew the world at every instant by momentary re-creation and destruction.

Thus the seeds cause this gigantic flower of delusion called the world to bloom at every point in time, abandoning it at the same instant. But the succession of seeds producing seeds demands the help of karma seeds, as we have said. These karma seeds come from the "perfuming" of the momentary present.

The true meaning of Yuishiki is that the whole of the world manifests itself now in this very instant. Yet this instantaneous world already dies in the same moment and simultaneously a new one appears. The world which appears one moment is transformed in the following and thus continues on. Everything in the entire world is *alaya* consciousness.

20

WHEN HONDA'S THINKING had evolved this far, everything around him took on an unanticipated appearance.

This particular day, he happened to have been invited to a villa in Shoto in the Shibuya district concerning a prolonged lawsuit and was waiting in the second-floor reception room. No lodgings were available, and when the plaintiff came up to Tokyo on matters of litigation, he stayed at the house of some wealthy man from his home region. The owner had long since left Tokyo for Karuizawa to avoid the bombings.

The administrative suit was being conducted with a leisureliness that stood above time. It had, in fact, been initiated by a law promulgated in 1899, and the origin of the dispute itself went back to post-Restoration days several decades earlier. The accused in this case was the government, and even the defendant's title had changed from Minister of Agriculture and Commerce to that of Agriculture and Forestry with the reorganization of the cabinet. Lawyers representing the plaintiff covered several generations, and now, if Honda, who had been entrusted with the case, won, according to the original agreement one third of the entire land accruing to the plaintiff would be his remuneration. However, he did not expect that the litigation would be over in his lifetime.

Thus he came to the Shibuya villa only to pass the

time, using the work as a pretext. In reality he came in anticipation of the polished rice and chicken that his client usually brought as a gift from the country.

The client, who should have long since arrived, was not there yet. He was no doubt having difficulty with the trains.

The June afternoon was too warm for his civilian uniform and gaiters, so Honda opened the tall, oblong English window and stood by it to catch some air. Having had no military experience, he could not to this day manage his gaiters properly, and they tended to slip off his legs and to bunch around his calves, giving him the sensation of dragging a pilgrim's bag around his legs when he walked. His wife Rié always feared that the loose gaiters might get caught in the crowded street-cars and trip him.

Perspiration seeped through the lumpy areas of the gaiters today. The vulgarly shiny summer uniform, made of some staple fiber, retained every crease, and Honda knew that the back of his jacket must be puckered into ugly wrinkles from sitting. But it was no use straightening it.

From the window, he could see all the way to the Shibuya Station area bathed in June light. The residential parts of the immediate vicinity had survived relatively intact, but the area from the foot of the plateau up to the station was freshly bombed ruins spotted with half-destroyed concrete buildings. The air raids that had razed the area had occurred only the week before, on the nights of May twenty-fourth and twenty-fifth, 1945, during which a total of five hundred B-29s had fire-bombed various residential parts of Tokyo. The odor of the conflagration still remained, and the memory of the hellish scene still lingered in the light of day.

The odor, like that of a crematorium, was mixed with more ordinary smells such as those from kitchens or bonfires, commingling with the pungent tang of chemicals as in a pharmaceutical factory or machinery. The smell of burnt-out ruins was already familiar to Honda.

Fortunately his house in Hongo had not yet been touched.

In the continuous metallic whine of bombs drilling through the night sky above, followed by a series of explosions and the release of fire bombs, he could always hear something inhuman, something like the voices of women cheering somewhere in the sky. Honda realized later that these were the cries of the damned.

In the burnt-out ruins, the debris had turned rusty, and the crushed roofs had remained untouched. Pillars of various heights stood everywhere like blackened pickets, and ashes crumbled from them to dance in the faint breeze.

Here and there something glittered brightly—for the most part, the remains of shattered panes of glass, glass surfaces burned and warped, pieces of broken bottles that reflected the sun. These little fragments harvested all the June light they could gather to them. Honda beheld for the first time the brilliance of the rubble.

The concrete foundations of houses were clearly limned under the crumbled walls. High and low, each was lit by the afternoon sun. For this reason, the entire ruin had the appearance of a type mold for a sheet of newsprint. But the predominant shade was the light reddish brown of a flowerpot, not the gloomy gray unevenness of a newspaper mold.

There was little greenery, for the area had been mostly commercial. Some half-burned trees were still standing along the streets.

Many shattered office buildings had paneless windows on this side, through which one could see the light reflecting in the glass on the far side, and the window frames were blackened, probably by the soot that had been deposited by the shooting flames.

It was a sloping area with a complex mesh of back streets on different levels. The concrete stairs and steps that remained led expectantly to nothing. Nothing remained either above or below them. In the field of rubble too there was no starting point, no destination; only the stairways adhered to direction.

All was quiet, but there were faint stirrings and things would rise softly. When he looked, it seemed like some hallucination, in which blackened corpses ravaged by countless vermin began to stir. They were ashes caught in the breeze, rising everywhere. There were white ashes and black ashes. Some floating ash adhered to a crumbling wall and rested there. Ashes of straw, ashes of books, ashes from a secondhand bookstall, ashes from a quilt maker's shop, floating about individually, commingling indiscriminately, moving, shifting over the face of the devastation.

An area of asphalt road gleamed blackly with water spurting from a ruptured main.

The sky was strangely spacious and the summer clouds immaculately white.

This was the world presented to Honda's five senses at this very moment. His plentiful savings had enabled him to accept only those legal cases that suited him during the war, and the study of samsara and reincarnation which entirely filled his leisure time seemed designed for the purpose of making this devastation manifest. The destroyer was Honda himself.

The vast panorama of devastation before his eyes, resembling the end of the world, was not the end itself, nor was it the beginning. It was a world that imperturbably regenerated itself from instant to instant. *Alaya* consciousness, perturbed by nothing, accepted this expanse of reddish ruin as one world, relinquishing it the next moment, accepting in the same way other worlds in which the color of destruction deepened with every day, with every month.

Honda felt no emotion as he compared this sight with the city as it had been. Only when his eyes caught the bright reflections of the fragments of broken glass in the ruins and he was momentarily blinded did he understand with the sureness of his senses that the glass, the whole ruin would disappear the next instant to make way for another. He would resist catastrophe with catastrophe, and he would deal with the infinite disintegration and desolation with ever more gigantic and all-inclusive instantaneously repeated devastation. Yes, he must grasp with his mind the instant-by-instant, inevitable total destruction and prepare for the carnage of an uncertain future. He was elated to the point of trembling with these refreshing ideas that he had gleaned from Yuishiki doctrine.

21

WHEN HIS TALK with the client was over, Honda took his gifts and started out for Shibuya Station. There had been reports of a large-scale bombing of Osaka by B-29s. Of late, rumors were frequently heard that western Japan was now the main target. Tokyo seemed to be having a momentary respite.

Honda thought of walking a little further as long as it was light. At the top of Dogen Hill was located the former estate of Marquis Matsugae.

As far as Honda knew, the Matsugae family had sold eighty acres of its total land-holding of one hundred and ten to Hakoné Real Estate, Ltd., in the early twenties. But half of the money obtained at that time was lost in short order when the fifteen banks it had been placed in collapsed. The adopted heir of the family, a profligate, quickly disposed of the remaining thirty acres, and the present Matsugae house was reputed to be an ordinary place built on something less than an acre. He had driven by the gate, but had not entered now that he had completely lost touch with the family. Honda was vaguely curious to know whether the house had disappeared in the air raid last week.

The road running along the burned-out buildings of Dogen Hill had already been cleared, and climbing the slope presented no difficulty. Here and there he could see where people had begun to live in their simple air-raid trenches which they had covered with half-burned lumber and pieces of zinc sheeting. It was close to dinner time, and smoke from the cooking fires was rising. Someone was replenishing a pot with water spouting from an exposed conduit. The sky was filled with the beautiful glow of evening.

From the top of the slope to the upper boulevard, the entire area of Minami Daira-dai had once been a part of the hundred-and-ten-acre Matsugae property. The former estate had recently been divided into small lots, but now it had been transformed into a vast, unbroken ruin, reacquiring under the spacious evening sky the grand scale of bygone days.

The single remaining building belonged to a detachment of military police, and soldiers with arm bands were constantly going in and out. Honda vaguely remembered that the edifice had once stood next to the Matsugae estate. And sure enough, the next moment he recognized the stone pillars of the Matsugae gate beyond.

From it, the remaining acre appeared extremely small, for the property had been divided among many tenant houses. The pond and the artificial hill in the garden appeared as poor miniature replicas of the once magnificent lake and the maple-covered mountain of the old estate. There was no stone wall in the back, and as the wooden fence had burned down, the expanse of devastated neighboring lots lay in view all the way to Minami Daira-dai. He realized that the plot had been reclaimed by filling in the former extensive pond.

An island had once occupied the center of the lake, while a waterfall poured into it from the maple-covered mountain. Honda had once crossed over to it by boat with Kiyoaki and from there had recognized the figure of Satoko clad in a light-blue kimono. Kiyoaki had been in the flower of his youth, and Honda too had still been young, much more so indeed than he remembered. There something had commenced and something had ended. But no traces remained.

The Matsugae estate had been restored by the ruthless, impartially destructive bombing. The contours of the land had changed, but across the desolate expanse Honda could still single out the location of the pond, the shrine, the main house, the Western-style wing, and the driveway in front of the porch. The outlines of the Matsugae house that he had frequented were clearly etched in his memory.

But under the billowing evening clouds the innumerable shriveled zinc fragments, broken slates, shredded trees, melted glass, burned clapboard, or the exposed chimneys of fireplaces standing lonely like skeletons, doors squashed into lozenge shapes—all were dyed a deep, rusty red. Collapsed and prostrate on the ground, their wild shapes that defied norms seemed like strange nettles sprouting from the land. The eeriness was further heightened by the evening sun which added to everything a distinctive shadow.

The sky was the vermilion of silk kimono lining with tufts of cloud scattered about. The color had penetrated to their very core, and their raveled edges radiated like golden threads. He had never seen such a sinister sky.

Suddenly he discerned in the vast ruin the figure of a woman sitting on a garden stone which had survived. The back of her somewhat shiny trousers made from lavender silk kimono material was transformed to *lie-de-vin* by the evening sun. Her black gleaming hair done in a Western style was wet, and her huddled figure appeared tormented. She seemed to be crying, but her shoulders were not shaken by sobs; she seemed to be suffering too, but her back gave no indication of anguish. She sat hunched up as though petrified. Her motionlessness lasted too long for someone merely lost in thought. Honda judged from the luster of her hair that she was probably middle-aged, perhaps the owner of one of the houses that had stood there, or possibly a relative.

He realized he should have to offer assistance if she had been overcome by some indisposition. As he drew closer, he saw a black handbag and cane which she had placed beside the stone on which she was sitting.

Honda put his hand on her shoulder and shook it discreetly. He half feared that if he used any strength the form would collapse into ashes.

The woman looked obliquely up at him. The face frightened Honda. From the gap that showed at the unnatural hairline he realized that the black hair was a wig. The harsh vermilion of her lipstick stood out against the powder which had been thickly applied to cover the wrinkles and the hollows of her eyes; it was drawn on in the old-fashioned court style, a peaked upper lip and a tiny lower one. He recognized the face of Tadeshina beneath this indescribably aged mask.

"You're Mrs. Tadeshina, aren't you?" said Honda without thinking.

"Who could you be?" said Tadeshina. "A moment, please," she added, hurriedly taking her glasses from her breast. He could see the Tadeshina of former days in her sly attempt to gain time by opening the sides and putting them over her ears. Under the pretext that she needed her glasses to see, she hurriedly tried to place him.

But the ruse was not successful. Even with the glasses, the old woman saw only a stranger standing before her. For the first time uneasiness and an old aristocratic prejudice—a mild chilliness she had learned to simulate so skillfully over the years—appeared on her face. This time she spoke with stiff formality.

"You must excuse me. I have quite lost my memory of late. I really have no idea . . ."

"I'm Honda. Thirty years ago I was a classmate of Kiyoaki Matsugae's at the Peers School, and I used to come to the house all the time."

"Oh, Mr. Honda! How good it is to see you! I don't know how to apologize . . . I'm sorry not to have recognized you. Yes, Mr. Honda, indeed. You look just as you did in your younger days. Oh, what a . . ."

Tadeshina hurriedly put a sleeve to her eyes. Her tears in former days had always been suspicious, but now the makeup under her eyes immediately soaked them up like a whitewashed wall in the rain, and a generous supply overflowed almost mechanically from her bleary eyes. Such tears, as abundant as an overturned tub of water, totally unrelated to either joy or sorrow, were much more believable than those of thirty years ago.

Nevertheless, her senility was preposterous. On her skin, hidden under the thick white powder, Honda could see the moss of decrepitude that covered her entire body, and yet he sensed her extraordinary mind still working diligently like a watch ticking away in the pocket of a dead man.

"It's good you're looking so well. How old are you now?" asked Honda.

"I'm ninety-four this year. I'm a little hard of hearing, but other than that I have my health and no ailments; my legs are strong, and I manage to get around alone with a cane. My nephew's family are looking after me, and they don't like to let me go out alone. But I don't really care when or where I die, so I like to get out as much as possible while I still can. I'm not at all afraid of the air raids. If I'm hit by a bomb or incinerated I'll die without any pain and without causing anybody any trouble. You may not believe it, but I feel envious of the bodies lying by the roadside these days. When I heard that the Shibuya area had been burned in the bombardment the other day, I simply had to see the site of the Matsugae estate. I slipped out of my nephew's house. What would the Marquis and the Marchioness say if they were alive to see this state of affairs! They were fortunate enough to die before experiencing any of this misery."

"Fortunately my house hasn't been burned yet, but I feel the same way about my mother. I'm glad she died while Japan was still winning."

"Oh dear! Your mother's gone too . . . I am terribly sorry to hear that, I had no idea . . ."

Tadeshina had not forgotten the emotionless, gracious civilities of her former days.

"What's become of the Ayakuras?"

After putting the question, Honda immediately regretted it. As he had expected, the old woman hesitated noticeably. However, whenever she showed any visible sign of emotion, it was usually lacking in sincerity and simply for exhibition.

"Yes, after Miss Satoko entered the orders, I left

the Ayakura family, and since then I've only attended Lord Ayakura's funeral. The Viscountess, I believe, is still alive, but after his lordship passed away she sold the house in Tokyo and went to relatives in Shishigatani in Kyoto. Her daughter . . ."

Honda felt a quivering in his heart and asked involuntarily: "Do you ever see Miss Satoko?"

"Yes, I've seen her three times in all after the funeral. She's always so kind to me when I visit her. She even invites me to spend the night at the temple. So sweet and gracious . . ."

Tadeshina took off her clouded glasses, quickly removed a coarse tissue from her sleeve and held it over her eyes for some time. When she took it away there was a dark ring where the powder had come off.

"Miss Satoko's well then?" said Honda again.

"She is, indeed. And—how shall I say?—she's more beautiful, more pure than ever, and her beauty becomes more serene as she grows older. Please visit her some time, Mr. Honda. Do, she'll be so pleased to see you."

Honda abruptly recalled that midnight drive from Kamakura to Tokyo alone with Satoko.

She was another man's woman, but she had been almost oppressively feminine then.

She had already had a foreboding of things to come ultimately and had expressed her readiness in preparing for them. Honda recalled, as vividly as though it had happened yesterday, that thrilling moment just before dawn when her profile had been framed by the car window with the foliage in the background flying past.

When he came back to reality, Tadeshina's face had lost its pretense of deference and she was scrutinizing him. Wrinkles like the lines in tie-dyed silk surrounded her bow-shaped lips, but now at either side her mouth was slightly pulled up in the semblance of a smile. Suddenly, in the two eyes—old wells in patches of snow—the pupils moved horizontally with a suggestion of the old coquetry.

"You were in love with her, weren't you? I knew it."

Honda flinched, more at the vestiges of Tadeshina's

coquetry than from displeasure at such a conjecture after so many years. To change the subject, he turned his thoughts to the gifts he had received from his client. It occurred to him that he might share a portion with her: a couple of eggs and a little chicken.

Tadeshina expressed her guileless joy and appreciation just as he had expected she would.

"Oh, my, eggs! How unusual to see eggs these days! I feel as if I haven't seen one for years! Heavens, eggs!"

The meandering, complex thanks that followed made Honda realize that the old woman must be given scarcely any decent food. He was further surprised when she again took out the egg that she had put away in her shopping bag. Holding it up against the fading twilight sky, she said:

"Rather than taking this home—you must excuse my poor manners—I would rather just eat it here . . ."

As the old woman spoke, she looked regretfully at the egg against the darkening sky. It smoldered in her trembling old fingers as the fading light touched its delicate, cold shell.

For some time Tadeshina caressed the egg in her hand. The noise in the area had abated, and only the faint sound of her dry skin rubbing against it was audible.

Honda ignored her search for a sharp corner against which to crack the shell. He was reluctant to help her in an action which was somehow objectionable. Tadeshina broke the egg unexpectedly skillfully on the edge of the stone on which she was sitting. Carefully bringing it to her mouth in order to lose none of its contents, she gradually lifted her face and poured it between her gleaming dentures gaping at the evening sky. The lustrous roundness of the yolk passing her lips was fleetingly visible, and her throat emitted an extremely healthy swallowing sound.

"My, this is the first nourishing food I've had in a long, long time. I feel revived. I feel as though the beauty

THE TEMPLE OF DAWN • 131

of my youth has come back. You might not believe it, Mr. Honda, but I was a famous beauty in my day."

Her tone had suddenly become frank.

There is a time of day immediately before dusk when the outline of every object becomes sharply delineated. It was just that moment. The lacerated edges of wooden beams in the wreckage, the freshness of the rents in the shredded trees, and the curled zinc sheets with their puddles of rain water—everything appeared almost unpleasantly vivid. In the extreme west only a horizontal line of scarlet was to be seen in the sky between two or three towering black burned-out buildings. Flecks of scarlet were also visible through the windows of the ruined structures. It was as if someone had turned on a red light in a deserted and uninhabited house.

"How can I thank you? Yoy have always been such a tenderhearted man, and you are still so kind. I have nothing to give you, but at least . . ."

Like a blind woman, Tadeshina hunted through her bag. Before Honda could stop her, she had taken out a volume bound in the Japanese style and thrust it into his hand.

"At least I want to give you this book. I have always treasured it and carried it with me. It is an efficacious sutra given me by a priest to ward off harm and illness. I am so happy to have run into you and to have been able to talk about bygone times. You'll probably be going out on air-raid days, and there are bad fevers about. But if you carry this sutra with you, you are sure to avoid any disaster. I should like you to keep it as a token of my appreciation."

Honda held the book up reverently to show his thanks and looked at the title on the cover. It was barely legible in the evening light.

Mahamayurividyarajni, "Sutra of the Great Golden Peacock Wisdom King."

22

EVER SINCE THAT DAY, Honda could scarcely contain his desire to see Satoko, but he knew that the urge came in part from Tadeshina's remark that she was still beautiful. He was deathly afraid of seeing a "ruin of beauty" like the ruins of the city.

But the war situation was deteriorating daily, and it was difficult to obtain train tickets unless one had connections in the Army, and a pleasure trip was out of the question.

As the days passed, Honda opened the *Peacock King Sutra* that Tadeshina had given him. He had never had the opportunity of reading any Esoteric Buddhist sutras before.

The opening passages gave explanations and rules for use in small, almost illegible print.

To begin with, the Peacock Wisdom King occupied the sixth position from the southern end of the Susiddhi Court in the Womb Mandala. As he is attributed the power of begetting all Buddhas, he is also called the "Peacock King, Begetter of All Buddhas."

When he consulted the Buddhist documents he had so far collected, Honda found that the deity had clearly originated in Hindu *shakti* worship. Since *shakti* rites were directed toward Kali, wife of Shiva, or toward Durga, the statue of the bloodthirsty goddess he had seen at the Kalighat in Calcutta was indeed the archetype of the Peacock Wisdom King.

When he discovered this, the sutra that had come into his possession by accident suddenly became of interest to him. Along with the use of *dharani* * and mantra in Esoteric Buddhist rites, the old deities of Hinduism had invaded the world of Buddhism by resorting to all sorts of transformations.

Originally the *Sutra of the Peacock Wisdom King* was

---

* Magic formulas. (Translators' note.)

believed to have been an incantation spoken by the Buddha, and it was supposed to ward off snakes or cure poisoning from their bites.

According to the *Peacock Sutra*:

When one Kissho, who had not been long ordained, was preparing kindling for the monks' bath, a black snake came out from under a strange tree and bit his right toe. He fainted and fell to the ground, his eyes turned up, and he foamed at the mouth. Ananda went to where the Buddha was and said: "How can he be cured?" Whereupon the Buddha answered, saying: "If you hold the *Sutra of the Incantation of the Great Tathagata Peacock Wisdom King,* clasp the monk Kissho in your arms, and make the proper hand signs as you chant the mantra, the poison will be harmless. Neither sword nor cane will be able to inflict injury. It will fend off all calamities."

Not only snake poison, but all fevers, all wounds, all pain and suffering were reputed abolished by this sutra. Simply chanting it was sufficient, and the mere thought of the Peacock Wisdom King did away with all fear, enemies, and calamities. Therefore, during the Heian period, only the Elder of the Toji and the Abbot of the Ninna Temple in the Imperial line were permitted to perform the Esoteric Buddhist rites of this sutra. During such ceremonies, fervent prayers were offered against all possible situations, from natural calamities to pestilence and childbirth.

The Peacock Wisdom King in the illustration was a gorgeous and sumptuous figure as though the personification of the peacock itself, so different from the bloody image of Kali, his prototype, with her protruding tongue and her necklace of severed heads.

His magic formula was said to imitate the cry of the peacock—*ka-ka-ka-ka-ka-ka-ka-ka-ka-ka-ka-ka*—and the mantra, *ma yu kitsu ra tei sha ka,* meant "Peacock fulfillment." Even the special hand gesture, which was called the "sign of the Buddha Begetter, the Peacock Wisdom King," and which was made by joining the two hands back to back, the two thumbs and the two little fingers pressed together, was both a description and imitation of the peacock's majesty. The gesture represented the shape of the peacock, the little fingers being the tail and the thumbs the head, and the rest of the fingers the feathers. The way the middle six fingers moved as the incantation was chanted depicted a peacock dancing.

A blue Indian sky trailed behind the Wisdom King on his golden peacock mount. A tropical sky with its impressive clouds, its afternoon ennui, and its evening breezes, all necessary for spinning a gorgeous and colorful illusion.

The golden peacock was seen from the front, standing firmly on its two legs. It had opened its wings and was carrying the Wisdom King on its back, guarding him by spreading its magnificent fan tail which stood in place of a halo. The king was sitting in the lotus position on a white lotus flower placed on the back of the peacock. Of the king's four arms, the first on the right held an open lotus; the second, the peach-shaped fruit of karma; the first hand on the left was held over the heart, its upturned palm supporting the fruit of good fortune; and the second, a peacock tail of thirty-five feathers.

The Wisdom King posed with compassionate countenance, and his body was extremely fair. The skin visible under silk gauze was enhanced by such magnificent jewelry as the crown on his head, the necklace around his neck, the earrings hanging from his ears, and the bracelets at his wrists. A cool weariness lingered on the heavy lids of the half-open eyes as though the deity had just awakened from an afternoon nap. Imparting boundless mercy and saving people without number might produce in one an emotion similar to the idle sleepiness that Honda had discovered in the bright, vast expanses of India.

In contrast to this absolutely white and serene image, the extended feathers of the peacock that acted as a halo were dazzlingly polychrome. Of the plumage of all birds, that of the peacock was closest in hue to the evening clouds. Like an Esoteric Buddhist mandala that rearranges a chaotic universe into an orderly one, the feathers presented the methodical organization of the riotous disorder of color seen in the evening clouds, their amorphousness, and the play of light upon them, in a geometric and patterned brocade. Gold, green, indigo, purple, brown—such dusky brilliance, however, indicated the end of the evening glow when the disk of the setting sun itself was no longer visible.

The tail feathers lacked only scarlet. If there were such a bird as a scarlet peacock and if the Peacock Wisdom King had been seated upon it, tail fully open, he would be none other than the goddess Kali herself.

Honda believed that such a peacock must have appeared in the evening clouds in the sky above the ruins where he had encountered Tadeshina.

Part Two

23

"YOU'VE PLANTED some beautiful cypresses," said Honda's new neighbor. "It used to be so barren and treeless here."

Keiko Hisamatsu was an imposing woman.

She was close to fifty, but her face, rumored to have undergone plastic surgery, retained an overly taut, shiny youthfulness. She was one of those exceptional Japanese who could speak informally to either Prime Minister Yoshida or to General MacArthur; she had long since divorced her husband. At the moment she had a lover, a young American officer in the Occupation Forces who worked at the camp at the foot of Mount Fuji. She had repaired her long-neglected villa at Ninooka in Gotemba and would occasionally come for a rendezvous or, as she said, "to write leisurely answers to long-neglected letters." Her villa stood next to Honda's.

In the spring of 1952, Honda celebrated his fifty-seventh birthday. For the first time in his life, he had acquired a villa. Guests had been invited from Tokyo for the opening that was to take place on the morrow. He himself had come a day early to oversee preparations and had invited his neighbor Keiko to inspect the garden that measured something more than an acre.

"I've been looking forward to the completion of your house as if it were my own," said Keiko, walking over the dead, frost-wet lawn, lifting her thin high-heeled shoes step by step like a waterfowl. "This grass was planted last year. How well it has taken. You set up the garden first and then took your time with the house. Only a true lover of gardens could do that."

"I had no place to stay, so I commuted from Gotemba to lay it out," replied Honda, looking like some Parisian concierge in his heavy, slightly raveled cardigan with a silk scarf wrapped around his neck against the cold.

Honda felt a certain discomfort with women like Keiko, who had lived a life of leisure. It was as though his pettiness were being seen through—the meanness of working and studying through life and now at the onset of old age suddenly trying to learn how to relax.

His being here, the proprietor of a villa, had been made possible by an antiquated section of a little-known law issued under the Imperial Seal on April 18, 1899, and entitled "Concerning the return of nationally owned lands, forests, and fields."

In July of 1873, a land-reform decree was issued, and government officials had gone from village to village attempting to ascertain the ownership of various holdings. Fearing they would be taxed, owners denied possession of certain tracts, and thus a great number of private holdings and commonages had become unattached and had been transferred to the government.

Much later, in view of the clamorous voices of regret and resentment, a law was passed in 1899, the second article of which stated that applicants for the return of land were required to prove previous ownership by producing at least one of seven records. One was called a "state document." And the sixth article of the code stated that all pertinent legal action would come under the jurisdiction of the Court of Administrative Litigation.

Many such suits were instituted in the 1890s, but the Court of Administrative Litigation permitted only one hearing, with no opportunity for appeal. And since there was no provision for supervision of the legal process, everything was done in a most leisurely fashion.

In any village in which communal lands had been confiscated because of a thoughtless lie, the Oaza, or administrative division, became the plaintiff in administrative litigation. Even if the village had been amalgamated into a township, the Oaza could claim possession and remain as an "owner district."

In the case of a certain village in the district of Miharu in Fukushima Prefecture, a suit was instituted in 1900, in which the government and the plaintiff went about the business most leisurely. Over a period of fifty years, the defendant had changed from Minister of Agriculture and Commerce to Minister of Agriculture and Forestry, and, one by one, successive lawyers in charge of the litigation had died, only to be succeeded by others. In 1940, a delegate from the district of the plaintiff village came to Tokyo to see Honda, who was already a well-known lawyer, and deposited the hopeless case in his hands.

The fifty-year deadlock was broken by the defeat of Japan in the war.

According to the new constitution executed in 1947, special courts were eliminated and the Court of Administrative Litigation was abolished. All administrative cases in process were transferred to the Tokyo High Court and treated as civil suits. As a result, Honda won the case without difficulty. It was nothing more than pure luck—being at the right place at the right time.

In accordance with the agreement which had been handed down through the years, Honda received as his fee for winning the case one third of all lands returned to the village. He had the choice of accepting this real estate or of converting it into cash at the going rate. He chose the latter. Thus he came into the sum of thirty-six million yen.

This event changed the very roots of Honda's life. During the war he had gradually grown bored with a lawyer's lot, and while retaining the widely respected name of the Honda Law Offices, he left all work to his younger partners and put in only an occasional appearance. His social life changed and so did his thinking. He could not take his good fortune seriously, coming so suddenly as he had into possession of close to forty million yen, nor could he be serious about the times that had made such a miracle possible. Therefore he decided to take the whole thing casually.

He considered dismantling and rebuilding his residence in Hongo, which would have been much better off burned in the raids, but he was already too disillusioned with the city to construct anything new there and expect it to last forever. Anyway, it would be burned to the ground in the next war.

His wife Rié preferred to sell the property and perhaps live in an aprtment rather than to continue on in the big old house by themselves. But Honda took the pretext of her sickliness for building a villa in a remote, sparsely populated spot where she could rest.

The couple went to see some land in the Sengokuhara area in Hakoné with an introduction from an acquaintance, but when they heard of the excessive dampness in the region they were frightened off. Guided by the chauffeur of the hired car, they drove over Hakoné Pass and explored the summer resort area of Ninooka in the Gotemba section that had been developed some forty years before. There were many villas belonging to former dignitaries. But after the war, they had closed their gates to avoid the American Occupation Forces near the Fuji Maneuvering Terrain and the inevitable women who followed them. Honda was told that in an area west of the villa district there was some barren land that had once belonged to the government but that had been turned over without charge to the farmers of the region as a result of the land reform. One could make a good buy there.

The entire area at the foot of Mount Hakoné was not covered by the volcanic lava as was that around Fuji. But it was barren land unfit for growing anything except perhaps cypresses. The farmers did not know what to do with it. Honda was delighted with one property where pampas grass and sagebrush covered a slope that gently descended to a valley stream. Mount Fuji was clearly visible.

Upon inquiry he found the price to be very reasonable and therefore did not follow Rié's suggestion to give the matter further thought. He made an immediate down payment for a parcel of a little over four acres.

Rié said that she did not like the unspeakably somber harshness of the land. She was afraid of melancholia. She knew instinctively that she had no use for such feelings in her old age. But to Honda, who was dreaming of pleasure, it was this very gloominess that was indispensable to him.

"It's nothing. If we clear the area and plant some greenery and put up a house, it'll be almost too cheerful," he had said.

Hiring carpenters from the area to build the house and employing people there to plant the trees and do the landscaping was a slow process, but it kept the expenses down. Honda retained from former days his habit of considering indiscriminate expenditure vulgar. Nevertheless, the pleasure of leisurely guiding a guest around and showing off his extensive property was surely an emotion born long ago in his boyhood when he had frequented the Matsugae estate. He did not mind the chilliness of early spring which stung the skin with the frigidity of the lingering snows of Hakoné, because it was the chilliness of his own garden; by the same token, the loneliness of only two people casting faint shadows on the expanse of lawn pleased him, because it was the loneliness of his own property. He felt as though he were grasping the real luxury of private ownership for the first time. Furthermore, it pleased him that he had come to it not through fanaticism, but completely by means of his own logical thinking and good timing.

Keiko's overly handsome profile held no trace of coquetry or reserve. She had the ability to make any man beside her—even the fifty-seven-year-old Honda—feel as though he were a mere stripling. It was a woman's power to impose on a fifty-seven-year-old man the apparent cheerfulness and sunniness of a youth bound by pure hypocrisy and vanity, one who kept up appearances at all costs, though uneasy and respectful with women.

From Honda's point of view, age was nothing to be taken into account. Until he was in his forties he had been conscientious about the plusses and minuses of age. Now, however, he had an actually casual and carefree idea of it. He was not surprised when sometimes he happened to discover clear signs of true childishness in himself, in his fifty-seven-year-old body. Old age was, somehow, a kind of declaration of bankruptcy.

He had grown terribly concerned about his health and terrified of his self-indulgence in emotion. If the function of reason was control, the urgent necessity for it had passed. Experiences were nothing but cleaned bones on a dinner plate.

Keiko stood at the center of the greensward, contrasting the view of Hakoné to the east with that of Fuji to the northwest. She exuded a stateliness which was best described as regal; the fullness of her suit coat, her erect neck, everything conveyed the air of a commanding general. Her young officer must surely be subjected to all manner of orders, including ones not so easy to execute.

Compared to the clear, snow-dotted ridges of Hakoné, Fuji, half covered by clouds, appeared ephemeral. Honda noticed that some optical illusion made it now higher, now lower.

"Today I heard a nightingale for the first time," said Honda, looking through the fragile withered upper branches of the thin cypress trees that he had purchased in the neighborhood and transplanted to his property.

"Nightingales come in mid-March," said Keiko. "You'll be able to see cuckoos in May. You can see as well as hear them, mind you. This is probably the only place that one can see and hear cuckoos at the same time."

"Let's go in. I'll build a fire and make some tea," Honda suggested.

"I brought some cookies," said Keiko, referring to the package she had left in the vestibule a short while ago. The Hattori Clock Shop at the corner of Owari-cho on the Ginza had been turned into a PX after the war; and Keiko, having free access to this facility, usually bought her gifts there. English-made cookies familiar to her since prewar days could be purchased there inexpensively. The thin, hard, plum jam sandwiched in them served to connect the afternoon teas of her childhood with those of the present.

"I have a ring I should like you to appraise," said Honda, starting to walk.

24

FRAGRANT DAPHNE still in bud surrounded the terrace, and the birdhouse built in one corner bore the same type of red tile roof that covered the main house. When they saw Honda and Keiko approaching, the tiny sparrows that had flocked around the feeder darted away chirping, as though pricked by needles.

Just inside the entrance stood another door with a stained-glass center, and to either side were windows latticed with orange panes like those of Dutch mansions in the late Edo period. One could indistinctly see inside through them. Honda liked to stand here and look at the interior sinking in the wistful colors of the evening sun, an interior he himself had meticulously designed, with its thick beams purchased from a rural house and transferred intact, the chaste North German antique chandelier, the paneled doors with simple line drawings of Otsu folk painting, footman's armor, and a bow and arrows—all bathed in the fading yellow light, exuding the feeling of some gloomy still life, as if some Dutch painter like Jan Treck had done a Japanese scene.

Honda invited Keiko to enter. He seated her in the chair by the fireplace and tried to light the kindling, but it would not catch. Only the fireplace had been planned by a specialist from Tokyo; it was well designed and never let the smoke reverse and flow back into the room. But whenever he tried to build a fire, Honda always realized that he had never in his life had the opportunity of mastering the simplest techniques or knowledge. Indeed, he had never even handled basic materials.

It was strange to learn this at his age. He had never once known leisure in his entire life. Thus he had obviously never made any contact with nature, with the waves of the ocean, with the hardness of trees, with the weight of rocks, and with the tools like ship's fittings, nets, or hunting rifles that workers came to know through their work, and the aristocrats, conversely, were familiar with through the graciousness of their living. Kiyoaki had turned his leisure not toward nature but only toward his own emotions; if he had matured, he would have grown into nothing but idleness.

"Let me help," said Keiko, bending down with dignity, after watching Honda's ineptness for some time, the tip of her tongue protruding between her hard lips. Her hips appeared almost limitless to Honda's upturned eyes. The blue celadon color of her tight skirt, filled like a gigantic vase of the Yi Dynasty, was enhanced by the cut of the suit that had a sharply narrowed waistline.

As Honda had nothing to do while Keiko occupied herself with the fire, he left the room to fetch the ring he had mentioned. When he returned, savage vermilion flames were already slithering up the logs, and pieces of kindling were gnashing their teeth in the coquettishly clinging smoke, while sap secreted from the freshly cut wood sizzled. The brick lining of the fireplace flickered in the firelight. Keiko calmly brushed her hands and observed the result of her efforts with obvious satisfaction.

"How is this?"

"I'm impressed," said Honda, extending his hand into the firelight and handing the ring to Keiko. "This is the ring I mentioned a while ago. What do you think? I bought it as a present."

Keiko withdrew her fingers with their red manicured tips from the area of the flames and scrutinized the ring in the fading light from the window.

"A man's ring," she said.

It was formed of a dark green, square emerald encircled by gold finely sculpted to depict a pair of protective *yaksha* with impressive half-bestial faces. Keiko moved the ring from her fingertips, probably to avoid the reflection of her red nails, and holding it between her fingers, slipped it on her index finger. Although a man's ring, it was the size for some delicate, dark-skinned finger; it was not overly large even on her.

"It's a good stone. But with old emeralds the inside fissures always effloresce in the long run. There's danger of fragility when the cloudiness rises from underneath. This one shows that condition. But still it's a good stone. And the carving is unusual. It'll be valuable as an antique."

"Where do you think I bought it?"

"Abroad?"

"No, in the ruins of Tokyo. At Prince Toin's shop."

"Oh yes, those days . . . But no matter what financial trouble the Prince might have had, for him to open an antique shop . . . ! I've been there two or three times myself. Everything interesting turned out to be something I had seen at relatives' long ago. But the shop had to close. I heard that the Prince was never there; the former steward who was acting as head clerk was running the show and stealing all the profits. Not a single member of royalty has started a successful business after the war. No matter what the property tax, they should have safeguarded what possessions they had left. There was always some promoter who would talk them into something. Especially Prince Toin, who had always been a soldier. He reminds me of the poor samurai who all went bankrupt after the Restoration."

Then Honda told her the history of the ring.

In 1947, Honda heard that Prince Toin had lost his title after the war and had bought up art objects cheaply from members of the former nobility overburdened with property taxes. He had opened an antique shop for foreigners. The Prince would not have remembered him even if Honda had gone to see him, but he had been moved to look in at the shop out of sheer curiosity without identifying himself. In a glass case, he discovered the ring of Princess Chantrapa, which the

Siamese prince Chao P. had lost in the dormitory of the Peers School thirty-four long years before.

It was obvious that the ring, which had been believed mislaid at the time, had in reality been stolen. The sales clerk, of course, did not disclose the origin of the object, but it must have come from the house of some former noble. The man who had had to sell it must have been a student at the school when Honda was there. He was moved by an old sense of justice to purchase it, wanting to return it himself somehow to the original owner.

"Then are you going to Thailand to give it back? To clear the name of your alma mater?" teased Keiko.

"I intended to someday. But it's not necessary now. The Princess has come to Japan to study."

"A dead girl here to study?"

"No, no, Chantrapa the second—Ying Chan, I mean," said Honda. "I've invited her to the party tomorrow. I intend to put the ring on her finger then. She's seventeen years old, with beautiful black hair and bright eyes. She speaks Japanese quite well; she must have studied hard before leaving her country."

25

THE NEXT MORNING Honda awoke alone in the villa, and for protection against the cold, donned a woolen scarf, a cardigan, and a thick winter coat. He crossed the lawn and walked to the arbor at the west end of the garden. More than anything else he had been anticipating watching Fuji at dawn.

The mountain was tinted crimson in the sunrise. Its tip glowed the color of a brilliant rose stone, and to his eyes it was a dreamlike illusion, a classical cathedral roof, a Japanese Temple of Dawn.

Sometimes Honda was confused as to whether he sought solitude or frivolous pleasure. He lacked something essential to become a serious pleasure-seeker.

For the first time somewhere within—and at his age!—a

desire for transformation had awakened. Having earnestly observed other men's reincarnation without so much as turning an eye, he had never brooded over the impossibility of his own. And now that he was reaching an age when the last glow of life revealed the expanse of his past, the certainty of its impossibility heightened the illusion of the possibility of rebirth all the more.

He too might do something unexpected. To this day all his actions had been predictable, and his reason had always cast its light one step ahead, like a flashlight held by someone walking along a dark road at night. By schemes and predictions he had been able to avoid surprising himself. The most frightening thing was that all mysteries, including the miracle of transmigration, finished by being cut and dried.

He needed to be surprised. It had become almost a necessity of life. If there were a special right in scorning reason and trampling it, he had the rational self-conceit to think that it was permitted only to him! He had to involve his stable world in some amorphous turmoil again, in something with which he was not at all familiar!

Honda knew very well that he had lost all physical qualifications for that. His hair had grown thin, his sideburns were streaked with white, and his stomach had swollen like remorse itself. All the characteristics of early old age which he had considered so ugly as a youth now marked his body unsparingly. Of course, even when young, he had never regarded himself as handsome, like Kiyoaki, but he had not thought himself to be particularly ugly either. At least he had not found it necessary to place himself among the negative numbers in a world of beauty and to construct his equations in consequence. Why was it that now when his ugliness had become so obvious, the world about him was still beautiful? This was indeed far worse than death itself; the worst death!

It was twenty minutes past six. Two thirds covered by snow, Fuji had brushed off the colors of dawn and stood against the blue sky in sharply etched beauty. It was almost too clearly visible. The texture of the snow was delicate, full of the sensitive tension of its undulations. It called to mind the fine play of lean muscle. Except for the lower slopes, there were only two slightly reddish black patches near the top and near the Hoei summit. The blue sky was hard and cloudless; had he thrown a rock, the sharp sound of stone hitting it would have echoed back.

This Fuji influenced all dispositions, controlled all emotions. It was the pure white essence of questionability itself that rose before him.

Honda's hunger sharpened in the tranquility. He looked forward to his breakfast of bread purchased in Tokyo and the soft-boiled egg and coffee he would make as he listened to the chirping of the birds. His wife was due to arrive with Princess Ying Chan at eleven o'clock to begin preparations for the party.

After breakfast he returned to the garden.

It was close to eight. Little by little small wisps of cloud had begun to rise like snow drifting on the other side of Mount Fuji. They spread stealthily, as if to spy on the near side, extending their tentacles as they progressed. Suddenly they were swallowed up by the ceramic blue sky. These seemingly insignificant ambushes were not to be ignored. Such clouds tended to regroup up to noon, repeating their surprise attacks and eventually covering the entire mountain.

Honda sat absentmindedly in the arbor until about ten o'clock. He had stored away the books that all his life had never been far from him and was dreaming of raw materials from which life and emotion had not been filtered out. He sat motionless, doing nothing. A cloud, which had appeared faintly to the left and which soon stopped at the Hoei summit, raised its tail like a leaping dolphin.

His wife, who he insisted be punctual, arrived at eleven o'clock in a clamorous taxi. Princess Ying Chan was not beside her. "Oh dear, you're alone!" said Honda at once to this bloated, sour woman as she removed several packages from the car.

Rié did not answer for a minute, but raised her eyelids like heavy sunshades.

"I'll explain later when I've more time. I've had so much trouble. Help me with these packages first."

Rié had waited until the designated time, but Princess Ying Chan had not made her appearance. This was after two or three telephone calls. She had finally phoned the only available contact, the Foreign Student Center, and was told that the Princess had not returned to her dormitory the night before. She had been invited to dine at the home of some Japanese family where a new student from Thailand was staying.

Rié had been worried and had considered delaying the time of her own arrival at the villa. But she had no way of informing Honda, since they did not yet have a phone. Instead, she had hurried to the Foreign Student Center where she left a note written in English with the caretaker, carefully explaining with a map how to get to the villa. If things went well, the Princess should arrive by the time the party started in the evening.

"Well, if that was the trouble, you could have asked Makiko Kito to help find her."

"But I couldn't possibly impose on a guest. Even she would have a hard time locating a girl from a foreign country she doesn't know at all and then bringing her all the way over here. And besides, you can't expect a celebrity like Makiko to go out of her way. She probably thinks she's doing us a favor just by coming."

Honda fell silent. He would reserve judgment.

When a picture is removed from the wall where it has long hung, it leaves a fresh whiteness the exact size and shape of the frame. The resulting image is pure, to be sure, but it is quite out of step with its environment; it is too strong, too insistent. Now that Honda had retired from his professional activities on the bench he had left all matters concerning justice to his wife. The whiteness of the wall was always claiming: I am just, I am right, who could possibly blame me?

To begin with, it was the wealth into which Honda had unexpectedly come and the ugliness of age which

Rié had begun to notice in herself that had removed the framed portrait of the quiet submissive wife from the wall. As her husband grew rich, Rié became afraid of him. But the more fearful she was, the more arrogant she became, showing unconscious hostility to everyone, talking constantly of her chronic kidney ailment, and yet more than ever wanting affection. This desire for love made her even more homely.

As soon as she arrived at the villa and had carried the packages of food to the kitchen, Rié began noisily to wash Honda's breakfast dishes. She was sure her fatigue would aggravate her illness and was preparing the excuse of being made to work too hard though no one had ordered her to do so. She kept doing what was harmful to her health, expecting Honda to stop her. If he did not do so now, things would be difficult later.

"Why don't you rest a while and do that later?" he said kindly. "We have plenty of time. Ying Chan really causes a lot of trouble, doesn't she? She was saying she wanted so much to help. After all that, I have to pitch in at the last minute."

"Your help will make things worse."

Rié returned to the living room wiping her wet hands.

In the dusky chamber where a patch of afternoon sun lay by the window, Rié's eyes under her puffy lids looked like the small holes in a woman's Nō mask. The regrets of a barren woman, uncured, worsening over the years, a body bloated with regress like a billowing tarpaulin. "I am right, but I'm a failure." The unchanging gentleness she had shown her deceased mother-in-law had come from this self-reproach. If she had had children, if only she had had many children, she would have been able to melt her husband with the accumulation of their soft, sweet flesh. But deterioration had long since begun in a world where propagation was denied, just as a fish cast up from the sea on an autumn afternoon gradually rots away. Rié shuddered before this rich husband of hers.

Honda had thoughtfully ignored the distress of his

wife, who was always hoping for the impossible. Now he could not bear the truth that he craved that too and in so doing was reduced to her level. But this fresh abhorrence made the existence of Rié quite important.

"Where did Ying Chan stay last night? Why did she stay away? There's a housemother at the Foreign Student Center and supervision is probably strict. Why did she? Who was she with?" said Honda, pursuing his thought.

It was simply uneasiness. It was the same daily unsettled feeling, the precise catagory of emotion he experienced mornings when he shaved himself badly or nights when he could not find a comfortable position for his head on the pillow. It was a far cry from concern for a fellow human; it was somewhat detached and yet it seemed to conform to an urgent necessity in life. He had felt as though some foreign object had been cast into his mind, something like a small black Buddha image carved in black ebony from the Thai jungles.

His wife continued to prattle on about insignificant details such as how to receive the guests and which rooms should be given to those who were spending the night. All that was of no interest to Honda.

Gradually Rié became aware that her husband's mind had wandered. In the past she had never felt any suspicion about her husband when he ensconced himself in his study, for it was certain that his law studies had bound him there; but now his absentmindedness signified the burning of an invisible flame, and his silence betokened some kind of scheme.

Rié's eyes followed her husband's gaze in an effort to find the source of his distraction. But there beyond the window lay only the garden with its dead grass on which two or three little birds had come to sport.

* * *

The guests had been invited to come at four, since Honda wanted them to see the view while the sun was still in the sky. Keiko came at one with an offer to help.

Both Honda and Rié were pleased with this unexpected assistance.

Among all her husband's new friends, strangely, it was only to Keiko that Rié opened up. She felt intuitively that Keiko was not an enemy. The reason was Keiko's kindness, her great bosom and huge hips, her calm speech. Even the fragrance of her perfume seemed to lend a sort of security to Rié's innate modesty, like the official red seal of approval stamped conspicuously on certificates hung in bakeries.

Seated next to the fireplace Honda, mellowed, opened the morning paper that Rié had brought from Tokyo, listening absently to the women's conversation in the kitchen.

The headline on the first page was: ENTIRE ADMINISTRATIVE TREATY APPENDICES, according to which sixteen American Air Force bases were to be retained after the Japanese-American peace treaty went into effect. Printed to one side was a talk by Senator Smith expressing American determination—OBLIGATION TO PROTECT JAPAN. WILL NOT TOLERATE COMMUNIST AGGRESSION. On the second page American economic trends were reported under the title DECREASE IN CIVILIAN PRODUCTION: NEW REVERSAL RESULTS FROM ECONOMIC SLUMP IN WESTERN EUROPE, which appeared in bold print and showed definite concern.

But Honda's mind was constantly brought back to Ying Chan's absence. He conjured up all sorts of situations and his unshackled imagination made him uneasy. From the most ominous to the most obscene, reality had the multilayered cross section of wood agate. He had never seen reality take such form insofar as he could recall.

Honda was startled by the loud crackling of the newspaper as he folded it. The page facing the fire was hot and dry. He idly mused that it was impossible for a newspaper to be so hot. The sensation was strangely bound with the sluggishness that lingered deep in his slackened body. Then the flames curling over a fresh log suddenly reminded him of the funeral pyres at Benares.

Keiko appeared in a large apron and said: "How about serving sherry and whiskey and water, and perhaps some Dubonnet for aperitifs? Cocktails are too much trouble. Let's not serve them."

"I leave everything up to you."

"And what about the Thai princess? We should have a few soft drinks in case she doesn't indulge."

"She might not come," Honda answered placidly.

"Oh?" Keiko said calmly and withdrew. Her impeccable courtesy made her perspicacity rather uncanny. Honda thought that one would often overestimate a woman like her because of this elegant nonchalance.

Makiko Kito was the first to arrive. She was accompanied by her pupil Mrs. Tsubakihara, in whose chauffeured car they had driven over the Hakoné mountains.

Makiko's reputation as a poetess was at its height. Honda had no standards for measuring poetic values; but when he heard Makiko's name repeated by the most unexpected people, he realized how highly she must be regarded. Mrs. Tsubakihara, from a former *zaibatsu* family, was about fifty, the same age as Makiko. But she showed deference to Makiko as if she were a goddess.

Mrs. Tsubakihara was in perpetual mourning for her son, a Navy ensign, who had died seven years ago. Honda knew nothing of her past, but she seemed like a sad bit of fruit pickled in the vinegar of grief.

Makiko was still beautiful. Her pellucid skin showed signs of aging, but it retained the freshness of lingering snow; and the creeping gray in her hair, untouched by artificial coloring, gave the stamp of sincerity to her poetry. Her behavior was natural, but she emitted a sense of mystery. She never overlooked strategic presents or dinner invitations to important personalites. She won over those who might speak ill of her. Though all real emotion had long since dried up, she preserved a lingering hint of sorrow and the illusion of being alone.

Compared to her grief, that of Mrs. Tsubakihara seemed immature. The comparison was indeed cruel;

Makiko's aesthetic sorrow, which had been distilled into a mask, produced masterpieces, while the fresh, unhealed grief of her disciple remained in a raw, unformed state, providing no inspiration for the creation of moving poetry. Whatever slight reputation Mrs. Tsubakihara enjoyed as a poetess would at once disappear were it not for Makiko's support.

Makiko extracted poetic emotion from the raw grief of this constant companion, drawing forth an abstracted sadness that no longer was the possession of anyone and labeling it with her own name. Thus, the unworked gem of sorrow and the skilled craftsman combined to bring forth innumerable masterpieces—mufflers that succeeded in concealing the aging necks that carried them year after year.

Makiko was irritated to have arrived early.

"The chauffeur drove too fast," she said, looking at Mrs. Tsubakihara beside her.

"Quite so. The traffic was not so congested as we expected."

"Let's see the garden first. We were looking forward to that," she said to Honda. "Please don't bother, we'll just take our time and stroll about and maybe write a little poetry."

Honda insisted on showing them around and took along a bottle of sherry and some tidbits, intending to serve them in the arbor. The afternoon had grown warm. Beyond the garden, which narrowed as it sloped gently to the valley, one could see Mount Fuji to the west. It was veiled by the cotton clouds of spring, and only the snow-clad summit was sharply limned against the azure sky.

"By summer I plan to have a swimming pool built in front of the terrace where the birdhouse is," Honda explained on the way.

But the ladies' response was chill, and he suddenly felt like a clerk at some inn escorting guests on a tour of the premises.

Artists and their ilk proved most difficult for Honda

to deal with. He had resumed relations with Makiko at the time of the fifteenth memorial service for Isao in 1948. Japanese poetry had not been the cause, as one might have expected. The former perfunctory relationship of counselor and witness (even though it held undertones of conniving) had actually blossomed into friendship, for they both held unvoiced affection for Isao. Honda was at a complete loss for words and had thus broached the inane subject of a swimming pool. Makiko with her pupil at her side stood facing the spectacle of Mount Fuji in the spring.

He knew that the women did not quite feel contemptuous of him, yet he realized they felt easy enough with him to act without constraint. He was outside their circle, alien to their way of life. He could easily imagine Makiko speaking to someone involved in a difficult case: "Mr. Honda's a friend of mine. No, he doesn't write poetry. But he's very understanding, and he's excellent in both civil and criminal cases. I'll speak to him for you."

But within, Honda was afraid of Makiko, and she probably was just as frightened of him. She had revived the old association with him in order to protect her name. Honda had no illusions as to her true character; he knew that she was quite capable of bearing false witness, of telling at the critical moment the most thoroughly believable lies.

Other than that, Honda was likable, unobjectionable to the women. How freely they talked in front of him, whereas they at once hid behind innocuous social chatter when Rié approached. Honda liked to observe these once beautiful, but no longer young women, their perpetual sad conversations, their confusion of their own sensuality with the past, memories and realities encroaching one upon the other, and their habit of distorting nature and reality to suit their whim. He also liked their ability to bestow automatic lyricism on everything beautiful they saw, like a bailiff stamping every piece of furniture he finds. As if this were a way of protecting themselves from whatever beauty they might perceive. Honda liked to see them romp and gambol like two inspired waterfowl who, having stumbled clumsily onto land, slip back into the water, exhibiting forthwith unexpected grace and nimbleness as they swim and dive with abandon. When they composed a poem, they would display unreserved freedom in mental sunbathing, quite without fear of the resultant exposure. It brought to mind the young Princess and the old ladies at Bang Pa In.

Would Ying Chan really come? Where had she stayed the night? Concern suddenly inserted a rough wooden wedge into his mind.

"What a beautiful garden! Hakoné to the east and Fuji to the west. It's a crime that you dawdle around without writing a single poem. While we're forced to produce poetry under the polluted skies of Tokyo, you read law books here. What an unfair world!"

"I gave up on legal books long ago," said Honda, offering them some sherry. The movement of kimono sleeves and the graceful motion of their fingers as the two women accepted the sherry glasses were extremely lovely. Actually Mrs. Tsubakihara slavishly aped Makiko, from the gesture of lightly holding up her sleeve to the way she curled her ringed fingers when picking up the glass.

"How happy Akio would have been to see this garden!" said Mrs. Tsubakihara, mentioning her dead son. "He adored Mount Fuji, and even before entering the Navy, he had a framed photograph of it in his study so he could always look at it. Such clean-cut, youthful tastes."

Every time she mentioned his name, the ripple of a sob touched her cheeks, as though a precision mechanism existed in the depth of her heart, automatically activated at every reference to him, independent of her wishes, and producing an unvarying facial expression. As an emperor's name is always mentioned with a reverent expression, the fleeting trace of sobs was practically synonymous with the name Akio.

Makiko had spread a notebook on her lap and composed a poem.

"You've already written one!" exclaimed Mrs. Tsubakihara, looking jealously at her teacher's bent head. Honda looked too. The slim, white, fragrant nape that had once attracted young Isao lingered like a fading moon in his eyes.

"That's Mr. Imanishi. I'm sure it must be!" cried Mrs. Tsubakihara, looking at the man crossing the lawn. Even from that distance, the white forehead and tall figure walking in the characteristically infirm manner, trailing its long shadow, were recognizably his.

"How horrible! He's sure to start that vulgar talk again. He'll ruin our enjoyment straightaway," said Mrs. Tsubakihara.

Yasushi Imanishi was about forty and a specialist in German literature. He had introduced the younger German writers during the war and now indiscriminately wrote all kinds of essays. Currently he was dreaming about the *Millennium of Sex* that he was going to write, but as yet there was no sign of his having done so. Probably he had lost interest in writing it now that he had discussed with everyone the details of its contents. What relevance the *Millennium,* which was altogether weird and gloomy, could hold for him no one could say. He was the second son of the head of Imanishi Securities and was living the comfortable life of a bachelor.

His face was pale and nervous, but he was congenial, talkative, and both the financial world and left-wing writers found him amusing. He really felt that he had discovered for the first time in his life something that suited his personality in this postwar iconoclastic period directed against established authority and convention. This was the struggle taken up by rugged, pale intellectuals. He advocated the political significance of sexual fantasy, which he had adopted as his specialty. Until then, he had been merely a Novalis-like romanticist.

Women liked the manner he had of gallantly spicing

his aristocratic ways with obscenities. Those who called him degenerate were only revealing that they were holdovers from feudal days. At the same time, Imanishi never failed to disappoint serious progressives by his silly future map of the *Millennium*.

He never spoke in a loud voice. For that presented the danger of taking matters from the area of delicate sensuality and transforming them into ideology.

The four guests passed the time in the arbor basking in the afternoon sun, while they waited for the others to arrive. The gurgling sound of the stream running just below insisted on intruding itself into their awareness. Honda could not help but remember the words: "Everything is in constant flux like a torrent."

Imanishi had called the kingdom of his fantasy "The Land of the Pomegranate." He had named it after the small, ruby-red bursting seeds. He claimed that he traveled to his kingdom asleep and awake, and everyone asked for news of it.

"What's happening in 'The Land of the Pomegranate' these days?"

"As usual the population is well under control. All sorts of problems arise because of the high incidence of incest. A single woman is often aunt, mother, sister, and cousin to the same man. As a result, half the babies are incredibly beautiful, while the other half are ugly and deformed.

"The beautiful children of both sexes are separated in infancy from the ugly ones and assembled in a place called 'The Garden of the Loved Ones.' The facilities are magnificent, a veritable paradise on earth. An artificial sun constantly gives out exactly the ideal number of ultraviolet rays. No one wears clothes, and all devote themselves to swimming and other physical exercises. Flowers bloom in profusion, and small animals and birds are never caged. The children there eat good nourishing food, but never grow fat, for they are checked weekly by medical examiners. They can only grow more and more beautiful. But reading is strictly forbidden. It spoils natural beauty, so the taboo makes sense.

"But when they reach adolescence, they're brought from the garden once a week to become objects of sexual amusement for the ugly ones outside. After two or three years of this sort of activity, they are destroyed. Don't you think it's true brotherly love to terminate life while beautiful people are still young?

"The creative powers of all artists in the land are utilized to develop various means of slaughter. That is to say, there are theaters throughout the country devoted to sexual murder, in which the beautiful boys and girls are cast in all manner of roles where they are tortured to death. They recreate all sorts of mythological and historical personalities who were sadistically murdered while young and beautiful. But of course there are many new creations too. They are nobly murdered in magnificent, sensual costumes, with splendid lighting, brilliant stage settings, and wonderful music; but usually they are toyed with by members of the audience before they are quite dead, and after that the bodies are consumed.

"The graves? The graves are right outside 'The Garden of the Loved Ones.' It's a beautiful place, and ugly deformed people stroll among the tombs on moonlit nights, lost in romantic moods. As statues of the beautiful ones are erected as gravestones, there's no cemetery in the world with so many beautiful bodies."

"Why do they have to kill them?"

"Because they're soon bored by living people."

"The people in 'The Land of the Pomegranate' are infinitely wise. They know very well that there are only two roles for humans in the world: those who remember and those who are remembered.

"Now that I have told you this much, I must inform you about their religion. Such custom is based on religious belief.

"They don't believe in rebirth in 'The Land of the Pomegranate.' Because God is manifest at the supreme instant of sexual climax, and the true nature of godliness lies in its unique appearance. There is no possibility that one would become more beautiful after rebirth, and that means that resurrection would hold no meaning. It's unthinkable that a faded shirt should be whiter than a brand-new one, isn't it? So the gods of 'The Land of the Pomegranate' are used once and thrown away.

"The religion of the country is polytheistic, but in a temporal sort of way; and countless numbers of gods squander their total physical existence, disappearing once they have expressed this highest moment in eternity. Now you know: 'The Garden of the Loved Ones' is a factory for making gods.

"To transform history in this world into a chain of beautiful events, the sacrifice of gods must continue infinitely. Such is the theology. Don't you think it's rational? Furthermore, the people display absolutely no hypocrisy; so beauty and sexual attractiveness are synonyms. They are very well aware that only through sexual desire may one approach God; that is, beauty.

"One possesses a god by means of sexual desire, and sexual possession occurs at the climax of pleasure. But an orgasm does not endure, therefore possession can mean only one thing: the unification of the unenduring with the ephemeralness of the object of sexual desire. The surest method is the elimination of this object at the moment of climax. Therefore, the people of the country are clearly aware that sexual possession is consummated in murder and cannibalism.

"It is certainly wonderful that this paradox of sexual possession controls even the economic structure of the country. The funadamental rule of possession is 'to kill the loved one,' which means that completion of any possession signifies simultaneous termination of possessing, and continued possession is a violation of love. Physical labor is permitted only to create beautiful physiques, and the ugly are exempted from it. Actually industrial production is completely automated and does not require human power. The arts? The only arts are found in the infinite variety of the murder theater as well as in the erection of statues to the beautiful dead. From the religious point of view, sensual realism is the basic style, and abstraction is completely rejected. Incorporation of 'life' in the arts is strictly forbidden.

"The approach to beauty is through sexual desire, but what records this moment of beauty for all eternity is memory . . . Now you have a rough understanding of the fundamental structure of 'The Land of the Pomegranate,' I think. The basic concept is memory, and in a manner of speaking, memory is national policy.

"Orgasm, a phenomenon something like a corporeal crystal, is further crystallized in memory, and following the death of the god of beauty, one can recall the highest degree of sexual excitement. The people live only in order to reach this point. Compared to this heavenly jewel, the physical existence of human beings, whether the lover or the beloved, the killer or the killed, is only the means of reaching this point. This is the ideal of the country.

"Memory is the sole matter of our spirit. Even should a god appear at the climax of sexual possession, then that god becomes 'the remembered one,' and the lover becomes 'the one who remembers.' Only through this time-consuming process is the presence of the god really proved, is beauty attained for the first time, and is sexual desire distilled into love that is independent of possession. *Hence, gods and humans are not separated in space, but there is a time lag between them.* Here lies the essence of temporal polytheism. Do you understand?

"Murder sounds harsh, but it is necessary for purifying memory and distilling it into its strongest concentrated element. Besides, these ugly, deformed inhabitants are noble, truly noble. They are experts in altruism; they live for self-denial. These lovers-cum-murderers-cum-rememberers live their roles faithfully, they remember nothing about themselves, but live only in adoration of the memory of the loved ones' beautiful death. Remembering becomes the single task of their lives. 'The Land of the Pomegranate' is also a country of cypresses, beautiful mementoes, and mourning; it is the most peaceful and quiet place in all the world, a country of recollections.

"Every time I go there, I think I never want to return to a place like Japan. The land is full of the sweetest, tenderest elements of humanity. It is a country of true humanism and peace. They have no such savage custom as eating the flesh of oxen and pigs."

"I would like to ask you one thing. You say that they eat human flesh, but what parts of the human body do they consume?" Makiko asked, amused.

"You know very well without asking," said Imanishi in a quiet, subdued voice.

Honda thought it more than comical that a former judge could listen without flinching to such manner of talk. He had never even dreamed that a man like Imanishi could ever exist. Had Cesare Lombroso, the criminologist, met him, he would have ordered him immediately banished from society.

Honda was repelled by Imanishi's sex-oriented interests, yet he himself indulged in another kind. If this were not a product of Imanishi's imagination, they should all be inhabitants of the sex millennium of the gods. It was a divine theatrical farce that God had made Honda live on as one who would remember, killing off Kiyoaki and Isao as those to be remembered. But Imanishi had stated that there was no rebirth. Samsara might be an idea standing in opposition to resurrection, and its characteristic might be its guaranteeing that life occur only once. In particular, Imanishi's theory that there was a time lag between human existence and God, and that man could meet God only in memory forced Honda to look back upon his own life and his travels; it evoked something vast and vaguely nostalgic.

What a man Imanishi was!

He intentionally exposed to the sun black inner deformities and was even pleased in so doing. He staked all on the sophistication of his nonchalant face, describing his blackness to others as though it did not concern him at all.

Honda, having long been a part of the legal world, concealed in his heart a certain romantic respect for the self-confident criminal. To be truthful, the confident criminal was extremely rare. Indeed, he had never met anyone who could be so classified except Isao.

It followed that Honda concealed feelings of hatred and contempt for repentant offenders.

Which was Imanishi?

He was probably never repentant, but he quite lacked the nobility of the principled criminal. By his vanity and sophistication he was trying to embellish the meanness of a man who has confessed and thus sought to achieve the advantage of both confession and sophistication. The ugliness of this transparent anatomical model! Honda, nevertheless, persistently refused to recognize the fact that he was somewhat attracted to Imanishi, that the invitation he had extended to him to come to the villa was rooted in a kind of envy for his courage. Furthermore, that he concealed this was not because of his conceit and fortitude in demeaning himself to the baseness of one who has confessed, but doubtless because of his fear of Imanishi's X-ray eyes. Honda had secretly labeled his own fear the "sickness of objectivity." It was the ultimate hell, filled with pleasurable thrills, into which a cognition that refused to act was finally precipitated.

The man has eyes like a fish, thought Honda, glancing surreptitiously at Imanishi's profile as the latter was talking triumphantly to the women.

Only after the sun had dyed the clouds to the left of Mount Fuji had all the guests assembled.

When the four made their way from the arbor to the house, Keiko's American lover, the Army lieutenant, was helping her in the kitchen. Shortly, the aging erstwhile Baron and Baroness Shinkawa arrived; then at intervals, Sakurai, a diplomat; Murata, the president of a construction company; Kawaguchi, an important newspaper man; Akiko Kyoya, a singer of French songs; and Ikuko

Fujima, a traditional Japanese dancer. Such a motley group of guests would have been unthinkable in Honda's former household. Honda's heart, too, was heavy: Ying Chan had not put in an appearance.

26

FORMER BARON SHINKAWA was seated in a chair by the fireside from which point he coldly observed the other guests.

He was now seventy-two. Grumbling and complaining without fail whenever he left home, he could not forego the joy of going out; at even his age his love for parties had not diminished. He had been very bored during the period of the postwar purges and had fallen into the habit of accepting all invitations. This had continued on into the post-purge years.

But now everyone considered him and his garrulous wife to be the most boring of guests. His sarcasm had lost its bite, and his epigrammatic expressions had become long-winded and shallow. He was never able to recall people's names.

"That . . . what was he called? . . . remember . . . he was often depicted in political cartoons . . . don't you remember? . . . a small, fat man, round as a butterball . . . what was his name? . . . a very common one . . ."

His listener could not help but recognize Shinkawa's losing battle with the invisible monster of forgetfulness. This quiet, but tenacious animal would occasionally withdraw only to reappear at once, clinging to Shinkawa, brushing his forehead with its shaggy tail.

At last, he would give up and continue his story.

". . . anyway, this politician's wife was a remarkable woman." But the episode in which the most important name was missing no longer held any flavor. Each time he would stamp his foot in sheer vexation, so anxious was he to impart to others the flavor of the tale he alone could savor. It was then that Shinkawa would be aware of a mendicantlike emotion, one he had previously never experienced. In his struggle to find someone to appreciate his simple punning jokes, as though begging for understanding, he had unconsciously become obsequious.

He was pathetically compelled to tear down the refined pride he had so long possessed, and gradually his prime concern became the assumption of an attitude of contemptuousness—something that he had exhibited most casually on the tip of his nose like cigar smoke in former days. But at the same time, he took great pains to avoid revealing this hidden contempt to anyone. He was fearful that he might not receive other invitations.

In the midst of a party, he would occasionally pull at his wife's sleeve and whisper in her ear:

"What a despicable pack. They don't know the first thing about how to speak of the indelicate in a refined way. Japanese ugliness is so complete it's almost impressive. But you mustn't let them suspect how we think."

Shinkawa's eyes suddenly became glazed before the flames in the fireplace; he recalled the garden party at the Marquis Matsugae's some forty years ago, proudly remembering that there too he had felt nothing but contempt for his host.

But only one thing had changed. In former times, the object of his contempt could do him no harm; but now just being there profoundly wounded him.

Mrs. Shinkawa was vivacious.

At her age she increasingly found an indefinable interest in talking about herself. Her search for listeners harmonized beautifully with the attempt to abolish class distinctions that was now in style. She had never once been concerned about the quality of her audience.

She paid exaggerated compliments to the singer of French songs as though she were talking to royalty, in return for which she obtained a hearing. She shamelessly praised Makiko Kito's poems and then imposed her own tale on the poor woman—once she had been complimented by an Englishman who had called her a poet. He had made the remark when she had compared the late summer clouds over Karuizawa to a Sisley painting.

Now, moved by some uncanny intuition, she began to talk about the garden party at the Matsugae estate as she joined her husband by the fireplace.

"As I think back, those were stupid and uncivilized times when expensive parties entailed nothing more than having a few geisha dance and make music at home. How unimaginative people were then. I must say Japan has made quite a bit of progress: the barbarous customs are gone and it's ordinary for wives to be included in social affairs. Look at them, the women at this party are no longer silent. Conversations that took place at garden parties used to be excruciatingly boring, but now the women converse very wittily."

But it was doubtful whether she had ever listened to anyone's conversation, either now or at any time in the past forty years. She had never tried to talk about anything except herself.

Mrs. Shinkawa suddenly left her husband's side. She cast a glance into a dark mirror mounted on a wall. Looking-glasses never frightened her. They all functioned as wastebaskets into which she could discard her wrinkles as she stood before them.

Jack, a first lieutenant in the Quartermaster Corps, was working hard. The guests looked with pleasure at this member of the "Occupation Forces" who was so gentle and loyal. Keiko treated him grandly, with incomparable regal skill.

Sometimes Jack would extend an arm and encircle her from behind, mischievously touching her breast. She permitted herself a calm, wry smile as she clasped his hairy, ringed fingers.

"Such a child. He's incorrigible," she said in a dry, didactic tone, looking around at everyone. Jack's posterior encased in his Army uniform was capacious, and the guests would compare it with Keiko's majestic buttocks, arguing which was the larger.

Mrs. Tsubakihara was still talking with Imanishi. She was taken aback to meet for the first time someone who completely scorned her precious sorrow, but she did not change in the least the idiotic expression of mourning on her face.

"No matter how much you grieve, your son will not come back to life. Besides you've a balloon in your heart so filled with grief that nothing else can possibly get in. It gives you a secure feeling, doesn't it? Let me be rude a bit more: you're convinced that no one else will do you the favor of filling your balloon, so you fill it yourself with homemade sorrow-gas that you pump into it at a moment's notice. That releases you from the fear of being bothered by any other emotion."

"What a horrible thing to say! How cruel . . ."

Mrs. Tsubakihara looked up at Imanishi from the handkerchief in which she muffled her sobs. He thought the look in her eyes was that of an innocent little girl who craved to be raped.

The president of the Murata Construction Company was offering a hyperbolic compliment to Shinkawa, hailing him as a great patron in the financial world. Shinkawa was irked to be assigned to the same category as the vulgar builder. Murata had erected immense billboards bearing his name on all the company's construction sites; the self-advertising was everywhere. But no one looked less like a construction expert. A pale, flat face revealed his background as a reformist bureaucrat of prewar days. He was an idealist who lived parastically off others. No sooner had he stopped clinging and achieved independent success in business than he discovered a bright, vast ocean where his inherent crassness could disport itself without restraint. Murata had made the dancer Ikuko Fujima his mistress. Ikuko was wearing a sumptuous kimono interwoven with silk and lacquer threads, and a five-carat diamond blazed on her finger; when she laughed, she held her neck and back rigidly erect.

"An extremely fine house, sir, but if you'd let me build it for you, I could have saved you a lot of money. What a shame," Murata repeated at least three times to Honda.

The diplomat Sakurai and the senior reporter Kawaguchi were discussing international problems, standing on either side of Akiko Kyoya. Sakurai's fishlike skin and Kawaguchi's, marked by age and spoiled by saké, provided a good contrast between the two and their careers. One was cold- and the other hot-blooded. They were discussing weighty problems, as men are wont to do in the company of women, in an effort to impress the singer Akiko. She, on the other hand, was completely oblivious to the subtle rivalry and inane vanity, constantly helping herself to the canapés, glancing alternately with her melancholic, dark eyes at the disheveled white hair and the overly groomed head. She pursed her mouth into the shape of an O and tossed one tidbit after another between her goldfish lips.

Makiko Kito took the trouble of going up to Imanishi and saying: "You have the most peculiar tastes."

"Must I get your permission every time I make love to your pupil? It's as though I were making love to my mother, I feel a kind of sacred tremor. At any rate, I'll never make the mistake of making love to you. What you think of me is written all over your face. I'm the type that repels you sexually more than any other, right?"

"You know very well you do."

Makiko felt relieved and spoke in a most charming voice. Then she laid a strip of silence between them, that resembled the black edge of tatami matting.

"Even if you should succeed in making love to her, you could never assume the role of her son. Her dead son is extremely sacred and beautiful to her; she is a holy priestess serving him."

"Well, I don't know. To me everything looks suspicious. It's blasphemy that a living person should continue harboring pure emotions and expressing them."

"That's why I say she is serving the pure sentiment of the dead."

"Anyway she does it out of her necessity to live. That already makes it suspicious."

Makiko narrowed her eyes and laughed in sheer repulsion.

"There isn't a real man at this party," she said. With that she left Imanishi as Honda called to her. Mrs. Tsubakihara was seated on the edge of a bench built into the wall, crying as she leaned back. Outside, the night air was extremely cold, and condensed droplets of moisture trickled down the panes.

Honda intended to ask Makiko to take care of Mrs. Tsubakihara. If her tears stemmed less from her painful memories than from the small amount of liquor she had consumed, she could well be a sentimental drinker.

Rié, her face pallid, approached Honda and whispered in his ear.

"There's been a strange noise. It started a little while ago in the garden . . . I wonder if I'm hearing things."

"Did you look?"

"No, I was afraid to."

Honda strode to one of the windows and cleared the steam from the pane with his fingers. Beyond the dead grass, above the cypresses, hung a spectral moon. A wild dog was snooping about, dragging its shadow after it. Stopping and curling up its tail, it threw out its furry white chest that shone in the moonlight and howled mournfully.

"That's it, isn't it?" Honda asked his wife. The cause of her childish fear had been too easily revealed and Rié did not immediately agree, but merely smiled a vague, indecisive smile.

As he listened further, two or three dogs responded from beyond the cypress grove.

The wind had increased.

27

IT WAS MIDNIGHT. From the window of his second-floor study, Honda watched a small, ghostly moon traverse the sky. Ying Chan had not put in an appearance. The moon had come instead.

The party had come to a close near midnight. Only the overnight guests still remained, gathered in a small circle. Gradually they withdrew to their assigned bedrooms. After the two guest rooms upstairs, came Honda's study, which in turn adjoined the master bedroom. Once she had seen the guests off, exhaustion had settled in, numbing Rié's body to the very tips of her swollen fingers. She had retired to her bedroom after bidding her husband good night. Alone in the study, Honda still saw the backs of his wife's hands which were so swollen they gave off a dull sheen. Rié had triumphantly shown them to him.

The malice spreading inside had pushed outward, swelling her skin, erasing the angularity of her hands, which had taken on a strangely puffy, childish appearance that stayed with him a long time. He had suggested a private celebration in their bedroom on the occasion of the housewarming, but he had been turned down. If his suggestion had not been vetoed, what would have happened? Something desolate must flow under that nauseous subcutaneous fat of kindness and sympathy.

Honda looked about his Western study, with its pretentious bright window and its clean desk. When he really worked hard, the study was never like this. Then it had an unmanageable disorderliness, like that of living itself, and it smelled like a chicken roost. Now, on the arty desk fashioned from a single zelkova plank an English writing set of Moroccan leather had been placed. In the pen plate were several pencils neatly sharpened, all in a line, embossed letters freshly shining like the insignia on cadets' collars. There was also his bronze

169

alligator paperweight—inherited from his father—and an empty letter box of meshed bamboo.

He rose frequently and crossed over to wipe the panes in the bay window with its curtains still open, for the moon shining through the glass was clouded and distorted by the heat in the room. He was certain that unless the moon were permitted to stay clear, the emptiness and disgust that flooded his heart would expand and expand, and the dark turmoil would be transformed into sexual desire. It astonished him to discover that it was just such a landscape that awaited him at the end of his life's journey. The dog's mournful bark sounded again, and the fragile cypress trees creaked in the wind.

It was some time since his wife had gone to sleep in the next room. Honda switched off the light in the study and walked over to the bookcases that flanked the wall of the guest room. Quietly he took down a number of Western books and piled them on the floor. What he had himself labeled the "disease of objectivity" now overcame him. The minute he surrendered to it he would be forced to antagonize all society which until now had been on his side.

But why? he wondered. This too was a part of the varied aspects of human behavior which he had objectively observed from the bench or from the lawyer's seat for so many years. How could it be that observing from those vantage points was perfectly legal, but looking as he would now a violation of the law? Observation in that manner had made him the object of approval by society, while watching like this was subject to reproach and contempt. If this were a crime, it was probably because he derived so much pleasure from it. Yet his experience as judge had taught him the pleasure to be found in a clear mind, devoid of private desire. And if that enjoyment was noble because it was not accompanied by any quickening of the pulse, could it be that the essence of criminality lay in the palpitation of the heart? This innermost response of a human being, this palpitation in the face of pleasure—could that be the most significant ingredient in any violation of the law?

All this was sophistry. As he pulled the books from the bookcase, Honda felt a throbbing in his heart similar to that of a young boy, and he was made sharply aware how weak and vulnerable his very existence was vis-à-vis society. He was alone and helpless. The forces that had held him high as on a scaffolding had now been removed. Like the sand trickling in an hourglass, the inexorable endless descent had started. In that case, law and society were already his enemies. Had he possessed a little more courage and were this not his own study but some corner of a park where young grass grew or perhaps a dark byroad speckled with the lights of houses, he would then in reality become a most shameful criminal. People would jeer: "The judge became attorney, and the attorney a criminal!" They would say that here was a man who had never stopped loving the court throughout his life!

Once the books were removed, a small hole appeared before him in the wall. The dusty, dark space was just large enough for his face. The dusty smell suddenly filled Honda's heart with keen memories of youth, striking the meager red sparks of the secret pleasures of childhood. He remembered the texture of the dark-blue velvet coverlet mixed with the odor of the toilet. The first obscene word he had discovered in a dictionary. All the melancholic, foul odors of boyhood. He discovered in his throbbing heart the faintest caricature of the noble passion that had urged Kiyoaki toward final catastrophe. Whatever it was, it was a single dark passage that connected the nineteen-year-old Kiyoaki and the fifty-seven-year-old Honda. As he closed his eyes, an illusion sprang up, in the darkness of the bookcase, of scattered particles of red flesh flying about like a cluster of mosquitoes.

The guest room next to his study was occupied by Makiko and Mrs. Tsubakihara. Imanishi occupied the chamber beyond. Honda had definitely sensed some sort of communication between the two rooms; he had heard doors opening surreptitiously and then the sound of muffled voices, scolding whispers, similar to spatterings on the surface of water. The noise stopped and then began again. Something was being precipitated on the plane that inclined into the depth of night, as though an ivory die were cast and was rolling down a tilted board.

He had an idea of what was taking place. But what met his eyes was more than he had imagined.

In the adjacent guest room twin beds had been placed parallel to the wall with the secret opening. The bed directly below the hole was almost completely out of his view, but the other was entirely visible. The night lamp was on, but the bed itself was veiled in shadow.

Honda was startled to see in the pale light a pair of wide-open eyes staring into his. They belonged to none other than Makiko.

She was sitting on the far bed clad in a white night kimono. The collar of the robe was primly closed, and her silvery hair shone dimly in the light that came from one side. She had cleansed her face of cosmetics, and its whiteness of former days had not changed. It still was clear and cold. Her age was revealed in the round shoulders where the plump flesh had drooped, but for the most part her confidence in the imperviousness of her being, never threatened through the long years, was obvious in the regular breathing of her breast. It was as if the essence of night were seated there, clad in white. Honda felt as though he were looking at Mount Fuji on a moonlit night. The gentle slope at the foot of the mountain was covered in the flowing creases of the blue-lined blanket. Makiko's lap was half hidden under the coverlet on which she languidly leaned her arm.

Her eyes, that appeared at first to have caught Honda's peeping gaze, were not really turned toward the hole. They were lowered and were gazing at the bed placed against the wall.

Seeing only her eyes, one would be convinced that Makiko was concentrating on the creation of a poem as she gazed into some river which happened to lie just beneath. It was that time of night when the human spirit could grasp a certain vivid turmoil in the air and would struggle to crystallize it. In making the effort, one's eyes would become like those of a hunter about to shoot. Seeing only her eyes, one could but feel the sublimity of her soul.

Makiko was not looking at a river or a fish, but at human forms writhing on the shadowy bed. Honda elevated his head until he struck the top of the bookcase in an effort to see down through the small peephole. He could in this way observe what was taking place on the bed beyond the wall. A man's thin, pale thighs were twined about those of a woman. Immediately below him were two heaps of withered flesh hardly bursting with vigor, swaying slowly like aquatic animals as they made contact. They gleamed damply in the faint light; the devourer was unmistakably being devoured; obvious trickery was going hand in hand with sincere tremors. Two mounds of moist pubic hair touched and separated; and a white patch where the light struck the woman's belly, as if a piece of white tissue had been inserted between the two bodies, pierced Honda's awestricken eyes.

Whatever the situation, Imanishi had shamelessly exposed the pitiful thighs of an intellectual in heat. True to his theories, the cheerless, rippling oscillation of his flat buttocks, between which appeared a wasted coccyx, was merely a momentary illusion. His obvious lack of sincerity angered Honda.

Compared to him, Mrs. Tsubakihara was earnestness itself; he could see her hands stretched out like those of a drowning woman, her fingers desperately grasping at Imanishi's hair. At last, she called her son's name. It was a suppressed, faint cry:

"Akio, Akio. Forgive me . . ." Her words were muffled in sobs, but Imanishi was not affected in the least.

Honda, suddenly recognizing the solemnity and loathsomeness of the situation, bit his lips. It was now clear. Whether Makiko had ordered her to perform or not, it was obviously not the first time that Mrs. Tsubakihara had been involved in this sort of exhibition for Makiko and probably only for her. This was the very essence of the teacher-student relationship between Makiko and Mrs. Tsubakihara, their contempt and dedication.

Honda looked at Makiko again. She was looking down serenely, her silvery hair shining and floating over her head. They were of a different sex, but Honda realized that Makiko was his exact counterpart.

28

THE NEXT DAY was beautiful and sunny. The Hondas had invited their three overnight guests and Keiko to drive in two separate cars to the Sengen Shrine at Fuji-Yoshida. Except for Keiko, they all planned to depart for Tokyo from there, and Honda had locked up before leaving the villa. Just as he was closing the door, he had the sudden premonition that Ying Chan would come during his absence; but that was most unlikely.

Honda had just been reading the *Honcho monzui,* "Compositions of Elegance Composed in Japan," which Imanishi had brought for him. Of course, he had wished to read the "Essays on Mount Fuji" by Yoshika no Miyako and had asked Imanishi to get him a copy.

"Mount Fuji is located in the province of Suruga; its peak, as if sharpened, towers high into the heavens." Such descriptions held little interest, but then a passage followed that struck Honda so strongly that it had long remained in his memory; he had not had the chance of reading it again since then.

An old man recounted: On the fifth day of the eleventh month in the seventeenth year of Jokan (A.D. 875), officials and people gathered to hold a celebration in accordance with tradition. The sun emerged around noon, and the sky was extremely beautiful and clear. As the spectators looked up to the summit of the mountain, they saw two beautiful women in white garments dancing together. Both were floating more than a foot above the peak. All the inhabitants of the land saw them.

It was not strange that such optical illusions should occur on a fine day at Mount Fuji, for it often produced various chimera. Frequently a quiet wind at the sloping foot of the mountain would develop into a strong gale at the top, carrying a mist of snow into the blue sky. It was probably this snow dust that had appeared in the form of two beautiful women to the inhabitants' eyes.

Fuji was cold and self-assured, but through its confident coldness and whiteness it permitted all possible fantasies. In ultimate frigidity is vertigo, just as delirium characterizes the extreme of reason. Fuji was a mysterious ultimate of perfection and its beauty verged on a vague lyricism. It was at once infinite and finite. It was quite possible that two beautiful women in white garments had danced there.

In addition, Honda was charmed by the fact that the spirit enshrined at the Sengen Shrine was a goddess called Konohana Sakuya.

Mrs. Tsubakihara, Makiko, and Imanishi rode in Mrs. Tsubakihara's car, and the Hondas and Keiko took the limousine Honda had engaged for his return to Tokyo. This was a natural arrangement, but Honda had vaguely wanted to be in the same car as Makiko and experienced a pang of regret. He had wanted to sit next to her and look into the intense eyes he had seen the night before, the eyes of a huntress ready to launch her arrow.

The drive to Fuji-Yoshida, however, was not an easy one. The national highway, the former Kamakura Road, climbed over the Kagosaka Pass from Subashiri and passed northward along Lake Yamanaka. It was mostly unpaved and mountainous. The prefectural boundary between Shizuoka and Yamanashi ran along the ridge of Kagosaka.

While Keiko and Rié sat next to each other and made their small woman-talk, Honda looked out the window with childlike earnestness. Keiko's presence was very useful in forestalling Rié's complaints. Rié had become like a bottle of beer that overflowed the moment the cap was removed. Since morning she had been objecting to the idea of driving back to Tokyo, insisting that not since childhood had she taken such a long, meaningless, and extravagant drive.

This same Rié became quite docile, even charming, as she talked with Keiko.

"You don't have to worry about kidney trouble," Keiko said bluntly.

"Do you think so? When I hear you talk like that, I'm rather encouraged. It's strange. I get angry when my husband speaks to me sweetly with his dishonest, exaggerated sympathy and pretended concern."

Probably out of tact, Keiko would never come to Honda's defense when Rié attacked him.

"Mr. Honda has no head for anything but logical thinking, and there's nothing you can do about it," said Keiko.

Once across the dividing line, one could see that the northern slope of the mountain was completely blanketed in hard-frozen snow that, in contracting, had become etched in a snakeskin pattern. It resembled the backs of Rié's hands when the swelling subsided.

At that moment, however, Rié had become more bearable to Honda. To be with two women who, in his hearing, were talking so unflatteringly—especially when one was his own wife—somehow provided him a passing feeling of contentment.

Beyond the Kagosaka Pass, a heavy layer of snow lay over everything, and the ground in the sparse grove at Lake Yamanaka looked as if it were covered by frozen crepe de chine. The pine needles were yellow, and only in the water of the lake was the color bright and clear. As he looked back, the white surface of Fuji, the origin of all the whiteness in this area, was glowing as if it had been brushed with oil.

It was about half past three in the afternoon when they arrived at the Sengen Shrine. As he glanced back at the three passengers emerging from the black Chrysler, Honda experienced an ominous feeling as if he were watching corpses suddenly rising from a black coffin.

This morning it was imperative for the three that they wipe clean the memory of the previous night. But confinement in the close quarters of the limousine for the entire journey had made the episode even more odious, like the waters of abdominal dropsy that accumulate immediately, no matter how frequently they are tapped. The three blinked as though bothered by the glare from the snow at the roadside. Nevertheless, Makiko was standing rigidly erect. Honda was repelled by the sight of Imanishi's sallow, unresilient skin. He had blasphemed against the beauty of that tragic fantasy of the flesh, of which he had spoken so elatedly the previous day; this had been proven by his complete lack of qualifications as a lover. He compounded the outrage by his conviction that his ugliness would remain undetected.

In any event, Honda had witnessed it. The one who sees and the one who had unknowingly been seen were already conjoined at the limits of this double world. Makiko glanced up at the gigantic stone torii with "Mount Fuji" carved on a framed rock and again took out the notebook she always carried for jotting down her poetical thoughts. A delicate pencil was permanently attached to it by a purple string.

Helping each other, the six walked along the damp, snowy path leading to the shrine. Here and there the sun penetrated through the branches, highlighting patches of snow. The lofty limbs of the old cryptomerias continued to release their dead brown needles that fell on the little heaps of tenacious snow. There was a misty light that made it seem that they were enveloped in a greenish haze. At the far end of the path a red torii surrounded by snow came into view.

This sign of divinity evoked in Honda the memory of Isao Iinuma. Again he looked at Makiko. Momentarily he felt he could forget her eyes at midnight, now that she was imbued with divine power. Isao, adored by those changing eyes, had perhaps been slain by them.

Keiko maintained a calm and self-possessed attitude no matter what she saw.

"How beautiful! Wonderful. How Japanese!" she said expansively.

Makiko actually seemed to wince on hearing her conclusive way of speaking and glanced at her somewhat fretfully. Rié detachedly watched from her position at the rear.

Each tottering step Mrs. Tsubakihara took along the path to the shrine gave her the appearance of a sorrowful crane with drooping feathers. She offhandedly refused the assistance proferred by Imanishi and placed her hand on Honda's arm. She was in no mood to compose poetry.

Her grief was too genuine to be a pose, and Honda was almost touched as he gazed down at her doleful profile. His eyes met Makiko's who had chosen that instant to glance from the other side at her dejected disciple. As usual, Makiko had discovered poetry in the woman's sad face lit by light reflecting from the snow. She composed a poem.

When they reached the sacred bridge that crossed the road to the top of Mount Fuji, Mrs. Tsubakihara spoke to Honda in a quavering voice.

"Please forgive me. When I think that this is the shrine of Mount Fuji I feel as though a smiling Akio should be meeting me. He was so fond of Fuji."

Her grief was strangely vacant; sadness seemed to blow through the empty woman like a gust of wind swirling through a vacant arbor. And she was almost inordinately quiet, quite like after a séance—devastation in the wake of the ghostly spirit. Her dry cheeks in the shadow of strands of hair appeared absorbent, like pieces of rice paper. Quietly, unhindered, her sorrow seemed to flow freely in and out through them almost like breath.

Observing this scene had made Rié forget her own illness. She was the very picture of health. Honda in such moments suspected that his wife was a hypochondriac, that even her swelling was probably not genuine.

The party finally reached the great red torii that towered nearly sixty feet high. When they had passed through it, they found themselves directly in front of

the pavilion where the sacred dances were performed;
it was surrounded by soiled snow that had been piled
in front of the red gate. Sacred rope was strung along
three sides of the pavilion under the eaves, and from
the tops of the tall cryptomerias a ray of clear sunshine
fell on the sacred strips of paper *gohei* which stood
out against the unpainted offering table on the floor.
The pavilion up to its latticed ceiling was lit by the
reflection from the snow, but the sunlight that reached
the paper was especially bright. The strips swayed lightly
in the breeze.

Momentarily Honda felt the pure white paper to be
alive.

Mrs. Tsubakihara's tears broke the spell. No one
was particularly surprised by the sound of her sobs.

No sooner had she caught sight of the holy paper
than she was stricken with fear. She ran to the front
of the red main shrine guarded by reliefs of Chinese
lions and dragons, and prostrating herself in prayer,
burst into tears.

Honda no longer wondered why her grief had not
healed so long after the war. He was witness to the
secret whereby, as yesterday, it was revived and fresh-
ened.

29

THE NEXT DAY, Keiko telephoned from Ninooka in
Gotemba. Honda was out. Rié was home in bed, still
exhausted from the party. When she heard it was Keiko,
however, she came to the phone.

Keiko had called to relate that Ying Chan had come
to Gotemba that day alone.

"When I was walking the dog, I saw a young lady
wandering about the gate of your villa. Somehow she
didn't look Japanese. I called to her, and she said she
was from Thailand. She told me she had been invited
by Mr. Honda but that she had been prevented from

coming. She arrived today because she thought that everyone was still here. I was surprised at her cheerfulness; but she had come alone all that way, and I felt sorry that she had to go back again. I offered her some tea at home and took her to the station. I've just returned from seeing her off. She said she would apologize to Mr. Honda after she got back to Tokyo. But she claims she doesn't like to use the telephone. Talking in Japanese on the phone gives her a headache. She's very charming. Her hair is so black and her eyes so large."

After chattering on, Keiko thanked Rié for the party again, added that she was busy preparing a poker game that night for her American officer and his friends, and then hung up.

Rié faithfully reported the entire conversation to Honda when he arrived. He listened, grimacing as if inhaling smoke. Of course he did not tell his wife that he had dreamt of Ying Chan that night.

One of the advantages of age was knowing how to be patient. Still he did have some social obligations in addition to work. He could not wait forever for the unpredictable Ying Chan. He could have entrusted the ring to his wife, but wanting to present it himself, he carried it in the inside pocket of his suit coat.

Some ten days later, Rié reported that during his absence Ying Chan had made a visit, the purpose of which had not been altogether clear. Dressed in her mourning kimono, Rié had just been leaving the house to attend the funeral of a former classmate when she saw Ying Chan entering the gate.

"Was she alone?" asked Honda.

"Yes, she seemed to be."

"It's too bad she made the trip. We'll have to invite her to dinner or something next time."

"I wonder if she'll come," Rié said with a vague smile.

Honda was fully aware that a telephone call would create psychological problems for Ying Chan. Thus he arbitrarily selected a date and sent her a ticket to the Shimbashi Theater, leaving it up to her whether she came or not. The road company of the traditional Osaka puppet theater had opened in Tokyo; he wanted her to see a performance. He sent her one of the matinee tickets he had bought, intending afterwards to take her to dine at the Imperial Hotel, which had recently been returned by the Occupation Forces to Japanese management.

The particular performance that day was *Mount Kagami* and *The Monkey Leader of Horikawa*. Having previously experienced her irresponsibility, he was not surprised when Ying Chan failed to put in an appearance. Sitting alone, he leisurely watched the scene known as "Women's Quarters." During the long intermission before the presentation of *Horikawa,* he strolled out to the garden. It was a fine, clear day and many people had come out to enjoy the fresh air.

He was impressed to see that the appearance of the audience here had, compared to several years ago, improved considerably of late. Perhaps it was because there were many geisha, but kimonos had become more sumptuous and ostentatious as memories of the terrible ruins faded. Women's tastes in these postwar days had become especially colorful, no matter what their age. There was a decidedly more opulent display of bright fabrics than in the audiences of the Imperial Theater during the twenties.

If Honda had been so inclined, he could have selected the most beautiful of the young geishas and become her patron. It would be a pleasure to buy her anything she requested and enjoy her coquetry, tenuous as a spring cloud . . . those tiny feet so neatly clad in white custom-made *tabi.* She would be a perfectly dressed doll in her kimono. All this could belong to him. But he could at once foresee the conclusion. Boiling water of passion would overflow and the dancing ashes of death would fly up to blind him.

The charm of this theater lay in the manner in which the garden gave onto the river; there during the hot summer months one could enjoy the cool breezes wafting up from the water. But now the river was stagnant, and barges and garbage floated slowly downstream.

Honda well remembered the rivers in Tokyo during the war with the bodies of those killed in the bombing drifting along. There was no longer any factory smoke, and the water had become ominously cleansed, reflecting the strangely blue sky overhead said to occur at the moment of death. In comparison, this muddied, polluted water was the very symbol of prosperity.

Two geisha were leaning against the balustrade, enjoying the river breeze. One was wearing a silk kimono with a small design scattered with cherry petals and a Nagoya cherry-pattern obi in black. It was most probably hand-painted. She was tiny with a round face. The other exhibited a taste for color in her choice of clothing. A cold smile played on her face from the bridge of her nose, which was slightly too high, down to her thin lips. The two kept up an incessant chatter, punctuated by exaggerated exclamations. Two curls of smoke mounted from their cigarettes—imported brands with gold tips—which they held between fingers that never fluttered in surprise.

Honda soon realized that they were surreptitiously looking at the opposite bank. The former Imperial Japanese Naval Hospital with its statue of some erstwhile admiral still on display had now been turned into an American military hospital and was filled with soldiers wounded in the Korean War. The spring sun gleamed on the half-open cherry blossoms in the front garden, under which young soldiers were being pushed in wheelchairs. Some walked with the aid of crutches, while others strolled about with only their arms in pure white slings. No voices called from across the river to the two exquisitely dressed young women, nor was there the sound of cheerful American whistles. Like a scene from another world, the opposite bank bathed in brilliant sunshine was completely quiet, manned as it was by the forms of maimed young soldiers purposely pretending nonchalance.

The two geisha obviously enjoyed the contrast. Covered in white powder and silk, indulging in spring idleness and extravagant living, they feasted on the spectacle of those who only yesterday had been the proud victors with their injuries, pain, dismembered arms and legs. Such subtle malice and exquisite viciousness were their specialty.

From his vantage point as a bystander, Honda could discern the extravagance of the contrast between the theater garden and the scene on the far bank. Over there existed the dust, blood, misery, injured pride, irretrievable misfortune, tears, heartache, and the mangled male sexuality of the soldiers who had controlled Japan for the last seven years; while on this side, women of the defeated country paraded their overrefined, arrogant sensuality, relishing the blood of the erstwhile conqueror's drenched in their own perspiration. They were flies eating at the wounds, spreading the transparent black wings of their *haori* like the wings of magnificent black butterflies. The river breeze was of no use to bring them together. It was easy to imagine the frustration of the Americans, who had so futilely shed their blood to create this useless brilliance to which they had no access, to engender the vanity and extravagance of this insensitive display.

"It really doesn't seem to be true," Honda heard one of the women remark.

"Yes. They're too miserable to look at. Foreigners are so big and all the more pitiful in that condition. But misery is mutual. We have gone through a lot."

"Well, that is what they get for biting off more than they can chew," the other woman coldly declared. They watched with intensified interest, but this soon passed and faded. As if in competition they each produced compacts and squinted obliquely into the mirrors as they powdered their noses. The heavily scented powder, caught by the river breeze, sifted down along the hem of their *haori,* to be carried even to the sleeve opening of Honda's coat. He noticed that the little mirrors, though covered with a thin film of powder, still managed to cast a wan reflection on the bush at his feet, quite like the fluttering of tiny ants.

The faint ringing of a distant bell signified that the curtain was about to rise on the next act. Only the final part of *Horikawa* remained. As he turned his steps back toward the theater, resigned that Ying Chan would not put in an appearance this late, Honda suddenly realized that he had experienced a sensual pleasure in her wonderful absence. Ying Chan was standing inside, half hidden in the shadow of a pillar; it was as if she were trying to avoid the light streaming in.

Honda's eyes had not yet adjusted themselves to the obscurity, and all he saw was the black of her hair and the luminous darkness of her large eyes as though they were a blur of opacity. Her hair oil gave off a strong fragrance. Ying Chan smiled, showing a blurred whiteness of lovely teeth.

30

THAT EVENING they had dinner at the Imperial Hotel. It had been devastated. The Occupation Forces had claimed to understand the creative genius of Frank Lloyd Wright, but they had not hesitated to cover the stone lantern in the garden with white paint. The pseudo-Gothic ceiling of the dining hall was even more gloomy and in worse repair than ever. The only patches of freshness were provided by the white linen cloths that glistened ostentatiously on the rows of dining tables.

When Honda had ordered, he immediately drew from an inner pocket the small box and placed it directly in front of Ying Chan. She opened it and cried out.

"It was inevitable that the ring should be returned to you." Speaking in the simplest language, Honda told her its history. The smile that flickered over her features as she listened did not always coincide with his narration, and it occurred to him that she might not be comprehending all he was saying.

Her breasts, visible above the level of the table, were, quite unlike her face which was childish, magnificently developed, like those of a figurehead on a ship. He knew without seeing that the body of one of the goddesses in the Ajanta murals lay beneath the simple student's blouse across from him.

The deceptively light but solid flesh seemed to have the weightiness of some dark fruit . . . the almost stifling black hair and the ambiguous, wistful lines from the slightly flared nostrils down to the upper lip . . . She seemed to be just as casually oblivious to the words that her body spoke as she was when she listened to Honda's recital. Her enormous, jet-black eyes transcended intelligence, and they somehow gave her the appearance of being blind. What mystery of forms! That Ying Chan should present to him a body that one sensed was overly fragrant was due to the spell of the distant jungle which reached as far as Japan. Honda felt that what people called blood lineage was perhaps a deep, formless voice that pursued one eternally. Sometimes a passionate whisper, sometimes a hoarse cry, it was the very origin of all beautiful physical forms and the wellspring of the charm they emitted.

When he placed the dark green emerald ring on Ying Chan's finger, he had the sensation that he was witness to the moment when the deep, far-off voice and the girl's physical being were at long last perfectly fused.

"Thank you," said Ying Chan with a fawning smile that might have marred her dignity. Honda realized that it was the expression that always appeared when she felt sure that her selfish feelings were understood. But no sooner did he try to capture it than the smile was already gone like a swiftly withdrawing wave.

"When you were a child you claimed to be the reincarnation of a Japanese boy I knew very well; you annoyed everyone by insisting that Japan was your real home and that you wanted to return. Now that you are here and that ring is on your finger, it means that for you too a great circle has been joined."

"I don't really understand," answered Ying Chan with not a trace of emotion. "I don't remember anything of my childhood. I really don't. They all tease me about having been slightly mad and laugh at me when they tell what you've just been saying. But I've completely forgotten everything. I went to Switzerland as soon as the war broke out and stayed there until the end, and the only thing I remember about Japan is that I used to love a Japanese doll someone gave me."

Honda felt an urge to tell her that it had been sent by him, but checked himself.

"My father told me that Japanese schools were good, so I came here to study. Recently I've had the idea that perhaps when I was a child I was like a mirror reflecting everything in people's minds, and I simply said what occurred to me. For instance, if you had an idea, it might have been reflected in me. That was probably what happened, I imagine. What do you think?"

Ying Chan had the habit of terminating a question with an English rising inflection. Her ultimas reminded Honda of the sharply curling tails of the golden serpents at the tips of the red Chinese-tile roofs of Thai temples reaching into the blue sky.

Honda was suddenly aware of a family at a nearby table. The head, probably some businessman, his wife and their grown sons were having dinner. Their fine clothes notwithstanding, he could discern something vulgar in their faces. He surmised that they had become wealthy through the Korean War. The faces of the sons were particularly flabby, like that of a dog that has just been awakened, and their lips and eyes reflected a complete lack of breeding. They were all noisily sipping their soup.

From time to time, the sons would nudge each other and steal a glance at Honda's table. Their eyes were mocking: an old man having dinner with a concubine that looked like a schoolgirl. Their eyes seemed to have nothing better to say. Honda could not but recall Imanishi's exasperating inadequacy that midnight in Ninooka and compare it to himself.

There are rules more severe in this world than those of morality, Honda felt at such moments. Unsuitable lovers were punished by the fact that they would never be the source of dreams, but merely evoke disgust in others. The people of those times when one knew nothing of humanism were surely much more cruel to all ugly creatures than modern man.

After dinner Ying Chan excused herself to go to the powder room, and Honda remained alone in the lobby. He suddenly felt relaxed. From that moment on, he could enjoy Ying Chan's absence without compunction.

A question sprang to his mind: he had not yet learned where Ying Chan had stayed the night before the housewarming.

She did not return to the lobby for some time. He remembered the occasion when the little girl had relieved herself at Bang Pa In surrounded by her ladies. Then he recalled the naked Princess bathing in the brown river along which coiled the roots of mangroves. No matter how hard he had stared, he had not been able to make out the three black moles he had expected to find on her left side.

Honda's wants were quite simple, and it would have been incorrect to label his emotion "love." He wished only to look at the completely naked form of the Princess, aware that the once flat breasts had ripened, thrusting out like the heads of fledglings peeping from their nest; to see how the pink nipples pouted discontentedly and how the brown underarms lay in faint shadow; to watch the manner in which the underside of her arms carried wave patterns like a sensitive, sandy shore; to be aware of how every step toward maturity progressed in the dusky light; and then to quiver in the presence of that body, comparing it to that of the little girl. That was all. In her belly, floating in pure softness, the navel would be deep-set like a small coral atoll. Protected by thick hair instead of *yakshas,* that which once had been sober, hard silence would now be turned into constant, moist smiles. The way her beautiful toes would open up one by one, the way her thighs would shine, and the way her mature legs would extend to support earnestly the discipline and dreams of the dance of life. He wanted to compare all of those with her figure as a little girl.

This was to know time, to know what time had wrought, what time had ripened. If those moles were not to be found on her left side after careful inspection, he would then fall in love with her completely and finally. Transmigration stood barring the way to his love, and samsara held his passion in check.

Awakened from his dreams by Ying Chan's return to the lobby, Honda suddenly voiced what was occupying his thoughts. Despite everything, his words were sharp with the pangs of jealousy.

"I forgot to ask. I heard that you stayed out all night before the party at Gotemba without reporting in at the Foreign Student Center. Was it at a Japanese house?"

"Yes, it was," Ying Chan responded without hesitation, sitting in the armchair next to Honda's, hunching her back a little and scrutinizing her beautiful legs that she held neatly together. "A Thai friend is staying there. The family all insisted I spend the night, so I did."

"It must be an entertaining household with a lot of young people."

"Not exactly. The two sons, the daughter, my Thai friend, and I all played charades. The father heads a big business concern in Southeast Asia, so they're very kind to Southeast Asians."

"Is your Thai friend a boy?"

"No, a girl. Why?"

Again Ying Chan abruptly raised the last syllable of her question.

Then Honda expressed disapproval that she had made so few Japanese friends. He warned her that living abroad made no sense unless she cultivated a variety of people in the country where she was studying. As she might possibly be uncomfortable having dinner with him alone, he offered to bring some young friends along the next time, unconsciously scheming for another opportunity to see her. He extracted from her a promise that at the same day the following week she would come to the lobby of the Imperial at seven o'clock. The thought of Rié made him hesitant to invite her to his own house.

31

HE RETURNED HOME. He got out of the car and felt the
drizzle moisten his temples. The houseboy met him in
the vestibule and informed him that Mrs. Honda was
tired and had retired early. He also reported that a per-
sistent guest had insisted on waiting more than an hour
and was in the small living room to which the houseboy
had been obliged to usher him. Did he recognize the
name Iinuma? asked the youth. At once Honda surmised
that the man had come to ask for money.

It was four years since Honda had last seen Iinuma
at the fifteenth anniversary memorial service for Isao.
At the time it was obvious that Iinuma was quite without funds after the war. Yet he had been favorably impressed by the tasteful, simple memorial service held at
a shrine.

Honda had at once thought it was about money, for
recently people who had not visited him for years would
turn up for no other reason than to ask him for funds.
Unsuccessful lawyers, former attorneys who had become
vagrants, unsuccessful court reporters—all came flock-
ing. Each had heard of Honda's good fortune and each
seemed to think he had some right to a share, since
Honda had come into the money by sheer luck. He
responded only to the requests of the truly humble.

When he entered the reception room, Iinuma rose
from the chair and made a deep obeisance, showing
the back of his wilted suit up to the nape of his gray-
haired neck. Playing the role of a poor man suited him
more than poverty itself. Honda urged him to sit down
and ordered the houseboy to bring whiskey.

Iinuma offered an obvious lie, saying that he had
been just passing by and could not resist the urge to
see Honda. One glass and he pretended to be drunk.
As Honda started to pour another drink, he held the
glass with his right hand and respectfully supported

the bottom with the left. This struck Honda unpleasantly. A rat often held his loot in just such a fashion. Then Iinuma found a cue to start his harangue.

"Well, it seems to me that 'following the reverse course' has come to be the cliché of the day. But the government will start revising the constitution by next year at the latest, I think. The reason everybody's talking about the revival of conscription is because there are really grounds for it. But the infuriating thing is that the foundation can't be brought out in the open and is still underground. By contrast, how do you like how powerful the Reds are getting? How about the disorders in the anti-draft demonstration in Kobé the other day? They called it an 'anti-draft youth rally,' but the strange thing was that a lot of Koreans took part. They fought against the police with not only rocks, but hot pepper, Molotov cocktails, bamboo lances, and everything else. I heard that some three hundred students, children, and Koreans invaded Hyogo Police Station and demanded the release of the ones who had been arrested."

He wants money, Honda thought, paying little attention to what Iinuma was saying. But, he deliberated, he must let Iinuma know that no matter how the New Dealers controlled things with their socialistic policies, no matter how much noise the Reds made, the basis of the private property system would never be shaken. The drizzle outside the window seemed to thicken as though a multilayered curtain of rain was enveloping the house. He had seen Ying Chan off to the Foreign Student Center in a taxi. Since then the thought had not left his mind that this spring rain must have seeped into her simple room in the students' quarters and made it damp. What sort of subtle effect would the humidity have on the girl's body that had matured in the tropics? How did she sleep? Facing the ceiling and breathing hard? Or coiled up with a smile on her lips? Or on her side like the golden reclining figure of Shakyamuni in the Nirvana Hall, arm under head, supine, showing the brilliant soles of her feet?

"The General Rally for the Banishment of Oppressive

Laws by the Kyoto Branch of the General Council of Japanese Labor Unions has got violent too," continued Iinuma. "At this rate, May Day this year isn't going to be any too peaceful; you just can't predict how much violence will break out. Red students take over school buildings in the universities and have confrontations with the police. And this, sir, right after the signing of the Japanese-American Peace Treaty and the Mutual Security Pact. How ironic."

He wants money, thought Honda.

"I'm all in favor of Prime Minister Yoshida's idea about declaring the Communist Party illegal," Iinuma went on. "Japan's in turmoil again. If we let things go on, now that the Peace Treaty is signed, we're going to be thrown headlong into a Communist revolution. Most of the American troops will be gone, and how are you going to control a general strike? I lose a lot of sleep over Japan's future. *What's learned in the cradle is carried to the grave* is true even now."

He wants money, Honda kept thinking. But even after several more drinks Iinuma still did not bring the subject up.

He talked briefly about his divorce two years ago, then suddenly changed the subject to bygone days, and started on a dogged confession how he would never in his life forget the obligation he felt toward Honda, who has given up his judgeship and volunteered to conduct Isao's defense without remuneration. Honda could not bear the thought of Iinuma talking about Isao and he hurriedly interrupted.

Iinuma suddenly took off his jacket. The room was not warm enough to be uncomfortable, but Honda presumed that he was drunk. He took off his necktie next and unbuttoned his white shirt, unfastening even his undershirt to expose a chest which had turned red from the alcohol. Honda could see the almost completely white hairs scattering the light like so many needles.

"To be honest with you, I came to show you this. I have no greater shame. If I could, I would have preferred to hide it from you all my life, but I have been thinking for some time that I would reveal it only to you and let you have a good laugh. I thought only you would really understand me, even my failures. You would know what kind of man I am. I'm honestly and truly ashamed, when I compare myself to my dead son who died so nobly. I have no words to express adequately the depth of my shame at still being alive like this."

Tears ran down his cheeks, and his words came pell-mell:

"This is the scar from when I tried to commit suicide right after the war. My mistake was thinking I might not succeed in committing seppuku, so instead I plunged a dagger into my chest, but missed my heart. I bled like a pig, but I didn't die."

As though showing off, Iinuma caressed the scar that glistened a purplish blue. As a matter of fact, even Honda could see that something had been irreversibly terminated. Iinuma's ruddy, coarse skin had puckered, surrounding the wound and closing it clumsily, underscoring the unsuccessfulness of the attempt.

However, Iinuma's obdurate chest, now covered with white hair, still was proud of what it had once been. Honda finally realized that it was not at all money for which he had come, still he did not feel ashamed for having misjudged his purpose. Iinuma had not changed. Honda found it understandable that even such a man as he should be compelled to distill and crystallize a desperate, soiled, and humiliating deed, that he should strive by so doing to transmute shame into a rare gem, and that he should gradually be overcome by the desire, the need to display it to a trustworthy witness. Whether he was serious or merely pretending, the fact remained that the purple scar on his chest was in the final analysis the only precious thing that remained in his life. Honda had been selected for the unwelcome honor of being witness to this noble action of many years ago.

Iinuma, seeming to have rapidly sobered, put on his clothes, aologized for having overstayed, and extended thanks for the drinks. He was about to leave when Honda stopped him. Wrapping up some fifty thousand yen in bills, he thrust the packet into the pocket of Iinuma's seedy coat despite the protestations of his visitor.

"In that case," said Iinuma finally, thanking Honda with extreme formality, "I accept your kindness with gratitude. It will be a privilege to use it to help revive the Seiken School."

Honda accompanied him to the entrance in the rain. Iinuma's silhouette disappeared through the side gate beneath the pomegranate leaves. It reminded him, for some reason, of one of those countless nocturnal islands that dot the gloomy waters around Japan. An outlying island with no water except the rain—mad, wild, starving.

32

FAR FROM THE PEACE he had expected on placing the ring on Ying Chan's finger, Honda was filled with fear.

He was concerned with the difficult question of how to conceal himself to view her nude. How wonderful it would be if, unaware of him, she would move about full of life or take her self-indulgent ease, revealing every secret in her heart, being completely natural. How wonderful to observe like a biologist every detail. But should his presence be known, then everything would at once collapse.

A perfect crystal of quartz, a glass bowl in which nothing exists but the free play of lovely, subjective being. Ying Chan should be in just such a bowl.

Honda was certain that he had played a part in the crystallization of Kiyoaki's and Isao's transparent lives. In them he had been the extended helping hand, even though it had proven ineffectual and useless. The important thing was that Honda himself had been unaware of his role; he had played his part quite naturally, as a matter of fact quite idiotically, though he himself was convinced that he had been intelligent about it. But after he had become aware! After a torrid India had unsparingly taught him, what help could he have rendered to life? What kind of intervention, what engagement could there be?

Furthermore, Ying Chan was a woman. Hers was a body which filled the cup to its very brim with the unknown darkness of charm. It seduced him. It attracted him constantly toward life. For what purpose? he wondered. He did not know, but one of the reasons was probably that the life to which he was attracted was destined to involve others through the charm it exuded; it was fated to destroy its own roots. Another reason was that he was obliged to realize completely this time the impossibility of involvement in another's life.

Of course Honda was convinced that having Ying Chan in a transparent crystal would constitute the core of his pleasure, but he could not separate that from his innate desire for investigation. Was there no way by which he could harmoniously reconcile these two contradictory tastes and overcome Ying Chan, this black lotus that had bloomed from the mud of life's flow?

In this respect, it would have been better if she had shown some clear sign of being the transmigration of Isao and Kiyoaki. Then Honda's passion would be cooled. Yet on the other hand, had she simply been a girl who had nothing to do with the mystery of rebirth Honda had witnessed, he would not have been so strongly attracted to her. Perhaps the origin of that strength which sternly held his passion in check and that of the extraordinarily powerful attraction existed together in the same samsara. The source of awakening and the origin of samsara and delusion were both samsara.

As he thought of it, Honda strongly wished that he were a man approaching the end of life, someone properly tied and totally complacent. Honda knew a number of such people. Many were discernment itself in turning a profit and rising in the world or in struggling for power; they were adept in grasping the psychology of formidable competitors. Yet when it came to women they were completely ignorant, even though they had slept with several hundreds. Such men were satisfied to surround themselves with the screens of women and flatterers whom they bought with their money and power. Like loons, the women would sit around, showing only one side of their faces. Such men are not free; they're in a cage! thought Honda. They sit in cages made of things that only *their* eyes can see, that void the world and shut it out.

Other men are somewhat wiser. They are rich, powerful, and more aware of human nature. They can know everything about a man, they can penetrate to the core of things by interpreting the slightest surface indication. Super-psychologists who master the taste of life by the bitterness of smartweed vinegar. Whenever they wish they can order the trees and rocks and shrubs shifted in their beautiful little yards, they possess diminutive, refined gardens made of well-organized and well-arranged extractions of the world and life: gardens of real connoisseurs. Such precincts consist of rocks of deception, crape myrtle of coquetry, horsetails of guileness, washbasins of flattery, small waterfalls of loyalty, and the craggy rocks of countless betrayals. They sit the whole day before such allegorical plots, soaking themselves in the quiet pleasure of having disarmed the world and life of all resistance. Yet like a pricelessly rare teacup filled with foaming light green tea they firmly grasp in their hands the bitterness and superiority of cognizant men. Honda was not such a man. He was neither self-satisfied nor secure. And yet he was no longer ignorant either. He had seen only the borderline between the knowable and the unknowable; still it was enough to make him aware. And uncertainty was an incomparable treasure that man could steal from youth. Honda had already taken part in the lives of Kiyoaki and Isao, and had seen forms of fate where it was completely meaningless to extend his hand. It was as if he had been deceived. From the standpoint of fate, living was like being swindled. And human existence . . . signified nothing but the lack of fulfillment, and that he had thoroughly mastered in India.

Nevertheless, the absolutely passive life or life's ultimately ontological form which is not commonly revealed had attracted Honda too much. And he was tainted by the extravagant concept that without such forms there was no life. He quite lacked the qualifications of a seducer. For seducing and deceiving were futile from the standpoint of fate, and "the will to seduce" was itself futile. When one recognized that there was no other form of living except to be naïvely deceived by fate alone, how was it possible to interfere? How could one even glimpse the pure form of such existence? For the moment, one could conceive of such a being only in its absence. Ying Chan, who was self-sufficient in her universe, she who was a universe in herself, must be isolated from him. At times, she was a kind of optical illusion, a corporeal rainbow. Her face was red and her neck orange, her breasts were yellow and she had a green stomach, blue thighs, indigo calves, and violet toes. Above her head was an invisible infrared heart, and below her firmly planted feet were the invisible ultraviolet footprints of memory. The extremity of the rainbow had fused with the heaven of death. She was a rainbow bridging the firmament of death. If "not knowing" was the first factor in eroticism, the ultimate had to be the eternally unknowable . . . death.

When the unexpected amount of money came into his possession, Honda thought like everyone else that he would spend it for his own gratification, but such money was useless for his most essential pleasure. Participation, caring, protection, possession, monopoly—all these things required money, and money had its use; but Honda's pleasure rejected all of them.

He knew that in inexpensive joys lurked thrilling pleasure. The feel of wet moss on the tree trunks in the grove where he had hidden himself, the subtle scent of dead leaves on the ground where he had knelt on a May night of the previous year in the park. The fragrance of young leaves was pungent and lovers lay disheveled on the grass. Auto headlights came and went ruthlessly on the road around the grove. Their beams illuminated the coniferous trees that were like the columns of some shrine and then would tragically and swiftly sweep down the shadowy shafts one after the other; he had shuddered as the light swept over the grass. Momentarily it picked out the almost cruelly sacred beauty of white turned-up underclothes. Only once Honda saw a ray of light pass directly across a woman's face with dreamy eyes. As he had glimpsed the reflection of a speck of light, they must surely have been open, if only partially. It was a ghastly moment when the darkness of human existence was abruptly unveiled, and he had inadvertently seen what he should not have.

To match his tremors with those of the lovers, to synchronize his palpitations with theirs, to share their fear, and at the end of such uniting, to remain an outsider who saw but was not seen. Celebrants of this furtive spying lurked here and there under the trees and in the bushes like crickets. Honda was one of these nameless men.

Young men and women . . . bodies entwined . . . white lower parts exposed. Tenderness of hands moving where the shadows were deepest. White buttocks of men moving like Ping-Pong balls. The almost legal authenticity of their sighs.

Yes, when the headlights momentarily peeled off the darkness of existence, the woman's face had been unexpectedly illuminated. But it was not the ones being observed who were startled, but those who watched behind the trees. When the distant and lyrical siren of a patrol car resounded far outside the night park, where the reflections of neon signs glowed like embers, the watched women did not leave off their debauchery, and their men infallibly raised their virile torsos like young wolves.

On one occasion Honda had lunched with an experienced lawyer, who passed on a bit of gossip he had overheard at some police station. The nasty scandal had never appeared in the papers. It concerned a highly respected man prominent in legal circles, who enjoyed the prestige and respect due his eminent position. He

had become an habitual voyeur and had been appre-
hended by the police. He was sixty-four years old. A
young policeman asked for his personal card, ruthlessly
demanding an account of the old man's offenses. The
hapless lawyer was literally shaking with shame as he
was forced to reconstruct in detail the setting of his vo-
yeurism. During this time he was sternly lectured by the
officer. As soon as the young policeman learned of the
offender's high social status, he ridiculed the poor man
for his own amusement, emphasizing the incredible gap
between the prestige he enjoyed and the sordidness of his
crime. He was fully aware that it was humanly impossible to bridge such a chasm, and yet he had tortured
the man. Under the upbraiding by someone young
enough to be his grandson, the old man had become obsequious, hanging his head and incessantly wiping his
sweaty forehead. After being stuffed with mud slung
by one so low in the governmental bureaucracy, he
was finally discharged. Two years later he died of cancer.

How would he have behaved? Honda wondered.

Honda was suppose to know all about the secret of
how to bridge such a hopeless abyss. The secret formula
from India should have proven effective.

Why hadn't the old judge been able to explain the
nature of his pleasure by using legal jargon?—a pleasure
so strong that it brought tears to the eyes, the most
modest pleasure in life. But even though Honda pretended
to listen casually and to regard it as a piece of amusing
gossip, he could not help wondering throughout the meal
whether there were not some deeper motivation behind
the subject his colleague had brought up. He took care
to smile contemptuously at the critical points just like
the narrator, but he was confused by the cruel contrast
between the solemnity of the pleasure produced and
the misery it evoked. Such an act was as worthless to
the world as a worn-out pair of straw sandals; yet solemnity was concealed in its very core, and that was true
of any kind of pleasure. As a result of that hour-long
ordeal, he had completely renounced the thrill of his

habit. Fortunately, that side of him was known to no one.

It could not be that he was oblivious to danger, because he had overtly humiliated his own reason. The real adventure of a dangerous action is reason, and courage too came from that.

If money could not guarantee security and purchase for him real thrills, then what could he do to grasp fresh life at his age? And yet his hunger for living seemed never to decrease but rather to sharpen with age.

Thus, though he did not wish it, it would be necessary for him to use some sort of intermediary. Even if Ying Chan should by some chance sleep with him, as long as what he really wanted was something she could never show him, then it would be imperative that he employ some roundabout, artificial method to obtain what he needed so much.

Tortured by these thoughts and unable to sleep, he would take out the *Sutra of the Great Golden Peacock Wisdom King,* which had for some time remained undisturbed, accumulating dust on his bookshelf.

At times he murmured the mantra that stood for the achievement of the peacock: *ma yu kitsu ra tei sha ka.*

It was merely a game of conundrums. If he had survived the war because of this sutra, then life sustained by such means seemed all the more worthless.

33

KEIKO SHOWED great interest in the story of the *Sutra of the Peacock Wisdom King.*

"You say that it's efficacious against snakebite? Then I'd love to learn it. There are lots of snakes in my garden at Gotemba."

"I remember just a little of the opening passage. It goes: *ta do ya ta icchi mitchi chiri mitchi chiribiri mitchi.*"

Keiko laughed. "Sounds like the song 'Chiribiribin.'"

Honda felt a childish vexation at her flippant reaction and fell silent.

Keiko had brought along a student from Keio University whom she introduced as her nephew. He was wearing an imported suit and an expensive imported wristwatch. He had narrow eyebrows and thin lips. Honda was startled to realize that his own eyes, when looking at this frivolous modern young man, had involuntarily taken on the censorious stare typical of the members of the old kendo team.

Keiko maintained her self-composure at all times. She gave directions to everyone in regal, placid tones. Any request made of her was followed by elaborate instructions.

Honda had found this out two days before when he had taken her to lunch at the Tokyo Kaikan to celebrate her return to the city. He mentioned his wish to introduce Ying Chan to some suitable boy, "aggressive" if possible. The one word gave the whole ploy away to Keiko.

"I see," she said. "It's inconvenient for you that she's a virgin. I'll bring you my incorrigible nephew the next time we meet. You won't have to worry about any aftermath with that boy. Later you'll be able to play the role of the gentle, sweet, overly kind comfidant and enjoy her at your leisure . . . what a wonderful plan!"

When Keiko said "wonderful," the wonderfulness always seemed to vanish. In pleasure she completely lacked emotion—had she been a prostitute she would have had to pretend. She was too methodical.

Keiko embarked upon an explanation of her nephew's modishness—his name was Katsumi Shimura. She told Honda that he sent his measurements to New York and through an American friend of his father's ordered Brooks Brothers suits for every season of the year. This anecdote alone told much about the young man.

While the story of the *Sutra of the Peacock King* was being retold, Katsumi gazed off into the distance, obviously bored. The lobby of the Imperial Hotel was like the entrance to a tomb with low projecting rocks cutting off the mezzanine; in the shop occupying a corner of the lobby gaudily colored American magazines and paperbacks bloomed in disarray like withered flowers left in a graveyard.

Aunt and nephew closely resembled each other in their inability to listen seriously to what anyone else might be saying. In the nephew's case this was due to mere rudeness, while in the aunt's it seemed to be part of her good manners. Keiko would have listened with the same casual indifference to confessions horrible enough to freeze a normal person to the very marrow.

"The trouble is . . . I don't know for certain that Ying Chan will really show up," said Honda.

"You've developed a phobia about that ever since the housewarming. Let's just relax and wait. If she doesn't come, we can still have fun. The three of us will go to dinner. Katsumi is not particularly the type to be overly anxious."

"Oh, yes . . . well, that's right," Katsumi answered vaguely with his typically overcrisp intonation.

Abruptly Keiko removed a stick of solid perfume from her handbag and rubbed it on her earlobes, from which hung jade earrings.

As though on signal, all the lights in the lobby went out.

"Tisk! A power failure," exclaimed Katsumi. What was the point of saying the power had failed when it already had, thought Honda. Some people spoke only as an apology for their laziness.

Keiko, of course said nothing. The perfume was returned to her bag and the catch clicked in the darkness. The sound seemed to open into a deeper darkness. In the gloom the firm, opulent, sovereign flesh of Keiko's hips seemed to expand secretly and limitlessly with the spreading fragrance of the scent.

The silence was only momentary. As though pushing aside the darkness, the artificially vivacious conversation of the shipwrecked immediately began.

"During the occupation," said Honda, "the American forces had priority on the use of what little electricity there was, so we couldn't help but have blackouts. Yet I'm surprised it goes on."

"Recently during a massive power failure," added Keiko, "I was passing through Yoyogi when I saw that only the American Yoyogi Heights was brightly lit; that one section floating over the darkness of the entire area made it seem like a town of people from another planet. It was beautiful but eerie."

It was dark, but the headlights of the traffic in the streets beyond the pond in the front garden cast light up to the revolving doors of the entrance. One door was rotating from the momentum of someone departing and the headlights shone like luminous stripes in underwater darkness. Honda felt himself quiver slightly as he recalled the scene in the park at night.

"You can breathe so freely and easily in the dark," said Keiko. Honda wanted to ask: And what about the daytime? Keiko's shadow loomed up and sped across the wall. A bellboy had brought candles and when they were placed in ashtrays on several tables the lobby became a veritable cemetery flickering with lights to welcome back the dead.

A taxi drew up at the entrance. Ying Chan entered, dressed in a lovely canary-yellow dress. Honda was astounded at the miracle: she was only fifteen minutes late.

Ying Chan was beautiful in the candlelight. Her hair melted into the darkness; the many flames flickering in her eyes and the brilliance of her teeth were even more lovely than in electric light. The front of the canary-yellow dress rose and fell with each breath, exaggerating the shadows.

"Do you remember me? I am Mrs. Hisamatsu. It's been some time since we met in Gotemba," said Keiko. Ying Chan did not even thank her for that occasion and only nodded charmingly.

Keiko introduced Katsumi, who offered his seat. Honda knew at once that the boy had been strongly impressed by Ying Chan's beauty.

She casually opened her hand on which she wore the

emerald, but not in any effort to show it off to Honda. In the candlelight the stone reflected a green like the wings of some iridescent insect that had just flown in. The protecting *yakshas*' impressive golden faces were angry and full of shadows. Honda interpreted the fact that Ying Chan had worn the ring as an expression of her sweetness.

Keiko immediately spotted the jewel and without ado drew Ying Chan's hand to her.

"How unusual. Is it Thai?"

She could not have forgotten her close inspection of the stone at Gotemba, but her manner was so natural and convincing it quite seemed to have slipped her mind.

Staring into a candle flame, Honda silently wagered with himself whether Ying Chan would tell that it had been a gift from him.

"Yes, it's from Thailand," said Ying Chan simply. He was relieved by the answer and charmed with the graceful naturalness of the entire episode he had created.

As though she had already forgotten about the ring, Keiko, taking the initiative, arose.

"Let's go to Manuela's. Since we shall be going to a nightclub anyway, we might just as well have dinner there. The food is quite good."

Katsumi was driving a Pontiac that had been purchased under some American name. It would take them less than two minutes to reach their destination.

Ying Chan sat beside the driver, and Honda and Keiko rode in back. Keiko's bearing when getting in and out of cars was spectacular. As far back as she could remember, she had always had the habit of climbing in before anyone else. She never sidled along on skirted hips to the far seat, but would aim at the place where she would be sitting and in one motion, without hesitation, deposit there her amphoralike buttocks.

Ying Chan's long black hair cascaded over the back of the seat, and from behind it was especially magnificent. It reminded Honda of black ivy hanging from the ramparts of some deserted castle. During the day, the inevitable lizard would be resting in the shade. . . .

Miss Manuela owned a small, fashionable nightclub in the basement of a building across from the Japan Broadcasting Association. The brunette Eurasian dancer cheerfully greeted her faithful customers as soon as she recognized Keiko and Katsumi coming down the staircase in the vanguard of the little party.

"Oh, welcome! Katsumi, too! You're very early tonight. Feel free to take over." At this early hour no one was to be seen on the dance floor, and the only music came across its emptiness like a north wind scattering the fragments of light from the mirror ball as if they were scraps of white paper flying about on midnight streets.

"Wonderful! We have the club to ourselves!" said Keiko, stretching her sumptuously ringed hands into the dark space. Over this sweeping exclamation, the gleaming wind instruments sounded sadly.

"Oh, don't bother," said Keiko, stopping Miss Manuela, who, in place of the waiter, was on the point of taking orders for drinks. "Do sit down." Katsumi stood up and offered her a chair. Only after he had done so did Keiko introduce Ying Chan and Honda, and referring to the latter, added: "This gentleman is my new friend. I've acquired a Japanese taste."

"That's fine. You're really too Americanized. It's better to get rid of some of that American odor."

Miss Manuela pretended to sniff around Keiko in an exaggerated way, and Keiko responded theatrically by acting ticklish. Ying Chan laughed heartily at these antics and nearly upset a glass of water on the table. Honda was a little perplexed, and he and Katsumi glanced at each other. On reflection, he realized that this was the very first time their eyes had met.

Keiko, as if suddenly remembering, recovered her dignity.

"Did you have trouble when the power failed a while ago?" she asked fatuously.

"Of course not. We serve only by candlelight," Miss

Manuela answered with a lordly air; and white teeth gleaming in the gloom, she turned her friendly smile to Honda.

Members of the orchestra would greet Keiko when they left their seats, and she would answer by waving her white hand. Everything rotated around her.

The four had dinner, and while Honda did not enjoy eating in dark places, he had no alternative. The blood oozing from his slice of chateaubriand should have been bright red, but it appeared dismally dark.

Customers began to increase in number. Honda was aghast when he imagined how others would regard him, acting young in a place of entertainment such as this. The sooner the revolution the better; people were saying there would be one.

Honda was caught by surprise when his three companions simultaneously arose. The two women had stood up to go to the powder room and Katsumi had risen in accordance with prescribed etiquette. Katsumi sat down again, and the man of fifty-seven and the other of twenty, left together in the midst of music and dancing, remained silent, looking in different directions, having nothing to say.

Suddenly Katsumi spoke up rather hoarsely: "She's charming."

"Do you like her?"

"I've always been taken by dark, petite, and glamorous types that can't talk Japanese very well. How shall I say? . . . I probably have somewhat peculiar tastes."

"Really?" Honda responded with a soft smile, yet he was repelled by Katsumi's words.

"What do you think about the body?" he asked.

"Well, I've never given it much thought. Do you mean sensualism?" the young man answered glibly, quickly lighting Honda's cigarette with his Dunhill lighter.

"For instance, suppose you have a bunch of grapes. If you grasp them too hard they'll be crushed. But if you hold them just so as not to bruise them, then the fullness of the skin will put up a subtle resistance to your fingers. That's what I mean by 'body.' "

"I think I understand," answered the young student thoughtfully, eager to act as an adult, doubtless bolstering his self-confidence with the weight of his memories.

"Fine if you do. That's all I meant," said Honda, terminating the conversation.

Later Katsumi asked Ying Chan to dance; they returned to the table after three consecutive numbers.

"I couldn't help but remember your theory about the grapes," Katsumi said to Honda with a look of innocence.

"What are you talking about?" Keiko asked. The conversation faded into the noisy music and was lost.

Honda never tired of watching Ying Chan dance, though he himself did not know how. In movement she was free of the handicaps of living in a foreign land and her natural disposition was happily revealed. Her slim neck, relatively small for her body, moved well. Her ankles were delicate and quick. She danced on her toes, and under her swaying skirt her beautiful legs, like two tall palms on a distant island, moved swiftly. Languidness and vitality constantly alternated; hesitation and liveliness shifted at every instant, and while she was dancing her smile never disappeared. When she whirled around at Katsumi's fingertips during a jitterbug number, her body had already turned, but the gleam of her white teeth still remained visible like a half moon.

34

THE WORLD was filled with ominous portents.

A riot broke out in front of the Imperial Palace on May Day. The police shot into the mob and the situation deteriorated. Six or seven demonstrators formed a group and attacked an American car, turning it over and setting it on fire. An assaulted policeman abandoned his white motorcycle, which was immediately burned. An American sailor, who had fallen into the moat around the palace, popped up and down in the water because whenever he lifted his head demonstrators threw stones at him. Flames sprang up all over the square in front of the palace. During the riot American soldiers stood guard with fixed bayonets at the General Headquarters in Hibiya and at the Meiji Life Insurance Building.

It was an extraordinary event. No one believed that things would end here, and everyone suspected that other, larger-scale riots must be in store for the future.

Honda did not go to his office in the Marunouchi Building that day and did not actually see the demonstration, but when he heard about it on the radio and read the details in the newspapers he felt the situation to be serious enough. He had spent the wartime period rather uninvolved, yet now in peace he could not ignore what was happening about him. He felt insecure with the three customary ways of investing money and resolved to consult about the future with a friend who advised him on financial matters.

The next day, unable to sit still at home, he set out for a walk. The early-summer sun was shining; nothing seemed out of the ordinary. Avoiding the old store that sold serious material such as legal books, he entered a shop in the front of which magazines were displayed in random piles. He had formed the habit over the years of always going to bookstores on his walks.

The multitude of tiles on the spines soothed him. Everything was stored away in the form of concepts. Human love and desire, political unrest were all committed to writing and lined up in tranquility. Furthermore, one could find anything one desired, from books on knitting to international politics.

He did not know why he felt so relaxed on entering a bookshop; it was a habit formed in childhood. Kiyoaki and Isao had had nothing like it. How had it come about? he wondered. Did he feel insecure unless he constantly surveyed the entire world? Was it obstinacy that would not let him recognize facts that had not been recorded in print? According to Stéphane Mallarmé, sooner or later everything would be expressed in writing. If the world ended up in a great beautiful book, it would never be too late to dash over to the bookstore after it had all been printed.

Yes, yesterday's events were already finished. Here there were no flames from Molotov cocktails, no shouts, no violence. One could not even sense the distant repercussions of bloodshed. An amiable citizen trailed by a child was hunting through the books; a fat woman in a light green sweater holding a shopping bag arrogantly asked if the latest issue of some women's magazine had not yet come out. In the back of the store a vase with an arrangement of irises—a hobby of the storekeeper —had been placed below a framed piece of unskilled calligraphy which read: "Reading is nourishment for the heart."

Honda circled around in the congested store, bumping into customers. As he could find nothing he liked, he went to the shelves on which popular magazines were displayed. There a young man in a sports shirt, apparently a student, was engrossed in a magazine. From a distance, Honda could see that he had been staring at a single page with extraordinary earnestness. Approaching on the right side of the youth, he casually glanced at the leaf.

He saw a poorly printed, opaque blue photogravure of a naked woman sitting tied with a rope and leaning to one side. The boy never took his eyes from the magazine which he held in his left hand.

Honda noticed that the youth was strangely rigid—the neck, profile, and eyes were somehow unnaturally strained like those of a figure in some Egyptian relief. Then he saw clearly that the youth's right hand which was thrust into his trouser pocket was violently and mechanically moving.

Honda left the bookstore at once. His stroll had been spoiled.

—Why had he had to do such a thing in front of people? Didn't he have the money to buy the magazine? If that were so, I would have paid for it myself and given it to him. Yes, why didn't I do that right away? I really shouldn't have hesitated to give him the money.

But Honda's thoughts changed in the interval between two electric poles by the roadside.

—No, I don't believe that that was the case. If he really wanted the magazine, it was cheap enough for him to buy just by pawning his fountain pen.

The magazine should not have been purchased and taken home. From this point on, Honda's imagination ran riot. For some reason the youth did not quite seem to be a total stranger.

Not wishing to go home and face his wife with such thoughts on his mind, he chose a roundabout way and continued straight on instead of turning when he came to the corner of the Methodist Church.

Probably the reason the youth had not taken the magazine home was not at all because his family was strict or because he had no place to hide it. Honda arbitrarily came to the conclusion that the young man lived alone in a rooming house. It was obvious that as soon as the youth returned home the loneliness eagerly awaiting him would jump at him like a house pet; and he would have been afraid to open the picture of the trussed and naked woman, to share his pleasure with the loneliness. There, probably, waited the absolute freedom of the prison which the youth had himself constructed. In the tiny space, barren and square, in the dark nest filled with the smell of semen, he must have been afraid to face the naked blue woman writhing under the tightening rope that crushed her breasts, her nostrils spread like the wings of a dove. It was like committing murder to face a tightly bound woman in such perfect freedom. Thus he had chosen to expose himself to the public gaze. He had wanted to project himself into the role of a man tied by the ropes of people's eyes and to face the woman bound in danger and humiliation. The odious conditions he had chosen represented the sine qua non as subtle and delicate as silk thread that is concealed in all sexual love.

The seductions of a very special, extraordinarily sweet vulgarity . . . The boy would not have been consumed with desire for the girl had she been a beautiful photographic model. Sexuality that storms day and night like a gale through the metropolis. A great dark over-abundance. The streets across which shoot the flames of Molotov cocktails. The great underground canal of hidden sexual passion. When Honda saw the imposing stone pillars of his house, standing since his father's days, he realized he would have to live in a fashion very different from the way his father had lived out his old age. When he pushed open the side gate and saw the great white magnolia flowers in full bloom on the tips of their tall branches, he suddenly felt the fatigue of his walk and wished he could devote the rest of his life to creating haiku.

35

HONDA SUGGESTED a talk with Keiko and Katsumi, inasmuch as he had to pick up a box of cigars which he had asked her to get. Katsumi drove to meet him at his office building. It was an early summer afternoon and the sun was strong.

Genuine Havana cigars were unavailable, but tobacco products from Florida could be purchased at the PX. Since Keiko would be shopping for cigars at the former Matsuya department store, now the PX, Katsumi informed him they were to meet her there.

Honda could not himself enter the PX, of course. He had Katsumi stop in front, and they watched the exits from the car window. Outside the white-curtained PX windows numerous caricaturists loitered about, hounding the American soliders who emerged. The young soldiers, apparently back from Korea, put up little resistance as they amiably stood to be sketched. Among them an American girl wearing blue jeans, probably on a shopping trip, was sitting on the brass rail of a window having her portrait done.

It was an interesting scene to watch while killing time in the car. The serious-faced American soldiers, looking

quite professional, posed for the drawings with no feelings
of shyness before the spectators. It was hard to tell which
was the customer. Spectators surrounded them, and
as soon as someone grew tired of watching and left,
another immediately took his place. The rosy faces of
the tall Americans stood out like the heads of statues
above the mass of bystanders.

"She's late," Honda commented to Katsumi as he
got out of the car to stretch his legs in the sunlight.

He joined the crowd to look at the American girl.
Hardly pretty, she was swinging her blue-jeaned legs.
She wore a short-sleeved plaid blouse that looked like
a man's shirt. A shaft of light falling through the building
fell diagonally across half of her freckled cheek and
was regularly deflected by the movements of her jaw
as she chewed a wad of gum. She was not particularly
cold or arrogant. The curious stares had not affected
her natural poise in the slightest, and the deep-set brown
eyes, as if propped open, gazed blankly into space almost
without moving.

She looked at the people as though she were watching
the air; such a girl might be someone Honda was looking
for. When he realized it, he felt a sudden stir of interest
like rapidly curling ends of hair that have been set on
fire. It was then that a man standing next to him spoke.
He had been glancing at Honda's face for some time.
"We've met somewhere before, haven't we?" he said at
length.

Honda saw a shortish, rodentlike man in a seedy
suit. His hair was cut straight at the temples, and his
restless eyes held the glint of an ominous obsequiousness.
At once Honda felt uneasy.

"Who could you be? I'm sorry, but I don't seem
to . . ." he said coldly.

"Don't you remember? We're peeping chums under
the trees in the park," he said, stretching to whisper
in Honda's ear.

Despite his efforts not to, Honda paled.

"What do you mean?" he said coolly. "You've
mistaken me for someone else." A bitter sneer instantly

appeared on the little man's face. Honda knew that this sneer was like cracks in underground strata that sometimes had the power of instantly toppling great buildings. But at the moment there was no real proof. And still better, Honda no longer had any prestige to guard. It was thanks to this sneer that he clearly realized his present lack of social position.

Honda shouldered the man aside and began to walk toward the entrance of the PX. Opportunely Keiko appeared.

She came out, breasts high, dressed in a purple suit and followed by an American soldier whose face was almost completely hidden behind a mountainous armful of paper bags. Honda thought it might be her lover, Jack, but it was not.

In the middle of the pavement, Keiko introduced Honda to the soldier, and referring to the latter, explained: "I don't know his name, but he was kind enough to offer to help carry my packages to the car."

Seeing Honda talking with an American soldier, the little man hastened away.

A huge, brilliant golden brooch, like the metal of the Great Order of the Chrysanthemum, shone on Keiko's breast. She marched straight up to the car where Katsumi was respectfully waiting in the May sunshine. He held the door open and playfully bowed her in.

The soldier handed the paper bags one by one to Katsumi, who staggered, barely able to hold them.

It was a fine spectacle. The crowd in front of the PX stood watching with gaping mouths, quite forgetting the caricaturists.

When the car started to move, Keiko waved to the courteous soldier and he responded. So did two or three other men in the crowd.

"What popularity!" Honda commented rather flippantly to show himself how quickly he could recover from the traumatic episode.

Keiko laughed contentedly and said: "There is kindness to be found everywhere." In great haste she took out a handkerchief heavily embroidered in the Chinese

style and blew her nose loudly like a Westerner. The
nose showed no signs of damage afterwards. It was
as high and magnificent as usual.

"That's because you sleep naked every night," said
Katsumi who was driving.

"What a rude thing to say! As though you've ever
seen me . . . By the way, where shall we go?"

Honda was apprehensive about walking around the
Ginza area lest they run into the small man again.

"Let's go to that new . . . what's the building? . . .
at the corner of Hibiya," he said irritably, unable to remember.

"You mean the Nikkatsu Hotel?" said Katsumi. And
soon, glimpsing the soiled mustard color of the river
through the crowd, they crossed the Sukiya Bridge.

Keiko was most kind and also intelligent, but that
she lacked a certain gentleness was obvious. Of any
subject—literature, art, music, or even philosophy—she
spoke with her extravagant feminine, pleasure-loving
enthusiasm as though she were talking about perfume
or necklaces. She never actually paraded her erudition
in art or philosophy, and her knowledge was not necessarily balanced; but in some fields her information was
quite thorough.

As he recalled, upper-class women of the late nineteenth and early twentieth centuries were either stuffy
self-appointed virtuous types or brazen minxes, so
Keiko's well-roundedness surprised him. But he could
foresee trouble for the man who became her husband.
She was never cruel, but in her one sensed a certain intolerable fastidiousness in little things.

Could that be a defense? But for what purpose? To
be sure, she had never been raised in such a way that
she would require armor. She had never found it necessary
to fight the world. Rather, the world always showed
her deference, and one felt in her a kind of purity that
was overpowering in its authority.

Keiko was congenitally incapable of distinguishing

between affection and favor, and thus anyone she granted a boon might assume that she loved him.

This occasion was no exception. On the mezzanine overlooking the lobby that resembled a new rugby field, Keiko, a glass of sherry before her, began giving instructions. Honda was overwhelmed. It was as though he were listening to a lecture in a course on French cooking on how to prepare a fowl named Ying Chan.

"You've seen her twice since then. How were things? How far do you think you can go?" she asked Katsumi first. Then she pulled out a large box of cigars, which she seemed to have forgotten about until that moment, and silently placed it in Honda's lap.

"How did it go? I think the time's almost ripe."

Honda traced the pattern on the cigar box with his fingers. It reminded him of the paper currency of some small European country, its gold coins and pink ribbons embossed in golden letters on a green background. He was conjuring up the aroma of cigars; he had not smoked for some time. Simultaneously he sharply repelled Katsumi's words. Nevertheless, he was surprised when he discovered himself enjoying the repugnance like an omen of something.

"Did you at least kiss her?" asked Keiko.

"Yes, once."

"How was it?"

"How was it . . . ? Well, I took her back to the Foreign Student Center and kissed her just a little behind the gate."

"Yes? And how was it?"

"She seemed pretty flustered. It was probably her first time."

"That doesn't sound like you. Couldn't you have gone further?"

"But she's special. She's a princess."

Keiko turned to Honda. "The best way," she said, "would be for you to take her to Gotemba. Why don't you say you're throwing a party and invite her to stay overnight? As late as possible. She can't very well turn you down because you know she's stayed out other nights;

and besides, she has to make up for the party she stood you up on. If she's alone with Katsumi she'll be on her guard, so you must go with them. Of course, Katsumi will drive. You can tell her that I'll be waiting in Gotemba. It won't be true, but I won't be inconvenienced . . . When you reach your villa she'll find it strange that no one else is there. But even so, a foreign princess can't possibly run away, so it must be left to Katsumi. You can leave her to him for the night and wait for your *canard à l'orange* to be ready."

36

IT WAS MIDNIGHT at Ninooka in Gotemba. After putting out the fire in the fireplace, Honda took his umbrella and strolled from the living room out to the terrace.

There, in front, the swimming pool had already taken shape, and the rain was beating on the rough concrete. It was far from completed, and even the ladder was not yet attached. In the light from the terrace the rainy concrete was the color of grayish liquid. The swimming pool was being constructed by workers from Tokyo, and progress was necessarily slow.

It was obvious even in the nocturnal darkness that the swimming pool was not adequately drained. Honda decided he must tell the contractor when he returned to Tokyo. The many puddles in the bottom of the pool were pelted by the rain, producing ripples that wretchedly captured the reflections of light from the distant terrace. Night fog rose from the western end of the valley and hung motionless in the middle of the green. It was extremely cold.

The unfinished pool had begun to look like a gigantic grave pit, big enough and more for a legion of skeletons. Actually it did not *begin* to appear, it had never been anything else. The water would splash up if skeletons were dropped to the bottom and then grow calm, and the dried bones would immediately soak up the water and become glossy and fresh. Old-time Japanese, on reaching Honda's age, would have thought of building a treasury storagehouse celebrating longevity. Honda was building, of all things, a swimming pool! It was a cruel attempt to float his sagging decrepit flesh in an abundance of blue water. Honda had acquired the habit of spending money only for games full of malice. How the Hakoné mountains and the summer clouds reflecting in the water of the pool would brighten his old age! And what a grimace Ying Chan would make if she ever discoverd that he had built it precisely because he wished to see her naked body at close hand in the summer.

Honda started to return to lock the doors, when, raising the umbrella, he glanced up at the lights on the second floor. Four windows were still bright. They were in the two guest rooms adjacent to the study next to which Ying Chan was staying. Katsumi occupied the room beyond that.

Despite the umbrella, raindrops soaked his trousers and seemed to penetrate to his knees. In the night chill tiny red flowers of pain secretly blossomed in his various joints. He imagined them to be something like miniature *higan-bana*. The bones that in his youth had modestly hidden in his flesh playing out their roles were now in his old age beginning more and more to claim existence. They had begun to sing and complain, breaking through the deteriorating flesh and attempting to escape from the stubborn darkness of the body. They were constantly watching for opportunities to dash into the outside world where they could bask in the sun as freely as the young leaves, rocks, and trees that enjoyed sunshine all the time. Doubtless they knew that the day was not far off when they would realize their dreams.

Watching the lights on the second floor, Honda suddenly became warm as he thought of Ying Chan disrobing. Did bones take on heat? Had the red flowers in his joints developed hay fever? Honda quickly locked the doors, turned out the lights in the living room, and stealthily went upstairs. He entered from the bedroom door so that he could proceed noiselessly to the study. He felt his way to the bookcases in the darkness. His hands trembled as he removed one after the other the thick foreign volumes. At last he put his eye to the peephole in the back of the case.

Ying Chan entered the circle of dim light humming a song; he had never craved for any moment so much as this. It was the yearning one felt while waiting for a calabash flower to bloom on the verge of a summer evening. It was the moment at which a slowly opening fan revealed its complete picture. Honda was going to see Ying Chan in a state that as yet had been seen by no one. This was what he wanted more than anything else in the world. By his act of watching, this unseen condition was already destroyed. Being seen by absolutely no one and being unaware of being seen were similar, yet basically different.

Ying Chan had been surprisingly calm when she arrived at the villa and learned that the plans for the party were untrue.

From the time of their arrival Honda had worried about the explanation he must make. Katsumi had left all that to him in order to remain blameless in the matter. However, explanations were unnecessary. When Honda started a fire in the fireplace and gave her a drink, Ying Chan smiled happily and asked no questions. She might have thought that she had misunderstood his Japanese when she had originally been invited. Invitations extended in a foreign language often lead to misunderstandings and confusion. The reason Ying Chan had renewed acquaintance with Honda when she first came to Japan was because the Japanese ambassador to Thailand, having heard from others about Honda's former connections with Thai royalty, had written a letter of introduction. He had requested that Honda speak Japanese as much as possible so that the Princess might improve her command of the language.

As he watched Ying Chan, who seemed quite unaware of any danger, Honda was filled with a kind of pity.

She was crouching by a fire in a strange country, involuntarily involved in a conspiracy of the flesh that was far from tender. The flames reflected on the sides of her bronze cheeks, and her hair seemed to smolder. Her constant smile and her beautiful white teeth produced in him an indescribable sense of pity.

"When your father was in Japan, he was always frozen in winter. He couldn't wait for summer. You must feel that way too."

"Yes. I don't like cold weather."

"Well, it'll last only a little longer. In two months it will not be very different here from summer in Bangkok. As I look at you now I remember your father in cold weather. And I remember when I was young," said Honda, going to the fireplace to flick the ash from his cigar. He stole a glance at Ying Chan's lap from above. Whereupon her knees that had been opened closed like sensitive mimosa leaves.

All three had pushed aside the chairs and were sitting on the rug in front of the fire, and Honda could see Ying Chan in her various postures. She could, for example, sit nobly erect in a chair or relax on her side, her lovely legs crossed on the floor, playing the seductive Western woman. But sometimes she would suddenly break these patterns and surprise Honda, as when she had first come to the fire. She had hunched her shoulders from the cold, thrusting out her chin, miserably burying her neck; the way she talked and waved her thin wrists in the air suggested a certain Chinese-type shallowness. She had gradually drawn closer to the fire and sat facing it like the women who sold fruit in the deep green shade of the tropical afternoon markets with the blazing sunlight before them. With both legs rigid, hips suspended in the air, she bent over so that her voluptuous breasts and full thighs pushed against each other. The center of gravity lay at the contact point of crushed breast and thigh, around which her body swayed slightly in an incredibly vulgar manner. At such times the tension on her flesh was concentrated in her buttocks, her thighs, her back, in all the ignoble places of her body, and

Honda sensed a sharp odor of wilderness like that created by the heaps of dead leaves in the jungle.

Katsumi feigned calmness, and the patterns of the cut-glass brandy tumbler reflected on his white hand, but he was obviously irritable. Honda disdained his sexual desire.

"It'll be all right tonight. I'll have your room very warm," said Honda, forestalling the question of her staying overnight before it came up. "There'll be two big electric heaters. Thanks to Keiko's connections we were given an electric capacity as big as the one at Occupation Forces' quarters."

But Honda did not explain why this Western-style house did not have a Western heating system or even a Korean or a Chinese one. People had suggested a wall system using coal instead of oil, which was so difficult to obtain. His wife too had liked the idea, but Honda had not agreed. Wall heating consisted of passing hot air through double walls, and it was essential for him to have the walls of only one thickness.

He had pretended to his wife that he was making the trip alone, claiming he wanted to do some research undisturbed. Her words when he was about to leave, ordinary considerate words, had remained in his mind like curses: "Don't catch cold. It's frigid at Gotemba. On a rainy day like this it'll be colder than you think. Take good care of yourself."

Honda put his eye against the peephole. His eyelashes, turning inward, pricked his thin eyelids.

Ying Chan had not yet changed her clothes. The night kimono that had been laid out still lay on the bed. She was seated in a chair in front of the mirror and was earnestly gazing at something. He first thought it was a book, but it was much smaller and thinner and looked rather like a photograph. Curious to know whose picture it was, he tried all angles, but he could not manage to see it.

She was humming a monotonous melody to herself. It sounded like a Thai song. Honda had heard such popular tunes in Bangkok, sung in the high, squeaky tone of a Chinese fiddle. It suddenly brought back memories of the brilliant metal links in the chains around the banks at night or the boisterous scenes of the canal markets in the mornings.

Ying Chan put the photograph in her purse and walked two or three steps toward the bed; that is, toward the peephole. Honda's heart leaped. It seemed as though she would break through the wall and attack him. But instead, she jumped up on the farther of the two beds which was still covered by a spread and leaped from it to the one by the wall, which had already been made up for her. He could only see her legs.

Ying Chan bounced two or three times on the bed, turning with each leap in a different direction. He could see that the seams of her stockings were twisted.

Her beautiful legs were encased in gleaming nylon; her calves were smooth and tapered to firm ankles. Her soles were still in contact with the mattress, and she bounced by lightly bending her knees, her fluttering skirt momentarily exposing areas far above her knees. On the upper part of her stockings, where the texture was different and the beige darker, garter buttons like pale green peas were visible. Farther up, the bare dark skin of her thighs was like a dusky dawn sky seen through a skylight.

As she jumped, Ying Chan appeared to lose her balance, and the legs before his eyes began to fall to the right as if to disappear; but she descended from the bed without mishap. This was probably her childish habit of testing an unfamiliar bed.

Next she inspected the details of the night kimono Honda had put out for her. She placed it over her dress and looked at herself from all angles in front of the mirror. Then she removed it and settled down in the chair before the mirror. With both hands she grasped the clasp of the gold necklace behind her neck and skillfully undid it. She raised her fingers before the mirror and started to take off the ring, but then stopped. For Honda, watching her mirror image, Ying Chan's slow movements and her expression were as if under water or possibly maneuvered by remote control.

Instead of taking off the band, she raised her hand high toward the ceiling light. The man's emerald ring, conspicuous on her finger, sparkled greenly, and the monstrous faces of the golden protector *yakshas* glowed.

Finally, reaching back with both hands, she began to undo the small hook above the fastener of her dress. Honda held his breath.

Ying Chan stopped her movement and turned her face toward the door on the right. It was being unlocked with the spare key Honda had provided and Katsumi was opening it. Honda bit his lip, vexed by the bad timing. If Katsumi had come two or three minutes later, Ying Chan would have had her clothes off.

The sudden apprehension of the innocent girl was transformed in the dim round frame of the peephole into a painting of a critical moment. She did not yet know who might be coming through the door. Perhaps a great white peacock would strut arrogantly in, filling the room with the fragrance of lilies. And the flutter of its wings and its cries, like the squeaking of a pulley, would transform the entire room into the quiet hall of the Rosette Palace that one afternoon . . .

But what entered the room was an overly affected mediocrity. Katsumi did not so much as excuse himself for opening the door without knocking, but awkwardly mumbled that not being able to sleep, he had come to talk with her. The girl, resuming her smile, offered him a chair, and the two began a long conversation. Katsumi spoke flatteringly in English and Ying Chan became suddenly talkative. Peeping through his hole, Honda yawned.

Katsumi placed his hand on hers, and as she did not withdraw it, Honda watched intently. But he could not maintain the position for long, for it strained his neck.

He leaned against the bookcase and tried to follow what was going on by the sounds. The darkness released his imagination, and in his thoughts things progressed step by step much more rationally than what was really happening in the room. In his imagination Ying Chan's disrobing had already begun, and her brilliant nakedness had flowered. When she raised her left arm and smiled, the three moles appeared on her left side, symbols of the stars in the seductive tropical night sky, symbols of his proscription. He covered his eyes, and the image of the stars immediately shattered in the darkness.

There was a stir.

Honda hastily put his eye to the hole and in so doing bumped his head on the corner of the bookcase. The noise worried him more than the pain, but the situation on the other side of the wall was beyond any concern about small noises.

Katsumi was holding onto a resisting Ying Chan. The two bodies struggled in and out of the circular field of the peephole. The girl's dress was unzipped and her brown, perspiring, angular back with brassiere straps was visible. She freed her right hand and lashed out with clenched fist. The green emerald sparkled like a flying beetle and scraped along Katsumi's cheek. He drew back, putting his hand to his face. Soon there was the noise of him opening the door and leaving the room. Ying Chan was out of breath. Looking about, she dragged away one of the chairs, probably to prop against the door.

Honda panicked. Katsumi, who pretended to be so mature, was really a spoiled child, and he might well come by to borrow a first aid kit for his cheek.

Honda went to work at once. One by one he returned the thick books to the bookcase and with the meticulousness of a criminal checked that none of the titles had been replaced upside down. He verified that the door to the study was locked, turned off the heater, and stole back to his bedroom. He changed into pajamas, threw his clothes on the dresser, and crept into bed. He was prepared to act like someone interrupted in sleep when Katsumi's knock came at the door.

This became an experience of Honda's unknown "youth." The swiftness and nimbleness of a dormitory student who has violated the rules and crept back to bed with an air of innocence. Though he lay quietly, his heart palpitated so rapidly that the pillow, alive, seemed to jump up and down. It did not quiet for some time.

Katsumi was probably hesitating whether to come to see him or not. This long hesitation must be the result of calculation, the weighing of the advantages and disadvantages of an impulsive visit. While he was waiting, but not really expecting Katsumi, Honda fell asleep.

* * *

The rain had stopped by morning and a golden brocade of sunlight cascaded through the gap between the curtains over the east window.

Honda wrapped a scarf about his neck and in his thick gown went down to the kitchen, intending to prepare breakfast for the young people. He found Katsumi already sitting in a chair in the living room neatly dressed.

"Well, you're up early," Honda called halfway down the staircase, glancing swiftly at his pale cheeks.

Katsumi had already built a fire in the fireplace. He did not actually seem to be hiding his left cheek, and Honda was disappointed not to see a large scar in the firelight. There was a light scratch that could be explained away by any simple story.

"Won't you sit down for a while?" Katsumi indicated a chair as though he were the host.

"Good morning," Honda said again in greeting and sat down.

"I felt I ought to talk with you alone. I got up particularly early," said Katsumi as if he had done Honda a great favor.

"And . . . how was it?"

"Good."

"What do you mean 'good'?"

"Just as I expected." The young man smiled, suggesting

something profoundly significant. "She looks like a mere child, but she really isn't."

"Did it seem like the first time for her?"

"I'm the first . . . My successors will be green with envy, I'm sure."

It seemed needless to pursue the matter further, and Honda changed the subject. "By the way, did you happen to notice, she has some peculiar marks . . . on her left side . . . three, almost artificially magnificent moles all in a line. Didn't you see them?"

A momentary confusion crossed Katsumi's smug face. Many answers were possible, and there was the question of saving face too. He quickly concluded that the telling of lies had better be sacrificed for a more important occasion. It was interesting to speculate on the many possible responses passing through the young man's mind. Suddenly Katsumi leaned back in his chair with an exaggerated gesture of surprise.

"You win!" he said in a high voice. "You're a hard man, Mr. Honda! I'm losing my grip. I was fooled by her English when she seemed to say that it was the first time. You know her body already!"

It was Honda's turn to smile suggestively.

"I'm asking whether you saw the moles."

The young man answered tensely. He was being pressed to test his feigned composure. "Of course I saw them. They were slightly wet with perspiration and all three of them moving together in the dim light. With her dark skin they had a sort of mysterious and unforgettable beauty."

Honda went to the kitchen and prepared breakfast of coffee and croissants. Katsumi volunteered to help, but his anxiousness to do so was quite uncharacteristic of him. As if forced by a sense of obligation, he set out the plates, asked Honda where the teaspoons were kept, and arranged them on the table. For the first time Honda felt something akin to friendship bordering on pity toward the young man.

They argued about who should take the breakfast

to Ying Chan's room. Claiming the host's prerogative, Honda placed the dishes on a tray and slowly carried it upstairs.

He knocked on Ying Chan's door. There was no answer. Putting the tray down on the floor, he opened the door with a duplicate passkey. Wedged shut by something on the inside, it was difficult to force.

Honda looked around the room filled with morning light. She was gone.

37

OF LATE Mrs. Tsubakihara had been meeting Imanishi frequently.

She was quite blind. She was unable to form intelligent opinions about men. Nor could she judge one by sight and tell what kind of person he was . . . pig or wolf or vegetable. And such a woman was trying to write poetry of all things.

If awareness of suitability was the indication of a proud love affair, no one could appease Imanishi's self-consciousness as much as this woman, blind to any kind of suitability. She had begun to love the forty-year-old man like a son.

No one was further than Imanishi from possessing physical youthfulness, freshness, or courage. He had a weak stomach, sallow, unresilient skin, and was quick to catch colds. His long body, devoid of developed muscles, was like a long, limp sash, and he swayed when he walked. He was, in other words, an intellectual.

It should have been very difficult to love such a man, but just as Mrs. Tsubakihara turned out bad poetry with such ease, so had she fallen in love with no difficulty whatever. In anything and everything, her lack of skill was brilliant. Her docility and self-admitted love of criticism made her listen happily to Imanishi's constant personal rebukes. In all things she espoused the concept that criticism was a shortcut to improvement.

As a matter of fact, Imanishi had something in common with her. He was not annoyed by her girlishness when she talked so seriously about literature and poetry in the bedroom, and he himself chose the same setting to make his ideological confessions. A strange mixture of profound cynicism and immaturity lay behind the sickly youthfulness that flashed across his face from time to time. Now Mrs. Tsubakihara believed that he liked to say things to hurt people because he was pure.

The couple always met at a spruce little inn recently built on the Shibuya Hill. Each room formed an independent building separated from the others by a small stream running through the garden. The woodwork was fresh and clean, and the entrance inconspicuous.

About six o'clock on June sixteenth their taxi pulled up in front of the Shibuya Station and, halted by the crowds, could proceed no farther. The inn was only five or six minutes away by foot, and Imanishi and Mrs. Tsubakihara left the car.

A massive chorus singing the "Internationale" overwhelmed them. Banners fluttered in the breeze: "Down with the Law on the Prevention of Subversive Activities!" From the bridge of the Tamagawa Line a large banner was suspended: "Yankees Go Home!" The faces of the people swarming over the square were flushed, cheerful, and lighthearted in their rush toward destruction.

Mrs. Tsubakihara was frightened and hid behind Imanishi, who despite himself felt drawn by fear and anxiety toward the crowd. Light streamed meshlike through the legs of the mob surging across the square, the thump of footsteps increased like a sudden shower, then screams pierced the chorus and the sound of irregular clapping grew louder—all happened simultaneously as the riotous night descended upon the massed demonstrators. It reminded Imanishi of the extraordinary shudder he invariably experienced at the onset of his frequent colds with the concomitant rise of fever. Everyone had the horrible sensation of being skinned like rabbits and of having their raw red flesh suddenly exposed to the air.

"Cops! Cops!"

The sound of voices spread and the crowd scattered in confusion. The chorus of the "Internationale" which had been a massive wave broke into fragments that lingered here and there like puddles after rain. And these were routed by cries as the rush-hour crowds and those singing inextricably commingled. White police vans roared up, stopping by the statue of the Faithful Dog Hachi in front of Shibuya Station, and members of the police reserve in dark blue helmets popped out of the vehicles like a flock of grasshoppers.

Clutching Mrs. Tsubakihara's hand, Imanishi ran for his life with the crowd that was struggling to get away. When he reached a store front on the opposite side of the square and had caught his breath, he was astonished by his unexpected capacity for running. He too had been able to run! he realized. Thereupon unnatural palpitations abruptly began and his chest ached.

Compared to his own, Mrs. Tsubakihara's fear, like her sorrow, was somewhat stereotyped. Clutching her purse against her breast, she stood at his side as though she would faint at any moment. The purple neon lights reflecting on her powdered cheeks seemed to transform her fear into iridescent shell work. But her eyes never wavered.

Imanishi slipped cautiously along the front of the store and looked across the roiling square in front of the station. Amidst the welling shouts and screams, the great illuminated clock on the station building serenely recorded the time.

A doomsday fragrance was rising. The world was turning red like the eyes of someone in want of sleep. Imanishi felt as though he were listening to the strange noises of silkworms in their raising room nibbling furiously away at mulberry leaves.

Then in the distance flames shot up from a white police van. Probably a Molotov cocktail. Angry red tongues and screams rose with the white smoke. Imanishi realized that he was smiling.

At length as they started to walk away from the scene, Mrs. Tsubakihara noticed something hanging from Imanishi's hand.

"What do you have there?"

"I just picked it up."

He opened what seemed like a dark rag as he walked along and showed it to her. It was a black lace brassiere, distinctly different from the type Mrs. Tsubakihara used. It must have belonged to a woman exceptionally confident of her breasts. It was a large-size strapless kind, and the whalebone woven into the cups exaggerated the bulkiness of the two haughty, statuesque hollows.

"How horrible! Where did you pick it up?"

"There, a minute ago, when I ran over to the store. I noticed something clinging to my foot. It must have been stepped on. It's all covered with mud."

"The dirty thing! Throw it away!"

"But how strange! How very peculiar." Imanishi was delighted with the attention of the curious pedestrians passing by and proudly exhibited the brassiere as he walked along.

"How could something like this fall off? Do you think it's possible?"

Of course it was not. Brassieres, even the strapless type, were firmly fastened by several hooks. No matter how low the neckline, the brassiere could simply not get undone and spill out. Buffeted by the crowd, the woman had torn it off herself or someone else had. The latter instance would be unlikely, and it was more plausible that the woman had done so of her own volition.

For what purpose, he had no idea. At any rate, amidst the flames, the darkness, the shouting, a pair of large breasts had been sliced off. Only their satin shell had come away, but the strong, resilient fullness of the flesh was clearly attested by the black lace molds. The woman had purposely shed her brassiere with pride. The halo had been removed, and the moon now appeared somewhere in the turbulent darkness. Imanishi had picked up only a halo, but by this act he seemed to capture— more so than if he had picked up the breasts themselves —their warmth, their cunning elusiveness, and memories of lust came swarming like moths about a lamp. Imanishi casually put the brassiere to his nose. The smell of cheap perfume had permeated the fabric and was still strong despite the mud. He supposed she must have been a prostitute specializing in American soldiers.

"What a horrible man you are!"

Mrs. Tsubakihara was genuinely angry. His spiteful words always held some note of criticism, but such a sordid act was mean and unforgivable. And this was not criticism but rather a snide insult. She had taken the measure of the cups in a glance and recognized Imanishi's implied disdain for her own aging, withered breasts.

Once away from the square in front of the station nothing had changed on the road from Dogen Hill to Shoto along which small, hastily built shops stood cramped in the ruins of the bombing. Already at this early hour drunkards were loitering about, and neon lights hovered like schools of goldfish above their heads.

"I must hurry to destruction; unless I do, hell will return," thought Imanishi. As soon as he had escaped from the danger, the ordeal flushed his cheeks. With no further reproach from Mrs. Tsubakihara, he had already let the black brassiere slip from his fingers to the road where the stagnant air was hot and humid.

Imanishi was obsessed with the idea that unless destruction came to him soon, the hell of daily life would quicken and consume him; if destruction did not come at once he would for yet one more day be subject to the fantasy of being consumed by dullness. It was better to be caught in sudden, complete catastrophe than to be gnawed by the cancer of imagination. All this might then be unconscious fear that unless he put an end to himself without delay, his indubitable mediocrity would be revealed.

Imanishi could see signs of world destruction in the most insignificant things. Man always finds the omens he wants.

He wished that revolution would come. Leftist or rightist, it made no difference. How wonderful if it would carry someone like him, a parasite of his father's insurance company, to the guillotine. But no matter how he might proclaim his own shame, he was not sure whether the masses would hate him or not. What would he do if they interpreted his confession as a sign of repentance? If a guillotine were to be built in the bustling square in front of the station and days came when blood flowed in the midst of all this mundaneness, he might by his death be able to become "the remembered one." He pictured himself being placed beneath the cutter—scaffold of lumber wrapped in red and white cloth like a lottery booth, adorned with banners announcing a special summer sale in the commercial district, and a large price tag "Special" pasted on the blade. He shuddered.

Mrs. Tsubakihara tugged at his sleeve as he walked along lost in fantasy, calling his attention to the gate of their inn. The maid waiting in the vestibule guided them in silence to their usual room. Once they were alone, Imanishi, still in turmoil, became aware of the gurgle of the stream.

They ordered a plain chicken dish and saké. While they waited through the usual time-consuming preparations of the inn, they usually indulged in some kind of physical exchange. But today Mrs. Tsubakihara forced him into the washroom and made him wash his hands thoroughly, letting the tap water run as he did.

"Go on. Go on," she said.

Imanishi did not at first grasp why he was made to wash his hands so repeatedly, but from her serious expression he gathered that it was because of the brassiere he had picked up.

"No, you must wash them better." She frantically covered his hands with soap and open the tap wide, disregarding the noise and the splashing on the copper sink. Finally Imanishi's hands felt numb.

"Don't you think that's enough?"

"No, it's not. What do you think will happen if you come near me with hands like that? Touching me means touching the memory of my son that is in me. You'll profane Akio's sacred memory, the memory of a god . . . with your dirty hands . . ." Turning quickly away, she covered her eyes with a handkerchief.

Rubbing his hands together under the gushing water, Imanishi glanced obliquely at her. If she began to weep, that was a sign that whatever it was had passed and that she was prepared to accept anything.

"I wish I could die soon," said Imanishi sentimentally as they sat drinking saké together later.

"So do I," agreed Mrs. Tsubakihara. Her skin, as transparent as rice paper, showed the faint crimson of approaching intoxication.

In the next room where the doors were open the rising and falling contours of the light blue silk quilt gleamed as if it were quietly breathing. On the table slices of abalone with artificial pink in the dusky folds floated in a bowlful of water. And good was simmering in an earthenware pot.

Without speaking, Imanishi and Mrs. Tsubakihara knew that they were both awaiting something—probably the same thing.

She was enraptured with the thrill of sin and its attendant expectation of punishment for these secret meetings behind Makiko's back. She imagined Makiko entering the room, brandishing the brush dipped in red ink with which she corrected poems. "This won't do as poetry. I'll watch. Now try to create poetry with your whole being. I am here to teach you, Mrs. Tsubakihara."

Typically Imanishi had wished to carry the affair to its culmination right before Makiko's disdainful eyes. That first night at Ninooka in Gotemba was the climax of his dream which his affair with Mrs. Tsubakihara must again attain. At the very summit of the climax, Makiko's penetrating eyes had fixed on them both like cold stars. At any cost, her stare was necessary to him.

Without her eyes Imanishi could not be rid of a feeling of pretense in his union with Mrs. Tsubakihara; they could never escape the complex of being an illicit couple. Those eyes belonged to the most authoritative and dignified of matchmakers, eyes of a perspicacious goddess shining in a corner of the dusky bedroom, they had united and yet rejected them, forgiven and yet disdained them. Such eyes controlled acquiescence by a mysterious and reluctant justice that was set aside somewhere in this world. Only under them was the basis of the couple's union justifiable. Away from them, the lovers were merely withered grass floating on the waters of phenomena. Their union was an ephemeral contact: a woman, the captive of an irretrievable and illusory past, and a man craving for an illusory future that would never come. It was like the dead clicking of Go stones in their container.

Imanishi felt that Makiko was already seated immobile, waiting, in the adjacent chamber into which the light of this room did not shine. The feeling of her presence became more and more urgent, and he felt that he must confirm it. He went to the trouble to check, and Mrs. Tsubakihara posed no question, probably feeling the same way as he. In a corner niche of the small room of four and a half mats an arrangement of purple irises floated like flying swallows.

* * *

As usual when they had finished their lovemaking, they indulged like two women in endless small talk as they lazed about. Imanishi, now sexually released, spoke of Makiko in his worst derogatory manner.

"Makiko's using you. You're afraid you can't be a poet in your own right if you split with her. As a matter of fact, that might have been true up to now, but you must realize that you've got to an important turning point. Unless you free yourself from her influence, you'll never be good."

"But if I'm conceited enough to be independent, I know my progress in poetry will stop too."

"Why have you decided that?"

"I haven't decided, it's true. Maybe it's just fate."

Imanishi wanted to ask whether her poetry had ever actually improved, but his good breeding would not permit such an impertinence. Yet the words he used to pry her free from Makiko held no sincerity. He had the feeling that Mrs. Tsubakihara had answered fully aware of that.

At length she pulled up the sheet and, after tucking it around her neck, recited one of her recent poems, turning her eyes toward the dark ceiling. Imanishi criticized it immediately.

"It's a nice poem, but I don't like the petty, smug feeling it gives of dwelling on the mundane; it lacks universality. The reason is probably the last phrase. 'The blueness of the deep pool' lacks imagination. It's too conceptual. It's not based on life."

"Yes, I suppose you're right. I feel hurt if I'm criticized right after creating a poem, but in a couple of weeks I can see its weaknesses. But you know, Makiko praised this one. Unlike you, she said the last part was good, though she thought that 'blueness *is* the deep pool' might be more in keeping."

Mrs. Tsubakihara's tone was condescending, as though she were pitting one authority against another. In high spirits she began gossiping in detail about her acquaintances and that always pleased Imanishi.

"The other day I saw Keiko. She told me something interesting."

"What?" Imanishi was immediately intrigued. He twisted from his position on his stomach and clumsily dropped long cigarette ash on the sheet around her breast.

"It's about Mr. Honda and the Thai Princess," said Mrs. Tsubakihara. "The other day he secretly took her and Keiko's nephew Katsumi, who is the Princess's boyfriend, to his Ninooka villa."

"I wonder if the three of them slept together."

"Mr. Honda wouldn't do anything like that! He's the quiet, intellectual type. He probably wanted to play the generous matchmaker for the two young lovers. Everyone knows he adores the Princess, but they couldn't even carry on a sensible conversation with such a difference in age."

"And what was Keiko's role in the affair?"

"She was nothing more than an innocent bystander, actually. She happened to be at her villa in Ninooka. Jack was off-duty and spending the night there. Suddenly, three o'clock in the morning, there was a knock at the door and the Princess dashed in. Keiko and Jack were awakened from a sound sleep; but no matter how much they coaxed, the Princess absolutely refused to explain the situation. They were at wits' end. The Princess asked them to let her stay the night, and they did. Keiko intended to get in touch with Mr. Honda in the morning, she said.

"With all of that, she got up late and rushed Jack back to camp after a cup of coffee. As she was seeing him off in a jeep at the gate, Mr. Honda came to the villa looking as white as paper. Keiko laughed and said it was the first time she had ever seen him so upset.

"She knew he was looking for Ying Chan and, wanting to tease him a little, asked what he was up to so early in the morning.

"He said that Ying Chan had got lost, and his voice even quavered. After a while, when Mr. Honda started home—he had given up the search—Keiko told him that Ying Chan had spent the night with her. Mr. Honda blushed like a schoolboy—and at his age!—and said: 'Did she really!' He sounded ever so happy.

"When Keiko took him to the guest room and he found the Princess still sound asleep, he nearly collapsed with relief. Ying Chan had not been awakened by all the commotion. She was buried in her black hair, her pretty mouth a little open and her long eyelashes closed. The exhaustion that had been so obvious on her face four or five hours before when she had rushed to the villa was now quite gone, and an innocent youthfulness had returned to her cheeks, and her breathing was peaceful and regular. As if in a pleasant dream she coquettishly turned over in her bed."

38

PRINCESS YING CHAN was once again unavailable for Honda. The moonless rainy season went on and on.

That morning, when he had seen the sleeping girl's face, he had not wanted to awaken her. Having asked Keiko to look after her, he returned to Tokyo. Ashamed of himself, he did not see the Princess nor did he hear from her.

When this apparently calm and peaceful period commenced, Rié began to show signs of jealousy.

"We don't hear from the Thai Princess these days," she would casually observe during a meal. Her words carried a certain sarcasm, but her eyes were earnestly probing.

Rié had begun to draw free-association paintings on a white wall which reflected nothing for her.

Honda was in the habit of brushing his teeth regularly mornings and evenings. He noticed that his toothbrush was frequently changed, well before it was worn out. He presumed that Rié, probably having purchased a stock of brushes of the same type, color, and hardness, changed them as she saw fit. But the changes seemed too frequent, and though it was of little consequence he brought the matter to her attention.

"How stingy you are! Isn't it funny for a millionaire to be saving on something like that!" she had answered, almost stammering in her anger. Not comprehending the reason for her fury he had let her alone. But later he realized that the toothbrushes were changed the mornings after nights when he came in late. Apparently Rié surreptitiously changed them after he had gone to bed. The following day she would carefully inspect the base of each shiny bristle of the old brush to determine whether there were traces of lipstick or the faint fragrance of a young woman and then discard it.

Honda's gums bled sometimes for one reason or another; and though he did not yet need a full denture, he occasionally complained of pyorrhea. How did Rié interpret the pink stains that sometimes discolored the roots of the bristles?

He was merely conjecturing, but there were times when Rié seemed like a kind of obsessed scientist devoting herself to creating some new compound from the oxygen and nitrogen in the air. She seemed bored with her free time, and yet her eyes and senses were sharp. Though complaining incessantly of headaches, she constantly patrolled with nervous steps the many corridors of the old house.

Once when the subject of the villa happened to come up, Honda remarked that he had built it so that she could recuperate from her kidney condition.

"Are you telling me to go to that graveyard by myself?" she had said in tears, misunderstanding.

She was right in recognizing Honda's love for Ying Chan that had begun ever since he had gone to Gotemba alone; she had come to this conclusion from his silence about the girl. But she never supposed that he had not seen her since then. She mistakenly assumed that he was seeing her in secrecy and therefore wanted to erase the name from Rié's thoughts.

Such tranquility was uncanny. It held the false stillness of a hideout for some fugitive emotion afraid of its pursuers. Rié intuitively felt that some exclusive, secretive banquet had been arranged to which she would never be invited.

What was happening?

She had judged correctly also when she thought something had occurred, although Honda himself felt that everything was finished.

Since Rié had completely stopped going out, Honda began to leave the house more frequently than ever, even though he had no purpose. He felt suffocated by the constant presence of his wife who always stayed in under the pretext of illness.

As soon as Honda left the house, Rié would suddenly come alive. Theoretically she should have been worried about the purpose of his unexplained outings, but she had been able to reconcile herself with her now familiar fears. Thus jealousy had become the basis of her freedom.

It was the same as love; her heart was always ensnared, trammeled. She tried to practice calligraphy for a change, but involuntarily her hand would write characters related to the moon . . . "moonshadows" . . . "mountain in the moonlight."

It was repulsive to her that a girl as young as Ying Chan should have such large breasts. She would conjure up from the characters for "mountain in the moonlight" that she had inadvertently composed a pair of mountains in the shape of breasts quietly bathing in moonlight. This was related to her memory of the Twin Hills in Kyoto. But no matter how innocent, Rié feared anything that evoked memories. She had seen the Twin Hills on a high-school trip; and when she recalled the sway of her own small breasts perspiring under the white summer uniform, she felt herself curl up.

Concerned with Rié's fragility, Honda had wanted to engage several servants. Rié made the excuse that her worries would be multiplied if she had to oversee so many people, and she had only two maids in the kitchen. The work there that she had loved for many years was now considerably lessened; besides it was not good for her legs to be standing for any length of time on a chilly floor. She had no alternative but to stay in her room. She took up sewing. The drawing room draperies were threadbare and she ordered some silk brocade from Tatsumura in Kyoto. From the fabric with its print of patterns copied from those in the Shoso-in at Nara, she sewed new curtains.

Rié lined the material carefully with a thick black cloth to cut out the light. Honda noted this as she worked.

"You'd think we were still at war," he teased. As a result, she became even more obstinate in completing what she had begun.

She was not concerned about light leaking out from the inside, but about moonlight seeping in.

Rié stealthily read her husband's diary when he was out and was infuriated when she could find no mention of Ying Chan in it. Out of reticence, Honda had developed the habit of not writing anything romantic in his diary.

Among her husband's documents she found an extremely old record entitled "Dream Diary." *Kiyoaki Matsugae* was written on it. The name was familiar to her, for Honda had frequently mentioned it. But he had never spoken about the diary, and of course, this was the first time she had set eyes on it.

Looking through it, she was amazed at the absurd fantasies. She carefully replaced it. Rié was seeking no fantasy. The only thing she believed could cure her was the truth.

When, on closing a drawer, a kimono sleeve is caught, the seams of the sleeve and the bodice will tear as one walks away. As similar experiences were repeated, the sleeves of Rié's heart were torn to bits. She was captivated by something, yet her heart was empty and listless.

The rain continued day and night. She could see from the window the wet hydrangeas. The pastel violet balls of flowers floating in the gloomy day appeared as her own soul gone astray.

There was nothing more insufferable than the idea that Princess Moonlight existed in this world. It was shattered because of her.

Rié had lived her whole life without once knowing the terror of emotions. Thus she was surprised by the eruption of the riotous feelings of solitude within her. The barren woman had given birth for the first time, but to something monstrous.

Thus it was that Rié learned that she too had imagination. What had never been used, what had rusted in a corner of her long and tranquil life was suddenly unearthed out of necessity and polished and sharpened. At any rate, anything born of necessity is accompanied by bitterness, and her propensity toward flights of fancy held no sweetness.

Imagination based on reality might have opened and freed a mind, but that which attempted to come as close to the truth as possible demeaned and dried it up. Furthermore, if that truth did not really exist, everything would at once be transformed into futility.

But imagining a crime in which there was some truth would do no harm. Rié's imagination was a double-edged sword. She believed that there was truth somewhere and she desired that it not exist. Thus her jealous imagination was trapped by its own self-denial, and yet could not tolerate its own existence. Just as excessive acidity in the stomach gradually eats away the stomach walls, so her imagination eroded the root of its own imaginativeness, and at the same time she was driven by a desire to be saved that was a scream for help. Truth. If there were truth, she would be saved! The desire that appeared at the end of such a one-sided obsessive search inevitably began to resemble an urge for self-punishment. Because that truth—if it really existed— would crush her.

But punishment sought and obtained naturally holds a sense of unfairness. Why should an attorney be punished? That would be a reversal. When what she craved finally came to pass, instead of the delight of fulfillment, dissatisfaction and anger would flare up. Even now she could feel the heat of the burning stake. She must not allow such injustice to occur. She must not expose herself to such incomparably exquisite pain. Suffering from doubt was already enough; why should she pile the pain of recognition upon it?

Desiring to search out the truth, and yet to deny it, wanting to deny the truth, yet seeking only salvation in it. Such emotion went forever around in circles, just as the stray traveler on a mountain road, intending to go forward, somehow always returned to the point he started from.

It was like being enveloped in fog where in one area the details are uncannily distinct. One follows a ray of light only to discover that the moon is not there, rather it is at one's back and what one sees ahead is its reflection.

Yet Rié had not completely lost all sense of self-examination. Sometimes disgusted with herself, she wanted to cover her face in shame. Yet she felt that it was none of her fault that she had turned into an ugly, unlovable being because of her husband. She felt that her husband had really changed her into something despicable because he had no desire to love her. When she arrived at this realization, hatred welled up in her breast like a gushing spring.

But in her state, she tended to avoid the truth of the matter that even if she had not been turned by jealousy into one so repulsive, there were other causes that had transformed her into what she now was, that even had she stayed unchanged she would no longer have been loved. Her husband was perforce to be despised, but from his own need to turn away from her charms, he could not help but change her into an unlovable creature.

Rié had taken to gazing for long periods into her mirror. Wisps of stray hair emphasized the unloveliness of her cheeks. Everything about her seemed artificial, including the swelling of her face.

Since she had become aware of the bulging years ago, she had made up rather heavily. She disliked the way her eyes looked hooded, and she would apply dark eyebrow pencil and thick powder. When they had been younger, Honda had teased her by calling her "Moonface." She was irked at being chided about her affliction, but the night he called her "Moonface" his affection had been particularly warm, and thinking her handicap had probably increased his feeling, Rié had begun to take pride in her face. But on reflection, the sexual passion inspired by her edema contained a certain, subtle cruelty. To be sure, on such nights his lovemaking was passionate, but in view of his admonition that she remain absolutely passive, he might have been entertaining the illusion of a several-day-old corpse with her swollen face.

The reflection in the mirror was a living ruin. Under her lusterless hair, a sinewy malice appeared on her moonlike features like the ribs of a round fan. Her face had gradually turned into one not of a woman, and whatever feminine roundness it had, persisted only in the swelling. Even that was the cold, faded, tiresome roundness of the moon in daylight.

To apply beautifying makeup now would only signal defeat. But being ugly was also a defeat. She had lost all desire for repairing the defects in her present face; so the dents remained dents, the ugliness ugliness, and everything continued tranquilly like the rise and fall of sand dunes. Rié thought that it might just not be her husband's fault that she was unable to tear herself away from jealousy, but the fault of the enormous boredom that enveloped her like heavy bedding. She felt that she would need a frightening amount of strength to push it away and indolently did nothing about it. But if she was so lazy why could she find not even momentary peace?

Rié suddenly remembered the winter beauty of Mount Fuji, which she had been able to see from the second floor of the house soon after her marriage. She had been told by her mother-in-law to bring down the dinner service reserved for the New Year's celebrations and had gone obediently up to the storage room on the second floor. She had seen Fuji from there. She had tied a red cord across her sleeves to keep them down as new brides did.

Rié noticed that the rain had stopped and the evening light was limpid. Thinking to dispel her worries by looking at Fuji, she went up to the storage room on the second floor for the first time in many years. She climbed over the stacked guest bedding and opened the window with its opaque glass panes. The postwar sky, unlike that of former days, was bright, but an isinglass cloudiness had settled everywhere. Fuji was not visible.

39

HONDA AWAKENED with a need to urinate.

Tattered ends of interrupted dreams.

He had felt like strolling about a small residential district of Tokyo with its rows of little hedged gardens. The houses were tiny, and in front of them bonsai had been placed on shelves in the yards; some had small flower patches bordered with shells. The gardens were damp and filled with the inevitable snails. Two children sat facing each other on the edge of a veranda drinking warm sugar water and savoring wafers with broken corners. It was one of those Tokyo districts from which such scenes had now totally vanished. He had come to a dead-end alley surrounded by hedges. A decrepit wooden wicket gate stood at the farther end.

When he opened the wicket and stepped in, it proved to be the bright front garden of an old-fashioned hotel, and a garden party was in progress. The manager with a Ronald Colman moustache came forward and bowed respectfully.

Just then the brilliant, pathetic sound of bugles rose from the buffet tent, the ground suddenly split asunder, and Princess Moonlight clad in a golden dress emerged on the wings of a golden peacock. The assembly applauded as the peacock flew over their heads making a bell-like sound with its wings.

Princess Moonlight's shiny, brown thighs astride the golden peacock exposed her privates, and in short order she sent down a shower of fragrant urine onto the upturned faces of the onlookers.

Why had she not gone to the toilet? Honda wondered. He must scold her for such outlandish manners. He entered the hotel in search of a bathroom.

Inside, the building was completely still and contrasted with the commotion outdoors.

The door of each room was unlocked and slightly

ajar. Honda opened each one and saw that every room was empty except for a coffin on the bed.

A voice told him that that was the toilet he was looking for.

Unable to contain himself longer, he entered a room and tried to urinate into the coffin, but he could not out of fear of committing blasphemy.

It was at that point that he awakened.

Such dreams were merely the pitiful signs of old age when the urge to urinate came at shorter and shorter intervals. After returning from the toilet, completely awake and clear-headed, he was taken up with recapturing the broken threads of the dream. He knew that there was undeniable happiness to be found there.

He wished to recapture the feeling of radiant joy by making it go on. In it a brilliantly pure, unreserved delight existed to the fullest. And the joy was real. If, even in a dream, Honda could not think that the joy of capturing an unrepeatable segment of time in his life was real, what else could reality be? When he glanced up to the sky he caught sight of the transformed figure of the Peacock Wisdom King set in a complete harmony of affinity and sympathy, soaring astride the golden peacock. Ying Chan was his.

The next morning even after he awakened, the happy feeling distinctly persisted, and Honda was in high spirits.

Of course, the dream that he had had in his second sleep was so vague and shapeless that he could not possibly recall it. He could only remember that it had contained none of the happiness of the first. But the brilliant light in this latter had pierced the accumulation of the second dream that was like a snowdrift and had stayed in his memory until morning.

All day he again thought of Ying Chan, using her absence as a lever. He was astonished when he realized that something like the passion of the youthful first love he had never known infused his fifty-seven-year-old body.

On reflection, falling in love for him was not only

extraordinary, but rather comical. By having closely observed Kiyoaki Matsugae, he knew full well what sort of man should fall in love.

Falling in love was a special privilege given to someone whose external, sensuous charm and internal ignorance, disorganization, and lack of cognizance permitted him to form a kind of fantasy about others. It was a rude privilege. Honda was quite aware that since his childhood he had been the opposite of such a man.

He had often observed the contrariness of human fate that let one individual participate in history out of ignorance and another fail to because of eagerness. Thus he believed that the greatest reason for not obtaining what one wished lay in the desire to obtain. Because Honda had never wanted money, millions had come to him.

That was how he thought. His inability ever to obtain anything was not the result of any shortcoming or innate flaw in himself, nor was it some bad luck he carried with him. It was his habit to formulate everything into laws, to universalize. So it was no small wonder that he set out to circumvent this particular one. It was his manner to do everything by himself, thus he could easily play both the role of legislator and violator. In other words, he limited what he wanted to what he could never get. If by chance he obtained the object of his desire, it invariably proved worthless. Thus he strove to attribute all manner of impossibilities to this object, to put it at as great a distance as he could. In other words, he kept a passionate apathy in his heart.

In the case of Ying Chan the shrouding in mystery of this thick-petaled Thai rose was achieved almost completely after the incident that night in Gotemba. It consisted in relegating her to some unattainable place, somewhere his perception could never penetrate. (In the first place, the length of his arm and that of his perception were the same.) The pleasure one gets by seeing necessarily presupposes some unseeable sphere. Honda felt that he had seen to the ends of the world during his experience in India. And he wanted to know the feeling of

an indolent animal licking its resin-smeared fur and re-
laxing in a pool of sunshine, sending its prey someplace
where the claws of perception could never reach. In trying to simulate such an animal, was he not trying to imitate God?

It was unbearable for Honda that his carnal desires
should so perfectly overlap with his desire for perceiving;
and he knew very well that love would never be born
in him unless he could separate the two. How could
a rose spring up between a pair of gigantic trunks entwined
and ugly? Love should not open up like a parasitic orchid
on either one with their shameless hanging roots, nor
from his insipid desire for perception, nor from his rank
fifty-seven-year-old lust. It was necessary that Ying Chan
should exist beyond the reach of his desire for perceiving,
that he deal only with the impossibility of his desire.

Absence was the best for this. It was indeed. It was
the only pure, perfect material for his love. Without
absence the nocturnal beast of perception would immediately begin to glare and soon tear everything apart
with its sharp claws. Biting into the unknown, transforming everything into familiar corpses, stepping into the
morgue of perception—this frightfully boring disease had
once been cured by India, had it not? What India and
Benares had taught him was that, escaping the ultimate
of perception, Ying Chan like a single remaining rose
should be locked tightly away at the back of a dusty
ebony shelf; he could pretend to know it already so
that it would escape the eyes of his perception. That
Honda had achieved. He had locked the cupboard himself, and it was by his will that he did not open it.

Long ago Kiyoaki, fascinated by the completely impossible, had committed an impropriety. But Honda
created the impossible so that he would commit no
violation of it. For the minute he attempted a violation,
beauty could no longer exist in this world.

He remembered the freshness of the morning when
Ying Chan had vanished. A part of himself had been
driven by fear, yet another part had enjoyed the situation.

Even after he had discovered that she was no longer in her room, he did not panic and at once summon Katsumi. He was totally engrossed in savoring her ubiquitous lingering fragrance.

It had been a beautiful sunny morning. The bed was rumpled. He detected in the minute wrinkles in the sheet evidence of where her feverish body had tossed and turned in her distress. Honda picked up a curly wisp of hair hidden under the swells of the blanket that was like a nest where some lovely little animal had suffered. He looked to see if there were traces of Ying Chan's transparent saliva in the hollow of the pillow that still held its innocent indentation.

Only then had he gone down to tell Katsumi.

Katsumi had turned white. Honda had no difficulty in concealing the fact that he was not at all surprised.

They decided to join forces to search for her.

It would be untrue for Honda to deny he was then entertaining the thought of Ying Chan's death. He did not believe she was dead, but in this sunny interval in the rainy season death wafted even in the wasted fragrance of the morning coffee. Something tragic enclosed the morning like a fine silvery edging. It was the proof of grace Honda had dreamt about.

Though he had absolutely no intention of doing so, he suggested to Katsumi that perhaps they should notify the police and enjoyed seeing the extremely alarmed expression this evoked.

Honda visualized with a thrill Ying Chan's body floating in the swimming pool that reflected the blue sky. He went out to the terrace and looked into the rain puddles in the excavation. He felt that the glass that demarcated the real from the unreal had been completely shattered that moment and that he could thus easily step into the world of the unknown. The universe could be anything that morning. Anything was possible: death, murder, suicide, even universal destruction right in the midst of the bright fresh panorama.

As he and Katsumi descended the narrow lane across the soaking lawn toward the mountain stream, Honda

enjoyed, in a swift flight of imagination, a foreboding
of his once considerable social prestige collapsing amidst
great fracas if a suicide scandal were to appear in the
newspapers. But this was riduculous exaggeration. The
incident had taken place only between Katsumi and
Ying Chan, and no one in the world knew anything
about Honda's peephole.

For the first time in many days one could see Fuji
beyond the garden. It was already a summer mountain.
Its snowy skirts had been hoisted unexpectedly high,
and the color of the earth in the morning sun glowed
like rain-soaked brick.

They looked in the stream; they searched in the cypress
woods.

When they left the grounds Honda suggested that
Katsumi go to Keiko's house where he just might find
her in. This he obstinately refused to do, offering instead
to check by car along the road to the station. He was
terrified of facing his aunt.

Honda himself was hesitant about visiting Keiko at
such an early hour, but it was unavoidable in this instance.
He pushed the bell. Surprisingly, she appeared, makeup
completed and dressed in an emerald-green dress and
a cardigan.

"Good morning," she said quite normally. "You're
looking for Ying Chan? She came over here while it
was still dark. She's asleep now in Jack's bed. Lucky
Jack wasn't here. What a scene if he had been. Since
she seemed upset, I gave her some chartreuse and let
her sleep. After that I was wide awake, so I just stayed
up. What a horrible man you are! But I asked no questions about what happened. Would you like to see her
lovely face while she's sleeping?"

Honda, still extremely patient, controlled his desire
to see Ying Chan. Neither she nor even Keiko had contacted him.

He was waiting for madness to take complete possession of him.

Reason was threatened by an extreme of anxiety,

and just as the old fox in the farce *Fox Hunt* jumped at his prey although he was quite aware of the danger of a trap, Honda was waiting for the moment when he would be driven into blind self-destruction despite his experience and knowledge, accomplishment and skill, reason and objectivity—or rather, he was waiting for the moment when the accumulation of them all would drive him to it.

Just as a boy must wait for maturity, so a fifty-seven-year-old too had to attend his own ripening; and that was toward catastrophe. When all the trees in the withered November thickets had lost their leaves and the underbrush had yellowed and when in the clarity of the winter sun the place appeared as white and dry as the Pure Land, like the snake gourd, a single spot of crimson among dead vines, he fervently awaited his ripening toward catastrophe.

Whether what he sought was a flamelike lack of discernment or death, Honda's age made it difficult for him to know. Someplace, he knew not where, something was being slowly and carefully prepared. And now the only thing certain in the future was death.

At this office in the Marunouchi Building, when he heard a young law clerk receiving a private telephone call, shielding it so that his superiors would not know, Honda was overcome by intense loneliness. The call was obviously from a woman, and the young man, concerned about those around him, pretended reluctance; but in the distance Honda could almost hear the clear, attractive voice of the young woman.

Probably the two shared a secret language and communicated with each other by using business jargon. Honda suddenly conceived a plan for firing the young man whose eternally well-groomed hair, romantic eyes, and arrogant lips were all so unbecoming to a law office.

The best time to catch Keiko, who spent her days going to luncheons, cocktail parties, and formal dinners, was now at eleven o'clock in the morning. After having overheard the young clerk, Honda was loathe to make the call from the small office in his loud voice. Saying he was going to do some shopping, he went out.

The shopping arcade in the Marunouchi Building was one of the few places where prewar Tokyo still lingered on, and Honda enjoyed window-shopping at the haberdasheries or selecting paper for calligraphy. Gentlemen, obviously prewar types, were hunting for reasonable purchases that would not be too hard on their pockets; they walked cautiously to avoid slipping on the mosaic floor that was particularly slippery after the rain.

Honda called Keiko from a pay phone.

As usual she did not answer at once, but he was positive she was at home. He pictured her magnificent, opulent back; she must be in her slip putting on makeup after having selected her attire for the luncheon party and was oblivious to the telephone.

"I'm sorry to keep you waiting," she said in her rich, leisurely voice. "I've been thoughtless not to call. Have you been well?"

"Quite well, thanks. I wondered if we could have lunch sometime soon."

"Oh, how kind! But you really want to see Ying Chan, not me."

Honda was at once at a loss for words and decided to wait for Keiko's lead. "I'm sorry I've troubled you. By the way, she never contacted me after that night. Have you seen her?"

"No, not since then. I wonder what she's doing. Isn't she taking exams or something?"

"I don't think she studies much."

Honda was amazed by his own ability to carry on the conversation so calmly.

"But you want to see her anyway," began Keiko. Then she thought for a moment. The interval of silence was neither heavy nor important. White powder was probably floating in the shafts of the morning light falling through the bedroom windows. Honda knew that she was not the kind of woman to feign mystery, so he waited, leaving everything up to her.

"I shall pose a condition, I think," she said.

"What is that?"

"Ying Chan escaped to my place and she trusts me completely. So if I tell her that I shall be present too, she won't turn you down straightaway. Is that all right?"

"What do you mean is it all right? I was going to ask you to do precisely that."

"I really want to let you see her alone, but for a while . . . Where shall I call to give you the answer?"

"At my office. I've decided to go there every morning from now on," replied Honda and hung up.

The world was transformed from that moment on. How could he bear to wait for the next hour, the next day? He made a little wager with himself: if Ying Chan wore the emerald ring when she met him, that would mean she had forgiven him; if she did not, that would signify the opposite.

40

KEIKO'S HOUSE was situated in the higher section of Azabu and was deep-set with a driveway that led up to the entrance. There was a semicircular Regency facade built by Keiko's father in memory of his youth in Brighton. One warm afternoon toward the end of June, Honda had accepted an invitation to tea and entered the mansion with the feeling of returning to prewar Japan.

Following a typhoon and thunder and rain, suddenly in the summer light, unusual for the rainy season, the quiet woods on the front grounds seemed to store remembrances of an entire period. He thought he was returning to nostalgic old music. This kind of mansion, now almost the only one remaining in the burned ruins, had become even more privileged, sinful, and gloomy by reason of its solitariness. It was just as though remembrances left behind by the times were to have their impact suddenly heightened with the passing of the years.

A formal invitation had come to him announcing that Keiko's house had been released by the American Occupation Forces, and that she wished to give a tea to celebrate the occasion. She did not touch on the matter of Ying Chan. Honda came bearing a bouquet of flowers. While the house had been confiscated, Keiko had lived with her mother in a separate dwelling that had once been the steward's, and she had never invited guests to visit in Tokyo during that time.

A servant in white gloves met him at the door. The circular entrance hall was high-domed. The cryptomeria doors on one side were painted with cranes, while on the other they opened onto a spiral staircase of marble that led to the second floor. Halfway up the stairs, in a dark niche, stood a bronze Venus with eyes demurely lowered.

The doors wtih the Kano-style cranes, both half open, led to the drawing room. He found no one there.

Light from a row of small windows brightened the room, and the panes were old-fashioned crystal surfaces that refracted rainbow colors. Further into the interior, one side recessed into a niche. Golden clouds had been painted all over the wall, on which hung a narrow scroll with calligraphy. A chandelier was suspended from the Momoyama-style latticed ceiling. All the small tables and chairs were splendid Louis Quinze—*d'époque*. The upholstery of each chair bore a different design; altogether they formed the sequence of a fête champêtre by Watteau.

While Honda was examining the chairs, a familiar fragrance came to him, and turning around, he saw Keiko standing there in a fashionable double-skirted afternoon dress of heavy mustard pongee.

"How do you like them? Aren't they antediluvian?"

"What a perfectly splendid mingling of East and West!"

"My father's taste rather ran to this sort in everything. But don't you think they're well preserved? The confiscation of the house couldn't be avoided, but I ran around and did what I could so that it wouldn't be destroyed by ignoramuses. Since they used the place for Army VIPs, they turned it back to me quite undamaged, as you can see. There are childhood memories for me in every corner. It was lucky that some of the country bumpkins from Ohio didn't run the place down. I wanted you to see it today."

"And where are your other guests?"

"They're all in the garden. It's hot, but the breeze is pleasant. Won't you come out?"

Keiko made no reference to Ying Chan.

Opening a door in one corner of the room, she stepped out onto the terrace that led to the garden. In the shade of the large trees cane chairs and small tables were scattered about. The clouds were extremely beautiful, and the colors in the women's clothes heightened the green of the lawn. Flowerlike hats swayed to and fro.

Upon approaching the group Honda realized that it was composed of old women; furthermore, he was the only male guest there. He felt out of place as he was introduced. Each time the pink hands, blotched and wrinkled, were extended, he hesitated to shake them; he was depressed by the accumulation of hands; they darkened his heart like a cargo of dried fruit in the hold of a ship.

Western women, apparently unaware of the gaping zippers on their backs, swung their broad hips and cackled with laughter. Their sunken eyes with brown or blue pupils were focused on things he could not locate. When pronouncing certain words they would open their dark mouths so wide that he could see their tonsils, and they gave themselves to the conversation with a kind of vulgar enthusiasm. One of them, snatching up two or three thin sandwiches with red manicured fingers, turned suddenly to Honda and announced that she had been divorced three times and wanted to know whether the Japanese divorced a lot too.

The colorfully dressed guests strolled about the grove to escape the heat and were visible through the trees. Two or three of them emerged from the entrance to it. There was Ying Chan accompanied by a Western woman on either side.

Honda's heart pounded as though he had stumbled. This was it, this palpitation was important; thanks to it, life had stopped being solid dead matter and was transformed into a liquid, even gaseous state. Just seeing her had done him good. Sugar cubes melted in tea at the instant of this palpitation; the buildings all became unsteady; all the bridges bent as if they were candy; and life became synonymous with lightning or with the wavering poppy in the wind or with the swinging of a curtain. Extremely self-centered satisfaction and unpleasant shyness intermingled as in a hangover, projecting Honda with one thrust into a dream world.

Escorted by two tall women, Ying Chan in a sleeveless salmon-pink dress, her black hair lustrous as jet falling over her shoulders, suddenly came out of the grove into the sunlight. Honda took double pleasure in being reminded of the Princess's picnic at Bang Pa In, when she had been attended by the old ladies.

Keiko, unnoticed, was standing at his side.

"How do you like that? Don't I keep my promises?" she whispered in his ear.

A childlike insecurity welled up in Honda, and he was afraid that he could not possibly go through the scene unless he depended completely on Keiko for help. Step by step, a smiling Ying Chan approached this incomprehensible fear. He was flustered by his concern to control his emotion before Ying Chan should reach him, but the closer she came, the more it grew. Honda was tongue-tied before he even tried to speak.

"Just act as though nothing ever happened. You'd better not mention anything about Gotemba," Keiko whispered in his ear again.

Fortunately Ying Chan's progress was interrupted in the middle of the lawn when another woman stopped her to chat. She seemed not to have noticed him as yet. Ten or fifteen yards away she swayed on the branch of time like a beautiful orange that could be reached in seconds, ripe, heavy with fragrance and juice. Honda examined everything about her: her breasts, her legs, her smile, her white teeth. Everything had been nurtured under the burning summer sun, yet inside, her heart was surely impenetrably cold.

When Ying Chan finally joined the group in the circle of chairs it was still uncertain whether she had really not noticed Honda or was pretending not to have.

"It's Mr. Honda," Keiko said encouragingly.

"Oh?" said Ying Chan, turning around with a perfectly relaxed smile. Her face in the summer light was revived and her lips were more relaxed and smiling. Her eyebrows flowed, and in the amber brightness of her face her large, black eyes were luminous. Her face was enjoying its season. Summer had relaxed her as though she were stretching self-indulgently in an ample bath. The naturalness of her pose was complete. As he visualized the hollow between her breasts under her brassiere perspiring as if in a steamroom, he could feel the summer concealed deep within her body.

When she extended a hand her eyes were expressionless. Honda took it somewhat shakily. She was not wearing the emerald ring. Though the wager he had made was with himself, he realized now that he had wanted to lose, to be coldly rejected. He was surprised to note that even rejection gave him a pleasant sensation and did not at all disturb his audacious reveries.

Ying Chan took up an empty teacup, so Honda stretched his arm and touched the handle of the antique silver teapot. But the heat of the metal made him hesitate. He probably was motivated by a fear that the destination of his action would be interrupted by a fog of insecurity, that certainly his hand would tremble, and that he might do something terribly clumsy. A servant's white-gloved hand immediately came to his rescue and relieved him of his concern.

"You look well, now that summer's here," he finally managed to say. While he was quite unaware of it, his manner of speaking was more polite than usual.

"Yes, I like summer." Smiling softly, Ying Chan answered as if out of a textbook.

The old ladies around her, manifesting their interest, asked him to translate the conversation. The fragrance of the lemon on the table and the smell of old bodies and perfume put Honda's nerves on edge, but he translated the conversation. The old ladies laughed meaninglessly, commenting that the Japanese word for summer made them feel decidedly warm, conjecturing about a possible tropical etymology for the word.

Intuitively Honda felt Ying Chan's ennui. Looking around, he saw that Keiko had already gone. Boredom was increasing in Ying Chan like a silent animal sadly rubbing itself against the sultry grass. This intuition of his was the only bond with her. She moved gracefully, smiling and talking in English, but he gradually began to feel that she wanted perhaps to tell him about her boredom. It was a kind of music made by the accumulation of the summer melancholy of her flesh, from her heavy breasts down to her beautiful light legs. It was constantly in his ears, high and low, like the faint hum of insects flitting in the summer sky.

But it did not necessarily mean that she was bored with the party. Rather, the aura of ennui filling her body could have been her natural state that the summer had revived. She was obviously quite at home in this ennui. Retreating slightly into the shade of a tree, she spoke with vivacity, holding her teacup, surrounded by old ladies who addressed her as Your Serene Highness. She suddenly took off a shoe and with one sharp, stocking-clad toe casually scratched the calf of her other leg with the exquisite balance of a flamingo, holding the teacup perfectly steady and not spilling a single drop into the saucer.

Momentarily Honda was confident that he could slip into Ying Chan's heart straight and smoothly, even if he were not forgiven.

"That was quite a feat." Honda found a momentary interval in the conversation and spoke in Japanese.

"What?"

Ying Chan raised questioning eyes. There was nothing more charming than her mouth, which, when given a riddle, responded with an instant "What?" like a bubble floating on the surface of the water, making no effort to solve it. She did not at all mind unintelligibility, so he should have the same sort of courage. He had prepared a note written in pencil on a page torn from a little memorandum.

"Please see me alone," he said. "During the day is all right. Only an hour will do. How about today? Can you come here?" He handed her the paper with the time and place written on it.

Ying Chan deftly avoided the observant eyes of the ladies and glanced at the paper in the sun. Her momentary effort at evasion made Honda happy.

"Are you free?"

"Yes."

"Will you come?"

"Yes."

Ying Chan's "yes" was almost too distinct, but it was accompanied by a beautiful smile that at once softened her answer. It was clear that she was thinking of nothing.

Where do love and hatred go? Where do the tropical cloud shadows and the violent rains that fall like stones disappear to? To be made to realize the futility of his suffering was stronger than being made to realize the futility of his occasional happiness.

Keiko had disappeared, but now she returned leading two guests into the garden from the drawing room as she had done when Honda arrived. One old woman, on seeing the beautifully kimonoed figures, one in light and the other in dark blue, made hard and rasping sounds of admiration with her parrotlike tongue. Honda turned to look. It was Makiko attended by Mrs. Tsubakihara.

Honda had been rapturously gazing at Ying Chan's jet-black hair suddenly blowing in the wind like a sail, and the arrival seemed particularly untimely. As they approached, the two greeted Honda first of all. "How lucky you are today," said Makiko coldly, looking around at the old ladies. "The only thorn in a bouquet of roses!"

Of course, the two women were introduced to the

Westerners and amenities were exchanged, but they were pleased to return to Honda, with whom they talked in Japanese.

When the clouds shifted and the shadows deepened on her hair, Makiko said: "Did you see the demonstration on June twenty-fifth?"

"No, I only read about it in the papers."

"So did I. They threw Molotov cocktails everywhere in Shinjuku, and some police boxes were burned down. It was a terrible riot, I hear. At this rate, I wonder if the Communists won't take over."

"I don't think so."

"But things seem to get worse every month; even homemade guns are appearing. I imagine that the Communists and the Koreans will soon turn the whole of Tokyo into a sea of flames."

"We can't do much about it, can we?"

"You'll have a long life because you don't worry," said Makiko. "But looking at the world these days, I wonder what would have happened if Isao had lived. I started to write a series of poems called 'June Twenty-fifth.' I wanted to write poetry at the lowest level, one on which it would be impossible to create; I'd been looking for material that could never be turned into poetry when I finally hit on this."

"You say you hit on it, but you didn't go to see it yourself."

"A poet has long sight, unlike people like you."

It was unusual for Makiko to talk in such a relaxed fashion about her own poetry. But her attitude was a kind of priming. She looked around and smiled into Honda's eyes.

"I hear you were pretty upset in Gotemba the other day."

"Who told you?" Honda asked, unperturbed.

"Keiko," said Makiko calmly.

"Come to think," she continued, "it might have been an emergency, but Ying Chan has a lot of nerve barging into someone's house in the middle of the night and banging on the lovers' bedroom door. Jack's a lovely boy to treat her so kindly. He's really a well-bred and charming American."

Honda was confused. He was certain that Keiko had said that morning: "Lucky that Jack wasn't here. What a scene if he had been." And now Makiko was talking as though he *had* stayed the night. It was either Makiko's misunderstanding or Keiko's lie. The discovery of Keiko's meaningless little falsehood gave him a secret feeling of superiority that he was reluctant to share with Makiko. He wanted to avoid the absurdity of getting involved in women's gossip. Furthermore, Makiko had thought nothing of perjuring herself in front of judges. Honda never lied, but at times he had the habit of ignoring some paltry truth gliding away in front of him like trash flowing down a little gutter. It was a small vice that dated from the days of his judgeship.

As he attempted to change the subject, Mrs. Tsubakihara came sidling up as though seeking Makiko's protection. He was surprised that her face had become so drawn in the short time since he had last seen her. Her sorrowful expression itself had a wasted look, her eyes were hollow, and her lips, garishly painted orange, made her utterly grotesque.

With a smile in her eyes, Makiko suddenly lifted her disciple's round white chin with one finger and showed it to Honda.

"She gives me such a difficult time, threatening me with her ideas of suicide."

Mrs. Tsubakihara let her chin rest on Makiko's finger as though she wished to remain forever in that position, but the latter immediately removed it. Mrs. Tsubakihara, looking across the lawn where an evening breeze was beginning to rise, half spoke to Honda in a thick voice: "But without talent how can one go on living?"

"If the untalented had to die, everybody in Japan would be dead," Makiko responded in amusement.

Honda observed this exchange with a shudder.

41

AT FOUR O'CLOCK two days later, the appointed hour, Honda was waiting in the lobby of the Tokyo Kaikan. If Ying Chan came, he intended to take her to the roof garden restaurant which had opened that same summer.

The lobby was a convenient place to wait inconspicuously for someone. The easy chairs upholstered in leather were spaciously arranged and he could spread the bound newspaper in front of his face. In an inside pocket Honda had three hand-rolled Monte Cristo Havanas which he had obtained after a long wait. Ying Chan would doubtless be there before he could smoke them all. No sooner had he seated himself in a chair than the windows darkened; his only concern was that the showers might come and they might be unable to have dinner in the roof garden.

Thus a rich fifty-seven-year-old man awaited a Thai girl. The realization ultimately saved him from his fear, and he felt that he had returned to a normal daily life. He was a kind of harbor and not by nature a ship. The only natural state of his existence, that of waiting for Ying Chan, was reestablished. It was almost the form of his very soul.

An older man of means who did not seek the simpler male pleasures. He was a troublesome being, and he easily made the decision to exchange the earth for his boredom; but on the surface he was the embodiment of modesty, a spirit that preferred to lie low in a delimited, hollow area. He had the same attitude toward history and eras, miracles and revolutions. Sitting on a covered abyss as though on a toilet, he simply smoked his cigar and waited. He depended on his opponent's will for a decision and only under such conditions did his dream for the first time assume a distinct shape. Then, though only through a peephole, he saw the ambiguous form of ultimate happiness. Could death take him to extreme happiness in this condition? If so, Ying Chan must be death.

Honda was ready to play the cards of apprehension or despair he held in his hand. This time of expectant waiting was like black lacquer inlaid with countless mother-of-pearl pieces of uncertainty.

From the cellarlike Grill Rossini on the same floor, the tinkling sound of silverware could be heard as tables were set in preparation for the dinner hour. Like the knives and forks in the waiters' hands that had not yet been separated, emotion and reason commingled in Honda; and not a single plan (a malicious tendency of reason) had been made—his will was still uninvolved. The pleasure which he had discovered at the end of his life entailed such an indolent abandonment of human will. As he thus relinquished it, the determination to engage himself in history that had so obsessed him since youth was also suspended in space, and history hung detached somewhere in mid-air.

A circus girl soaring on her trapeze through the blinding height of timeless, dark hours, the skirt of the white skintight tunic fluttering . . . Ying Chan.

Outside the window it had grown dark. Two transients and their respective families were exchanging interminable greetings beside Honda; they lasted so long that he felt almost faint. A young couple, apparently engaged, were stonily silent like two manic depressives. Through the window he could see the stir of tree branches along the street, but the rain seemed not to have come. The wooden binding of the newspaper felt in Honda's hands like an extremely long shinbone. He smoked the three cigars. Ying Chan did not appear.

At long last he ate a reluctant meal and made his way to the Foreign Student Center. His behavior was against all good sense.

He entered the simple, four-storied building in Azabu. In the entry hall two or three dark-skinned, sharp-eyed youths in short-sleeved shirts of a large plaid were reading poorly printed Southeast Asian magazines. Honda went to the front desk and asked for Ying Chan.

"She's out," the clerk answered automatically. The response seemed too quick to be genuine. As Honda asked two or three questions the sharp-eyed youths all stared at him. The stifling night air made him feel as though he were in the waiting room of some little tropical airport.

"Could you tell me her room number?"

"It's against the rules. You can see the students only in this lobby and only by their consent."

When Honda gave up and left, the young men returned to their magazines. Brown ankles jutted out sharply like thorns from all pairs of crossed legs.

He could walk freely through the front garden, but no one was there. The sound of a guitar came from a brightly lit room on the third floor, and the windows were open wide to the humid weather. A melody sung in a high but soft voice resembling a high-pitched Chinese viol twined around the sounds of the strings like a yellowed vine. Listening to the sad voice, Honda recalled the unforgettable nights in Bangkok just before the war.

If only he could slip in, he wanted to go through every room, for he did not believe that Ying Chan was out. She was everywhere in the humid evening darkness of the rainy season. In the faint fragrance of flowers that had probably been cultivated by foreign students, in the distinct yellow gladioli or the pale violet of the Roger's bronze leaf intermingling in the dark . . . Minute elements of Ying Chan floating all about gradually coalesced into shape and solidified into her being. He could sense her even in the faint whir of mosquito wings.

Most of the windows were dark. Only one room at the corner of the third floor cast a bright radiance through moving lace curtains. Curious, Honda gazed at the window. Someone was standing just inside looking down at the garden. The wind caused the curtains to flutter and he caught a fleeting glimpse. It was Ying Chan wearing a slip. Involuntarily he ran toward the window and came directly under a street lamp. Ying Chan seemed shocked on recognizing him. Immediately the light was turned off and the window was closed.

Honda leaned against the corner of the building and waited a long time. The minutes dripped away and the blood throbbed in his temples. Time dripped like drops of blood. He pressed his cheek against the thin blue moss growing on the concrete, letting it cool his hot old cheeks.

After a while, a rustling like that of a snake's tongue sounded from the third-floor window. It was slowly opened, and something soft and white fell at Honda's feet. He picked it up and opened a piece of crumpled white paper. Inside was a wad of cotton large enough to fill his palm. It seemed to have been pressed into a compact mass, for as he released the outer wrapping it swelled like something alive. Honda fumbled with the layers of cotton. Inside lay the emerald ring protected by the golden *yakshas*.

He glanced up to the window again, but it was tightly closed and there was not the faintest ray of light.

When he left the Foreign Student Center and came to his senses, Honda realized that he was only a couple of blocks from Keiko's. Customarily he did not use his car for his rendezvous. He could summon a taxi, but he decided to punish himself by walking in spite of the pain in his back and hips. Even if she were not in, he could not possibly go straight home without first knocking at her door.

Were he young, he would have cried aloud as he walked. If he were young! But he had never cried when he was young! He had been a promising youth who thought he should use reason to bring success to himself and others instead of wasting time in shedding tears. What sweet sorrow, what lyrical despair! He permitted himself to feel like this only in a hypothetical past tense. By so doing, he eradicated all authenticity from his present emotion. If only sweet romanticism were allowed to one of his years! But neither now nor when he had been young had his makeup permitted anything of sweetness to himself. His only recourse was to daydream about a different kind of self in the past. How different? It had been quite impossible to become a Kiyoaki or an Isao.

If Honda's imagination let him dream that he would have been of this or that personality were he only young and thus served to protect him through the years at every dangerous emotional point, then his reluctance to recognize his present emotional condition was probably the result of such self-denial in his youth. At any rate, it was impossible for him to cry aloud as he walked—not when he was young and not now. In anyone's eyes this old gentleman in his Burberry coat and Borsalino would appear to be just a nocturnal stroller, whimsical, solitary.

Thus, as a result of the unpleasant self-consciousness that made him to refer to all emotions only indirectly, Honda had become so safe that he no longer had to worry about self-consciousness. It had become possible for him to act on any impulse or any desire, however shameless. If one studied his every action, one might conclude incorrectly that he was a man who acted on impulse. His hasty trip to Keiko's house along this nocturnal road, threatened at any moment by heavy showers, was one of his idiotic impulses. As he walked, he felt the urge to thrust his hand down his throat and, as though drawing a pocket watch from his vest, extract his heart.

It was improbable that Keiko would be home at this hour of the night, but she was.

Honda was at once shown into the resplendent drawing room. The Louis Quinze chairs with their straight backs would not let him relax, and he felt he was about to pass out from sheer exhaustion.

The cryptomeria doors were half open just as they had been the other day. The night solitude in the drawing room was enhanced by the overpowering brilliance of the chandelier. Through the window he saw the lights of the town twinkling through the far end of the grove in the garden, but he did not have the energy to walk over and out. It was better to endure the demoralizing heat and disintegrate in perspiration.

He heard Keiko's footsteps as she descended the spiral marble staircase to the entrance hall. She was wearing a colorful mumu with a long train. She entered the drawing room and closed the door with the cranes behind her. Her black hair was standing erect as if in a storm, flying about, shapelessly swollen, making her face with its light makeup appear unusually small and pale. She walked around among the chairs and sat down facing Honda in front of the niche with its mural of golden clouds. Cognac had been placed on the small table between them. Beneath the hem of her dress peeked her bare feet in bedroom slippers adorned with bouquets of dried tropical fruit. The red lacquer of her toenails was the same color as the large hibiscus flowers on her black mumu. Nevertheless, the abundance of dark hair standing on her head in front of the golden clouds added immeasurably to the gloom.

"Please excuse me. My hair looks mad. Your sudden visit upset even that. Unfortunately I just washed it a little while ago. I was going to set it tomorrow. You men don't know about such ordeals. But is something wrong? You look pale."

Briefly Honda told her what had happened, but he was disgusted to be speaking like a defense lawyer. He could not escape the habit of describing logically, inductively, even in this matter of such burning urgency. His words were useful only for arranging events into some sort of order. He had wanted to appeal to her by wordless, senseless screams for help. At least he had until he entered the house.

"The moral of the story is not to rush into things, it would seem," said Keiko. "I told you to leave everything to me. I don't know what to do either. Even so, Ying Chan was very, very rude. I wonder if that's the way in the South where she comes from. But I know that you're quite taken with her capricious manners." She offered him cognac and said: "And what are you suggesting I do?"

She did not sound at all annoyed, but displayed her characteristic melancholy enthusiasm.

Honda was slipping the ring on and off his little finger. "I would like you to return this to Ying Chan and ask her to accept it. The separation of this ring from her body makes me feel as though the relationship between her and my past is permanently severed."

Keiko was silent, and Honda feared that she was angry with him. She held the glass of cognac at eye level and watched how the once rippling liquid gradually slipped down the concave surface of the snifter, forming viscous, transparent cloud patterns. Her large eyes under the black mountain of hair were almost frightening. Her serious expression was too natural for someone trying to suppress a sardonic smile. Honda thought that her eyes were like those of a child who has watched the crushing of an ant. "I came to ask you merely to do that," he said encouragingly. "That's all."

He was gambling on an extremely trivial exaggeration. Where could he find pleasure except in a kind of ethical principle not to neglect the ludicrous? He had picked Ying Chan out of this garbage pail of a world, and though he ached to possess her he had not so much as laid a finger on her. He was seeking to intensify this idiocy to the point where his lust would intersect the orbits of the stars.

"Why don't you forget about the girl?" said Keiko finally. "Just the other day I heard she was dancing cheek to cheek with some vulgar student at a *thé dansant* at the Mimatsu."

"Forget her? I can never do that. Leaving her alone is allowing her to mature."

"And I suppose you have the right to stop her from maturing. How about your previous feeling that you didn't want her to be a virgin?"

"I thought it would change her overnight into a completely different woman. But that failed, thanks to your stupid nephew."

"He's quite a fool, isn't he," said Keiko, breaking into laughter. She examined her long nails through her glass in the light of the chandelier. They were painted with red lacquer and shone through it, glowing within the convexity like a small, mysterious sunrise.

"The sun's coming up, see!" said Keiko, indicating her glass. She was drunk.

"A cruel sunrise," Honda murmured, ardently wishing that the fog of shabbiness and irrationality would completely envelop this overly bright room so that he would be unable to see a thing before him.

"What would you do if I turned you down?"

"My future would be completely black."

"What an exaggeration!" Keiko put the glass on the table and thought a while longer. She murmured something about always being in the position of helping others. After a while she said:

"The real problem deep down is always childish. When a man makes up his mind, he'll set off on an African expedition to look for a single misprinted stamp."

"I think I'm in love with Ying Chan."

"Oh dear!" Keiko laughed loudly, quite unconvinced. There was a decisive note in her voice when she spoke again. "I understand now. You need to do something absolutely simple and silly right now. For instance—" She lifted the hem of her mumu a little. "For instance, how about kissing the arch of my foot? It'll cheer you up . . . studying the foot of a woman you don't love at all. Don't worry, I've just taken a bath and I'm quite scrubbed. It won't hurt you."

"If this is in exchange for my request, I'll be glad to oblige right now."

"All right, go ahead. It'll do you good to try something like that just once . . . in view of your well-known pride. The credit side of your reputation will be even further enhanced."

Keiko was obviously carried away by her passion as a preceptor. She stood directly under the splendid chandelier and with both hands brushed back her abundant hair, causing the sides to wave like elephant's ears.

Honda tried in vain to smile. He looked around and

slowly bent down. The pain in his hip increased sharply, so that he crouched and prostrated himself on the carpet with grim determination. From this viewpoint, Keiko's sandals resembled religious paraphernalia guarding the firmly planted, slightly sinewy arches of her feet. Clusters of brown, tan, purple, and white dried fruit hung over the vermilion toenails. As Honda put his lips close to the sandaled feet, they artfully drew away. Ultimately, unless he lifted the hem of the hibiscus skirt and thrust his head underneath, his lips could not reach the arches of her feet. Putting his head inside, he found that the mumu was filled with the faint warm fragrance of perfume. Suddenly he was in unknown country. When he raised his eyes after having kissed Keiko's feet, the light was all dark vermilion through the flower print, and two beautiful white columns with pale patterns of veins stood before him. In the distant sky hung a small black sun sending out disheveled black rays.

Honda twisted clear and stood up with difficulty.

"There. I've done my part."

"And I'll do mine," said Keiko, accepting the ring with a serene smile becoming to her age.

42

"WHAT ARE YOU DOING?" Rié called from the house to her husband, who had still not come in for his breakfast.

"I'm looking at Fuji," he answered from the terrace. The voice remained directed not toward the room but rather toward the mountain beyond the arbor at the western edge of the garden.

It was six o'clock of a summer morning, and Fuji was flushed the color of wine. Her contours were hazy. Like powder painted on the nose of a child in preparation for a summer festival, a brush mark of snow was visible around the eighth station.

After breakfast, Honda went out again, wearing only

a pair of shorts and polo shirt, and lay down beside the swimming pool under the brilliant morning sky. He playfully scooped up some water.

"What are you doing?" Rié called again as she cleaned away the breakfast things. This time he made no answer.

From the window Rié glared at this evidence of madness in her fifty-seven-year-old husband. In the first place, she did not like the way he was dressed. A man in the legal profession should never wear shorts. His stiff, emaciated white legs stood out below them. She did not fancy his shirt either. As if in punishment for wearing a polo shirt without possessing the virile fullness of youth, the sleeves and back drooped limply. She had come to the point where she took interest in seeing just how far her husband would go in his follies. It was a sort of perverse pleasure as in bearing down on an aching tooth.

Sensing through his back that his wife had given up and retreated to her room, Honda gazed to his heart's content at the beauty of the morning scene reflected in the pool.

Cicadas had begun to sing in the cypress grove. Honda raised his eyes. Mount Fuji which had had an alcoholic flush had now turned a rich purple. It was eight o'clock, and in the graduated greens of the foothills floated the faint contours of woods and villages. As he looked at the deep blue of Fuji in summer, Honda invented a little game he could enjoy alone. It consisted in visualizing a midwinter mountain in midsummer. After staring at the dark blue Fuji for a while, he would then suddenly shift his gaze to the blue sky to one side; the afterimage on his retina would turn completely white and momentarily he could see a pure milky mountain in the blue sky.

After discovering the way to create this illusion, Honda came to believe that there were two mountains. Beside the summer Fuji there always existed a winter one; in addition to the real image, an essence of the mountain, pure white, also existed. As he shifted his gaze to the swimming pool, he saw that the reflection of Hakoné occupied a much greater area than that of Fuji. The mass of mountain covered with green was hot and stifling. Birds flying through the sky reflected in the water and a familiar nightingale visited the feeding box.

Yes, yesterday he had killed a snake near the arbor. It was a striped one some two feet long, and he had killed it by crushing its head with a rock so that it should not frighten the guests expected today. The little massacre had occupied his entire day. Blue-black steel springs, the image of the smooth, writhing body of the snake struggling against death lingered in his mind. Knowing that he too could kill something gave him a gloomy sense of power.

And the swimming pool. Again Honda stretched his hand and troubled the surface of the water. The reflection of summer clouds shattered into fragments of frosted glass. The pool had been completed six days before, but no one had yet used it. Honda had been here with Rié for three days, but under the pretext that the water was cold he had not once been in.

His sole reason for constructing the pool had been to see Ying Chan naked; nothing else mattered.

The sound of hammering could be heard in the distance. Keiko's house was being remodeled. Since her place in Tokyo had been released by the Occupation Forces, Keiko came less and less to Gotemba, and somehow her relationship with Jack had cooled. Honda's new house had stimulated her sense of competition, and she had started to remodel her own on a grand scale, almost to the extent of building a new one. She maintained that she would not be able to live in it during the summer and would probably spend the season in Karuizawa.

Honda, leaving the swimming pool to avoid the sun that was growing gradually stronger, with difficulty opened the beach umbrella planted in the middle of a table. He seated himself on a chair in the shade and again directed his gaze to the surface of the water.

The morning coffee still provided a numbing sensation at the back of his head. In the bottom of the twenty-seven by sixty foot pool, white lines showed through the ripples of blue paint, reminding him of the lime markings and mint-scented saromethyl ointment inextricably associated with the athletic competitions of his distant youth. A clean white line was drawn geometrically on everything, and from it something started and something ended. But the memory was faulty. Honda had had nothing to do with athletic competition in his youth.

Rather the white line reminded him of the center marking running down a highway at night. He suddenly remembered the little old man who had always carried a cane on his night excursions into the park. The first time he had met him on a sidewalk swept by the dazzling headlights of automobiles, the old man was walking with his chest thrust out and an ivory-handled cane on his arm. If he had walked normally the cane would have dragged on the ground, and he had raised his bent arm unnaturally high so that his posture was even stiffer. The fragrant May woods lay to one side of the walk. The little man looked like some retired Army officer carefully concealing his now valueless decorations in the inner pocket of his jacket.

The second time he had happened on him in the darkness of the woods, Honda had observed in detail the cane's function.

When lovers met in the woods the man would usually press the woman back against a tree and begin to caress her. Seldom was the reverse true. And so when a young couple was thus involved the little man would take up his position on the opposite side of the trunk.

In the darkness not far from where Honda happened to be, he could see the cane's U-shaped ivory handle gradually edging around the tree trunk. He peered into the darkness, watching the floating white shape. When he discovered that the handle was ivory, he knew at once to whom it belonged. The woman's arms encircled the man's neck, while his arms met behind her back. The oily hair on the back of the man's head glistened in the beams of the passing headlights. The white handle roamed for a while in the darkness, and then as though having determined its course, it brushed the hem of the woman's skirt. Once the garment was hooked, the cane lifted it skillfully and quickly with one sweep up to her waist. The woman's white thighs were exposed, but he did not make the mistake of being found out by touching them with the cold ivory.

Then the woman whispered: "No, no." And finally: "It's cold." But the man, in seventh heaven, made no answer, and the woman seemed not to notice that his arms were completely occupied in embracing her.

This cynical and debasing mischief, this dedicated selfless cooperation always brought a smile to Honda's lips whenever he recalled it. But when he remembered the man who had spoken to him some time ago in broad daylight at the entrance to the Matsuya PX the slight edge of humor was replaced by a chilling sensation of fear. It was outrageous that his pleasure might disgust others and thereby subject him to their everlasting repugnance and further that such disgust might one day grow to be an indispensable element of pleasure.

Chilling self-disgust fused with the sweetest allurement . . . the very denial of existence joining with the concept of immortality that can never be healed. This unhealable existence was the unique essence of immortality.

Returning to the edge of the swimming pool, he bent down and took the flickering water in his hands. This was the feel of the wealth he had acquired at the end of his life. As he felt the darting arrows of the aestival sun striking his bended neck, it was as though he were the target of the enormous malice and derision of the fifty-seven summers of his life. It had not been such an unfortunate existence. All had been guided by the oar of reason, and the reefs of destruction had been skillfully avoided. To claim that he had not had a happy moment would be pure hyperbole. Nevertheless, how boring the voyage had been! It would be closer to his true feelings if he dared exaggerate and say that his life had been spent in complete darkness.

To declare his life unrelieved black seemed to express

a certain acute sympathy toward it. (Three was no compensation, no joy in my association with you. Though I not once asked for you, you imposed your tenacious friendship and coerced me into this outlandish tightrope walking called living. You made me frugal with my infatuations, gave me ridiculously excessive possessions, transformed justice into wastepaper, converted reason into mere furniture, and confined beauty to its shabbiest form.) Life strove mightily to exile orthodoxy, hospitalize heresy, and trap humanity into stupidity. It was an accumulation of used bandages soiled with layers of blood and pus. Life was the daily changing of the bandages of the heart that made the incurably sick, young and old alike, cry out in pain.

He felt that somewhere in the brilliant blue of the sky over this mountainous region were concealed the gigantic, supple white hands of a sublime nurse engaged in futile daily treatments and demanding chores. The hands touched him gently and again encouraged him to live. The white clouds floating in the sky over Otomé Pass were dazzlingly new, almost hypocritically hygienic white bandages that had been strewn about.

Honda knew that he was sufficiently objective about himself. To other people, he was among the most wealthy lawyers and in a position to enjoy a leisurely old age. This was a reward for having dispensed impartial justice, and there was no record of graft to mar his long life as judge and attorney. Thus he was regarded, if with some envy, at least with no reproach. It was one of those belated remunerations that society sometimes bestows on a persevering citizen. At this point in life, if his little vice were to come out in the open, people would dismiss it with a smile, regarding it as one of those harmless human foibles in everyone. In short, he had everything that was desirable in the eyes of the world, except perhaps children.

The couple had talked about adopting a child, and they had been urged to do so by others, but Rié had grown reluctant to discuss the matter and Honda too had lost interest after he had come into his property. He suspected that people were just after his money.

Voices came from the house.

He listened, wondering whether a guest might have arrived so early in the morning. But it was only Rié talking with Matsudo. Soon the two came to the terrace and looked out over the undulations of the lawn.

"Look," said Rié. "The lawn over there is so uneven. When you look at Fuji that slope by the arbor is the most conspicuous area of all. The uneven grass will be an embarrassment. A prince is coming, you know."

"Yes, madame. Shall I mow it again?"

"Would you please."

The chauffeur, a year older than Honda, walked to the end of the terrace to get the mower from the little storage room where the garden tools were kept. Honda had hired Matsudo not so much because he liked him, but because he appreciated the experience the chauffeur had driving government cars throughout the war and even after it.

His extremely sluggish manner, his faintly arrogant way of speaking, and the absolutely calm attitude of a man whose daily life was based entirely on the principle of safe driving—everything irritated Honda. (You think you can succeed in life simply by being as discreet about things as you are in driving, don't you? Well, you're wrong.) As he watched the old chauffeur he realized that Matsudo probably believed his employer to be the same kind of discreet person that he was. And Honda felt offended as though the chauffeur were drawing a rude caricature.

"Sit down here. You have plenty of time," Honda called to Rié.

"Yes, but the chef and waiters will be here soon."

"They'll be late as usual."

After hesitating slightly, like a thread loosening in water, Rié reentered the house to fetch a cushion. She feared that her kidneys might take cold from the iron chair.

"Chefs and waiters and . . . I can't stand those people

ruining the house," she said, seating herself in the chair next to Honda.

"If I were like Mrs. Kinkin and loved flamboyance, how I should have enjoyed this style of living!"

"You bring up such ancient subjects!"

Mrs. Kinkin had been the wife of the most celebrated lawyer in Japan not long after the turn of the century. A former geisha, she was famous for her beauty and extravagance. Frequently she could be seen riding a white horse. And she raised eyebrows by wearing long geisha kimonos to funerals. When her husband died, she committed suicide, desperate that she could no longer live in the luxury to which she was accustomed.

"I hear Mrs. Kinkin kept pet snakes and she always carried a little one about in her purse. Oh, I forgot. You said you killed one yesterday. It would be terrible if a snake appeared while the Prince is here." She called to Matsudo who was walking away with the lawn mower: "Matsudo! If you find a snake, get rid of it, but please don't let me see it."

Watching the movement of her throat as she shouted, there where age was so ruthlessly illuminated by the reflection of the pool, Honda suddenly remembered Tadeshina, whom he had met in the ruins of Shibuya during the war. He recalled the *Sutra of the Peacock Wisdom King* that she had given him.

"If you are bitten by a snake, all you have to do is to chant this spell: *ma yu kitsu ra tei sha ka.*"

"Really?" Without a trace of interest, Rié sat back in the chair again. The sound of the mower engine which began immediately permitted them the choice of silence.

Honda took for granted the pleasure his old-fashioned wife showed about the forthcoming princely visit, but he was surprised at her calmness when she learned about the expected arrival of Ying Chan. For her part, Rié was hoping that her long suffering would come to an end if she were to see Ying Chan at her husband's side.

"Tomorrow Keiko will be bringing Ying Chan along to the opening of the swimming pool, and they'll stay with us overnight," Honda had said casually, and she had experienced a kind of tingling pleasure. Her jealousy had been so deeply fraught with uncertainty that her distress, dissipating with every second, was like waiting for thunder after seeing a flash of lightning. What she had feared had fused with what she so anxiously awaited, and the realization that she need wait no longer cheered her.

Rié's heart resembled a river sluggishly flowing through a vast and desolate plain, eroding its banks. And now, about to enter the unknown sea, it contentedly deposited its muddy sediment at the river mouth. It was here that it would cease being fresh water and would be transformed into the bitter saline sea. If one increases the volume of an emotion to its limits, its nature changes of its own accord; the accumulation of suffering which had seemed to destroy her was suddenly transformed into a strength for living—an exceedingly bitter, exceedingly stern, but suddenly expansive blue strength —the ocean.

Honda had not noticed that his wife had been changing into an unrecognizably bitter and hard woman. The Rié who had tortured him by her ill-humored, silent quest was in fact no more than a chrysalis.

On this bright morning she felt that even her chronic kidney ailment was considerably better.

The distant, lazy sound of the mower made the eardrums of the silent couple vibrate. It was a silence totally alien to that of the picturesque old couple who no longer needed to converse. With some exaggeration Honda interpreted the situation in this way: they were two bundles of nerves leaning against each other and in so doing just managed to avoid collapsing to the ground with a metallic crash. It was as though they were both, with difficulty and in silence, acquiescing to their condition. If he had committed some brilliant crime, he would at least have been able to feel that he was soaring a little higher than his wife. But his pride was deeply hurt when he realized that both his wife's suffering and his own joy were of the same stature.

The second-floor guest-room windows reflecting on the surface of the water had been opened to let in the air, and the white lace curtains were fluttering. Tonight Ying Chan was expected behind that window, the one from which she had climbed to the roof in the middle of the night and nimbly jumped down to the ground. The act made him think that she could only have sprouted wings. Had she not really flown away when he had not been watching? How could one be sure that Ying Chan astride a peacock, unobserved by him, had not freed herself from the bondage of this existence and been transformed into a being beyond time and space? He was clearly enchanted by the lack of any proof that she had not and the impossibility of ascertaining that indeed she could not. When he reached this conclusion he realized the mystical nature of his love.

The surface of the swimming pool seemed as though some fisherman had cast a net of light over it. His wife was silent, her little swollen hands so like those of a Japanese doll lay on the edge of the table half covered by the shadow of the beach umbrella.

Honda could immerse himself in his thoughts.

The reality of Ying Chan was limited by the Ying Chan he could observe. She was a girl with beautiful black hair and a constant smile and a penchant for not keeping promises, yet a very determined young woman of impenetrable emotions. It was certain that the Ying Chan one saw was not all there was. For Honda, longing for the Ying Chan he could not see, love depended on the unknown; and naturally perception was related to the known. If he drove his perceptions on and with them plundered the unknown, thereby increasing the area of the known, could his love be achieved? No, it would not work that way, because his love strove to keep Ying Chan as far away as possible from the talons of his perception.

Since youth Honda's hunting dog of perception had always been extremely astute. Thus the Ying Chan he knew by seeing corresponded to his powers of perception.

Nothing but his ability to perceive made her existence possible.

Therefore his desire to see Ying Chan in the nude, a Ying Chan unknown to anyone, became an unattainable desire divided contradictorily into perception and love. Seeing already lay within the sphere of perception, and even if Ying Chan was not aware of it, from the moment he had peeped through the luminous hole in the back of the bookcase, she had become an inhabitant of a world created by her perception. In her world, contaminated by his the moment he laid eyes on it, what he really wanted to see would never appear. His love could not be fulfilled. And yet, if he did not see, love would forever be precluded.

He wanted to see a soaring Ying Chan, but bound by his perceptions, she did not soar. As long as she remained a creature of his perceptions she could not violate the physical laws governing them. Perhaps, except in dreams, the world where Ying Chan soared naked astride a peacock lay a step beyond and did not materialize because Honda's perception itself became a screen and was defective, an infinitesimal obstruction. Then how would it be if he got rid of the obstruction and changed the situation? That would mean the removal of Honda from the world which he shared with Ying Chan, in other words, his own death.

It now became clear that Honda's ultimate desire, what he really, really wanted to see could exist only in a world where he did not. In order to see what he truly wished to, he must die. When a voyeur recognizes that he can realize his ends only by eliminating the basic act of watching, this means his death as such.

For the first time in his life the significance of suicide for a cognizant man carried weight in Honda's mind.

If he denied perception as his love directed and tried to escape from perception infinitely, attempting to take Ying Chan to a territory beyond his reach, resistance by perception meant sure suicide. It would mean Honda's exit from a world contaminated by perception, with Ying Chan left behind. But at the very moment of his departure she would stand radiantly before him; nothing was so predictable as this.

The present world was one Honda's perceptions had created and thus Ying Chan inhabited it too. According to the precepts of the Yuishiki School, it was a world created by Honda's *alaya* consciousness. But the reason he still could not give himself completely to this doctrine was because he was too attached to his perceptions and was unable to agree to consider their root as the eternal *alaya* consciousness that discards the world one instant without regret and renews it the next.

Rather Honda thought of death as a game and was intoxicated by its sweetness. Incited by his perceptions, he dreamed about the supreme bliss of the moment of suicide, when the Ying Chan who had been seen by no other person would appear in all her brilliant, pure amber nudity like a resplendent moon rising.

Didn't "fulfillment of the Peacock" mean precisely this? According to the *Rules for Depicting the Peacock Wisdom King,* the *sammaya-gyo,* or the distinguishing symbol that represents the divinity's main vow, is described as a half-moon above the Peacock's tail; and above that a full moon is depicted. Just as the half-moon waxes into the full moon, so the learning of the Law is fully achieved.

What Honda wished might indeed be this Peacock fulfillment. If all love in the world were as incomplete as the half-moon, who would not dream of the full moon rising above the Peacock tail?

The sound of the mower stopped and a voice was heard from the distance: "Is this enough?"

Like a couple of bored parrots on their perch, the Hondas turned awkwardly to look toward the voice. Matsudo stood there in his khaki overall, and Fuji was already half hidden in the clouds behind him.

"Well, don't you think that's sufficient?" Rié said to her husband in a low voice.

"I suppose. We can't ask too much of the old man," responded Honda.

With both hands he formed a circle of approval, and Matsudo, understanding, slowly rolled the mower back to the house. The sound of a motor came from the gate on the Hakoné side and a station wagon entered the grounds. It was the car from Tokyo bearing the chef, three waiters, and an abundant supply of food.

43

HONDA HAD NOT YET invited the older inhabitants in the neighboring houses despite the fact that he was the newest comer to the View-on-Fuji Villas at Ninooka. The older inhabitants had kept away from their villas, frightened by rumors that public morals had been corrupted by the bars that had opened for the American soldiers near Gotemba. These establishments had brought in their wake call girls and pimps and low-class prostitutes who wandered about the training grounds armed with Army blankets. This summer the owners had begun to trickle back and Honda had invited some on the occasion of the opening of the pool.

The oldest villa owners were Prince and Princess Kaori and the aged widow of Kanzaemon Mashiba, founder of the Mashiba Bank. Mrs. Mashiba had announced that she would bring along her three grandchildren. There were several other guests from the area. In addition to Kieko and Ying Chan, Imanishi and Mrs. Tsubakihara were expected from Tokyo. Makiko had replied quite early that she would be traveling abroad. Under ordinary circumstances Makiko would have been accompanied by Mrs. Tsubakihara on her trip, but this time she had chosen another disciple as her companion.

Once a servant became a permanent employee, Honda was amused to note, Rié could drive her rather mercilessly, though she never gave up her sweet smile for outside help such as the chef and the waiters. She spoke politely and showed consideration in everything, anxious to prove to herself and others that she was beloved by one and all.

"Madame. What are we to do about the arbor? Shall I prepare drinks there too?" asked one of the waiters, already dressed in his white uniform.

"Please do."

"But it will be difficult for just the three of us to cover so much ground. Would it be satisfactory if we just left ice in the thermos bucket and requested the guests to help themselves?"

"Surely. The ones who stray as far as the arbor will probably be young couples anyway, and it might be just as well not to disturb them. Be doubly sure not to forget the mosquito repellent when it starts to get dark."

Honda was truly shocked to hear his wife speaking in such a manner. Her voice was pitched unnaturally high and her words floated on the air. The frivolity she had presumably despised more than anything in the world over the years now so infused her voice and words that he suspected her of sarcasm.

The alert movements of the waiters in their white uniforms seemed to have charged the household with straight lines. Their well-starched jackets, their youthful efficiency of movement, their apparent respectfulness, and their professional polish turned the household into a strange and refreshing world. All private matters were swept aside, and arrangements, consultation, commands, and orders flew about as if they were indeed the butterflies in whose shape the white napkins had been folded.

A buffet had been set up beside the pool to permit the guests to eat in their swimming suits. The familiar appearance of the house had instantly changed. Honda's treasured desk, covered with a white tablecloth, now served as an outdoor bar. Although he himself had directed the alterations, once underway they turned into a kind of violent transformation.

Driven back by the gradually intensifying sunlight, he watched everything in amazement. Who had planned all this? And to what end? To spend money? to invite impressive guests? to play the role of the complacent bourgeois? to boast of the completed swimming pool? As a matter of fact, this was the first private pool in Ninooka either before or since the war. There are many generous people in this world who will forgive another's wealth if only they are invited to his house.

"Dear please put these on," said Rié, bringing him a pair of dark-brown summer worsted trousers, a white shirt, and a bow tie with tiny brown polka dots. She placed them on the table under the beach umbrella.

"You want me to change here?"

"Why not? There are only the waiters. Besides, I'm going to ask them to take an early lunch break now."

He took up the bow tie, the extremities of which were shaped like gourds. Holding one end between two fingers, he playfully held it up to the light of the swimming pool. It was an informal, miserable, limp strip of fabric. It reminded him of the procedure of the "summary order" of a police court. "Notification of summary procedure and demur of the accused." It was Honda himself who most detested the approaching party . . . except for one ultimate kernel, one scintillating point of hopelessness.

Old Mrs. Mashiba was the first to arrive with her three grandchildren. These consisted of an unmarried girl and her two extremely ordinary, bespectacled, and studious-looking younger brothers, one a senior and the other a sophomore in college. The three immediately retired to the dressing rooms where they changed into swimming suits. The grandmother, wearing a kimono, remained under the umbrella.

"While my husband was alive, especially after the war, we fought at every election. I always voted Communist just to spite him. And then I was a great admirer of Kyuichi Tokuda."

The old widow adjusted her kimona collars incessantly or nervously tugged at her sleeves like a grasshopper ducking its head and rubbing its wings. She was reputed to be a completely unconventional and entertaining person; hidden behind mauve glasses, sparkled prying eyes, relentlessly speculating on the finances of one and all. Exposed to her cold gaze, everyone felt as if he were her dependent.

The three young people who returned dressed for swimming possessed bodies typical of good families, modest and sleek-limbed. One after the other they jumped into the water and in a relaxed way began swimming. Honda regretted above all that Ying Chan was not to be the first to enter the water in his pool.

Soon Rié came from the house escorting Prince and Princess Kaori, who were already in their bathing suits. Honda apologized for having been unaware of their arrival and for not having come up to greet them. He scolded Rié for not warning him; but the Prince merely shook hands, dismissing the whole matter, and went into the water. Mrs. Mashiba watched this exchange with a bemused look as though she were observing boorish people. After the Prince had circled the pool once and climbed up on the edge, she spoke to him from where she was in her shrill voice: "How young and manly you are, Prince! Ten years ago I should have challenged you to a race."

"I may not be up to you even now, Madame. Just swimming fifty yards and I'm already out of breath, as you see. Anyway, how wonderful that we can swim in Gotemba, though the water's a trifle chilly."

He shook the drops from his body as though sloughing off ostentation. Black dots spattered on the concrete.

The Prince himself had not noticed that people sometimes regarded him as cold because of his great efforts to behave on all occasions with the nonchalance and informality that had come after the war. When it was no longer necessary to maintain dignity, he became confused about human relationships. Confident because of his elite position that he had the right to dislike tradition more than anyone else, he slighted those who held it in esteem in this day and age. That might have been all right if when he remarked that someone showed no progressiveness it had not come to mean the same thing as when he had commented in former days that someone was too low-born. The Prince rated all progressives, as he did himself, as "sufferers in the fetters of tradition." Thus, paradoxically, the next step would have him thinking of himself as a commoner.

When the Prince removed his glasses before swimming, Honda saw his face for the first time without them. They were for him a rather important bridge to the world. When his bridge was removed, his plain face held a certain vague melancholy, parly because of the glare. It was a melancholy where the gap between long-gone nobility and the present was somehow confused, out of focus.

In contrast, the Princess, slightly plump in her bathing suit, was imbued with natural grace. When she floated on her back and raised one arm and smiled, she looked like some innocent, lovely waterfowl happily swimming against the background of Hakoné. One could but assume that she was one of those rare people who knew what happiness was.

Honda was mildly irritated by the Mashiba grandchildren who, having emerged from the water, now surrounded their grandmother and were conversing politely with the Prince and Princess. The subject of the young people's conversation was exclusively America. The oldest girl talked about the fashionable private school where she had studied, and her younger brothers only about the universities where they were going once they had graduated from their respective Japanese colleges. Everything was America. Television was already widespread there . . . how nice if that were true of Japan . . . but at the present rate it would probably be over ten years before they enjoyed television here . . . and on and on . . .

Mrs. Mashiba did not like conversations about the future. She interrupted immediately.

"You're all laughing at me, thinking I'll not be here to see it anyway. Very well, then. I'll appear as a ghost on your screens when you're watching every night."

The manner in which the grandmother ruthlessly controlled the young people's conversation was extraordi-

nary, as was the way the youngsters immediately fell
silent and listened the moment she spoke. Honda thought
they were like three intelligent rabbits.

The host was becoming skilled in greeting his guests
as they appeared one after another in their bathing suits
at the entrance to the terrace. On the other side of the
pool, flanked by two couples from neighboring villas,
Imanishi and Mrs. Tsubakihara clad in street clothes
raised their hands in greeting. Imanishi was wearing
an aloha shirt with a large print design in which he
was completely out of character, while Mrs. Tsubakihara
wore her usual black kimono of silk gauze that resembled
a mourning outfit. She was striving for effect: a single
ominous black crystal set in the brilliance of the swimming
pool. Honda saw through her right away and concluded
that Imanishi had put on his ludicrous shirt to flout
his simple mistress who was always trying to play roles
quite unsuited to her.

Lagging behind the animated guests in their bathing
suits, the couple slowly walked along the edge of the
water that made their black and yellow reflections rock.

The Prince and Princess knew Imanishi and Mrs.
Tsubakihara well. The Prince frequently attended postwar meetings of the so-called cultural elite and was
on sufficiently friendly terms with Imanishi to talk quite
informally with him.

"That amusing man has just arrived," he remarked
to Honda.

As soon as Imanishi was seated, he took out the crumpled wrapper from a pack of imported cigarettes, threw
it away, and drew out a new package. When he had
stripped off the wrapping, he tapped the bottom and
skillfully extracted a cigarette. "I can't sleep at all
these nights," he said perfunctorily as he put it to his
lips.

"Are you worried about something?" the Prince asked,
placing the plate from which he had just been eating
on the table.

"Not especially. But I've got to have someone to
talk to in the middle of the night. We talk and talk

until morning, and when the sun comes up we feel like committing suicide. Then we solemnly take sleeping pills. But we wake up and nothing has happened. The morning's the same as ever."

"What sort of conversations do you have night after night?"

"There's ever so much to talk about if you know that this is going to be your last. We cover every possible subject in the world. What we've done, what others have done, what the world has experienced, what mankind has gone through, or things a forgotten continent has dreamt of for several thousands of years. Anything will do. There are all kinds of subjects. The world is going to end tonight."

The Prince looked most interested and questioned further.

"But if you're alive the next day, what do you talk about then? You've covered everything."

"That's no problem. You just talk it all over again."

Amazed by this answer that sounded as though Imanishi were putting him on, the Prince fell silent.

Honda stood to the side listening. He did not know how serious Imanishi was. "By the way, what ever happened to the Land of the Pomegranate?" he asked, recalling the weird tale he had once heard.

"Ah . . ." said Imanishi, turning his cold eyes on him. His face looked more dissipated than ever these days, and it contrasted strangely with the colorful Hawaiian shirt and the American cigarettes, creating, Honda felt, the impression of a certain type of interpreter who worked for the Occupation Forces. "It's been destroyed! It exists no more."

This was his usual manner of speaking and the statement in itself did not surprise Honda. But if the millennium of sex, once called the Land of the Pomegranate, had perished in Imanishi's illusions, it also had to disappear in the mind of Honda, who hated these fantasies. It existed no more. Imanishi was guilty of slaughtering the fantasy, and Honda could imagine how he must have been intoxicated by the fanciful bloodletting in destroying the kingdom he had created. He could picture the harrowing scene that night. He had created by words and destroyed by words. Although the kingdom had never possessed reality, still it had once manifested itself somewhere, and now it was destroyed by cruel whim. Seeing Imanishi's drug-roughened yellowish brown tongue lick his lips, Honda vividly pictured imaginary mountains of corpses and rivers of blood.

Compared to the desires of this sallow weakling, his own wants were far more quiet and modest. Yet they were equally impossible of fulfillment. Seeing Imanishi who showed not a trace of sentimentality and hearing him announce with his typically affected nonchalance the destruction of the Land of the Pomegranate, Honda was pierced to the core by the frivolousness of it all.

But his thoughts were immediately interrupted by Mrs. Tsubakihara speaking in his ear. The fact that she whispered in a particularly low voice bespoke the fact that she had nothing of importance to relate.

"This is just between you and me. You know that Makiko's in Europe, don't you?"

"So I hear."

"I'm not talking about the trip itself. I just wanted to tell you that she didn't invite me to go with her this time. She took some vulgar and untalented pupil along. But of course I'm not criticizing that. Only she didn't tell me anything about her going. Can you believe it? I went to see her off at the airport, but I was so overcome I couldn't say a word."

"I wonder why she didn't mention it. The two of you were practically inseparable."

"We were not only inseparable, she was my goddess. And my goddess deserted me.

"It's a long story, but when her family was in great difficulty after the war—her father, a poet too, was an officer—I came to her assistance before anyone else. I asked her advice in everything. I concealed nothing from her. And I think I lived and wrote poetry just as she wished me to. The feeling of body and soul joined to a goddess kept me alive, though I was a mere shell after I lost my son in the war. My feelings didn't change at all even after she became so famous, but the only bad thing was that there was too much of a gap between her talent and mine. Or rather it became even clearer than ever to me after I was deserted that I had not had a shred of talent to start with."

"That's not true, I'm sure," said Honda, to be polite, squinting in the light from the swimming pool.

"No, I know it now perfectly well. There's no harm in facing it, but it's clear to me that she must have known from the very beginning. Can you think of anything more cruel? Knowing that I was completely without talent, she led me around by the nose, made me obey all her commands, and sometimes patted my back and used me as much as she wished. Then she discards me like an old shoe and goes off to Europe with some other wealthy, fawning disciple."

"Let's put aside the question of your talent. Makiko possesses outstanding ability and you know that's always accompanied by ruthless cruelty."

"Just as a goddess is cruel . . . But, Mr. Honda, how can I go on living after being deserted by a goddess? Without the one who knew my every thought and deed, what can I do?"

"How about religion?"

"Religion! It's no use believing in some invisible god who possesses no risk of treachery. It won't work if I can't have one who watches over me and tells me to do this and not that, who leads me by the hand into every action, and from whom I can conceal nothing, before whom I am purified and feel no shame."

"You'll always be a child . . . and a mother."

"Yes, Mr. Honda, I shall indeed."

Already tears were brimming in Mrs. Tsubakihara's eyes.

The Mashiba children and two new couples were in the swimming pool at the moment. Prince Kaori joined them, and they tossed about a large rubber ball with green and white stripes. The sound of splashing water, the shouting, and the merry laughter added brightness to the diffused light in the pool. The swaying blue surface was whipped up, breaking into a flurry of whitecaps. The water that had been licking quietly at the corners of the pool was now rent by the muscular shining backs of the swimmers, who made deep gashes in its sparkling surface. These instantly closed again and were transformed into quivering swells that engulfed those in the pool. The spray that rose among the shouting on one side produced countless oily rings of light on the other, all elaborately contracting and expanding.

The green and white striped ball, the instant it flew among the swimmers, appeared in chiaroscuro. The color of the water, the tones of the bathing suits, even the people playing there were unrelated to human feelings of any depth. Yet this amount of water and its movement, the laughter and the shouts of the people, somehow all evoked a feeling of tragedy in Honda's mind. He wondered why.

Could it be because of the sun? He looked up to the sky where the light appeared distorted by the deepness of the blue, and began to sneeze. Just then Mrs. Tsubakihara addressed him in her familiar tearful voice, muffled by the inevitable handkerchief that covered her face:

"What a good time they're having! Who would have imagined during the war that this would ever be possible. I wanted so much to have Akio experience this . . . at least once."

It was after two when Rié escorted Keiko and Ying Chan onto the terrace in their swimming suits. After having waited so impatiently and for so long, Ying Chan's appearance seemed to Honda much too routine.

Keiko, in a bathing suit with black and white vertical stripes, seemed voluptuous from across the pool. It was difficult to believe that she was nearly fifty years old. The Westernized life she had led from her childhood had helped to produce long and shapely legs totally unlike those of other Japanese women. Her carriage was excellent, and when seen in profile talking with Rié her curves flowed with statuesque majesty, and the sovereignty of buxom flesh was apparent in the symmetry of the swelling breasts and buttocks.

Ying Chan provided an idea contrast beside her. Clad in a white suit, she was holding a white rubber bathing cap in one hand and pushing back her hair with the other in a relaxed pose, one leg extended beyond the other. In her manner of placing her leg slightly forward, visible from a distance, was a kind of tropical asymmetry that excited people. Strong and yet slim, the long thighs supporting a well-developed torso somehow imparted a feeling of precariousness. In this she was most different from Keiko. In addition, the white suit brought out the brownness of her skin. The encased breasts and their dusky ripeness reminded Honda of the fresco at the Ajanta cave temple depicting the dying dancer. From this side of the pool he could clearly see her teeth gleaming whiter than her bathing suit when she smiled.

As she drew nearer, Honda stood up to greet this girl he had so eagerly awaited.

"Now everyone's here," said Rié, hastening over, but he made no reply.

Keiko greeted the Princess and waved to the Prince in the pool.

"I'm exhausted after the experience," she said in her rich, smooth voice, showing no sign of fatigue. "I'm too bad a driver to take the car from Karuizawa to Tokyo, pick up Ying Chan, and come all the way over to Gotemba. We're lucky to be here at all. I wonder why all the cars steer clear when I drive. It's like driving in no man's land."

"They're obviously impressed by your dignity," said Honda. For some reason, Rié laughed nervously.

In the meantime Ying Chan, oblivious to everyone, stood with her back to the table, her hands playing with her white cap, enchanted by the water tossing in the light. The inner surface of the white rubber cap gleamed occasionally as though it were oiled as she toyed with it. Honda was utterly captivated by the sight of her body, and it was only considerably later that he finally noticed something green glittering on one finger. It was the emerald ring with the golden guardian deities.

The instant he saw it, Honda's joy knew no bounds. It was a sign that she had forgiven him and that the Ying Chan who wore the ring had become the Ying Chan of former times. The rustling of the forest at the Peers School in Honda's youth, the two Siamese princes and the melancholy of their eyes, the announcement of Princess Chantrapa's death which had been received toward the end of summer in the garden at the southern villa, the long flow of time, the audience with the young Princess Moonlight in Bangkok, the bathing at Bang Pa In, the ring that had surfaced again in postwar Japan—the entire past was woven into a golden chain that linked up with his longing for the tropics. Only when she wore the ring did Ying Chan form a series of brilliant melancholy leitmotifs constantly stimulated in his intricate memories.

He heard the humming of bees close to his ear and caught the fragrant odor of the breeze that reminded him of roasted wheat, the unmistakable scent of summer. The Hondas were not particularly fond of flowers, and the garden had none of the beauty of Fuji's summer plains where pinks and gentians bloomed. But in the fragrant wind the scent of these fields and the dust stirred by the American Army maneuvers, at times dyeing the sky above yellow, delicately commingled.

Ying Chan's body was breathing at Honda's side. Not only that, but it welcomed summer as if hypersensitive to its special infection; she was infected by summer from head to toe. The texture of her skin resembled the glow of some strange Thai fruit sold on the marketplace in the shade of the mimosa. It was a bare body that in time had ripened and matured, signifying some accomplishment or promise.

As he reflected, he realized that the last time he had seen her unclothed was when she was seven, twelve years ago. The childish, slightly distended belly, which he remembered so vividly, had now flattened, but as if in compensation, the little pat chest had developed voluptuously. As she was preoccupied with the noise in the pool and was standing with her back turned toward the table, Honda could observe in detail the cords which, tied at the nape of her neck and falling down both sides, connected at the hips, the area in between forming a lovely straight line of bare back down to the crevice of her buttocks. Just above he could see the descending curve hesitate briefly at her coccyx, like the quiet basin of a small waterfall. The covered buttocks had the roundness and exquisiteness of a full moon rising. The cool of night seemed contained in the exposed flesh, while brightness appeared to radiate from the hidden flesh. The parasol barred her smooth skin with light and shadow; one arm in the shade was like bronze, but the other in the sun was like the polished surface of Chinese quincewood. Yet the skin, repelling both air and water, was not merely smooth, it had the moistness of amber orchid petals. The bone structure, which at a distance appeared delicate, was actually strong and well proportioned, though small.

"Well, shall we go in?" said Keiko.

"Yes, let's." Ying Chan looked back vivaciously and smiled. She had been waiting for these words.

Then she placed the white swimming cap on the table and raised her arms to put up her lovely black hair. The quick, rather negligent movement afforded Honda, who was in a good position, the opportunity of seeing under her arm the lower part of her side. The top of the suit was cut like an apron, and the part over her breasts had a cord passing through it and around the back of her neck, where the two ends were tied and then caught by loops at the back. The bib was cut low enough to reveal the rise of her breasts, and her sides were hidden only by the narrow sashlike ends which formed the loops for the cords at the back. Therefore, though the lower side was always visible, when her arms were raised, the narrow strips of fabric were displaced, fully exposing parts previously hidden. Honda saw that the firm expanse of skin there was no different from other areas. Not a single imperfection or blemish. She was unperturbed even in the sun, and not a suggestion of a mole was discernible. Joy welled within him.

Ying Chan forced the gathered mass of hair under the bathing cap and set out for the swimming pool with Keiko. By the time Keiko realized that she was still holding her cigarette and had returned to the table, Ying Chan had already entered the water. Assuring himself that Rié was nowhere about, Honda whispered in Keiko's ear as she stooped to crush her cigarette in the ashtray:

"I see she's wearing the ring."

Keiko said nothing, but winked knowingly. Little wrinkles, usually invisible, appeared at the corners of her eyes.

While he was gazing rapturously at the two swimmers, Rié returned and seated herself at his side. Intently watching Ying Chan leaping like a porpoise out of the sparkling water and plunging back in, a smile on her face, Rié said in a grating voice:

"With a body like that she ought to have a lot of children."

44

IN THE LIBRARY that night Honda could not interest himself in the usual books.

In a seldom-opened desk drawer he found a copy of *Court Proceedings*. For lack of anything better to do, he started reading. It concerned the sentence delivered in January, 1950, designating Honda as the legal possessor of his present holdings.

He opened the large file, which was bound by a black cord, on an English escritoire covered with Moroccan leather.

Main clause: Decision no. 9065 of 15 March 1902 by the Ministry of Agriculture and Commerce and National Forestry, whereby nationally owned land is nonreimbursable is hereby reversed. The defendant shall return to the plaintiff those national forests itemized elsewhere. Legal costs are to be borne by the defendant.

Nothing was more miraculous than the fact that the forests and mountains in a region of Fukushima prefecture, which originally had had no connection whatever with Honda, should now comprise the bulk of his wealth and support the disintegration of old age. Although it so happened that he had achieved victory, it had little to do with the original suit that had been brought in 1900, turned down once in 1902, then tenaciously pressed for half a century regardless of the vicissitudes of history. The cryptomeria forests, which people never frequented at night, and their damp undergrowth had again and again repeated their natural life cycle to afford him the manner of life he led today. How would some stranger passing through the forest early in the century have felt if, moved by the nobility of the treetops thrusting into the blue sky, he were to discover that their only raison d'être was to support a man's follies fifty years later?

Honda listened. The sounds of insects were still rare. His wife had gone to bed in the adjacent room. The house was pervaded with the coolness that suddenly follows the coming of night.

The party to celebrate the opening of the pool had ended about five o'clock, and all the guests except Keiko and Ying Chan were to return to their own homes. But Imanishi and Mrs. Tsubakihara obstinately refused to leave. They had come with the intention of staying overnight. As a result both dinner and sleeping arrangements had had to be replanned. Mrs. Tsubakihara was oblivious to the inconveniences she created.

The Hondas, Keiko, Ying Chan, Imanishi, and Mrs. Tsubakihara made their way to the arbor, where they stayed for some time.

Honda's original project had been to assign Keiko to the outer guest room and reserve the inner one next to the study for Ying Chan, but the change of plans required that he assign the second room to Imanishi and put Keiko in with Ying Chan. That scotched the scheme to use the peephole to observe Ying Chan sleeping alone. With Keiko there she would certainly be more reserved.

The words and phrases of the court documents conveyed no meaning to him.

Sixthly, in item 15 of Instruction no. 4, "Others shall be recognized as de facto owners under the regulations of the Tokugawa government and those of each fief" signifies that in addition to the cases of recognized possession set forth in items 1 to 14, when it can be ascertained that possession was generally recognized, the property may be returned to the recognized owner. "General recognition" means . . .

He looked at the clock and saw that it was already five or six minutes past twelve. Suddenly his heart stopped as if he had stumbled over something in the darkness. Hot, indescribably sweet palpitations commenced.

They were familiar to him. When he had lurked in the park at night, when what he had been expectantly awaiting was about to happen before his eyes, his heart would begin to palpitate as if pestered by a swarm of red ants.

An avalanche. A somber avalanche of honey that, overpowering everything with its suffocating sweetness, crushed the pillars of reason; all emotions were transmuted into these mechanical, rapid palpitations. Everything melted. It was useless to struggle against them.

Where did this avalanche come from? Somewhere there existed the secluded dwelling of carnal desire, and when it sent forth orders from afar, no matter how defective the antenna, it stirred sensitively; and abandoning all, one instantly responded. How alike were the voices of pleasure and death! When one is summoned, all work at once becomes unimportant. As on a ghost ship abandoned by its crew, be it the entries in the log, the uneaten food, the half-polished shoes, the comb left before the mirror, or even the partially knotted ropes—everything breathes of the mysteriously departed men, everything is left as it was in the haste of departure.

The palpitations were signs of welling desire. Manifestly only ugliness and disgrace lay in store, yet these palpitations had the richness and the brilliance of a rainbow; something indistinguishable from the sublime burst forth.

Something indistinguishable from the sublime! That was the villain. Nothing was more unattractive than the fact that both the force moving one to the noblest or most just of deeds and that inspiring the most obscene pleasure and the most ugly dreams should spring from the same source and be accompanied by the same warning palpitations. Base desires merely cast base shadows, and if the temptation of sublimity did not flash in these initial palpitations, a man could still maintain a calm pride in life. Perhaps the root of temptation lay not in carnal desire but in this pretentious illusion of silvery sublimity, this vague and mysterious half-hidden peak among the clouds. It was the birdlime of "sublimity" that first ensnared a man and then made him yearn with unbearable impatience after the vast light.

Honda, unable to endure it longer, stood up. He peered into the obscurity of the adjacent bedroom to be sure that his wife was asleep. Again he stood alone in the bright study. Since the dawn of history he had been alone in this study, and he would still be alone in it when history came to an end.

He extinguished the light. The moon was bright, and the furniture took on vague contours; the desk made of a single piece of zelkova wood gleamed as though its surface were covered with water.

He leaned against the bookcase on the wall dividing the study from the next room, listening for signs of movement. He could hear something, but it did not seem to be that they were still up and talking. It was conceivable that, unable to sleep, they might be conversing, but not a single distinct word filtered through to him.

Honda removed some ten Western books from the shelf to free the opening of the peephole. The number of books and the titles were always the same. They were invariably old leather-bound tomes with gilt lettering on law in German that had come to him from his father. His fingers could tell each and every one by the difference in thickness. The order in which he removed them never varied. He could guess the exact weight of each and he knew the odor of accumulated dust. The touch and the weight of these solemn and imposing volumes and the precision of their arrangements were the indispensable formalities of his pleasure. There was no more important ceremony than that of reverently removing these stone walls of concepts and transforming the grim pleasure he would have in reading them into his wretched infatuation. Carefully, making no noise, he lowered each volume to the floor. With each book the pounding of his heart increased. The eighth was a particularly heavy tome. When he pulled it out, his hand felt numb from the dusty golden weight of the pleasure he experienced.

He completed the task faultlessly and then placed his eye to the peephole without bumping his head. The subtlety of this skill was also of great consequence. How important each of these trifling matters seemed! As in some ritual, no detail could be omitted so that he might glimpse this other brilliant world. He was a lone priest left in the darkness. Strictly adhering to the ceremonial procedures long rehearsed in his head—he was plagued by the belief that if he should forget any part of the ritual the whole structure would collapse—he carefully put his right eye to the hole.

One of the bedside lamps seemed to be lit and a dim light mottled the room. He had been clever to have Matsudo move the wall bed so that both now stood in his field of vision.

In the dusky light inextricably entangled limbs writhed on the bed immediately before him. A white plump body and a dusky one lay with heads in opposite directions, exhausting their wanton desires. It was a position naturally assumed when the mind tied to the flesh and the brain that engendered love attempted to obtain balance by reaching out to the farthest point in order to taste the wine fermented by that love. Two heads of black shadowy hair were intimately pressed against two black pubescent mounds also filled with shadows. The annoying wisps of disheveled hair strewn across the cheeks had become signs of love. Smooth, burning thighs lay in intimate contact with smooth, burning cheeks, while the soft bellies heaved like moonlit inlets. He could not hear distinct voices, but a sobbing, neither pleasure nor sorrow, vibrated the length of the torsos. Breasts now abandoned by the partners innocently turned their nipples toward the light, trembling at times as though under an electrical charge. The depth of the night concealed in the aureoles around the nipples, the distance of the pleasure that made the breasts shudder, testified to the fact that every atom of their bodies was still isolated in maddening aloneness. They were feverishly striving to come closer, toward a greater intimacy, to fuse one into the other, but to no avail. Far away Keiko's red-lacquered toes flexed as if she were dancing on a sheet of hot iron, and yet they merely trod the empty twilight.

Honda realized that the room was filled with cool mountain air, but he felt as though the center of a furnace lay beyond the peephole. A shining furnace. He regretted that Ying Chan's back that he had examined so carefully during the day at the pool, perspiration flowing slowly down the spine, was turned toward him. Shortly the perspiration was diverted from its channel and trickled down the dark flank against the bed. It seemed as though he could smell the fragrance of some rich, ripe tropical fruit that had just split open.

Keiko shifted her body slightly to be on top, and Ying Chan tilted her neck, thrusting her head between Keiko's shining thighs. Naturally her breasts came into view. Her right arm encircled Keiko's hip, while her left hand gently caressed her belly. Intermittently little nocturnal lappings could be heard licking the banks of the harbor.

So beautiful was Ying Chan's sincerity that he was seeing for the first time that Honda even forgot to be surprised by this so treacherous conclusion to his love.

Her closed eyes were turned toward the ceiling, and her forehead was half buried in Keiko's sporadically convulsing thighs. Keiko's mimosalike hair almost completely covered her lovely, peaceful nostrils, now no longer cold and narrow. Ying Chan's bow-shaped upper lip was open and moist, and a busy sucking movement extended from her delicate chin to her cheeks that gleamed darkly. Presently Honda saw a line of tears flowing like some living animal from the shadow of her long eyelashes along her tightly closed eyes and down her cheek.

Within the limitless movement of waves everything was directed toward an as yet unknown summit. The two women seemed to be desperately striving to reach ultimate limits neither had ever dreamt of or hoped for. Honda felt as if there were some unknown pinnacle poised in the space of the dark room like a brilliant crown. It was probably the Thai full-moon diadem suspended there above the two writhing women; only Honda's eyes were able to envision it.

The bodies of both women alternately extended and contracted and then collapsed as they buried themselves gain in sighs and perspiration. The crown floated indifferently in the space which their straining fingers almost reached. When the envisioned summit, that unknown golden limit was manifest, the scene was completely transformed, and Honda could see the two women entangled beneath his gaze only in their suffering and torture. They were battered by the dissatisfaction of the flesh, their gathered brows were filled with pain, and their hot limbs seemed to writhe as though trying to escape from what seared them. They possessed no wings. They continued their futile thrashings to escape from their bonds, from their suffering; and yet their flesh firmly retained them. Only rapture could bring release.

Ying Chan's beautiful, dark breasts were drenched in perspiration, the right one crushed and disfigured beneath Keiko's body, while the left, heaving vigorously, lay voluptuously on her left arm with which she was caressing Keiko's belly. On the constantly trembling mound the nipple slumbered, and with the perspiration the sphere glowed as if bright with rain.

At that moment Ying Chan, perhaps jealous that Keiko's thigh had freedom of movement, raised her left arm high and grasped it as though to claim it as her own. She placed it firmly over her head as if she could do without breathing. The imposing white thigh completely covered her face.

Ying Chan's whole side was exposed. To the left of her bare breast, an area her arm had previously concealed, three extremely small moles appeared distinctly, like the Pleiades in the dusky sky of her brown skin that resembled the dying evening glow.

Honda was shocked. It was as if his eyes had been pierced with arrows.

Just as he ducked his head and was about to leave the bookcase, he felt a light tap on his back. On withdrawing his head he discovered Rié standing there in her nightdress, her face frighteningly pale.

"What are you doing? I suspected as much."

Honda felt no guilt as he turned his perspiring forehead to his wife. He had already seen the moles.

"Look. Look at the moles . . ."

"Are you telling me to peek?"

"Go ahead. It's just as I thought."

Caught between dignity and curiosity, Rié hesitated for some time. Ignoring her, Honda walked to the bay window and seated himself on the built-in bench. Rié put her eye to the peephole. Having been unable to see his own posture when he had done the same thing, Honda could not bear to witness the demeaning position of his wife. Nevertheless, they had come to the point of sharing the same deed.

He looked for the moon concealed by a cloud through the metal screen in the bay window. Behind the cloud, edged in light, the moon sent forth beams in all directions and cloud clusters trailed away in similar stateliness. The stars were few, and he saw only one shining brightly, scarcely touching the tops of the cypress trees.

When Rié had done peeping, she lit the lamp in the room. Her face was shining with joy.

She walked to the bench and sat down. Already she was cured.

"I'm stunned. . . . Did you know about that?" she said in a warm, low voice.

"No. I just found out."

"But you said it was just as you thought."

"That's not what I meant, Rié. I was talking about the moles. Some time ago you raked through my study in Tokyo and read Matsugae's diary, didn't you?"

"*I* hunted through your study?"

"It doesn't matter. I'm asking if you read Matsugae's diary."

"I . . . I don't remember. I'm not interested in other people's diaries."

When Honda asked her to bring him a cigar from the bedroom, she obediently followed his command. She even lighted it, shielding it with her hand from the wind that came through the window screen.

"The key to transmigration is in Matsugae's diary. You saw them too, didn't you? The three black moles on her left side? Those moles were originally on Matsugae."

Rié, thinking of other things, was indifferent to what Honda was saying. She probably thought her husband was looking for excuses. Honda pressed her, wishing them to have the memory in common.

"Well, you did see them, didn't you?"

"I can't say. But the scene was horrible. You never know about people, do you!"

"That's why I'm saying that Ying Chan is the reincarnation of Matsugae."

Rié gazed at her husband with pity. It was only natural that a woman who believed herself cured should try in turn to act as such. This woman who had so savagely confirmed reality was now ready to infect her husband with the roughness that burned her skin like salt water. Rié was no longer the Rié of old. Although she had once desired to transform reality she had wisely learned to believe in it. She had learned that without changing herself, the world could be transformed through observation. She rather looked down on her husband's world, without realizing that she had in fact become a co-conspirator by having been a voyeur too.

"What's all this about reincarnation? How ridiculous! I didn't read any diary. At any rate, I've finally calmed down. Your eyes must have been opened too, but I was suffering from something that didn't exist at all. I was wrestling with an illusion. Now that I realize it, I suddenly feel tired. But everything turned out for the best. There's nothing to worry about any more."

The two were sitting at either end of the bench, an ashtray between them. Honda, concerned that Rié might be cold, closed the window; the smoke from his cigar slowly eddied up under the light. They were silent, but the silence was not the same as that which had occurred that morning.

Their hearts were bound together by the odiousness of what they had observed, and Honda felt momentarily how good it would have been if they could have been like so many other couples in the world, if they could flaunt their impeccable moral rectitude like immaculately white aprons across their chests, sit at table three times a day and proudly eat to their satisfaction, if they could assume the right to disdain other things in the world. But in reality they had merely been transformed into a couple of voyeurs.

Yet each of them had not seen the same thing. Where Honda had discovered reality, Rié had found out her illusions. The process whereby they had reached this common point was the same for both in that they had not yet recuperated from their fatigue and their work had been futile. What remained now was mutual consolation.

After a while Rié yawned so widely one could see to the back of her mouth.

"Don't you think we should start thinking about adopting a child?" she said most appropriately, combing back her disheveled hair.

Death had flown from Honda's heart the moment he had seen Keiko and Ying Chan together. Now there was reason to believe that he might be immortal. "No," he said with determination, plucking a piece of tobacco from his lip, "it's better to live by ourselves. I prefer not having any heir."

Honda and Rié were no sooner awakened by a violent pounding on the door than they smelled the smoke.

"Fire! Fire!" a woman was shouting. When the couple, joining hands, ran out the door, the second-floor corridor was already filled with swirling smoke, and the person who had roused them was gone. Covering their mouths with their sleeves, the two ran coughing and choking down the stairs. The pool with its water flashed through Honda's mind. They would be safe only if they could reach it without delay.

As they burst out onto the terrace and looked at the pool, they saw Keiko holding Ying Chan and crying to them from the far side. That the fire was already sweeping through the house was obvious, for though the lights had not been turned on, the reflections of the two women were nonetheless clearly visible on the surface of the water. Honda was amazed by the personal appearance of both Keiko and Ying Chan. Their hair was disheveled, but both were wearing the dressing gowns they had brought with them. Honda was clad only in his pajamas and Rié was wearing her night kimono.

"I woke up coughing because of the smoke. It must have come from Mr. Imanishi's room," said Keiko.

"Who knocked on our door?"

"I did. I knocked on Mr. Imanishi's too, but he hasn't come down. What shall we do?"

"Matsudo! Matsudo!" Honda shouted, and the chauffeur came running along the edge of the swimming pool.

"Mr. Imanishi and Mrs. Tsubakihara are in there. Can't you go help them?"

They looked up and saw flames shooting out of the second-floor windows along with dense white smoke.

"That's impossible, Mr. Honda," the chauffeur said, carefully considering the situation. "It's too late now. Why didn't they get out?"

"They must have taken too many sleeping pills," Keiko remarked. Ying Chan buried her face in Keiko's breast and began to cry.

Apparently the roof had caved in, for flames shot high into a sky filled with flying sparks.

"What are we to do with the water?" said Honda helplessly, looking at the swimming pool that was so reddened with reflected flames and sparks that it would seem that in touching the water one's hand would be burned.

"Yes, I think it's too late to put out the fire, but perhaps we should douse the valuable pieces in the living room. Shall I bring a bucket?" asked Matsudo without making a move.

Honda was already thinking of something else.

"How about the fire department? I wonder what time it is now."

No one had a watch. They had all been left behind.

"It's three minutes past four. The sun will be up soon," said Matsudo.

"How provident of you to have thought to bring your watch," Honda said sarcastically, regaining his assurance as he discovered he was capable of sarcasm even in such circumstances.

"It's an old habit. I always sleep with my watch on," placidly answered the properly dressed Matsudo.

Rié, dazed, had seated herself in a chair next to the folded beach umbrella.

Honda saw Ying Chan remove her face from Keiko's breast, hastily fumble through the breast pocket of her dressing gown, and take out a photograph. The gloss of the picture was enhanced by the flames. Glancing distractedly at it, he saw that it was a completely nude Keiko leaning against a chair.

"I'm glad this was not burned," said Ying Chan,

smiling. As she looked up at Keiko, her white teeth gleamed in the light of the flames. His memory functioned amidst a welter of thoughts, and Honda recalled the scene just before Katsumi had broken into her bedroom. This was the same treasured picture that Ying Chan had been looking at then.

"Silly," said Keiko, tenderly putting an arm round her shoulder. "What did you do with the ring?"

"The ring! Oh, I've left it in the room," Honda heard her say distinctly. He was seized by a fear that the flaming silhouettes of his two friends might appear in the far windows of the second floor, screaming in terror. They were most certainly dying there. Probably they were already dead. This might well be why the fire gave the impression of quietness despite the grating and roaring.

The fire engine still had not come. Honda thought of the telephone in Keiko's house which was being remodeled and sent Matsudo running over to call the Gotemba Fire Station at Nimaibashi.

The holocaust had enveloped the entire second story, and the first floor was filled with smoke. As the wind happened to be coming from the direction of Fuji to the northwest, smoke did not blow toward the pool, but the dawn chill crept up the spines of the onlookers.

The fire changed at every instant. Mingling with sounds like colossal footsteps amidst the flames came the intermittent noise of things bursting. With each sound Honda associated some burning object: now a book, now the desk. He visualized pages turning over, swelling like roses.

The volume of fire increased in proportion to the smoke. The heat could be felt even on this side of the swimming pool, and the rising hot air carried up cinders and sparks. During the short time before they turned to ash, the cinders were gold, reminding one of the flutter of golden wings of fledglings leaving their nest. It seemed as though things were departing. In one area of the sky radiant with soaring flames, the outlines of the cloud banks hidden in the dusky light of dawn were now defined.

A roaring, probably caused by falling beams on the second floor, rose from the house. Then a section of outer wall was rent by flames, and a window frame engulfed in fire fell into the pool. The subtle decorative flames imparted to the falling black object the momentary illusion of being a window of the Marble Temple in Siam. A sizzling pierced the air as the frame plunged into the water. They jumped back from the pool.

The house, gradually losing its outer walls, took on the appearance of a gigantic burning bird cage. Tatters of delicate flame fluttered from every chink and every crack. The house was breathing. It was as though the source of a deep and vigorous life breath existed within the flames. From time to time the shape of some familiar piece of furniture, some former lifelike shadow would appear in their midst, but it would collapse instantly covered in brilliance and turn into joyfully dancing flames. The upsurging fire would suddenly shoot out like a snake's tongue only to disappear again into the smoke, while red faces of flame would suddenly appear from the dense black fumes. Everything happened with incredible rapidity, fire and fire joined hands, smoke wrapped about smoke, all attempting to reach a single summit. The upside-down burning house dropped mixtures of flame deep into the swimming pool, and the limpid dawn sky was visible through the tips of fingers of fire.

The wind changed direction and smoke blew toward the pool, sending the spectators further from the water. Although they could not detect it with certainty, and although no one mentioned it, they knew surely that the odor of burning human flesh was present in the smoke, and they covered their nostrils with both hands.

Rié suggested that it would be best to go to the arbor since dew was falling. The three women, turning their backs on the fire, started toward the arbor across the lawn just mowed the previous day. Honda remained alone.

He felt insistently that he had seen this somewhere before.

Flames reflecting in the water . . . burning corpses . . . Benares! How could he not have dreamed of recapturing the ultimate he had seen in that holy land?

The house had turned into kindling and life had become fire. All triviality had turned to ash and nothing but the most essential was important, and the hidden, gigantic face had turned up its head abruptly from the flame. Laughter, screams, sobs were all absorbed in the clamor of the flames, the crackling of wood, the distorted panes of glass, the creaking of the joints—sound itself was enveloped in an absolute quiet. Roasted tiles cracked and fell, one by one the fetters were released, and the house turned into a brilliant nakedness hitherto unknown. The light cream section of outer wall on the first floor which had not yet burned suddenly wrinkled and turned brown; and at the same time, the fire thrust violently through a light smudge of smoke. The smooth speed of transformation into flames and their shiftings in finding an escape were unimaginably exquisite.

Honda brushed sparks from his shoulders and sleeves. The surface of the swimming pool was covered with embers and ashes that swarmed like duckweed. But the brilliance of the fire penetrated everything, and the purification of the Mani Karnika ghat was reflected mirror-fashion in this small, limited area of water, in this sacred pool created for Ying Chan's bathing. What was different here from the funeral pyres reflected in the Ganges? Here too were fire and wood, and the two human bodies, slow to burn, were doubtless writhing and threshing in the flames. They no longer felt pain; the flesh merely imitated and repeated the forms of suffering as it resisted destruction. Such were the two corpses. This was precisely the same as that clear fire in the evening dusk at the floating ghat. Everything was being rapidly reduced to constituent elements. Smoke rose high into the sky.

The only thing missing was the face of the sacred white cow that had turned and stared straight at Honda from the other side of the flames.

When the fire engine arrived, the fire had already died down. Nevertheless, the firemen conscientiously hosed the house. A rescue was attempted, but they found the two corpses completely incinerated. The police arrived and requested Honda to verify the scene of death. But as the staircase had collapsed, it was difficult to reach the upper floor, and Honda gave up. On being told of the habits of Imanishi and Mrs. Tsubakihara, the officer in charge commented that the cause of the fire had probably been their smoking in bed. If they had taken sleeping pills about three, then the time of the drug's maximum effect would have coincided with the onset of the fire, doubtless starting from a lit cigarette dropped on the quilt. Honda did not accept the idea of suicide. When the officer spoke of "double suicide," Keiko, listening at one side, broke into unrestrained laughter.

When things settled down a bit, Honda would have to present himself at the police station to make a deposition. He was sure to be busy today. He must send Matsudo out to purchase food for breakfast, but it would be some time yet before the stores opened.

As there was no other place to go, everyone gathered in the arbor. In her faltering Japanese Ying Chan brought up the subject of a snake she had seen as she ran from the fire. It had appeared on the lawn and slithered away with unusual speed, the distant fire glinting on its oily brown scales. Listening to her, all of them, especially the women, felt even more the penetrating chill of the air.

Just then, Fuji the color of red tile at dawn, one sparkling brush mark of snow near its summit, appeared before them. Even under these circumstances Honda's eyes shifted involuntarily from the red mountain to the morning sky immediately beside it. The habit was almost unconscious. He could clearly see the distinct form of a winter Fuji.

45

IN 1967, it happened that Honda was invited to a dinner party at the American Embassy in Tokyo. There he met the head of the American Cultural Center in Bangkok. His wife, somewhat over thirty, was Thai, and people said that she was a princess. Honda was sure that she was Ying Chan.

Ying Chan had gone home shortly after the fire at Gotemba in 1952 and Honda had had no news since then. Momentarily he believed that she had unexpectedly returned to Tokyo after fifteen years as the wife of an American. This was not impossible, and it would be quite typical of Ying Chan to pretend not to know him at all when she greeted him at their introduction.

He looked at her several times during dinner, but the woman obstinately spoke no Japanese. Her English was that of a native American. Deeply engrossed, Honda made completely irrelevant answers on several occasions to the woman seated next to him.

Following dinner, liqueurs were served in another room. Honda approached the lady who was wearing a rose-colored dress of Thai silk and for the first time had the opportunity of talking with her alone.

He inquired if she knew Ying Chan.

"I do, indeed! She was my twin sister. But she's dead now," she said brightly in English. Impulsively he asked how she had died, and when.

The lady said that after she returned from her studies in Japan, Ying Chan's father discovered that she had benefited little from her stay, and he had tried to send her to the United States to study. But Ying Chan had not agreed and had chosen to live in her residence in Bangkok surrounded by flowers. She died suddenly in the spring at the age of twenty.

According to the lady-in-waiting, Ying Chan was alone in the garden, standing under a phoenix tree with its smoky vermilion flowers. Although there was no one else there, she was heard laughing. The lady-in-waiting thought it strange that she should be laughing all by herself. Clear, innocent sounds that rose in the sunny blue sky. The laughter ceased and almost at once turned into shrill screams. The lady-in-waiting rushed up to find Ying Chan on the ground, her thigh bitten by a cobra.

It was an hour before the doctor arrived. In the interval, her muscles slackened and she lost all motor control. She complained of sleepiness and double vision. Spinal paralysis set in and she began to salivate. Her breathing slowed while her pulse quickened and became irregular. Ying Chan had gone into final convulsions and died before the doctor arrived.

About the Author

ON NOVEMBER 25, 1970, Yukio Mishima committed *seppuku* (ritual suicide). Forty-five years old and at the peak of a brilliant literary career, he had that morning written the last word of the final novel of his tetralogy, *The Sea of Fertility*. "The tetralogy is his masterpiece, as he knew," Donald Keene has said.

Mishima had written much about suicide and early death, and often told his friends he wished to die young. After he conceived the idea of *The Sea of Fertility* in 1964, he frequently said he would die when it was completed. In fact the second of the four novels, *Runaway Horses,* is a remarkable literary rehearsal of his *seppuku.* Just before his suicide, he wrote his closest friends that he felt empty, having put into the tetralogy everything he thought and felt about life and this world. "The title, *The Sea of Fertility,*" he told Keene, "is intended to suggest the arid sea of the moon that belies its name. Or I might say that it superimposes the image of cosmic nihilism on that of the fertile sea."

Mishima's works have been compared to the works of Proust, Gide, and Sartre, and his obsession with courage and the manly virtues has been likened to Hemingway's. Arthur Miller said, "I felt Mishima had an admirable style. He was surrealistic. He was very erotic. He had an economy of means to create enormous myths—his novels are compressed visions." A British magazine called him "one of the outstanding modern writers of fiction, possessing a complex, subtle and frightening imaginative power."

He was often wrongly called a rightist because of his private "army" of a hundred unarmed young men, but it was not on the blacklist of the careful Japanese police because it had never been involved in violence and differed from conventional rightist organizations. It was a theatrical fantasy conceived by a poet, as was his death, about which Selig Harrison of the Washington *Post* wrote, "He forced the Japanese to

310

consider where they are going more dramatically than anyone else since World War II, and he has done so with a distinctively Japanese symbolism."

Mishima was born into a samurai family and imbued with the code that apotheosized complete control over mind and body, and loyalty to the Emperor—the same code that produced the austerity and self-sacrifice of Zen. Much of the tetralogy shows that he viewed the self-seeking arrogance and corruption of the militarists of the thirties (and their contemporary successors) as traitors to the samurai code.

His first novel was published in his school magazine when he was thirteen. A perceptive teacher encouraged him and persuaded a magazine to publish a story, *The Forest in Full Bloom*, in 1941, when Mishima (a pen name the teacher suggested) was sixteen. Three years later, when he entered Tokyo Imperial University, his first collection of stories was published under the same title and pen name. The first printing sold out in a week. In 1946 he brought two essays in manuscript to Kawabata, later the Nobel Prize winner, whose protégé he became. Altogether, 257 books by him, including 15 novels, have been published in Japan, and 77 translations here and in Europe.

Mishima reverenced and mastered the martial arts of Japan, creating a beautiful body he hoped age would never make ugly. He began to practice body-building in 1955, and *kendo* (dueling with bamboo staves) in 1959. In 1966 he took up *karate* as well. By 1968 he had become a *kendo* master of the fifth rank.

He traveled widely and often, and two travel books and many collections of articles are among his works. He also wrote countless short stories and thirty-three plays, in some of which he acted. Some ten films have been made from his novels; *The Sound of Waves* (1954, American edition 1956) was filmed twice, and one of the director Ishikawa's masterpieces, *Enjo*, was based on *The Temple of the Golden Pavilion* (1956, American edition 1959). Also available in English are *Five Modern Nō Plays* (1957) and the novels *After the Banquet* (1960, American edition 1963), *The Sailor Who Fell from Grace with the Sea* (1963, American edition 1965), *Forbidden Colors* (1951, American edition 1968), and *Thirst for Love* (1950, American edition 1969). The first novel of the tetralogy, *Spring Snow*, was published in 1972, and the second, *Runaway Horses*, in 1973.

About the Translators

E. DALE SAUNDERS, translator of Kobo Abé's *The Woman in the Dunes* (1964), *The Face of Another* (1966), *The Ruined Map* (1969), and *Inter Ice Age 4* (1970), received his A.B. from Western Reserve University (1941), his M.A. from Harvard (1948), and his Ph.D. from the University of Paris (1952). He is at present Visiting Professor of Japanese at the University of Paris VII. He is regularly Professor of Japanese at the University of Pennsylvania and has also taught at International Christian University, Tokyo, and at Harvard University. Among his publications are *Mudrā: A Study of Symbolic Gestures in Japanese Buddhist Sculpture* (1960) and *Buddhism in Japan* (1964).

CECILIA SEGAWA SEIGLE was born in Tokyo, Japan. She received her A.B. from Western College for Women, her M.A. in English from Bryn Mawr College, and her Ph.D. from the University of Pennsylvania in the field of Oriental Studies. In addition to her activity as a translator, Mrs. Seigle is head of the Far Eastern Desk at the Franklin Institute Research Laboratories in Philadelphia.